Prai~~se for Elmer Kelton~~

"Kelton's latest is a bowl-of-beans book; it ain't fancy, but it sure is filling, and it goes down good."

—*Texas Monthly* on *The Smiling Country*

"Elmer Kelton, a wily old cloudburst, imbues his Westerns with ancient myths and modern motifs that transcend cowboys and cattle trails."

—*The Dallas Morning News*

"One thing is certain: as long as there are writers as skillful as Elmer Kelton, Western literature will never die."

—*True West* magazine

Forge Books by Elmer Kelton

SHOTGUN

{ and }

SIX BITS A DAY

Elmer Kelton

FORGE®

A TOM DOHERTY ASSOCIATES BOOK | NEW YORK

SHOTGUN AND SIX BITS A DAY

Shotgun copyright © 1969 by Coronet Communications, Inc.
Six Bits a Day copyright © 2005 by the Estate of Elmer Kelton

Shotgun was originally published in 1969 by Paperback Library as *Shotgun Settlement* by Alex Hawk, a pseudonym of Elmer Kelton.
Six Bits a Day was originally published in 2005 by Forge books.

A Forge Book
Published by Tom Doherty Associates, LLC
175 Fifth Avenue
New York, NY 10010

www.tor-forge.com

Forge® is a registered trademark of Tom Doherty Associates, LLC.

ISBN 978-0-7653-7770-8

Forge books may be purchased for educational, business, or promotional use. For information on bulk purchases, please contact Macmillan Corporate and Premium Sales Department at 1-800-221-7945, extension 5442, or write specialmarkets@macmillan.com.

First Mass Market Edition: April 2014

Printed in the United States of America

0 9 8 7 6 5 4 3 2 1

{ Contents }

SHOTGUN

{ ONE }

The hostler at the Two Forks Livery & Grain paused in his listless pitching of hay as he saw two riders move down from the crest of the limestone hill. Harley Mills rubbed a sleeve over his sweat-streaked face and speculated as to whether he was fixing to get some customers. Hot as it was, and seeing as the stable didn't belong to him, he had as soon not have business get out of hand. It hadn't lately. With this drought on, people were playing it close to their belts. They weren't coming to town when they didn't have to, because money was tight. He went back to his halfhearted efforts until one of the horses in the corral thrust its head over the top plank and nickered. An answer came from out on the road. Mills put the hayfork aside and stepped through the gate.

The two men were strangers to him. "Mornin'," he said. "From the looks of the dust on you, you've come a ways. I expect them horses could stand a feed."

No one replied. The hostler stared a moment at a rust-bearded man hunched on a streak-faced bay, then his reddish eyes were drawn to the taller rider, a gaunt, sallow-faced man who studied him in dark distrust. The hostler felt a sudden misgiving and wished they had passed him by.

The man said, "You're Harley Mills."

The hostler swallowed, puzzled. "That's right. But I don't know you. Or do I?"

The rider said, "You didn't used to swamp stables. Time I remember you, you was cowboyin' for old man Blair Bishop."

"Used to. He fired—we come to a partin', years ago." Harley Mills searched the seldom-explored recesses of his whiskey-dimmed memory. Something in those deep-set black eyes reached him. His jaw dropped.

The rider responded with a hard grin. "Know me now, don't you?"

Mills nodded, dry-mouthed and nervous.

The tall man said evenly, "Then I reckon we'll leave these horses with you. Me and Owen, we're goin' to go wash some of the dust down. You take good care of them now, Harley, you hear? Good care." Mills could only nod. The tall rider swung to the hoof-scuffed ground and shoved the leather reins into Mills' numb hands. He reached back to his warbag tied behind the saddle and fetched out a cartridge belt. He took his time putting it on while the hostler stared at the .45 in fearful fascination.

The man asked, "Things ain't changed much in ten years, have they?" Mills shook his head, a knot in his throat. The rider queried, "Blair Bishop still figurin' hisself the big he-coon?" The hostler's eyes gave him the answer and he added, "Well, things can't stay the same forever. Come on, Owen, we're past due for that drink."

Harley Mills barely glanced at the red-bearded Owen

as he took the second set of reins. He watched the tall man stride up the street, looking at first one side of it, then the other. Mills led the horses into the corral, slipped the saddles and bridles off and gave the mounts a good bait of oats. His fingers touched a saddlegun in a scabbard as he swung the tall man's saddle onto a rack, and he jerked his hand back as if he had touched a hot stove.

Done, he shut the corral gate behind him and struck a stiff trot up the street to the courthouse. He almost ran down the county clerk as he rushed through the hall and into the door of the sheriff's office. He gestured excitedly at the graying ex-cowboy who looked up startled from his paperwork.

"It's Macy Modock," he blurted, gasping for breath. "Macy Modock is back in town."

The sheriff poked his head through the door of the Two Forks Bar & Billiard Emporium. Looking around quickly, he spotted the two men seated at a small table. He stared a moment, his heavy fingers gripping the doorjamb. At length the tall man spoke to him. "Come on in, Erly. Wondered how long it would take you."

Sheriff Erly Greenwood moved solemnly, his sun-browned face pinched into a frown. He halted two paces from the table, gave the red-bearded man a quick glance, then gazed at the other. "What you doin' here, Macy?"

"Havin' a drink. Share a little sunshine with us?"

"You was in the pen, Macy. How come you out?"

"I was turned out. Got all the proper papers right here in my pocket." He tapped his shirt. "Care to look?"

The sheriff nodded. "Maybe I better." His frown

deepened, and his moustache worked a little as he read. "You didn't serve out all the term they gave you."

"Good behavior, Erly. Surprise you I could behave myself?"

"Damn sure does. I figured you'd get in a fight and some other prisoner would stomp your brains out. Hoped so, as a matter of fact."

"But here I am back in Two Forks, like a bad penny."

"I want you out, Macy. Have your drink, get your horses fed, then ride on out. I don't want to ever see you again . . . not in this town, not in this country."

Macy Modock studied his half-finished drink, a little anger flaring before he quickly forced it back. "Erly, if you'll read that paper a little closer you'll see it says I done paid up all I owe. I can come and go as I please, here or anywhere else. And after all, I'm a property owner in Two Forks. I come to see about my property."

"After ten years? That old saloon you had is half fallen in. Kids broke out all the windowlights the first week you was gone. Wind took off most of the shingles, and rain has done the rest."

"The land it sets on is mine. I come to see after my property. There can't nobody quarrel over that."

Erly Greenwood shifted his weight from one foot to the other. His jaw worked, but it was a while before any words came out. "Macy, we've had a nice quiet town here the last few years."

Modock nodded. "You're puttin' on some belly."

"Just you listen to what I tell you. If you've come to settle up any old scores, I won't have it."

A hard smile came to Macy Modock's thin, cheek-sunken face. "I got no grudge against you, Erly. You just done what you was told. The boss man snapped his fingers and you jumped. That's how it always was, them days. He still snappin' his fingers, Erly?"

Anger leaped into Erly Greenwood's face. "He's a good man, Macy. Anything he done to you, he done for good cause. If you've come back to raise hell . . ."

Macy Modock glanced at his red-whiskered companion. "Like I told you, Owen, things ain't really changed. The years go by, people get older, but everything else stays the same."

The sheriff's voice carried an edge. "I want you out of here."

"When I get ready. Who knows? I might take a notion to rebuild."

Conviction came to Erly Greenwood. "You've come to get even with him, Macy. Don't you try."

Modock grunted. "You was just a cowboy when Blair Bishop had that badge pinned on you. You're still just a cowboy."

"That's a matter of opinion. Don't you crowd me."

Modock stared at him coldly. "If there's trouble between me and Blair Bishop, it'll be when he comes huntin' me, not me huntin' him."

Macy Modock turned away from the sheriff. He poured himself a fresh drink and held it in his hand, admiring the amber color as if he had dismissed the sheriff from his mind. Greenwood turned on his heel and left.

The smile came back slowly to Modock's line-creased mouth. "And Blair Bishop *will* come huntin' me, Owen. I'll *make* him hunt me. And when I shoot him in self-defense, not even a Two Forks jury can touch me."

{ TWO }

Blair Bishop lay on his back beneath the lacy shade of a tall mesquite tree and rubbed his right hand. Why was it, he wondered ruefully, that when a man got of an age where he ought to be able to stand back and breathe good, enjoy what he had built for himself and take the pleasure of turning responsibilities over to his sons, he had to start putting up with things like rheumatism? If it wasn't in his hands, it was in his hips. If it wasn't in his hips, it was in his legs. There wasn't a part of his body that hadn't at one time or another been fallen on, rolled over or kicked by a horse.

He looked past his big gray mount, tied to a limb of the mesquite. "See anything yet, Hez?"

Hez Northcutt, sitting on a leggy dun, stood in his stirrups and squinted. "Somebody's comin'. Looks like it's probably Finn bringin' old Clarence and that sorry crew of his."

Blair Bishop pushed slowly to his feet, wincing a little as a rheumatism pain lanced through his hip. Damn it, he wasn't too far past fifty. A man ought not to have to put up with this till he was old. He took off his hat and rubbed a sleeve across his sweaty brow, then pulled the spotted old Stetson down firmly over his thick gray hair. He squinted toward a wire corral full of bawling cows and restless calves, the dust rising thick and brown and drifting away in the hot west wind. This was a corral he used twice a year in branding the Double B onto his cattle that ranged this part of his land. But the cattle in the pen didn't wear that brand. They carried a C Bar. They were thin, their ribs showing through.

This had been a hard year for all cattle, Bishop's and everybody's. Beyond the corral, stretching for miles and disappearing into the shimmering heatwaves, lay grassland brown and short, thirsting for rain. The only thing green was the mesquite trees, which had deep roots and could outlast any other living plant except the cactus.

August had come, and it hadn't rained since March. Even that had been little more than a shower, following a dry winter. The brass of the summer sky showed little sign it would yield up rain for a long time yet.

Young Hez Northcutt slipped a pistol out of its holster and spun the cylinder, checking the load. "Hez," Blair spoke gently, "you can put that thing up. You'll have no use for it today."

Hez looked at him dubiously, plainly hoping. "You sure, Mister Bishop?"

"Clarence Cass will threaten and whine, but he wouldn't fight a blind jackrabbit. And them boys with him, they're just on a payroll. They won't bloody theirselves for the likes of Clarence."

The cowboy put the pistol away.

From behind the corral, where he had been looking over the cows, another young man rode up on a stocking-legged sorrel. He turned his gaze a moment toward the dust rising on the wagon road, then looked down regret-fully at the broad-shouldered rancher. "Dad, we're treatin' old Clarence awful rough."

"Clarence Cass is a user, boy. He's like a parasite tick that gets on a cow's ear and sucks blood till it busts it-self. He'll use you for all he can get out of you and then complain because you didn't give him more. Now and again you got to treat him rough. It's the only way you can tell him no."

Allan Bishop drummed his hand against his saddle horn. His voice was testy. "Still looks like we could've gone and talked to him."

Blair Bishop put his hands on his hips and leaned back, stretching, wishing he could work the rheumatism out. Impatience touched him, but he tried not to let it take over. Hell, the boy wasn't but twenty-two. At that age, even Blair had still harbored notions about the inherent good-ness of all men, goodness that would just naturally come out of its own accord if you would but reason with them. Blair Bishop had eventually had all such notions stomped out of him. His son hadn't, yet. Blair knew some men had it in them to do the right thing, and some didn't. The latter you had just as well not waste your time with. Minute you turned your back to them they would be whittling on you.

Blair thought his son made a good picture sitting there in the saddle. Strong shoulders, straight back, an earnest young face and square chin. In a lot of ways he looked like Blair had looked, maybe twenty-five years ago. Ex-cept Blair had never been that handsome the best day he had ever lived. Allan had inherited some looks from his mother's side.

And a little contrariness, too, Blair thought. It never come from me; I never been contrary in my life.

"Allan, one of these days this place will belong to you and your brother, Billy. He's too young yet to take on the tough end of it, but you're not. You know as well as I do that we've tried talkin' reason to old Clarence. Now it's your place to stand with me when we *show* the old beggar."

Allan's jaw was set hard.

Blair shrugged, losing patience. "All right, let's talk straight. It ain't old Clarence you're thinkin' about; it's that girl of his. Forget it, boy."

"Anything that hurts the old man hurts Jessie."

"So it'll just have to hurt her. You better forget about her, boy. She won't bring you nothin' but problems."

"You don't know her."

"I know the old man. I never knew the girl's mother, but I expect if she was much she never would've married Clarence. I been a stockman all my life. I know that if you breed a scrubby stud to a scrubby mare, you get a scrubby colt."

Anger leaped into Allan's face and he pulled his horse away, turning his back on his father.

Blair clenched his teeth. Maybe he oughtn't to've talked so rough, but he knew no way except being blunt. Though people didn't always agree with Blair Bishop, they never misunderstood him. He watched silently as his son moved the sorrel down the wagon road to meet the oncoming riders.

Hez Northcutt said: "I'm about his age, Mister Bishop. Maybe *I* can talk to him."

Blair shook his head. The cowboy had a point, but Blair rejected it. Blair had long had an easy partnership with both his sons. He still had it with Billy, who was about fifteen. But somehow the last couple or three years he had lost that open-handed relationship with Allan. At a time when two men ought to draw closer together, why was it they tended instead to pull apart? Why was it a father had to become a stranger to a son?

"He'll come around," Blair told the cowboy. "Just stubborn. Got that from his mother, God rest her."

Blair's foreman, Finn Goforth, spurred ahead of the riders so he could reach Blair Bishop first. On the way he passed Allan, and he spoke to him. If Allan replied, Blair couldn't tell it. Finn, fortyish and graying, took a curious glance back over his shoulder at Allan. "I fetched them, Mister Bishop."

"How did Clarence take it?"

"Like we'd poured coal oil in his whiskey barrel. He's bellyached all the way over here. I'll let you listen to him now; I'm sick of it."

Blair said, "I didn't figure on listenin'. I figured on doin' the talkin'." He scowled, watching his son pull up even with the Cass girl. "I wish I could talk to *him*," he complained.

"Allan's full growed," Finn commented. "You've always taught him to think for himself. You wouldn't give three cents for him if he didn't."

"Sure, I want him to think for himself," Blair said. "But I want him to think like *I* do."

Skinny Clarence Cass rode in front, hunched over in his saddle like a loose sack of bran. A short way behind him came a girl on a sidesaddle, her long dark skirt covering all but the ankles of her leather boots. Bringing up the rear were two Cass cowboys, in no hurry at all. Blair Bishop watched his son talking to the girl. At the distance he couldn't hear, but Allan's gestures made it plain he was apologizing.

Blair could tell by the pinch of Clarence's shoulders that the little man was fit to chew a horseshoe up and spit it out. A humorless smile came to Blair as he took a few steps forward. "Howdy, Clarence."

Cass reined up, his face splotched red from anger and the heat of the ride. "Bishop . . ." He had a thin neck, wattled like a turkey's.

Blair found himself smiling a little broader. He was actually enjoying this confrontation, and the realization surprised him a little. "I do believe we've got some of your cattle in that pen yonder."

Clarence Cass's anger was too much for him to hold. "Blair, you're a harsh man and a poor neighbor. An occasional beef critter of mine strays over onto your land and you abuse them and me like you was the Lord Almighty. One of these days you'll overstep yourself."

"There's more than an occasional critter in that pen; count them yourself. There's somethin' past a hundred head. And they didn't drift. Finn and Hez found where they was pushed through a cut fence. There was footprints all around where that wire was pinched. Cass footprints, I'd judge."

Cass blustered. "You got no proof of that."

"A man needs proof for court. I ain't goin' to court. I'm holdin' court of my own." Bishop's smile was suddenly gone. "Now you listen to me, Clarence, because I'm only goin' to tell you once and I don't want you to ever say you didn't hear. Your country is overstocked; I tried to tell you that last spring. Now your cows have eaten off all your grass and drunk up most of your water. You're tryin' to get them through by havin' them take mine. But I got barely enough to see my own cattle through till fall, and if it don't rain by then I'm in trouble same as you are."

For a moment he was distracted by sight of Jessie Cass. He saw her open her mouth as if to speak, then drop her chin. Well, he thought, at least she's got the decency to feel shame over the stunt her father tried to pull. Blair saw his son reach out and take Jessie's hand and squeeze it, reassuring her. "Damn it, boy," he wanted to say, "we got to stick together on this thing." But he couldn't rebuke his son in the presence of Cass and his crew; it would demean them both. He would wait.

He turned back to Cass. "Now you listen to me, Clarence. You've had all the free grass and free water you're goin' to steal from the Bishops. From this day on, we're goin' to watch our fences close. Any of your cattle we find over here, we'll run till they're ready to drop. For every dollar's worth of grass you steal, you'll lose five dollars worth of beef. We'll run them till there's no run left in them, then we'll put them back across the fence. Now, you think you can remember that?"

Clarence Cass looked as if he was about to suffer a stroke. He tried to argue, but he couldn't. He tried to curse, but only a half-intelligible gibberish came out. His Adam's apple bobbed up and down in anger and frustration, but he sat there and took Blair's tongue-lashing without striking back.

Blair glanced at the two Cass cowboys, not expecting any trouble from them. Cass didn't pay enough to get anything but his men's contempt. Blair suspected these cowboys would gleefully blab the whole story as quickly as they could get to town. Blair looked at them and jerked his chin toward the corrals. "Them's your boss's cows in there. Go drive them back where they belong."

The two rode over to the dusty corral and swung the wire gate open. One went in and pushed the bawling cattle out while the other waited beyond the gate to get them started in the right direction. Blair Bishop swung stiffly onto his big gray horse and stood ready to see that none of the cattle cut back or ran off. They were of a common strain, mostly Longhorn, a kind progressive ranchmen were trying to breed up and get rid of. He spotted a leggy, lanky C Bar bull in the bunch. That was one reason he hated so badly to see Cass' cattle come over here, apart from the fact that he was short of grass and water himself. Bishop's place was under fence now, and he was buying better bulls to upgrade his herd. Every time a C Bar bull came over, it meant some of Blair's cows were going to fetch up a scrubby calf.

Somehow Clarence Cass got his voice back and his courage up. "You're a greedy man, Blair Bishop. You're a selfish man and no neighbor at all."

Cass' opinion of Blair was of no concern except as a matter of idle curiosity. "How do you figure that, Clarence?"

"Anybody can tell you've had all the luck. It rained more on you than it did on me. You made more grass than I did. I don't expect the Lord really intended to favor you over me; He'd of wanted you to share."

"We both had the same rain, Clarence, and that was mighty little. Difference is, you abused your land. Now you're payin' for it. Let's don't bring the Lord in on the argument."

A little distance away, Allan Bishop sat on his horse near Jessie Cass. They weren't talking; Jessie was looking shamefacedly at the ground.

Clarence Cass said harshly, "Well, if you ain't sharin', then I ain't."

"What do you mean by that?"

"That boy of yours, he ain't goin' to have nothin' from my little girl. You tell him that. You tell him if he don't leave my little Jessie alone, I'll fill his britches with buckshot."

"Don't look to me like she wants to be left alone."

"You just tell him, Blair Bishop. I wouldn't have her marryin' into no family that won't help a neighbor."

"Marry?" Blair was startled. That was the first time the thought of marriage had occurred to him. "Hell no, I wouldn't have it either. If my boy was to pull a stunt like that, I wouldn't let him *or* her back on the place."

Cass glared. "You don't think a Cass is good enough for your boy?"

"I sure as hell don't. Now, your cows are on their way, Clarence. I'd be much obliged if you'd go with them. And take your girl."

Cass started to ride off but paused for a last word. "Someday you'll be wishin' you had a good neighbor."

"I been wishin' that for years."

{ THREE }

B lair Bishop sat there awhile, watching the cattle move slowly toward Cass country, the heavy dust clouding them over and hiding them much of the time. He pitied the cattle, because he knew they would find little to eat where they were going. But if he let them stay here, they would simply starve themselves and his own as well, for if Clarence Cass got by with a hundred, he would push in a hundred more. There was no bottom to the man's shabby greed.

Hez Northcutt said, "Want me to trail along and see that they all get there, Mister Bishop?"

"Yes, Hez. And take Allan with you."

Hez looked away. "Allan's gone. Rode off toward the house."

Irritated, Blair said, "All right, go ahead. Stay behind them and don't get into no trouble. Just let them know you're back there watchin' them. That'll be enough." He turned toward the foreman, black-moustached Finn Goforth. "Finn, you and me, we'd just as well go in."

Ahead of him a long way, he could see Allan riding alone, nursing his anger.

Marry! Blair clenched his big aching fist. Sure, that Jessie was a fetching-looking girl. He had wondered sometimes if Clarence was really her father or if perhaps her mother had had a secret. Jessie was better looking than what a boy was apt to find down on Silky Row in Two Forks. But to be foolish enough to marry her! Maybe he had been giving Allan too much benefit of the doubt.

Blair Bishop had always been a summer man. Cold weather had a way of creeping into his bones, but give him hot weather and he was in his element. The sweat broke free and easy, and it seemed to take out some of the rheumatism with it. He enjoyed the touch of the hot west wind against his face, cooling him as it reached through his sweat-streaked shirt. Pride always welled up in him when he rode along letting his gaze reach from north to south, east to west, knowing that everything he could see from here was his. Droughty though it was, he had earned every foot of it, and he wouldn't ever want to give it up to anyone but the sons for whom he and Elizabeth had struggled so long. Blair had taken trail-drive money to buy the first of his holdings a long time ago, leasing state and school land to go with it. In later years, as school lands went up for claiming, he had gotten his cowboys to homestead claims. They proved them up for the required three years. Then, if they didn't want to keep the land, they sold it to Blair for a profit. A few had kept, but most had sold. Gradually the Blair Bishop ranch had grown. And with it Blair Bishop had grown too, certain he had the world by the tail on a downhill pull.

What he hadn't counted on was running out of water. The whole south end of his place was dry. In a dozen places he had dug wells in hopes of finding underground water, but it wasn't there. He found only caliche and dry

sand. On the south half of the place he depended upon
dug surface tanks to catch and hold runoff water when it
rained. Now all these tanks were dry but one. The cattle
on his entire south ranch depended upon water from one
place—the Black Bull Tank.

If he could just get through this drought, Blair had
sworn, he wouldn't be caught in this kind of trap again.
He was going to have a lot more good tanks to catch and
hold water. He would never again have all his chips riding on the Black Bull Tank.

He jerked his thumb to the right. "Let's go by and see
how that new tank is comin', Finn."

They could see the dust before they saw the tank site.
Blair heard the scrape of metal against hard-packed
earth. A black dog came barking to meet them. A man
shouted lustily, and a pair of mules trudged out onto a
mound of fresh-turned earth, pulling a long-handled
fresno loaded with dirt. A man in overalls jerked up the
handle, flipping the fresno forward to dump its load
upon the mound, the dust swirling about him. The mules
moved quicker, relieved of the heavy burden. The man
shouted at them again, pulling the lines and turning
them back down into a broad basin he was laboriously
hollowing out of the ground. He didn't see the horsemen
until they rode up on the mound. He pulled the mules to
a halt and wrapped the lines around the fresno handle.
He stepped forward, taking off his hat and wiping sweat
onto a dirt-crusted handkerchief he had used too many
times already.

"Evenin', Mister Bishop. Evenin', Finn."

Blair Bishop nodded. "You're comin' along fine with
it, Joe. That tank'll catch a right smart of water if it ever
decides to rain again."

Joe Little shook his head. "A right smart. But it don't look much like rain today. I may be able to build a dozen more like this before we ever see a drop."

"I hope not. I wouldn't have nothin' left to pay you with, nor no cattle to drink out of it."

A boy walked across the basin carrying a jug wrapped in a wet towsack to keep its contents cool. "You need a drink of water, Joe? Howdy, Finn. Howdy, Dad."

Blair looked at him without surprise. "Billy, I thought I sent you to the south line camp with a wagonload of supplies."

"I already been. On my way back I thought I'd stop and help Joe awhile."

Billy looked a lot like Allan, except he was several years younger and not yet as big. One thing about it, Clarence Cass didn't have any daughters Billy's size, so maybe that was one worry Blair wouldn't have to put up with as Billy got older.

When the water jug had been passed around, Blair swung down and stiffly dropped to one knee to feel the earth in the bottom of the basin. "You reckon this one'll hold water, Joe?"

"There's caliche under it, but I ain't got it scooped down to that depth yet. I think it'll be all right."

"I sure hope so. If there's one thing this drought has taught me, it's that it's as bad to run out of water as to run out of grass. This country tends to be shy of both."

Joe Little nodded. He was a small man with a grin as bright as all sunup, his teeth shining through thick brown dust and three weeks' growth of whiskers. "Me and my mules, we can't make it rain, Mister Bishop. But if it does rain, we can sure see to it that you're fixed to catch water."

"Fine, Joe. We'll be gettin' in. You comin', Billy?"

Billy Bishop shook his head. "I'll be in for supper. I still got time to spell Joe with his mules an hour or so first."

One thing about Blair's boys, Allan and Billy both . . . they weren't afraid of work. In Billy's case it wasn't so much that he liked building tanks as it was that he liked being around Joe Little. Joe had more good stories than a man could listen to in a year. Blair always figured he made most of them up as he went along, which was harmless enough if the listener realized that and didn't take them for more than they were worth. Billy needed to learn sooner or later that not everything he was told in this world was Bible-sworn truth.

Finn Goforth glanced back over his shoulder, watching Billy take over the fresno and bring it across the basin for a fresh, deep bite of earth. "Mister Bishop, you sure Joe Little is a good influence on that boy?"

"What do you mean?"

"Him bein' a reformed bank robber and all. At least, I hope he's reformed."

"He ain't given me no reason to doubt him. He works like hell."

"He's got reason to owe you. You was the only one around here would give him a job after he come home from the pen. But that don't mean he might not take a notion someday to try it all over again. It'd be a bad experience for Billy."

Blair shrugged. "I don't think Joe would ever do that, not anymore. Anyway, a boy's got to learn for himself that it's not all rosy the way they write it in books. He's got to learn that people will lie to you, steal from you, cheat you . . . maybe even kill you. I don't think he'll learn that from Joe, except maybe the lyin' part, and Joe's lies don't mean any harm."

When they reached the barn at headquarters, Blair found Allan sitting in the shade of the building patching a stirrup leather. Blair unsaddled his big gray and watched a moment as the animal rolled in the dust, ridding itself of the saddle's itch. Blair walked into the barn and flung his saddle up onto its place on the rack, hooked the bridle over the horn and dropped the wet blanket over it all. He walked back out and stood a moment in silence, waiting for Allan to say something. Allan didn't look at him.

"Son, I'll ask Chaco to get supper fixed a little early. I'm hungry as a wolf."

Allan only glanced at him, then went back to his work. "I'll eat at the bunkhouse with the boys tonight," he said tightly.

Blair rubbed his stiff, aching right hand. "Boy, what we done today, we done out of necessity. I told you. You know that old man."

"You don't have to tell me anything about Clarence Cass."

"What goes for him goes for his kin."

Allan looked his father in the eye. "I'll agree with everything you say about Clarence. But you don't know nothin' at all about Jessie."

"Know the bull, and you know the calf." Blair turned slowly, his hip hurting a little, giving him a slight limp as he strode toward the white frame house with the tall narrow windows that he had built for Elizabeth after so many years of dugouts and picket shacks. She hadn't lived long enough to see the first coat of paint start to peel.

He saw a man sitting on the front gallery, and he paused a moment to squint. Blair couldn't recognize him at the distance, but he didn't quicken his pace. He had found long ago that good news would keep, and bad news didn't get any better for rushing it. This could be a cattle buyer, which would be good news, or it could be the tax collector.

He found it was neither. "Howdy, Erly," Blair said as he mounted the steps. "How's the high sheriff?"

Erly Greenwood had pushed up from the rawhide-bottomed straight chair and stood at the top of the steps, hand outstretched. "Evenin', Blair. How's yourself?"

"Younger than ever, except for a little rheumatism. You ain't reached that stage in life yet." He studied the sheriff with pleasure. "You're lookin' good, Erly. That Alice must be feedin' you well. Been a long time since you been out our way. This calls for a drink." He pushed open the carved front door with its oval glass and shouted, "Chaco, bring us a bottle out here."

Chaco Martinez fetched it. Blair offered it to Erly, but the sheriff motioned for Blair to take first drink. Blair did. He sighed in pleasure, wiping his sleeve across his mouth. "Some things fade as the years go by. Others just get better. Good whiskey and good friends, that's two things that always pleasure a man." He watched Erly tilt the bottle, then dropped his dirty hat on the floor and settled into the rocking chair he kept on the gallery for enjoying the evening breeze. "Chaco'll have supper ready directly. Looks like if you don't stay the night, I'm liable to have to eat by myself."

"I'll stay. I'd be half the night gettin' back to town."

Blair noticed that the warmth faded from the sheriff's face, and a worried frown replaced it. Blair considered. No, it wasn't election year; something else must be eating on him. Blair said, "We miss you out here, Erly. I've got good help, mind you, but I don't reckon there's ever been a better cowboy on this place than you was. Before you started puttin' on weight, that is."

Erly nodded. "I suppose I was a fair to middlin' hand. Times, I wish I was cowboyin' again. Seemed like then I always knew what to do."

"And now you don't?"

Erly shook his head. "Right now I'm in the water up to my neck, and it's still risin'. I got to tell an old friend some bad news, and I also got to tell him there's not a damn thing I can do."

"You talkin' about me, Erly?"

"You, Blair. I come to tell you Macy Modock is back."

Blair Bishop stopped rocking the chair. He sat in silence a minute or two, remembering, oblivious to the rising breeze riffling his thick gray hair. "You seen him, Erly?"

"Seen him and talked to him. Acts like he's back to stay." While Blair chewed his lip, the sheriff said, "I told him to keep right on movin', but I got no authority to make him do it. He's out free and legal. Long's I don't catch him breakin' the law, there's not a thing I can do about him, accordin' to the statutes." He paused. "There's a thing or two I could do *outside* of the statutes. With a man like Modock, I don't think there's many would criticize me."

"What could you do?"

"A man with his record, it'd be easy to trump up somethin' on him."

"You wouldn't want to do that, Erly."

"But I'd do it if you asked me to."

Blair Bishop passed the bottle to him again. "You know I wouldn't ask you. I wouldn't want you to."

"I didn't figure you would. So that leaves Modock sittin' there and us sittin' here, wonderin' what he's got on his mind."

"He didn't give you no idea?"

"Blair, he swore ten years ago that you'd pay for havin' him put away. He had a real good system goin' for him . . . a busy saloon, a cattle-runnin' business, even a little bit of bank robbery on the side. Hadn't been for you, I never could've nailed him. It was you that hired the special prosecutor and run all his sidekicks out of the country so the jury could get up courage to convict him."

"There's not much he could do except come right out and kill me. I doubt that he cares to hang."

"He wouldn't of come back here if he didn't have somethin' on his mind. He's still got a little money, Blair. It's been settin' in a bank drawin' interest all the time he's been gone. He could go someplace he wasn't known and set himself up decent. But he's come back here."

Blair Bishop scowled, remembering how it had been before Macy Modock was sent away. "So it leaves us out on the end of the limb."

"And Macy Modock with a saw in his hand."

Blair looked at the bottle, decided he didn't want another drink and offered it to Erly. The sheriff shook his head. Blair said, "Well, I don't intend to sit here and sweat, wonderin' about him. I'll go back to town with you in the mornin'. I'll talk to him myself."

The sheriff fretted. "I don't know if that's a good idea. It might come to a shootin'."

"Not if I don't take a gun with me." He held up his

rheumatic right hand. "Look at that. Most times I can't even hold a pistol anymore, much less shoot one."

"It puts you at a bad disadvantage, Blair."

"But it puts him there too. He can't shoot a man that ain't got a gun and couldn't use one if he had it. He didn't come out after ten years in the pen rarin' to go right back."

They dismissed Macy Modock from conversation, but he remained on both their minds during the long periods of silence between the subjects they drummed up to talk about. Billy Bishop came home finally, face and clothes covered with dust from the tank-building job. Chaco Martinez met him at the gallery and made him strip off the clothes right there and walk around back to wash before he came into the house. That, Blair thought, was what Elizabeth would have done had she lived. Chaco, cranky but competent, was no substitute for a wife and mother, though without him Blair didn't know how he would have managed the house and the care of two boys.

Blair kept looking for Allan to come up from the bunk-house, but his older son never showed. Finally he said to Billy, "Why don't you go tell your brother it's time for him to go to bed?"

Billy Bishop avoided his father's eyes. "He's not here, Dad." Pressed, he added, "He was saddlin' up a horse when I came in. Said he had an errand to run. I don't figure you sent him on any errand, Dad."

Blair shook his head, for both he and Billy knew where Allan had gone. Billy held his silence awhile, then put in, "Dad, maybe you ought to get to know Jessie better. Maybe she's not as bad as you think."

"I'm not sayin' she's bad, son. I'm just sayin' she was foaled in a poor stable."

There never was a time that Blair Bishop could walk into this house without Elizabeth crossing his mind. Times like this he missed her most of all. Maybe a mother could have talked to a son in a way a father couldn't.

{ FOUR }

He was up before daylight next morning. He met his sons and Erly Greenwood in the kitchen, where Chaco Martinez was frying up steak for breakfast, humming a Mexican song about the dark ties between love and death. Blair hadn't slept much, and he guessed his face showed it. He fastened his gaze on Allan. "Son, you went someplace last night."

"Yes, sir, I did."

"You know I don't want you goin' there no more."

"Dad, I've never argued with you. I don't intend to. So that's one subject I just don't want to talk to you about."

"We *will* talk about it."

"*You* can. I'm not goin' to listen." Allan got up and started toward the door. Blair waited until Allan had his hand on the doorknob. He called, "Come on back, boy, and eat your breakfast. We'll talk about it another time."

Blair Bishop hadn't lost many battles in his life. He had an uneasy feeling he was going to lose this one. Sure, he could do one thing; he could flat forbid Allan ever to go to the Cass place again. And likely as not Allan would pack up and leave the ranch, then do what he damn well pleased. That, Blair knew, was what *he* would have done if the same situation had occurred twenty-five or thirty years ago. But of course it hadn't. Elizabeth had been one thing. A daughter of Clarence Cass was another.

The sheriff had not mentioned Macy Modock to Blair's sons or to Chaco, who would quickly blab it. Blair made a point to say nothing. Time enough for that after he had a chance to meet Modock face to face.

He sensed that people were watching him as he rode into Two Forks with Erly Greenwood. The word about Modock must have gotten around by now. Those people who had lived here ten years ago wouldn't have any trouble remembering. The rest had no doubt heard enough. He rode through town, tying up beside Erly at a hitchrack in front of the courthouse. The hostler from the Two Forks Livery & Grain came shuffling toward them as fast as he could move without breaking into a trot.

"Mornin', Mister Bishop. Reckon Erly's told you?"

Blair nodded. "He told me."

"It was me that seen Macy first, Mister Bishop. I knowed he meant trouble, and I went straight to the sheriff. I knowed that was what you'd of wanted me to do, and I done it."

Blair decided Harley Mills was casting around for some kind of reward. He also knew that anything he gave Harley would wind up being spent or traded for whiskey. Blair had given Harley a good chance once and had seen him drink it up. Blair Bishop was not much given to second chances. "Thanks, Harley. Where's Macy at?"

"A little while ago he was settin' in the Bar & Billiard Emporium. Had a redheaded feller with him. They come to town together. They both got guns on." The hostler had glanced at Blair's hip and saw no pistol there. He began to realize Blair didn't intend to give him anything, and he showed his disappointment.

"All right, Harley." Blair couldn't tell whether Harley was concerned about him or just wanting to be sure he saw the whole show. He suspected the latter. He looked a moment toward the saloon, dreading.

"Well, Erly, I guess this is what I come for."

"I'm goin' with you."

"No, you're not. I told you, you bein' there with a gun—or even that badge—might trigger somethin' off."

"What if he shoots you, Blair?"

Blair Bishop came close to making a dry smile. "Then I reckon you can come on over."

The ride into town had stiffened Blair's legs, and he walked slowly, that cursed limp plaguing him. Damn it, why couldn't a man go into his autumn years with a little dignity? His mouth went dry as he neared the building. Blair Bishop had never feared any man, and he didn't fear Macy Modock. But he disliked trouble and would ride around it when he could. Whether this meeting meant trouble or not, he knew it was a cinch to be unpleasant. He'd already had enough unpleasantness to do him for a lifetime.

The heavy bartender stepped out the front door and moved to meet him. His long moustaches drooped, and his bushy eyebrows were knitted in concern. "Mister Bishop, you know who's in there?"

Blair nodded. "I know."

"You and me been friends a long time, Mister Bishop. I don't want nothin' happenin' to you in my bar."

"Nothin's fixin' to happen. I'm goin' to talk to him, is all."

"He's been settin' there like he was waitin' for somethin'. You, maybe. I don't like the feel of it."

"If he's waitin' for me, there's no use me puttin' things off."

"You ain't packin' no gun, Mister Bishop, but he is. And so's that mean-eyed one he's got with him. They could kill you in a second."

"That's how come I left my gun at home. There won't be no trouble."

The bartender glanced at the door. "All right, Mister Bishop. But I got my shotgun behind the bar, loaded and cocked. If that Modock makes one bad move, I'll let him have both barrels."

Blair nodded his thanks. He stepped up onto the little wooden porch and through the open door. He sensed the bartender coming in behind him and moving to his place behind the bar. Blair Bishop blinked, then saw three men seated at a little table. He gave the red-bearded one a brief glance and pegged him for a gunfighter. That cinched it; Modock hadn't come here looking for sunshine and pretty songs. He turned to the tall, lanky man with the black eyes and unlighted cigar.

"Macy. Been a long time."

"Ten years, two months and twenty-one days. I counted them every one."

It relieved Blair that Macy made no move to shake hands, for Blair had no intention of doing it. He noted that the ten years had been hard on Macy Modock. The man seemed to have aged twenty since he had left here. He was thinner, his cheeks sunken in, his shoulders a little drooped. Macy's hair was shorter than he used to wear it . . . prison cut, Blair figured. And it was sprinkled with gray where once it had been coal black. But his eyes hadn't changed. They had always looked hard as steel. They were framed in darker circles now more than ever before, and if anything, they were harder.

Modock motioned toward the red-bearded man. "This here is Owen Darby. We was partners, you might say, back in *school*. We worked on the same pile of rocks."

Blair nodded. That fit his first appraisal.

Modock motioned toward a thin, black-suited little man on the other side of him. "Bishop, you ain't yet said good mornin' to Judge Quincy."

Blair said, "I *never* say good mornin' to Judge Quincy."

The little man's lip turned down in an angry scowl. In Bishop's view, Quincy was a cheap, scheming lawyer who made his living defending the indefensible and hunting for loopholes in the statutes. He had never been a judge in his life, and he never would be one unless the government went plumb to hell. Someone had hung the name on him as a cheap saloon joke, and it had stuck to him ever since. Folks said "Judge" with a bit of a snicker.

Modock said, "I'll grant you the judge didn't have much luck defendin' me, but then he was up against the best legal talent that a rich man's money could buy. He's had pretty good luck in some other cases, though. I count him as a friend."

Every man to his own kind, Blair thought. "I come to town because I figured you and me might have somethin' to talk about, Macy. Do we?"

"I don't know. What do you think?" Modock seemed to sense that he held all the cards. "Bothers you, don't it, me bein' here?"

"Like knowin' there's a rattlesnake under my porch and not bein' able to get at him. It bothers me that they

ever let you out. It'd bother me knowin' you was anyplace, Macy, except in jail. But you're here, and I want
to know what you're plannin' to do."

Modock took the cigar from his mouth, eyeing Blair
Bishop levelly, his own eyes unreadable. "Can't say that
I've made up my mind. If I do, maybe I'll let you know."

"If you got any notions about gettin' even with me,
Macy, you better forget them. What I done to you, you
had comin' in spades. I don't want trouble with you, but
I won't stand still for no foolishness."

Macy dipped the end of his cigar in his whiskey glass,
soaked it a moment, then shoved it back into his mouth.
"Now, what do you think I might do to you, Bishop? You
was a big man before, and you're bigger now. Got you a
fine ranch, lots of cattle. And me, what have I got to show
for all that time? Ten years cut out of my life, cut out of
me the way you'd rip the guts out of a catfish."

"You've still got a little money, Macy, from what I
hear. And you still got time. You could do a right smart
for yourself if you was of a mind to."

Macy grinned, his teeth clamped on the cold cigar.
"And I will, Bishop; you can just bet I will."

Blair felt his hackles rise. "You'd do better someplace
else. Take your money and go where they don't know
you."

"But I couldn't collect what's owed me if I was to go
someplace else. And I'm figurin' on collectin', Bishop.
From you, most of all." He used the cigar as a pointer,
jabbing it toward Blair. "I had ten years to study about
you, and believe me I done a lot of thinkin'. For a long
time if I'd of had the chance, I'd of just come back and
shot you dead wherever I found you. But gradually it
come to me that there's better ways of killin' a man than

shootin' him. There's ways to kill him off an inch at a time till there's nothin' left of him but a little dab of cold sweat. I decided that's what I'd do to you, Bishop, just whittle away at you.

"I see you ain't wearin' a gun. Probably haven't in years. But before I'm done, you'll wear one. Maybe in the end you'll get so desperate you'll come gunnin' after me and I can finish the job nice and legal, in self-defense."

Color surged into Bishop's face. His arthritic right hand convulsed. There had been a time if anyone had talked to him like that he would have shot him on the spot. But that had been a long time ago, before the years mellowed him, and before an accumulation of old pains and injuries half crippled him. He said quietly, "I'm sorry it's this way, Macy. I expected it would be, but I'm sorry just the same." He turned, his big Mexican spurs jingling as he limped heavily across the pine floor and out onto the porch. A strong dread rose up in him, and a helplessness.

He walked across the street to where the sheriff waited beside the tied horses. Bishop didn't speak, so Erly Greenwood did.

"Talkin' to him didn't help, did it?"

Bishop shook his head. "The hate's as strong as it ever was."

The sheriff suggested, "What I told you yesterday still goes. Just say the word and I'll trump up somethin'."

"It'd never set right with you, Erly, or with me. No, we'll just wait, and we'll hope. Sooner or later he'll make a mistake."

"By that time," said Greenwood, "you could be dead."

* * *

Modock got up from his chair and walked to the door to watch Blair Bishop limp across the street. He saw him in conversation with the sheriff. Modock chewed the cigar savagely, his hard eyes glittering with the pent-up hatred of ten hellish years.

The red-whiskered Owen Darby spat at a brass bowl and missed. "You got your stomach churnin', Macy. I can hear it from where I sit. If I hated a man that much, I'd just shoot him and be done with it."

Modock glanced around at the heavy bartender and decided to ignore him. He didn't give a damn what a bartender thought. "Did you ever get so hungry for somethin', Owen, that when you finally got it you ate it slow and spaced it out to make it last as long as you could?" When Darby shook his head, Modock said, "No, I expect you never did, so you can't begin to understand. *You* kill a man quick, the way a wolf does. If it's a man like Bishop, I'd rather do it slow and play with him awhile, like a cat."

A young woman walked by in the street. From the scarlet hue of her crinolines, Modock surmised she might come from down on Silky Row. "Talk about hungry . . . a man don't know how long ten years can be when he never feels the touch of a woman, never hears the laugh in a woman's voice. That's somethin' else Blair Bishop owes me for . . . ten years without a woman." He glanced at the bartender. "Things still alive on Silky Row, the way they used to be?"

The bartender made no attempt to hide his dislike. "Just about. But I doubt *you're* as alive as you used to be."

Modock grunted and walked back to the table. He stared at the little lawyer. "Judge, how long you think it'll take you to go through all them deeds of Bishop's?"

Quincy sat rigid, ill at ease in the company of these two. "Some time. And it'll require some money too. A task like this is not undertaken lightly."

"You'll get your money; I promised you that. Find me the right flaws in them deeds and you'll get a lot *more* money." He leaned over the table. "Let me down and you'll eat every law book in your office, one at a time."

"Mister Modock, you have no right . . ."

Modock punched his finger into Quincy's breastbone hard enough to bring pain. "I don't give a damn about rights. You just do what I tell you!"

{ FIVE }

Joe Little put the can of tomatoes on the ground, opened the blade of his pocketknife and punched a hole through the tin. He punched a second at a right angle, the ends of the slits coming together in a V. He pushed the cut part down with his thumb and offered the can to Billy Bishop. Billy, trained to defer to his elders, shook his head. "You first."

Little tilted the can up and took a long swallow. He passed it over to Billy. "Boy," he said, "you got to quit bringin' me stuff like this out of your old daddy's pantry. He's furnishin' me grub enough."

"Not tomatoes or peaches or stuff like that. Anyway, he can afford a can of somethin' now and then."

"I don't know. If it don't rain pretty soon, he might not be able to buy nothin'. You got to quit it, Billy. That's stealin'."

"It's not stealin' when you take it out of your own house. That's not like stealin' cattle, or takin' from a bank, or . . ." He broke off short, realizing he was edging into deep water. "Anyway, Dad knows about it. He's seen me. And you deserve somethin' special once in a while. This is hard work, buildin' tanks."

Joe Little studied the can awhile in silence. "Did I

ever tell you, boy, about the time I shared a can of tomatoes with John Wesley Hardin?"

Billy smiled. "Just happens you did. Only, the last time
you said it was Billy the Kid."

Joe Little frowned. "I believe you're right. It *was*
Billy the Kid. What I shared with Wes Hardin was a pot
of coffee."

Joe's black dog set in to barking and trotted across the
newly dug basin. Joe stood up to look. He almost dropped
the can. He said something under his breath, his eyes going wide.

Billy jumped to his feet. "What is it, Joe?" Joe didn't
reply, so Billy looked for himself. A hundred yards away
came two men on horseback. They were strangers to Billy.

Joe said: "If I didn't know better, I'd swear that was
Macy Modock, but he's in jail."

Billy shook his head. "No, he's out. You hadn't heard?"

"I ain't heard nothin' but a hooty owl and you in a
month of Sundays."

"They been talkin' a little around the ranch. They
don't say much that I can hear. I remember there was
hard feelin's once between him and Dad. Is he back to
make trouble, Joe?"

"I don't know, boy." Joe Little shook his head. "Anywhere he's at, he's goin' to make trouble." He sagged a
bit.

Billy looked at him in surprise. "You know Macy
Modock?"

"I know him, boy. I've stretched the truth a mite about
some of them other fellers, but I sure as hell know Macy
Modock. We was . . . in *school* together. Shared a room
awhile, so to speak."

"You mean you was cellmates?"

Joe Little dropped any pretense. "We was cellmates. For me, it was like bein' denned up with a rattler."

Macy Modock and Owen Darby eased their horses down into the basin and rode across to where Little and Billy stood on the fresh-made dump. Modock lifted his hand and made a dim sort of smile. "Howdy, Joe. Folks in town told me you was workin' out here."

Joe looked at first one man, then the other, worry creasing his dust-powdered face. "Folks in town talk too much. How do, Macy, Darby . . ." There was no greeting in his voice. The black dog sniffed suspiciously around the strange horses and backed off, as if deciding that if his master didn't like the company, he didn't either. He barked again from a careful distance.

Macy Modock stared at Billy. "I'd judge by the looks that this boy would be a Bishop. Howdy, boy."

Billy Bishop had been raised to be civil right up to the moment he swung his fist. "How do, Mister Modock."

Modock's attention stayed with Billy. "I swear, he sure does favor his old daddy. I bet that old man sets a heap of store in you, don't he, boy?"

Joe Little took that for an implied threat. "Macy, this boy is a friend of mine. You leave him alone."

"I'm a friend of yours too, Joe."

"That all depends, Macy. It all depends."

Modock watched the boy a minute longer, then said, "Button, I got somethin' to discuss with my old friend Joe Little. Don't you reckon you could find you somethin' to do while we talk? Go work them mules and that fresno, maybe."

Billy looked uncertainly at Joe. Joe silently motioned with his chin for him to go ahead. Reluctantly Billy walked down into the basin where the mules waited patiently, in no hurry to work again. Joe Little moved off of the dump on the side away from the wind so the dust wouldn't reach him. Modock and Owen Darby followed him a-horseback. Joe turned and said curtly, "You said you wanted to talk. I don't see we got anything to talk about, but go ahead."

"Maybe we *ain't* got anything to talk about, but I thought I'd come see for myself if it was true what I heard . . . that Joe Little was sweatin' hisself into the ground for Blair Bishop."

"I'm bein' paid a fair wage. I got over two hundred dollars in the bank. That's more money than I ever had in my life before . . . legally."

"Two hundred dollars? Why, friend, you made that much money once in an hour."

"I said legally."

"If I remember right, Blair Bishop helped put you away, same as he done me."

"I had it comin'. I been ashamed ever since for what I done."

Modock's eyes narrowed. "Joe, I thought you had more in you. That black dog of yours yonder . . . if a man was to take a double of a rope to him, he'd tuck his tail between his legs and run. And it looks to me like that's just what you done too. You've tucked your tail."

"I'm doin' honest work and earnin' an honest dollar."

"Workin' for a man who helped send you to jail. A man who probably despises you and'd tell you so if he didn't need you to bend your back for him."

Fear began to touch Joe Little, because he knew this pair was up to something, and he sensed they had a place in it for him. Otherwise they wouldn't have come out here. Macy Modock was not a man to waste his time on people he couldn't use. "Macy, if you got any notions that include me, forget it. I'm stayin' right where I'm at."

"Followin' a plow or a fresno, lookin' a pair of mules in the rump all day? I thought you had more ambition."

"I have. Someday it'll be my own mules, my own place."

"But still mules. You're a damn fool, Joe Little. I'm sorry we wasted our time."

"I'm sorry too. I'd of been happier if I'd never laid eyes on you again the rest of my life."

Anger came into Modock's dark-circled eyes. "Next time you're kissin' Blair Bishop's boots, remember we offered you a chance to get out. Goodbye, Joe. We'll see you in hell."

"Keep a place warm for me. You'll probably get there before I do."

Macy Modock drew rein and took a long look down toward the headquarters of the Clarence Cass place. "That's a greasy-sack outfit if ever I seen one," he muttered to Owen Darby. "A man can't have no pride to live in a place like that when he could do better." The house was small and plain, evidently put up by somebody who didn't know much about carpentering and didn't learn much on the job. It showed no evidence that it had ever known paint. The corrals were of brush, mostly, some of the fences leaning. One wild bull could have torn the whole thing out by the roots.

"Fits the rest of his country," Darby put in. "Whole place looks like it'd been sheeped into the ground."

"Not sheep," Modock said. "Just too many cattle. Dry weather come, the place couldn't feed them all."

A thin, sharp-hipped Longhorn steer eyed the riders warily and clattered off into a motte of live oaks, his tail high. He looked weak enough to fall if he tried to run very hard. Modock scowled. "I remember this place the way it used to be. Cass didn't have it then. We stole some pretty good cows off of the old boy who did."

"How come he left?"

"Went broke. They split up his country and sold it off to people like this Cass."

"Maybe you helped break him."

"Maybe. It was his lookout, not mine. It's every man's place to take care of hisself. If he can't do it, he ain't got no sympathy comin'." Modock took a long sweeping look over the land. "If it'd rain some, I could make a good place out of this, Owen . . . if it was mine. And maybe before we're through, it'll *be* mine."

They rode up to the barn first, where Modock saw a man lounging in the shade, a rawhide chair tilted against the wall. It seemed to Modock that the wall might have had a little lean to it, but he wasn't sure. He wouldn't be surprised, judging by the rest of the outfit. He spotted another man asleep farther out, under a wooden water tank that stood on a platform beside a cypress-vaned windmill. "Evenin'. We're lookin' for Clarence Cass."

The cowboy jerked awake, pushing the hat back out of his face and blinking sleepily. Modock had to repeat. The cowboy pointed. "He's up at the house. Clarence, he usually takes him a little nap in the heat of the day."

That didn't surprise Modock either. From the looks of the place, he would judge that nap ran from noon till about sundown.

Owen Darby said, "If you *was* to take over this place, I don't know what you'd want with it."

"It could be fixed up. Needs some changes made. Them lazy cowboys is the first thing I'd get rid of."

Riding toward the small house, Modock caught a quick glimpse of a young woman out back, hanging clothes on a sagging wire. He glanced at Darby in surprise. Nobody had mentioned to him about a girl out here. He turned back for a second look at her, but she had disappeared quickly into the house. "Owen," he said quietly, "place already looks better."

He swung down and looped his leather reins over a fence picket. Darby took his time, following behind as Modock strode up to the house, narrowed eyes sweeping everything in sight. The door was wide open, but Modock thought it best to observe the amenities, for now. He knocked on the door frame.

From inside, he could hear the woman's voice, speaking low, and he could hear a sleepy, confused grumbling. Broke up the old man's nap, he knew. Presently Clarence Cass trudged to the door, trying to shove his shirttail into his waistband without bothering to unbutton his britches. He blinked at Modock without recognition. "You-all lookin' for somebody?"

Modock spoke with what pleasantness he was able to muster. "Yes, sir, we're lookin' for Clarence Cass, the owner of this place. You'd be him, I judge."

"Yes, sir, reckon I would."

"We'd be right favored if we could have a drink of cool water out of your cistern, sir. Then we'd like to talk some business with you."

"With me?" Cass, not completely over his nap, blinked uncertainly. "Sure, the cistern's right yonder. You-all cattle buyers?"

"No, sir."

"Then what business you got with me?"

Modock walked over to the cistern and turned the handle to lower the bucket into the well. He cranked it up again, conscious that Cass was waking rapidly now, and trailing him in his socks. He took his time about drinking the water, then passing it on to Darby, letting the old man's curiosity build. Cass repeated, "What's this business you was talkin' about?"

Modock turned to face him and motioned that they ought to go over and sit down in the shade. It was Cass' place, but already Modock was beginning to call the turn. "Mister Cass, I understand you had some difficulty the other day with Blair Bishop."

Cass for a moment eyed him with suspicion. "I'd say that was my business. Anyway, I ain't finished with Blair Bishop yet."

Modock nodded. "That's why we came. I'm Macy Modock. This here is my friend Owen Darby."

Realization came, and Cass' mouth went open. "Modock! Didn't know you was anywheres around. I've heard about you."

"Mostly lies, I expect, sir. There was a time I had a standin' in Two Forks . . . in this whole country. It was taken away from me by schemers and liars. Oh, I'll grant you, Mister Cass, I sure ain't no preacher. I expect when I get to the Pearly Gates, it'll take some talkin' to get me through. But I'm not near what some have painted me. Some like Blair Bishop . . ." He paused. "You should know, sir. I understand he's maligned you too."

Cass nodded vigorously. "One of these days my patience'll wear thin."

Modock reached into his pocket and took out a couple of cigars, handing one to Cass, biting into the other himself. "I thought maybe it already had. I thought you might be ready to do somethin' about it."

"I will. One of these days I damn sure will."

"It could be one day *soon,* if you was of a mind. Some folks in town, they told me you'd be a real good man for me to get together with. They said you was a man who knew what he wanted and wasn't afraid."

Cass' vanity was quickly touched. "Who was it said that?"

"Some folks." Modock took out a match but didn't light the cigar. He simply chewed it while his narrowed eyes studied Clarence Cass. Feeling he had lucked upon a sympathetic ear, Cass began to unburden himself of all the injuries he had suffered at the hands of the rich and overbearing Blair Bishop. Modock listened attentively, nodding every so often and speaking softly, "That's just the way it was done to me."

Owen Darby couldn't listen to it. Scowling, he walked off to poke around the place for himself.

At length Cass ran down, and Modock said, "I can tell you've got a just grievance, my friend. And I can tell that the folks in town was right. You're the man I been lookin' for."

Cass reached down and pulled up a saggy sock. "What did you have in mind for me to do?"

"Just string along with me . . . back me up in whatever I say. We'll get even with Blair Bishop."

A sudden worry tugged in Cass' face. "But how? You ain't figurin' on killin' nobody, are you?"

"Killin'? The thought never once crossed my mind. I'd sooner scrub floors in the meanest dive in town than to kill somebody. No, what I got in mind will give us a chance to whittle Blair Bishop down, to break him piece by piece. You'll be in on it; you'll have the satisfaction. What's more, you'll have a chance to pick up some of the pieces when they fall. You'd like to have part of the Bishop ranch, wouldn't you, Mister Cass? You got a chance to get it."

"The Bishop ranch." A glow came into Cass' eyes, and he began rubbing his knuckles, enjoying the thought of it. "He's always lorded it over me, Blair Bishop has. He's got a better country, had better rain, always had all the luck when there's been others just as deservin' that the Almighty has passed by and left needful. It'd sure pleasure me . . ." He broke into a crooked grin. Modock guessed that was a sight few people had ever seen. Cass said, "I'm with you, Mister Modock. What'll I do?"

"First off, you'll let it be known around that me and Owen, we're on a deal to buy in as partners with you."

Cass' eyebrows raised. "You ain't, are you?"

"Of course not. There won't be no papers signed. Later on you can say we backed out by mutual consent. But we need a base to operate from, a reason for some of the things I figure to do. You with us, friend?"

"*With* you, Mister Modock."

They shook hands, and Owen Darby came back. Modock said, "See there, Owen, I told you this was the man."

Clarence Cass straightened his bent shoulders and stood every bit of five and a half feet tall. "I'm proud you come, Macy. I never been one to brag; I always been one to keep my silence. Still waters runs the deepest, I've always thought."

"Truer words was never spoke, partner."

Cass turned toward the house and called: "Jessie! I

want you to put a pot of coffee on for these men." The girl came hesitantly to the door. Modock stared, his dark eyes widening for a moment. She was seventeen, maybe eighteen, eyes blue, face slender and nice-featured, hair the soft brown of a good Morgan colt. And her figure . . . she was coming into the full bloom of womanhood. Modock kept staring, the pulse quickening in him. He'd visited down on Silky Row a little since he had been back in Two Forks, but that was tarnished merchandise. This, he sensed, was fresh goods, untried, unspoiled.

Cass introduced the girl to the two men. "Girl," he said, "Macy and Owen here, they're talkin' about goin' in as partners with us. I want you to fix them some coffee." He reconsidered. "No, by Godfrey, this calls for somethin' better than coffee. This calls for whiskey, and I got a new bottle still uncorked."

Modock took the bottle, but he didn't need it. The girl was enough for now, as long as he had been without. He watched her move about the house, and he decided. This ranch wasn't the only thing of Clarence Cass' that Macy Modock was going to have!

{ SIX }

⟨⟨⟨⟨

In the darkness, Allan Bishop almost rode upon Joe Little's tank-building camp. He reined up sharply at the unexpected sight of Joe's mules hobbled on the short grass. The mules stirred in the pale moonlight, and in camp Joe Little called, "Who's out yonder?"

Allan's first impulse was to keep quiet and bluff it out, to make Joe think it was just a loose horse ambling by in the night. But he remembered Joe kept a shotgun in camp. He decided he'd be better off not finding out how good a shot Joe was.

"It's me, Joe. Allan Bishop."

"Allan!" Joe Little came out of the shallow basin where he had spread his bedroll. He wasn't carrying the shotgun. "Boy, you lost?"

Allan shook his head and dismounted. "I'd forgot you'd moved over here to start a new tank. If I'd thought, I'd of ridden way around and not bothered you."

"Your daddy decided he needed a second watering here close by the old Black Bull Tank. There's enough water gets down this draw sometimes to fill two tanks and leave plenty over." He eyed Allan suspiciously. "How come you out in the night thisaway?"

"Just ridin', Joe."

Little tilted his head. "Ain't but a mile or so yonder to old Clarence Cass' fence. That's where you're headin', ain't it?"

Allan nodded, uncomfortable.

"I'm not faultin' you, Allan. Ain't been many years since I was doin' the same. I know the way your pulse beats, but the way I heard it, Clarence said you wasn't to go over there no more, and Blair Bishop said the same thing."

"I'm of age, Joe. So's Jessie, pretty near." Allan's voice tightened in resentment. "Why don't they leave us alone, Joe? We're not hurtin' nobody. We got a right to lead our own lives."

"You're too young to understand it if I told you, and Blair Bishop's too old to understand your side of it. Maybe I'm at just the right age . . . halfway between. Your daddy thinks he's doin' what's best for you. As for old Clarence, he's a miserable little whelp, and deep down I expect he knows it. Your old daddy has shamed him. Clarence hasn't got the guts to lash out at Blair, but in his eyes you're still a button. His kind can always kick a dog or a kid."

"Sorry I bothered you, Joe. If anybody asks, you didn't see me."

"You watch out for that old man."

Allan rode away thinking he knew why his brother Billy liked to visit with Joe Little. Joe had been through the grinder. Joe understood.

It went against Allan Bishop's grain to go on the *cuidado,* to sneak around like a coyote. He had grown up watching his father meet everything and everybody head on, his shoulders square and his jaw set. He doubted that Blair Bishop had ever gone to a back door or followed the moonlight shadows in his life. They would probably bury Blair Bishop with his hat on.

But Allan found himself approaching Clarence Cass' place from the back side and stepping to the ground, tying his horse in the darkness of the mesquite brush a hundred yards from the barn. Allan paused in the edge of the shadow, looking around before he set out to cross the open strip that lay between him and the brush corrals. The house lay beyond, and so did a rough-lumber shed. Allan doubted he would be seen.

He waited a long time, wanting to roll a smoke but fearing the flare of the match might betray him. He leaned on the fence and stared at the lamplighted windows of the house. Presently he saw a quick movement, something passing between him and the light. In a moment a slender figure came around the corner of the corral and paused. A girl's voice reached him gentle and quiet. "Allan!"

"Over here, Jessie." He walked to meet her and swept her into his arms. He kissed her savagely, for the wanting was stronger now that they had been forbidden to each other. They said little at first, for all the love words had been spoken so many times before. At length, Allan said, "I've got a good mind to march up to the house and tell your old daddy I'm takin' you and he can go to hell!"

"What about your *own* daddy?"

"I'd tell him the same thing, if he pushed me."

"No you wouldn't. You respect him too much; you don't really want to hurt him. As for mine, I know what he is. But still, he's my father. So we'll wait."

"This business of meetin' in the dark, it's no good, Jessie. I feel like some kind of a criminal. I expect you do too."

"We got to do it this way or not see each other at all."

"We don't have to say nothing to either one of them, you know. We could just up and leave and not speak to anybody."

"It'd be the same thing, almost. Later on we'd be ashamed. We got a whole life to live together, Allan. We don't want to start it wrong."

"I don't know how long I can wait, Jessie. Seein' you this way, it sets me afire."

"Then maybe you better not be a-comin' over here again for a while."

"Not seein' you would be even worse."

She shook her head and buried her face against his chest.

"I don't know what the answer is, Allan. We just got to wait awhile. I don't know what my daddy would do for himself if I was to leave him."

"The whole place would come apart. If you hadn't worked like a span of mules, it'd already be gone. Sooner or later you got to leave him. He won't never be no readier for it than he is tonight."

"I'm afraid to leave him right now. Things are wrong out here. They been wrong ever since Macy Modock came."

"I hear he's bought into partnership."

"That's what he and Dad say. I haven't seen any money change hands. There's somethin' wrong; I can't figure out just what. Dad hangs on him like a hound dog to a master, and yet I can tell that somehow Dad's afraid of him too. First thing Modock did was to fire our two cowhands. I could tell Dad didn't intend for him to do it, but Dad just stood there and didn't say a word. Modock's gradually takin' this place over. Dad's losin' his grip on it."

"I can't figure out what a man like Modock wants with a place like this. There's lots of better ones if he wanted to ranch."

"He's not a rancher. I don't know what he is exactly, but he's not a rancher. He scares me, Allan. He scares me to death."

"Has he done anything . . ."

She shook her head. "No. But did you ever get a sudden feelin' you was in danger, and then see a rattlesnake? An instinct, sort of. Times I get that feelin'. I look around, and there's Macy Modock watching me."

"All the more reason I ought to take you away from here."

"No, Allan, not for a while yet, anyway. If there's somethin' wrong, I don't want to leave my dad here by himself. We'll go when it's time. Till then we just got to wait."

She kissed him again. He caught her hands as she started to leave. He held them a moment, saw she meant what she had said, then reluctantly let her go. She turned once at the corner of the corral and looked back at him. Then she was gone.

Allan Bishop went to his horse.

In the shadows, Macy Modock stood watching the girl. He had followed her when she left the house with an excuse about seeing that the chickens were shut up. He had seen her take care of that chore before dark. Modock had stood back far enough that he could not make out the words, but he could hear the soft exchange of talk between boy and girl. He had trembled as he watched the girl move into Allan Bishop's arms. Watching her now as she walked slowly toward the house, it was all he could do to keep from striding after her, overtaking her, setting claim upon her and letting the fire in him run its course. But the slow fire of his hatred burned steadier, and it prevailed. There were other things to be done first.

He looked toward the brush where the young man had gone, and where hoofbeats trailed away in the night. It would be easy to ride after Allan Bishop, to kill him and fling his body upon Blair Bishop's porch. What better way to punish the man than by robbing him of his son?

But Modock knew that would cut vengeance short. That would put him on the run. Maybe he would have time to kill Blair Bishop, and maybe he wouldn't.

No, he would wait. All things would come to him in their own due course. He would kill Blair Bishop, but it would be in his own time, and under conditions of his own choosing.

{ SEVEN }

A full moon sent long shadows slanting out ahead of three riders. They moved in an easy trot across the rolling land, unshod hoofs raising dry dust to pinch the nostrils of horses and men. One man kept hanging back and looking nervously around him, twisting his skinny frame first one way, then the other.

"Macy, I oughtn't to be with you on this. If old Blair Bishop was to catch me on his country of a night, he'd turn me wrongside out. You know he's bound to miss them cattle sooner or later. You know who he'll suspicion first."

Macy Modock glanced at Owen Darby, then growled impatiently at Cass. "I wisht you'd quit your bellyachin', Clarence. I've listened to about all I'm goin' to. Hush up or I'll set you afoot, and then maybe he *will* catch you."

"Old Bishop . . . when he gets mad, he don't fool around."

"Clarence . . ." Modock's voice carried threat.

But Clarence Cass had bottled up too much anxiety to quit talking.

"You got no right to make me come along with you on a thing like this. I ain't stole none of Bishop's cows, and I didn't want to be no part of what you're fixin' to do tonight."

Modock grunted savagely. "I figure as long as we're partners we ought to share everything, the risk as well as the spoils. You been grinnin' like a possum, watchin' the boys ride out of a night to haze off Bishop stock. It tickled you, long's you wasn't a part of it. Now I figure it's time you *became* a part of it. You'll be a better partner, Clarence, once you've got your own feet muddied a little, same as ours. You won't be as apt to change your mind about things, or go around talkin' when you ought to be a-listenin'. Now catch up and stay up!"

They reached the fence. Modock dismounted, took a pair of wire pinchers from his saddle and pulled out the staples that held the wire. He had to remove them from two posts to make the wires loose enough that he could press them to the ground and let the horses walk over onto the Double B side of the fence. Clarence Cass held back, and for a moment Modock thought he would have to go fetch him. But Cass came finally, complaining all the way.

"What'll we do if Bishop catches us?"

"What'd he be doin' out this time of the night? He's gettin' on in years. He needs his rest."

"I'm as old as he is. I need mine too," Cass whimpered, watching Modock put the staples back in place so the men's entry would not so easily be noticed. They would ride out this way again, but they might not hit the same place in the fence. "Besides, I don't like leavin' that little girl of mine there all by herself with them men of yours on the place. Can't ever tell what ideas'll come into the mind of men like that."

"You know damn well what kind of ideas they have. But I told them I'd put a bullet in the man that touches her. Besides, they got an errand of their own. They'll go out and pick up some more of them Double B cattle tonight."

"Bishop won't hold still when he finds out somebody's takin' his cows."

"He's got too many anyway, dry as it is. Besides, he can't tie it to me and you, Clarence. He won't find no tracks leadin' to our place."

Cass winced. "Our place? It's still my place."

Modock nodded. "I find that awful easy to forget." He rode in silence awhile, then asked, "You sure we're headed in the right direction for that tank?"

Cass' shoulders were slumped in resignation. "I told you. The Black Bull Tank lies yonderway. It ain't fair, really. It sets on a draw leadin' out of my country. Old Bishop catches the water that runs off of my place, and he won't share none of it."

"You could build a tank of your own and stop most of the runoff."

"I will one of these days. Just never have had the time."

Modock spat, his contempt bubbling close to the surface. "You sure this tank has got a weak bottom in it?"

"I'm sure. Harley Mills cowboyed for him a few years. He told me how much trouble they had at first, makin' it hold water. It kept seepin' down through the bottom. Finally they brought all the Double B horses over here and held them in the tank bottom half a day, millin' them around so their hoofs would pack the ground. Nothin' packs like a remuda of horses."

"If we crack that tight bottom, won't take long for the water to seep right on through. Give it a few days and Bishop's Black Bull Tank will be nothin' but a black *mud* tank."

A dog barked, and Macy Modock hauled up on his reins. "What's a dog doin' way out here in the far side of a pasture?"

Cass shrugged. "Stray."

Modock listened, suspicious. "You sure you ain't led us wrong? You sure you ain't led us to a house or a line camp?"

"I'm sure. I tell you, Macy, I know where I'm at. There's not a soul lives within miles of here."

The dog barked again a time or two, but Modock couldn't spot the animal in the moonlight. He noticed that the cattle trails began converging, so he satisfied himself Cass was leading them to the tank. Presently he rode up on the dam. A few cattle which were bedded down around the water rose nervously to their feet and began to edge away. Modock whistled. No wonder Blair Bishop was so proud of this tank. Even low, it still held a considerable body of water, enough to keep his cows awhile longer if nothing unexpected happened to it.

Modock was here to see that something did happen to it. He reached into his saddlebags and pulled out three sticks of dynamite. Handing the leather reins to Owen Darby, he knelt to set the fuses, each a slightly different length. Digging a hole in the dry earth just at the edge of the mud, he laid down the stick with the shortest fuse and packed the earth around it. He walked around the tank, pausing to set a second. At the far side he placed the third, then lighted the long fuse. He came back to the second and touched it off, finished by lighting the first, then took his horse from Darby and swung into the saddle.

"We better move off a ways. These horses will throw a fit."

The first explosion made the earth tremble. Modock's horse tried to pitch. Clarence Cass' simply wanted to run. It was all Cass could do to stop him short of a full stampede. The last two explosions came close together. Modock could hear the mud splatter onto the tank dam. He heard the clatter of cattle stampeding away into the protecting brush.

It took him a minute to get his horse under control, then he forced the reluctant animal back to the tank. Where the charges had been set, Modock saw three sizable holes gradually filling with water. He was counting on the tremors having sent cracks through the tightly packed bottom. They couldn't be seen beneath the water, but Modock was confident they were there. Cass and Owen Darby rode up beside him. Cass said, "The water's still in it."

"It'll take time. Several days, more than likely. But it'll go."

"Bishop'll see them holes. He'll see the mud scattered all over."

"The mud'll dry in the hot sun tomorrow, and the cattle will tromp it back to dust. As for the holes, he can't prove they wasn't pawed by bulls lookin' for a fight."

"In his own mind, he'll know."

"Sure, he'll know." Modock grinned. "I *want* him to know that it's me and not just hard luck. But there won't be a blessed thing he can do about it, not a thing he can prove."

They started back toward the fence, Modock whistling tunelessly, letting his mind run free with all manner of good and violent dreams, the taste of triumph sweet as wild-bee honey.

The dog came charging at them unexpectedly out of

the mesquite, barking its challenge. Modock's horse, still unstrung by the explosions, went straight up. Modock took a hard, dirt-eating fall but somehow held on to his reins. He jumped to his feet, holding desperately to the struggling horse. The breath half knocked out of him, Modock managed to slap the barking dog and send it retreating. He cursed, reaching for his pistol but realizing that if he fired a shot, the horse would probably get away from him. He managed finally to get a foot into the stirrup and swing back into the saddle. He spurred the horse viciously, at the same time hauling hard on the reins to keep the animal from getting its head down to buck again.

A voice came from the mesquite. "Macy Modock! I ought to've known it'd be you."

Modock's pistol was in his hand, and he bent low over the horse's neck, hoping not to present an easy target. "Who's that?" he demanded, half panicky at the thought of being caught.

Tank-builder Joe Little rode out of the brush, shotgun pointed toward the three horsemen. He commanded the dog to heel, then approached Modock. The muzzle of that shotgun looked big as a coffeepot. Modock stared in disbelief. "What're you doin' here, Joe?"

"I got a camp over yonder, buildin' another tank for Blair Bishop, below the Black Bull." He glanced contemptuously at Clarence Cass, whose chin had dropped to his shirt collar in the agony of discovery. "First blast woke me up. Thought it was thunder, till I looked up and seen the moon and the stars. The other two blasts come, and all of a sudden I knowed. Raise your hands, Macy. You others too. You'll answer to Blair Bishop."

Modock was recovering from surprise, and he began

calculating odds. He didn't like that shotgun. Even if he fired his pistol and hit Joe, he knew the shotgun blast would probably tear him in two. "It's a long ways from here to the Double B headquarters. You better ride off and forget you seen us, Joe."

"I wish I could forget I *ever* seen you, Macy, much less shared a cell with you. It takes a lowdown form of a man to dynamite another man's waterhole and starve his cattle to death. I figure you're goin' back where you come from, Macy, and takin' company with you."

"I made you an offer a while back, Joe. It still stands. Go in with us and get that land you wanted. You might even get some of the Bishop country you been workin' so hard on. Use your head, Joe, and you can wind up bigger than you ever thought of."

"Blair Bishop's a friend of mine. You, Macy, are no friend to anybody." He motioned with the shotgun. "Easy now, and slip them cartridge belts off. Drop them careful."

Modock caught a signal in Owen Darby's face. He couldn't tell exactly what Darby had in mind, but he knew Darby was about to try something. Modock lagged, fumbling with the belt buckle. Darby undid his and slipped the belt and holster loose from his hip as if to drop it. Instead, he flipped it into the face of Joe Little's horse. The horse shied away, forcing Joe involuntarily to grab at the saddle horn and let the shotgun dip.

Modock's right hand streaked back from the buckle and came up with the pistol. He held it almost point-blank at Joe Little's chest. Horror came into Joe's face as he tried desperately to bring the shotgun back into line.

Modock fired. Joe rocked back. His horse jumped in

terror. Joe Little slid out of the saddle and hit the ground with one leg crumpled.

Clarence Cass sat stupefied, watching Joe Little gasp away his life. Modock swung to the ground and kicked the shotgun away in case there was still any inclination on Joe's part to use it. But Joe was beyond thinking.

Joe's black dog growled deep in its throat and lunged in fury at Macy Modock. Instinctively Modock threw up his arm. The dog's teeth sank into it. Modock swung the pistol up under the dog's belly and fired. The dog fell away, kicking. Cursing violently, a cold rage flowing over him, Modock fired twice more into the shaggy body.

"Nothin' I hate worse than a damned dog . . ."

He rubbed his arm where the sharp teeth had dug in, bringing blood.

Cass tried to speak, but only a few terrified gasps came. Modock looked up to see Owen Darby catching Joe's runaway horse and bringing it back. Darby looked down at Joe's body. "This sure queers things, Macy. What you goin' to do now?"

Modock shook his head. "I'm tryin' to think. Just shut up and let me study it out." He cursed silently. Damn Joe Little and his stupid meddling. Modock wished Joe hadn't been here; not that he had any regret for the killing itself, but only that it made for an unexpected complication. He had felt no regard for Joe Little when they were in prison together, no more than he felt for anyone else beyond whatever use he might be. It was these unforeseen surprises that always seemed to get a man caught. It was hard to prepare for them.

Modock straightened, deciding he saw a way out. "Owen, you was sayin' the other day you wished you could break into that wooden box of a bank in Two Forks."

Darby nodded. "But you said we had bigger fish to fry, and I might ruin the whole setup."

"All of a sudden I'm changin' my mind. I think it'd be a great idea now for you to bust that bank. Our friend Joe Little was in the pen for doin' that very thing. If he was to disappear right after the bank was robbed, what do you reckon folks would think?"

Darby began to smile. "That's why I like to ride with you, Macy. You can take a disaster and make a winnin' hand out of it."

"We'll take him and his horse and make sure they're never found. Clarence, you get down here and help me with him."

Clarence Cass was almost crying, his throat quivering as he kept trying for voice. He made no move to leave his saddle. Modock railed at him without effect. Darby swung down and helped Modock lift Joe Little's body across the saddle, the frightened horse pulling its head around, its eyes spooked.

Darby asked, "What about our tracks?"

"No way we can rub them all out. We'll just have to hope that nobody will come along till the cattle and the wind have covered them up. Unless somebody's lookin' for tracks, they ain't apt to notice them anyway."

"We can't leave that dog layin' there."

"We'll drag him off into the brush. There won't nobody find him."

Voice came at last to Clarence Cass. "You killed him! You killed him! They'll hang us now for sure!"

Modock glanced at Darby, knowing Darby had been wishing Modock would let him shut the little man up for once and for all. Sooner or later they would have to do something permanent about Cass, but not until all advantage had been taken of him. "Clarence, you quit your cryin'. Get a head back on your shoulders. Anything we done, *you* done."

"I didn't come for no killin'."

"Neither did we, but you got it, and you're in it up to your Adam's apple. Anything that happens to us happens to you too."

"Macy, I didn't know you was goin' to drag me into a thing like this. Just blowin' up a tank was all. That's what you said, just blowin' up a tank. Now I want you off of my ranch, out of this country."

Angrily Modock reached down to Joe Little's warm body and came up with blood thick on his fingers. He smeared it onto Clarence Cass' hand. Cass drew back trembling, trying desperately to wipe the blood onto his trousers. Modock said, "It won't wash off, Clarence. So from now on, your life depends on us. You'll keep your mouth shut and do everything I tell you. Everything! Else you might just wind up where Joe Little is. Come on, let's get out of here!"

{ EIGHT }

The sun was starting down in the afternoon sky when Sheriff Erly Greenwood and a deputy rode into the yard of the Double B headquarters. Blair Bishop lay on a blanket on the breezy gallery of the ranchhouse, taking gratefully what little comfort he found on a hot summer day. Time had been when his conscience would have hurt him a little, napping like this when there was work to be done. But as the years went by it seemed easier to deal with his conscience on such matters. No matter how much work a man did, it was never enough anyway.

The sound of hoofs brought Blair's gray head up from the pillow. He raised up slowly, stretching, then got to his feet and invited Erly with a broad wave of his hand. "Come on up and shade awhile, Erly. It's hotter than the hinges of hell out in that sun."

Greenwood could well remember when Blair Bishop wouldn't have taken time for a noonday siesta, but that had been before the ranchman had come to terms with ambition and had learned to accept the natural rhythms of life. He climbed the steps and shook hands with the ranchman. The deputy followed his example. Blair, in his sock feet, led them into the house for a drink of cool water. Then they came back out onto the gallery, for the house caught and held much of the afternoon heat entrapped despite its tall, narrow windows.

. "Blair," the sheriff said, "I come to talk to Joe Little."

Blair told him Joe was building a surface tank out close to the Black Bull. Greenwood asked him, "Seen him today?"

"He seldom comes to headquarters, just when he needs somethin'. My boy Billy drops by and keeps him pretty well stocked on groceries and things . . . includin' the best stuff out of my own pantry. What do you want with Joe?"

"Somebody busted into the bank last night. Got off with somethin' like four to five thousand dollars."

"Joe wouldn't . . ." Blair's eyes narrowed. "He paid off what he owed the state. He wouldn't do nothing like that again, Erly. He's got a good job, got friends . . ."

"How long would it take him to make four or five thousand dollars, Blair, workin' a team of mules in this heat, sweatin' himself to death on another man's land? You can see how some of the old quick-money notions might get to preyin' on Joe's mind."

"Did anybody see him?"

"Not exactly. There was a cowboy layin' drunk in an alley. He saw the robber. Said it could have been Joe."

"Could have been? With a drunk cowboy, it *could* have been Ulysses S. Grant or Robert E. Lee."

"Just the same, I sure want to talk to Joe. He's the first one lots of folks in town thought of. If I don't talk to him, some of them are liable to come lookin'."

Blair nodded. "I'll get Billy to hitch a team to the buckboard, and we'll ride with you over there."

* * *

They found Joe's camp beside the half-finished tank, the mules hobbled to graze on the scanty grass. Blair Bishop knew the moment he saw the mules that something was wrong. He exchanged glances with Billy and found the same conviction in the boy's eyes. Joe was always working at this time of day. Those mules didn't get the hobbles until sundown. Blair didn't have to say anything. Erly Greenwood read the signs the same way. The sheriff asked, "Does he keep a horse?"

Blair didn't answer, but Billy did. "He's always got a horse. I don't see it anyplace around."

Erly Greenwood's face went grave as he looked over the deserted camp. "You know, don't you, Blair? We'll have to send out word on Joe Little."

Billy protested. "Dad, Joe wouldn't rob nobody. He told me a dozen times he'd rather starve than to do anything like that again."

Blair sensed the desperation in Billy's voice, a silent cry for faith, for Billy had thought the sun rose and set in Joe Little. "Boy," he said unconvincingly, "maybe it's not the way it looks. Maybe old Joe just up and went somewhere."

Erly Greenwood said, "Blair, there's no use kiddin' him. Billy's old enough to take things the way they come." He turned his attention to Billy. "Think hard now, son. Do you remember anything he might've said about places he'd like to go to, things he'd like to do?"

Billy shook his head defensively. "No, sir. He said he was goin' to buy a place of his own. That's all he ever said he wanted, was a place of his own."

The sheriff commented, "Four to five thousand dollars would buy a man a right smart of a little place. He'd have to go a far piece, though. He must've said some-thin', Billy."

"Nothin'. I tell you, he didn't say nothin'."

Erly Greenwood studied him apologetically but uncon-vinced. "All right, son, but if you think of anything later on, let us know. We want to help Joe; we got no wish to hurt him." He shook Blair's hand, gripping it lightly be-cause of the rheumatism, but bringing pain just the same. "Sorry, Blair, I can't say I was in favor of you ever brin-gin' Joe Little here in the first place, but I'll say this: I liked him."

"You got your job to do, Erly. Want us to help you look for tracks?"

"Any helpful tracks will be the ones goin' *away* from the bank, not the ones he made goin' to it. We'd be was-tin' our time out here."

Sitting slumped on the buckboard seat, Blair sorrow-fully watched them ride off in the direction of town. The leather lines slacked from Billy's listless hands. Blair looked at his son. "Boy, sometimes life's hard that way. People we like, people we trust, they do things we can't understand, things that hurt us. It don't help to blame them. It ain't right to blame a man unless you try on his boots and walk awhile in his tracks. Whatever was drivin' Joe, it was somethin' more powerful than we know. Ain't right for us to feel hard about him."

"I'm not feelin' hard about him, Dad. I know he didn't do it."

Blair shrugged, not knowing what else to say. "Some-times we just got to accept the things that are and not ask questions. This is one of those times." He rubbed his aching hand, wanting to busy his mind on other matters and hoping to get Billy occupied too. "Long's we're this close, let's go over and take a look at the Black Bull Tank. It does me good to see a place that's still got water."

The tank's banks were too steep for the buckboard, so Blair climbed heavily out and walked. Billy followed him. At the top of the dam, Blair stopped in surprise. He glanced at Billy, shock in his square face. "Boy, that tank ain't got half the water in it that it had the other day."

Billy's jaw dropped. "I was over here just day before yesterday. It still had lots of water in it. Somethin's happened. It's gone plumb to hell."

That wasn't language Blair had taught Billy to use, though he used it liberally enough himself. He never even noticed this time. In dismay he trudged down toward the water line. He bogged in heavy black mud almost to his boottops. "Right here's where the water line was a day or two ago. Cattle didn't drink this much, and it don't evaporate this fast."

He knelt painfully, touching the wet ground with his hand as if somehow that would give him a hint to what had gone wrong. He got up slowly, feeling as if a mule had kicked him in the stomach. Billy looked at him in alarm. For a moment Blair thought Billy's expression was a reflection of his concern over the water, but he realized that wasn't it, at least not the main part of it.

Billy said, "Dad, you better go sit in the buckboard awhile. You've turned as white as skim milk."

"I'm all right, boy, I'm all right." Blair looked at the water again, still mystified. He started around the edge of it, looking for a line that might indicate a crack in the dam. He didn't see anything.

He didn't see the hole, either, until he fell into it and went to his knees. Billy ran to help him, but Blair pushed to his feet alone, wiping the mud from his hands onto his already muddy trousers. "Damned bulls," he muttered, "pawin' holes where a man can fall in them. If they ever come up with a substitute, I'll never have a bull on the place again."

Billy observed, "They been doin' a lot of fightin', seems like. There's another bull hole over yonder."

"Bunch of bulls around here are sure in need of a shippin'," Blair growled. Pawing holes was bull nature, but at a time like this Blair had no patience with it. He glanced across the tank and became aware of a third hole which looked about like the other two. Of a sudden, suspicion hit him. The impact was almost as hard as the initial one of seeing the tank nearly dry.

"Billy, somethin' strike you funny about them bull holes?"

Billy shook his head. "Nothin' strikes me very funny right now."

"Aside from the fact that there's three of them showed up all at the same time, and the fact that they're kind of deep, don't it seem peculiar to you that they're in the edge of the mud instead of out where the sand is a little dryer? An old bull ain't goin' to stand and paw mud when there's dry ground all around him."

Billy blinked in confusion. "What you tryin' to say, Dad?"

"I'm not sure. It's just a feelin' that's come over me, or maybe somethin' I smell. There's more here than meets the eye."

"You think Joe Little went and did somethin'? He wouldn't, Dad. He wouldn't hurt us thisaway."

"Not Joe Little. I was thinkin' of Macy Modock."

"Joe would've known about it. He'd of told us . . ."

Billy's eyes widened as the implication hit him. "Unless Modock done somethin' to him." He grabbed his father's arm. "Dad, we got to catch up to Erly Greenwood and tell him."

"Tell him what? We'd have to prove it first."

"But maybe Joe's in trouble and needs our help. No tellin' what that Modock might be doin' to him."

Blair knew now. Though he had nothing stronger than instinct to go by, he knew. "Whatever it is, boy, he's already done it. Macy Modock is a hard man. Whatever he felt like he had to do to Joe, it's over and done with."

"You think he killed him?"

"You'd best make up your mind to it, Billy. I'll bet everything I own. If Modock was out here and Joe caught him, then Joe is dead."

Billy's hands trembled as the enormity of the idea took hold. Tears welled into his eyes. "Then let's go after Modock. Let's kill him!"

Blair Bishop firmly took his son's arm. "No, son, that's not for us to do. Time was when it would've been the thing, but that time is gone. We'll go tell Erly Greenwood what we think. The fixin' of it is up to him."

"Joe Little was our friend."

Blair Bishop's eyes were bleak, and he knew a moment of temptation. "If I was your age and time was rolled back a few years, I'd do just what you're sayin'. But I ain't, and it ain't, and we can't. Let's get to the buckboard. If we push, maybe we can catch Erly."

They did, and Greenwood came back for a look around. What he saw did not incline him to agree. "I don't see a thing that supports you, Blair. If there was any tracks, they're gone. If them holes was blowed or dug, there's nothin' to show for it. For all I can tell, they're just what they look like . . . a sign the bulls was fightin'. The trouble with you and Billy is that you don't want to accept the truth when it stares you in the eye. Joe Little got tired of workin' and robbed that bank. You've got Macy Modock so heavy on your mind that you're ready to blame him for everything but the drought. If he's tryin' to make you sweat, he's doin' a good job of it. I bet you ain't slept a full night in peace since he came back. Now he's givin' you nightmares in the daytime."

That was strong talk coming from Erly Greenwood, who had always handled Blair Bishop with a respectful deference. But Greenwood had a looted bank in town to worry about, and the weather was hot, and he'd made a lot of extra miles that weren't taking him any closer to the man who had done the job.

Angered, Blair said, "I got a strong feelin' about this thing, Erly. You won't find Joe Little, not on this earth. If you want to find that bank money, you go to Macy Modock."

Greenwood kept his impatience in check; Blair had to give him credit for that. "Blair, I'll see you again soon's I get some time. Awful sorry about that tank."

{ NINE }

The Black Bull Tank had become only a mudhole. Blair had known that as soon as he had seen the cattle standing around the tankdam. There had been far too many for this early in the day. Usually they began gathering in the afternoon and watered, then lay around until the cool of the evening brought them back to their feet and set them to looking for grass. Blair could tell these cattle had been here since yesterday, and they were thirsty. He rode up on the dam, his two sons flanking him. What he saw confirmed his fears.

"Well, it's gone, boys. The trap's drawin' shut."

Allan nodded gravely. Billy stared, the consequences not quite so apparent to him as to his father and his older brother. "We'll just have to take them somewhere else," he said.

Blair Bishop nodded sourly, still convinced Modock had brought this trouble on him. "It means we'll have to double up cattle on another place that's already in trouble itself." He pondered a moment. "We'll haze them over onto the Harley Mills pasture. At least there we got a couple of windmill's still pumpin' all right."

Allan said, "Grass is awful short over there, Dad."

"It's short everywhere. But there's water, at least." He

rode down the dam, waving his hand and hollering at the cattle. His sons fanned out on either side of him and did likewise. One cow remained. She was out twenty feet in the mud, hopelessly mired to her belly. Trembling, she shook her head angrily at the horsemen. She had obviously been here for some time, struggling vainly, fighting this mud. She was in a hostile mood toward all the world.

"Allan," Blair called, "I graduated from this kind of chore a long time ago. I'll let you do the honors. Billy, you keep gatherin' the rest of them cattle."

Allan stepped to the ground and tightened his cinch for a good pull. He rode to the edge of the mud, swung his loop and sailed it around the cow's horns. Taking up the slack, he dallied the end of the rope around his saddle horn and spurred away. The horse scrambled for footing, pulling hard. The cow's neck stretched and she bawled in rage, but the mud held her.

Blair said, "I was afraid it wouldn't be that easy. You'll have to get in there with her. Hand me your rope."

Allan took it philosophically, for this was part of a cowboy's work. Using a few choice words to describe the ancestry of a brute stupid enough to get herself into such a predicament, he took off his boots and waded into the mud.

Blair's horse was bigger and stronger than Allan's. Blair always rode a big horse, for he was an older and heavier man. He dallied Allan's rope around his saddle horn. The cow slung her head, trying vainly to reach Allan with her horns. He got behind her and grasped her tail. Blair spurred. As the horse strained against the rope, Allan lifted the cow's hindquarters. The first try didn't move her much, but on the second she somehow got her feet under her and began adding to the struggle what little strength she had left. She moved forward gradually at first. Then she broke loose from the mud's tight grip and came scrambling up out of it. On dry ground, she went to her knees. Her tongue was hanging out, and she was bawling in rage. Allan eased up to get the rope off, but she was ready to fight anything which moved. She slung her head and missed him only an inch with her sharp horns. Allan dodged back, cursing her. She got to her feet and charged him. There was nothing for Allan to do but run toward his horse, barefoot, muddy to his thighs. The horse didn't like the looks of either him or the cow, and he shied away.

Blair put his own horse between Allan and the cow and took another dally farther down on the rope. He rode away fast, jerking the cow off of her feet. While she was down, Allan slipped the rope off. He lost no time picking up his boots and getting back into his saddle. He would stay barefoot till the mud dried enough that he could rub it off.

Blair and Allan watched the cow slowly struggle to her feet. She stood shaking, tongue out and drooling saliva as she faced them in frustration and anger, tossing her head in belligerence.

"Never fails to happen," Allan said. "Do one a favor, and she turns on you."

"Female. A lot of females will do you that way. Cow, human, or whatever."

The cow decided she had made her point, and she moved weakly up over the dam to seek out her sisters. Allan looked at his father. "You tryin' to say somethin', Dad?"

Blair shrugged. "Yep, and you know what it is."

"I told you before, Dad, there's no use us talkin' about Jessie. Nothin' you say is goin' to change the way I feel about her. And I'm goin' to keep right on seein' her. I wish you wouldn't crowd me."

"If it was just seein' her, boy, that wouldn't be so bad. But it's more than that. One of these times you'll feel called upon to marry her. Sure, she looks pretty good to you now, mostly because you ain't seen a lot of other girls and got nothin' to compare by. I swear, I'd almost rather see you spendin' your time down on Silky Row in town. At least nobody there would try to tie on to you. Everybody would know just where she stood."

Allan stopped his horse. He looked his father in the eye, a quality Blair had taught him from the time he was big enough to walk. "Dad, I never lied to you, and I won't lie to you now. When the time is right, I'm goin' to marry Jessie Cass. Now, you can accept her, or you can tell us both to leave. I hope you'll accept her, because she's a good girl. But even if you don't, that won't change anything. I'll marry her. You won't stand in my way, and neither will anybody else."

Blair Bishop felt anger. He had raised his boys not to talk back to him. But he had also taught them to be straightforward and not back off from a problem. Blair struggled to put down his anger. Allan didn't seem to be in any hurry about this. Maybe something would come along to help Blair open his eyes for him before it was too late.

Blair retreated, but he didn't surrender. "Billy's probably havin' trouble tryin' to push them cattle all by himself. We better go give him a hand."

Along the way they picked up foreman Finn Goforth and cowboy Hez Northcutt, who had been riding missions of their own. The cattle drove sluggishly at first, their thirst making them contrary, and their instincts tugging them back toward the tank where they were used to watering. Every so often an animal would turn back, and only a rope would stop her. Billy was the one who most often used the rope. He was at an age when a rope had a rough appeal to him and nothing was so much fun as to stand a runaway steer on its rump. Irritably, for he was thirsty too, Blair grouched at him about rough-handling the stock. Billy would explain that he couldn't afford to let them get away.

They missed dinner, for moving these cattle to water was more important than getting back to the headquarters for a noon meal. A cowboy was conditioned to accept such things. The good of the stock was always paramount over the needs of the man.

Late in the afternoon the tall windmill showed on the short-grass prairie. It seemed to shimmer and dance in the heatwaves playing along the horizon. Riding point, Blair Bishop thought he saw a cloud of dust ahead of him, and the movement of cattle. He blinked and lost sight of it in the heat. Eyesight going bad, he decided. Looked like when the rheumatism got hold of him, it was bound to take everything else. By now he was tired and hot and thirsty and irritable. So was everybody else on the drive. He hadn't heard a man speak a word in an hour, except to use the Lord's name in vain against some recalcitrant critter.

But directly Finn Goforth trotted his horse up from the flank and pulled in beside Blair. "Do you see somethin' odd up ahead of us?"

Blair grunted. "Thought I did, but I lost it. Mirage,

I figured, or just my own eyes. Times anymore I'm not worth killin'."

Finn pointed. "It ain't no mirage."

Blair sat up straight in the saddle. He stared a moment, glanced at Finn in disbelief and looked back again. "Finn, somebody's movin' cattle."

"There's nothin' up yonder but Double B range. There's not anybody supposed to be movin' cattle here but us."

Anger surged red into Blair's square face. "Rustlers! In broad open daylight!"

Finn Goforth shook his head. "That's the first thought that came to me. You know we been losin' some cattle lately, a few here, a few there. Started about the time Macy Modock come back. But they'd have to have a lot of gall to come so far onto Double B country in the daytime when there'd be so much chance of a Bishop man runnin' onto them. I can't hardly believe they'd be stealin' cattle now. Tonight, maybe, after the moon comes up, but not now."

By instinct Blair Bishop reached for his hip. He didn't have a pistol, hadn't worn one in years. He looked back at his two sons and Hez Northcutt. "Nary a gun in the whole bunch of us, Finn, except that carbine you carry under your leg. Let me have it, and I'll ride up and see what the hell is goin' on."

Goforth shook his head. "With that hand of yours, you couldn't lever it. One shot is all you'd ever get. I'll go with you, Mister Bishop, and I'll keep hold of the rifle."

Blair flexed his right hand. It was painfully stiff. Finn was right. Blair looked over his shoulder and signaled for Allan to come up on the run. He could tell that Allan had seen the other string of cattle too. "You go tell Billy and Hez to keep pushin' this bunch. The three of us are ridin' on to see what this is all about."

He swung into an easy lope that would give Allan a chance to catch up with him. The thought fleetingly crossed his mind that if it *was* cow thieves, and they were armed, one saddlegun wouldn't be much persuasion against them. But the thought was not enough to slow him. It had been said of Blair Bishop in his younger days that he would charge hell with a bucket of gypwater. Armed or not, he had seen few men who would stand against him long.

Between the three men and the windmill lay a barbed wire fence. Originally the four sections of land where the windmill stood had been homesteaded at Blair's suggestion by Harley Mills when Harley was a Double B cowboy. He had gone through the state requirements, then had sold the place to Blair and gone off to get gloriously drunk. He had never been completely sober since, and Blair had been obliged to fire him.

Next to the Mills land was a similar place Blair had bought from a homesteading cowboy named Abernathy. Unlike Mills, Abernathy had taken his money and bought a string of steers. He threw them in with a trail herd bound for the railroad and was drowned trying to swim a creek. In his honor the land was still known as the Abernathy place, though it had been in the Bishop name for years.

A double-width wire gate was marked by three tall posts. Blair moved toward them, but he saw other riders were going to get there first from the far side of the fence. Behind the riders came a large herd of slow-moving cattle, obscured by heavy gray dust. Blair recognized a tall, gaunt man whose black hat was pulled down almost over his eyes. "That's Macy Modock. Let me have that rifle, Finn."

Goforth demurred again. "I don't want to see you killed, Mister Bishop, so I better keep it. Any time you want him shot, just give me the word."

Someone dismounted and threw the two gates wide open, then climbed back onto his horse. Macy Modock pulled up into one of the gates and stopped, waiting. Beside him was the red-bearded one Blair remembered as Owen Darby. Darby had a saddlegun lying across the pommel of his saddle. Two other riders flanked them, facing toward the Bishops and Finn Goforth. None looked much like preachers.

Macy Modock held up his hand as Blair Bishop neared. It wasn't a gesture of peace; it was a sign to stop.

"Macy," Blair spoke angrily, "this here is my land, and I'll wager them yonder is my cattle. Now what the hell are you up to?"

Modock gave him that dry, flat, dangerous smile of his. "You're right, Blair Bishop, up to a point. Them is your cattle, and that where you're at is your land. But this where I'm sittin', it's not your land anymore; it's mine. I'm movin' your cattle off of it."

The surprise struck Blair Bishop like a fist. He hesitated, wondering if the thirst and the heat hadn't affected his hearing. "Your land? It's mine, and it has been for years."

Macy Modock patiently shook his head. That smile clung, ugly and threatening. "You thought it was. You thought you had defrauded the state. But after all this time you been caught up with, Bishop. You're losin' it, and I've filed claim on it."

Finn Goforth held the carbine. "Just say the word, Mister Bishop . . ."

If Blair had held the rifle at that moment, he probably would have shot Macy Modock out of the saddle, or tried to. But he didn't and perhaps that helped him take a better look at the three men who sided Modock. Finn's first shot would have to be a good one; he would never live to fire a second. "Stay easy, Finn," Blair rasped. He had no wish to lose a good foreman and longtime friend. To Modock he said, "If you think I'm goin' to stand still for you takin' four good sections of my land . . ."

Macy shook his head. "Not four . . . *eight*. Them other four sections yonder was filed on by a feller name of Abernathy. You're losin' those too. Owen here has filed on that land."

Blair flamed, "You're not bluffin' us, Macy. We got thirsty cattle comin', and you're standin' in the gate. Pull aside."

Macy's hand moved back near the pistol at his hip. "The only cattle passin' through that gate is the ones behind us, and they're goin' out, not in."

"Those eight sections have got about all the dependable water left on this ranch, Macy. They're the only place, almost, where a man can find well water just about anywhere he digs. I'm not givin' them up to nobody."

"You don't have to give them up; they're bein' *took*. You see, Bishop, you thought I was the only enemy you had. You thought when you sent me up that you didn't have any enemy left who could hurt you. But you didn't think about Judge Quincy. A little old dried-up wart like that couldn't do you no damage, you thought. But you wasn't payin' attention."

Blair Bishop listened, stewing.

Modock went on: "This land was homesteaded by Abernathy and Mills. They swore they met all the state's requirements, and they got the deeds. But did you ever look at the fine print on them papers, Bishop? No, of course you didn't. You thought anything a Bishop could get his hands on was safe forever. But there's fine print that says if there's fraud in connection with them home-steads, they can be taken back and put up for somebody else to claim."

"There wasn't no fraud."

"It was common knowledge around here that you was in collusion with them cowboys when they filed on that land. Before they ever done it, they agreed to sell the land to you. You held them to it."

"There never was any such agreement. I told them when the time came I'd like to buy and would pay them a good price. I never told them they had to. There was a couple who didn't. They're still my friends."

Finn Goforth was one of them, but Blair saw no need mentioning the fact to the likes of Macy Modock. Finn had decided he wanted to keep his land as something to build on for his own future. He was still working for Blair, letting Blair use his land under lease and letting the lease payments stack up as savings in the Two Forks bank to buy a cow herd someday.

Modock said, "We got a signed affidavit from Harley Mills. He says him and Abernathy never actually lived on their land the way they was supposed to. They lived in the Double B bunkhouse the whole blessed time."

"They both set up shacks on their land. They lived in them the way the law specified."

"I ain't seen no shacks."

"We taken them down and reused the lumber."

Modock grunted sarcastically. "Sure. That'd sound good in court. Can you produce either man to swear he lived in the shack?"

"You know Abernathy's dead. As for Harley Mills, he'd sell his soul for a barrel of whiskey. How much did you give him?"

"Harley says you got him to swear false testimony, then forced him to sell to you or you'd expose him and get him sent to jail."

"Harley lied. He lived up to the law, same as the others. He taken his money and drank it up. That's why he's swampin' a stable."

"He claims you got what you wanted from him and then fired him."

"I had to let him go because he was drinkin' too much. You better not depend on Harley for a witness. He'll be drunk when you need him."

"I got his affidavit. What have *you* got, Bishop? I tell you what you *ain't* got; you ain't got this land no more. *We* have. And we're movin' you off it today."

Finn Goforth said deliberately, "No you ain't," and he raised the saddlegun. That was a mistake. Owen Darby's carbine fired. The horses jumped in fright. Blair saw Finn rock back in the saddle, discharging his carbine harmlessly in the air. He doubled over and slid to the ground.

"Finn!" Blair shouted. He tried to dismount, but his big gray was crow-hopping excitedly. Blair's stiff legs went out from under him as he hit the ground, and he went down on hands and knees almost under the panicked gray horse. A hoof barely missed him before Blair could crawl away and struggle painfully to his feet.

Allan was already on his knees beside the foreman

and was turning Finn over. Finn's face was going gray. Blood flowed from a wound deep in his shoulder.

Blair picked up Finn's fallen carbine. He tried feverishly to lever a fresh cartridge into the breech, but his crippled hand betrayed him. He couldn't get a grip. He cursed wildly, furious at the hand, furious at Macy Modock. But the hand wouldn't function. Forcing it brought only pain.

Glancing up, he saw three men's guns leveled at him and knew that if he had been able to lever a cartridge, they would not have let him live to fire it.

Macy Modock raised his hand and motioned for his men to lower their weapons. "Not yet, boys, not yet. Comes time to do the honors on Blair Bishop, I want to do it myself."

Blair stood openmouthed and raging, the sweat rolling down his dusty face, pain lancing through his hand from trying to force it to do something of which it no longer was capable. "Modock, I swear to God . . ."

"Just go on and swear, Bishop. Ain't another damn thing you can do."

Allan's anxious voice reached Blair. "Dad, Finn's hard hit. He won't live long if we don't get this blood stopped."

A cold chill ran through Blair Bishop as he realized how close he had come to being killed, standing there with that useless rifle in his hands. He dropped it and turned back to Finn Goforth. Allan ripped Finn's shirt open to expose the wound.

Billy Bishop and Hez Northcutt had abandoned their cattle at the sound of the shot and came loping up excitedly. Hez jumped off to see about Finn. Billy glanced at Finn, saw the blood, then spotted the saddlegun lying on the ground. He reached for it, but Blair managed to grab him.

"Boy, don't touch that rifle! Can't you see they're fixin' to kill you?"

Billy cried in fury: "He's the one that killed Joe Little. Now he's shot Finn."

Macy Modock said coldly, "Go on, Blair Bishop, let him pick it up."

Blair sensed they wouldn't withhold fire against Billy. They would cut him to pieces. Blair pushed Billy back, putting himself between the gunmen and his son. "No, Modock, you're not goin' to get at me by killin' these boys of mine."

Allan methodically wadded a handkerchief against Finn's wound, trying to stop the blood. When that handkerchief was soaked, Blair handed him one from his own pocket. If the wound didn't kill Finn, those dirty handkerchiefs probably would, Blair thought darkly.

"Billy, you and Hez ride up to the ranch. Billy, you go to town and fetch a doctor to the house. Get word to the sheriff too. Hez, you load up the buckboard with blankets and bring it here in a run. Allan and I'll take care of him the best we can till you get back."

Billy said, "How about them cows?"

"The hell with the cows. We got to save Finn."

The young cowboys rode off together in a lope that Blair knew was likely to kill both horses if they didn't slow down. They would, when excitement gave way to judgment. Allan and Blair carried the foreman gently to the shade of a thin mesquite tree and laid him on the ground. The blood gradually stopped.

On the other side of the gate, the riders arrived with the cattle they were pushing for Macy Modock. Blair watched in helpless anger as they drove them through the double gate and then chased them into a run that would carry them a considerable distance out across a waterless pasture.

Modock rode over and looked down from the saddle, the hard smile still making a slash across his thin face. "Too bad about your man. Owen Darby's slippin' in his old age. Time was when he'd have got this feller in the heart and you wouldn't have to be fussin' over him this-away. You'd just dig a hole for him, is all."

"Did you dig a hole for Joe Little?"

Modock never changed expression. "You ain't found it, have you?"

Blair said, "Soon's I get Finn took care of, I'll be back. I'll bring plenty with me."

Modock was unmoved. "It ain't your land no more. It's mine, or fixin' to be. Judge Quincy's been over at the Statehouse the last four days. I got a wire from him that he had everything fixed. That land is mine and Owen Darby's. We're goin' to put the Cass cattle on it."

"They don't just take a man's land away without goin' to court."

"If you want to press it, I reckon you can have your day in court. But you'll lose. Judge tells me that's a cinch. And meantime, as they say, possession is nine points of the law. I sure as hell got possession. And I got some boys yonder tough enough to see that I keep it."

"Without that land, I got a bunch of cows that don't have water to drink. You won't keep me off."

"Seems to me I heard about my partner Clarence Cass tryin' to tell you he had the same problem. And I remember what you told him. So I'm tellin' you the same thing, Blair Bishop, with one extra addition: any of your men tries to come onto my land, I'm givin' my boys orders to shoot him."

Blair Bishop stared at Finn's saddlegun, still lying where it had been dropped. From here, if Allan would lever a cartridge into it for him, Blair was almost sure he could shoot Macy Modock as the man rode away. Blair made a move toward the rifle then stopped, knowing he couldn't do it that way.

He might curse himself the rest of his life for missing the chance, but he couldn't shoot a man in the back. Not even Macy Modock.

{ TEN }

For the better part of an hour the doctor labored in flickering light while first one man then another held a lamp close. But finally he straightened in resignation, wiping a handkerchief over his bald head and his sweat-glistening face. "I'm sorry, Blair. Did all I could, but Finn Goforth is gone."

Cold lay in the pit of Blair's stomach. Even as he had paced the parlor floor, pausing periodically to stare blackly out into the darkness, he had known it would end this way.

The doctor said, "If I'd been close by when it happened, maybe I could've saved him. Even then it would've been close." He began putting his instruments into his bag.

"Doc," Blair rasped, wanting comfort and not knowing where to find it, "it's midnight. No use you ridin' to town now. We got a bed for you and a couple of stiff drinks to help settle you if you need them." The doctor nodded his acceptance. "God knows I need them."

Blair added, "Could be we'll need you again anyway. When we've done right by Finn, we'll be goin' back over there."

"With the few men you've got?"

"I'll have more. I'm fixin' to send the boys out to round up all the friends we can muster."

The doctor poured a liberal drink out of a bottle Blair fetched from a cabinet. He sat down wearily, taking one stiff drink that twisted his face, then sipping easier on the rest of it while he pondered. "You have two sons, Blair. Tomorrow one of them—maybe both—could be lyin' here where Finn is."

"It's our land. It'll be the boys' land one of these days . . ." Blair rubbed his cramped, aching hand. "Maybe not so long off."

"Your land. And you'd expect your friends to come and die for it with you? That's a lot to ask of friendship, Blair."

"No more than I've done for some of them." He didn't have to tell the doctor how it had been in earlier days, about the Comanche raids and the like. Doc knew. "This fight ain't just for me or my boys; it's for all these people. You remember how bad it used to be when Macy Modock was here before. If we let him get a foothold, it'll be the same way again."

"You're still not the law, Blair. We've got a duly elected sheriff in this county. It's up to him to handle it."

Blair's left fist doubled. His right one couldn't. "Erly can't do it all by himself." He turned to his sons, to Hez Northcutt and to chunky Chaco Martinez. "Saddle up. You got some ridin' to do."

He stepped out onto the gallery with them. From the darkness came the sound of a running horse. Blair motioned for the others to wait. "Could be the sheriff," he said. Nobody had been able to find him earlier. The lawman was still scouring the country for Joe Little.

The horse loped into the open yard, and Blair saw the

flare of long skirts. He frowned as Jessie Cass reined to
a stop and jumped down in front of the house. Her eyes
went straight to Allan. "Allan," she cried, "are you all
right?"

Allan hurried down the steps and grabbed her into his
arms. "Jessie, what're you doin' here?"

"I heard them say they'd shot somebody. They didn't
say who. I was scared to death it was you. I'd of died if
it was you."

Blair Bishop watched hard-eyed as Allan held the girl
tightly. "It was Finn. He's dead, Jessie."

"Dead?" She sobbed quietly. "I've been afraid it
would come to somethin' like this. I've been tryin' to
tell Dad . . ."

Blair moved stiffly down the steps. His voice was cold.

"You go on home, girl, and you tell your daddy somethin' else. You tell him he picked himself the wrong partners if he has any notion of gettin' his greedy hands on
some of the Double B for them scrubby cattle. You tell
him a good man died here tonight, and I'm holdin' him
responsible right along with the others."

Jessie turned from Allan, but she still held his hand.
"He can't do anything," she said brokenly. "All those
men . . . bad men . . . they've got him scared to open
his mouth. They're breakin' him down, Mister Bishop.
They've taken over."

"He asked for it. He let it start. I got no sympathy for
Clarence Cass, but one thing I'll sure as hell promise him:
I'm goin' to protect what's mine. He ain't goin' to get any
of this land, either by stealin' it or by marryin' off his
daughter to it. If I got to bury your old daddy along with
the rest of them, then that's just what I'll do. You go tell
him that, girl."

"Please, Mister Bishop, you've got to understand how it is . . ."

"I *know* how it is. I lost one good man findin' out. I got a strong hunch I lost another and just can't prove it. So you go tell him what I said. Tell him if he's got half the brains God gave a jackrabbit, he'll pack up and leave this country on the fastest horse he's got. And you better go with him."

Allan tightened his hold on the girl's hand. "Jessie's not goin'."

Blair's eyes narrowed. He gave the girl a long, hard look, then turned to Allan. He thrust his jaw forward. "Boy, we got a good man dead in yonder. I don't want to ever see Clarence Cass' miserable whinin' face again, and I won't have this girl around to remind me of him." To the stricken girl he said evenly, "Now get on that horse and go home, girl. Don't you ever come here again!"

Crying, she tried to leave. Allan held her. Stubbornly he faced his father. "I've told you how it is with us. Anywhere Jessie goes, I go with her!"

That shook Blair Bishop. He said, "You know what we got to do tomorrow. If we don't do it, Finn died for nothin'. Would you turn your back on us at a time like this?"

"Not unless I was forced to it. Don't you force me."

"The choice is yours. I don't want that girl here. Not now and not ever."

Allan eyed his father an awful moment, then the girl. He gripped Jessie's hand so hard she flinched. "Jessie, I got a duty here. I'll see it through. When it's done, I'll come for you and we'll *both* leave this country. You go on home and get your things ready. Chances are I'll be there sometime tomorrow."

Blair Bishop swallowed, but he tried not to let the bitter disappointment show. He turned away from the couple and walked out into the yard, struggling for control over the grief and anger which shook him. He could hear Allan talking softly to the girl. "He's speakin' for himself," Allan was saying, "but not for me. Soon as I go to fetch you, you can say goodbye to that place. You won't ever have to go back there."

Blair didn't look, but he could tell Allan was helping the girl onto her horse. "Allan," she said, "be careful. Those men had as soon kill you as look at you. Maybe a little rather."

"I'll be careful. You do the same."

The horse moved away. Presently Blair heard his oldest son walk up beside him. "She's gone, Dad, and you won't have to look at her again. Soon's we get this quarrel with Modock over with, I'll be leavin'."

"It's your choice to make, son," Blair said stiffly.

"Always remember, I didn't want to make it."

By daylight the first people came. A neighbor brought a pine coffin that he had stayed up through the post-midnight hours to build. His wife had padded the interior of it with dark velvet cloth. The men filed through the Bishop parlor to view Finn Goforth in the simple coffin. Then they gathered on the gallery in angry silence, for Finn had been a man without an enemy, except those he inherited through Blair Bishop.

Blair sat in the parlor quietly receiving the people. Few women came, because what lay ahead this day was for the men to do. Nobody talked about it, but Blair sensed it was strong on everyone's mind. Mentally he tallied the men as they arrived. About ten o'clock he pushed painfully to his feet. He looked a minute into the faces of men he counted as friends—ranchers, cowboys, people from town. They had come to side him in his hour of need, for they realized it was their hour too.

Allan Bishop waited with the rest. Blair wished that he could undo what had been said in the dark of night, but it lay between them like a strong adobe wall. He nodded at Allan. "Let's go, son."

Billy Bishop came out of his bedroom, shotgun in hand.

Blair caught his arm. "Billy, you're not of age for this. When we've finished buryin' Finn, you're comin' back to the house."

"I'm old enough. There's not nobody can shoot this thing any better."

Blair's voice carried in it a firmness that plainly brooked no argument. "You're stayin' home, son."

The burial was soon over. Without saying anything, Blair Bishop limped out and swung heavily upon his big gray horse. The other men followed suit. The only sound was of stamping hoofs and creaking leather. For a moment Blair caught the reluctant look in Billy's eyes. Blair wanted to know *one* son would be home when he came back . . . if he came back.

He set out with a dozen riders behind him. Before he had gone a mile, he picked up three more. They moved in a stiff trot, saving the horses but steadily putting the miles behind them. Blair led them in an arc that would allow them to pick up most of the cattle. The ones Modock had herded out of the pasture probably would be scattered in the general vicinity of the gate, wanting back in for the water they were accustomed to. The others which Blair and the men had driven yesterday probably would be strung out halfway to the Black Bull Tank by now, instinct taking them back.

The horsemen picked up the scattered cattle as they found them and bunched them gradually, pushing toward the double gates. The animals were dry now, slobbering for want of water. They moved sluggishly, instinct telling them they were being pushed away from water rather than toward it. The dry ground went to powder beneath the scraping of their sharp hoofs, and dust rose in a choking veil of gray.

Finally Blair could see the tall gateposts which marked the location of the fence. And he could see the dark figures he knew were horsemen, waiting to stop them. "This time, Macy Modock," he muttered, "you'll move aside or get trampled."

The day was hot, but the sweat which broke over him was cold. He counted the men at the gate. Six. He had them outnumbered by more than two to one. He said nothing. He simply touched spurs to the big gray and moved into an easy swinging lope, leaving the cattle. Without looking back, he knew the men behind him would follow his lead. The thought gave him satisfaction, knowing he had friends strong enough in their faith to follow him into the muzzles of professional guns. But the responsibility was heavy too. For half a moment he felt the hard tug of strong doubt. But this left him in a rise of bitterness as he recognized the thin form of Macy Modock slacked on his horse just beyond the wire gate.

Blair pulled a shotgun out of his saddle scabbard. He had left his rifle at home because he feared his right hand would allow him poor use of it, at best. But he could handle this shotgun. For one shot, at least. He would make that shot a good one, or he would never get a second.

His horsemen pulled up on either side of him, presenting a broad, massive line bristling with weapons. Blair studied the men across the fence. Each had a rifle or a pistol in his hands. Mostly rifles.

We can't help but win, he thought, *but there's liable to be some good men fall.*

The alternative was to be able to convince Modock of the hopelessness of his situation, and failing this, to get Modock with a first shot that might—given luck—be the only one fired. One more man dead among Blair's good friends was one more man too many.

Maybe Modock would see reason when he looked into all those guns.

One of the wire gates lay on the ground, thrown back out of the way. A horseman rode through it, his hand raised. Blair felt surprise. This was sheriff Erly Greenwood.

"Erly," Blair said, "my boy told me he couldn't find you last night."

"I got in awful late. What I found didn't cheer me none. Blair, you got to call this off."

"*Me?* You get Macy Modock to call it off. He's the one makin' the grab, startin' the trouble."

Erly Greenwood appeared considerably agitated. Blair surmised he had been arguing with Macy Modock before the ranchers arrived. He probably hadn't gotten anywhere with Modock. *The only thing Modock understands is a .30-.30 slug, or a dose of buckshot*, Blair thought.

The sheriff appeared almost in despair. Blair hadn't slept any last night, and he guessed the sheriff hadn't either. Greenwood said, "Blair, you got to back off. Somebody'll get killed here sure as hell."

Blair shook his head. "I come to put my cows back

where they belong. They're goin' through that gate, Erly, before the sun's an hour higher."

"You got good men with you. Friends of yours, friends of mine. You don't want their blood on your conscience."

"They know what's at stake here. They know what it might cost. They figure this is for them as well as for me. Them thirsty cows back yonder are mine. But next week or next month they could be somebody else's. We've decided we're goin' to stop the thing before it ever really starts. We'll stop it here."

"I'm askin' you to back away, Blair."

Blair frowned, beginning to be puzzled. "You askin' me as a friend, Erly, or as the sheriff?"

"As a friend first. If you won't do it as a friend, then I'll ask you as the sheriff."

"Them cows yonder, they can't wait much longer. They're dry. I'm takin' them to water. That's my land."

"Maybe it's not, Blair."

Blair stared, incredulous. "You better explain that."

"Judge Quincy got in from the Statehouse. Brought a court order with him. It's an injunction to keep you off till there can be a hearin' on whether you got legal title or not."

"Legal title? I've had title for years."

"Seems like Quincy dug up somethin' that casts a shadow over your deeds, Blair. The court orders everything held still till there can be a hearin'. Now, I'm askin' you again to turn back."

"Erly, you wouldn't side with Modock."

"You know me better than that. But I got to uphold the law, and a court order's the law. So back off, Blair, please."

"And if I don't?"

"Then I got to try and stop you."

"You wouldn't shoot me, Erly."

"But I might block that gate till you shoot *me*."

Dry-mouthed, Blair looked awhile at Erly Greenwood, then at the barbed wire fence and at the windmill far beyond it. He looked at the riders who faced him across that fence, and most of all he stared at Macy Modock, the hatred aboil in him.

"This is twice now you've let me down, Erly."

"Not through any choice of mine, Blair. I'd resign this badge before I'd hurt you. Right now I'm just tryin' to keep you from hurtin' yourself."

"What about my cows?"

"You push them up to the gate and I'll make Modock drive them to the mill for water, then bring them back to you. But you keep your men on this side."

"One waterin' saves them for one day. What about tomorrow?"

"I don't know, Blair. Honest to God, I don't know what you're goin' to do about this problem."

"Modock may not want to water them even this once."

"Right now he needs the law. He's usin' me and knows it. I'll tell him he'll do it or I'll shoot him."

Blair pondered, all his instincts telling him to fight, to make this a showdown and get it over with while the odds heavily favored him. Another time, they might be heavily against him. He studied the guns across the fence and felt his hands cold-sweaty against his own shotgun.

We could do it, he thought, wanting to go ahead. *We could do it so easy . . .*

He watched Macy Modock running his ready hand

up and down the rifle he held lying across the pommel of his saddle, its muzzle vaguely pointed in Blair's direction. Blair gauged the distance and knew he would have to move closer for this shotgun to take good effect.

To move closer, he would have to ride over Erly Greenwood.

Blair looked to one side of him, then to the other, at the men who had come to cast their lot with him. Guilt touched him, for if he backed away now, he was letting them down.

But he couldn't go against Erly. His shoulders slumped. "All right, Erly. But don't you let me down a third time."

He saw triumph in the way Macy Modock relaxed, letting the rifle droop, and resentment roiled in Blair Bishop. To Greenwood he said, "You make it clear to him that I ain't givin' up, not by a damn sight. I'm just backin' off this time because you asked me to. We'll give the court a chance." His eyes narrowed. "But the court better come through right, because that's my land, and I won't stay off of it long."

He turned his horse and started back toward the herd, to bring it up to the gate as Erly had said. One of his neighbors spurred up beside him. "You don't have to call it off on our account, Blair."

"It's over with, John. At least, for today it's over with."

The neighbor frowned, looking over his shoulder toward the fence. "Then it's over for good and all. Ever give Modock a toehold, the only way you'll be shed of him is to kill him."

They brought the cattle and turned them through the gate. Blair could tell Modock had no inclination to receive them and drive them up to water, but Erly Greenwood brooked no argument, and at the moment Modock was heavily dependent upon Greenwood's reluctant backing.

Gradually the neighbors dropped out and began riding away, saying little or nothing to Blair Bishop, talking little even among themselves. Blair watched them silently, sensing the disapproval of many who had come here angry enough to fight. To them, Blair had backed down. Blair Bishop, the old warhorse, was showing his age.

It shook his self-confidence, for in his own mind he still didn't know whether he had been wrong or right. Maybe he should have gone ahead and carried through his threat. Now it was too late. The moment had come, the iron had been hot, and he had not struck. The moment might not come again.

Maybe they *were* right. Maybe Blair Bishop *was* showing his age. Maybe he should turn it over to his sons.

But he couldn't do that. Billy was not of age. And Allan was standing firm on his promise. The confrontation over and the danger past, Allan had ridden away to get Jessie Cass.

Blair hung his head, beaten.

{ ELEVEN }

The confrontation at the fence hadn't turned out the way Allan Bishop had expected. He had thought Blair Bishop's show of strength would have put a quick end to it, either in a volley of gunfire or by Macy Modock's capitulation in the face of heavy odds. He had really anticipated the latter, for Modock might have been vindictive and he might have been greedy, but he was not a fool. What Allan hadn't expected—and knew his father hadn't either—was Erly Greenwood's being forced to take a position that gave the decision to Modock.

Now the question remained unresolved; the problem bore on Blair Bishop heavier than ever. Allan felt a keen sense of guilt, leaving this way when it was plain his father faced deeper trouble. He knew how it would look; many would call him a quitter, deserting Blair Bishop in his hour of greatest need. Allan hadn't wanted it this way; Blair had made the ultimatum. Given any way out, Allan would have stayed and seen it through. But not at the risk of losing Jessie Cass. No telling what things were like at the Cass place anymore. Allan had made up his mind he wouldn't leave her there another day, another night.

He wished he had taken time to go to the ranch for a

wagon. He figured the ranch owed him that much, for as a Bishop son he had never drawn any regular wage. But maybe now would be a good time to fetch Jessie, when Modock and his crew and Clarence Cass were occupied watering the Bishop cattle and driving them back out of the contested pasture.

Allan had no particular fear of Modock. He realized the man was reputed to be fast with a gun, and word had drifted down that Owen Darby was fast too. But Blair Bishop had always maintained and taught his sons that speed wasn't the only thing which mattered. Coolness and deliberation counted for a lot. Allan figured he had both, but he had never had occasion to test them under fire. The deliberation part told him if he could avoid a fight, he was that much better off. And getting Jessie out while everybody was gone might be a good way to sidestep trouble.

Don't run from a fight, Blair had taught his sons, but walk away right gingerly if you can.

He rode boldly up to the small, slipshod frame house that seemed to show a slight lean toward the east. West wind was pushing on it all the time, Allan thought. Somehow the whole character of Clarence Cass seemed reflected in his poor drab house.

"Jessie," he called, "you in there?"

Jessie Cass had already seen him. She ran out, almost stumbling on the wooden doorstep. He took her into his arms a moment, then released her. "You got a horse here you can ride, or have we got to ride this one double?"

Surprised, she said, "You're really takin' me away from here?"

"Told you I was."

She had been crying; he could tell by the redness of her eyes. "The fight," she asked quickly, "is it over?"

"It never started. It's a standoff of sorts, but I reckon Modock has got a little the better of it."

Her voice was bitter. "I wish somebody would kill him. If somebody doesn't, there'll be other men die."

"That's no way for a girl to be a-talkin'."

"You haven't been here. You haven't seen him and listened to him. He's a little bit crazy, Allan."

He could tell by the way she spoke of Modock that she was afraid of him. "You won't be troubled by him no more. You got anything you need to pack, anything we can carry horseback?" He knew she didn't have much. Everything she owned could have been stuffed into a cowboy's warbag without crowding the pucker-string. Cass had never been one to spoil his daughter by teaching her vanity and a taste for worldly goods.

"I'll pack it," she said, "while you go saddle my horse for me. You'll find him grazin' down yonder in the draw, most likely."

Riding out, Allan saw a man standing in the open door of the shed, swaying. He recognized Harley Mills, once a Double B cowboy, mostly now a stable-sweeping drunk. Resentment touched Allan as he thought of Mills' falsely swearing that his homestead claim had been fraudulent.

"What're you doin' out here, Harley?" he demanded, but Mills didn't answer him and didn't have to. Allan could guess. He decided the man represented no threat to him and Jessie, so he rode on down to the draw. He found the horse, tossed a loop over its neck and led it back to the shed. Mills watched indifferently while Allan flung the sidesaddle onto the dun and led it to the house. Jessie came out carrying a faded carpetbag. "My mother's," she said. "It's about all she left me except a cheap ring and a locket."

"And the prettiest face in the country," Allan told her. He gave her a lift into the saddle. She looked around a moment, tears welling into her eyes. He asked her, "Any regrets?"

"I hate leavin' Dad. He's in trouble."

"Nothin' your stayin' could do to help him out of it." But Allan could respect her feelings, for he had the same kind himself regarding Blair Bishop.

"Where we goin'?" she asked.

"To town. I figure we'll get married there. Wouldn't be proper for us to go ridin' around all over the country together without we do the right thing first. And I got some money of my own in the bank. I thought I'd get Mister Karnes there to give me a letter of some kind so we can draw against it wherever we go. Then we'll just strike out a-lookin'. I'll find me a job on a ranch somewheres."

She said gravely, "You don't want to leave your old daddy any more than I want to leave mine."

"We got any choice?"

"I reckon not."

"Then we better be movin'. Longer we wait, the more likely we'll run into your daddy's friends."

They had already waited too long, but they didn't find out for a while. They rode side by side several miles, saying little, exchanging occasional glances but mostly keeping their own individual counsel, mulling over the intolerable conditions that had brought them to this necessity of riding away when neither really wanted to.

"Things'll work out," she said after a time. "You'll see."

He found no conviction in her voice, and there was none in his. "Sure they will."

It was on his mind that either probably would turn and go back if the other would but suggest it. Increasingly he knew he didn't want to go like this, and neither did she, leaving so much uncompleted, so much trouble still in the air. He was on the point of saying so when he saw riders coming toward them on the Cass wagon road.

Jessie gasped, "Modock!"

Allan stopped. He looked around quickly, but he saw no way to avoid the riders without running. It was contrary to all his upbringing to run. He hoped Modock still had the sheriff with him, for Erly Greenwood would see to it that there was no trouble. As the riders neared, he sagged. The sheriff must have gone back to town. Allan told Jessie, "Stay back a little. If there's a fight, I'll need room."

Clarence Cass was the first of the riders to speak after they closed the distance and stopped their horses in a crescent around Allan. He looked at his daughter in sharp surprise. "Jessie, what you doin' out here thisaway? I've told you I don't want you havin' no truck with this Bishop."

She didn't answer him. Modock spoke. "Ought to be plain enough to you, Clarence. It's plain to me. That boy yonder's a true son of his old daddy. He was fixin' to steal that little girl from you."

Allan said defiantly, "Jessie and me, we're goin' to town. We're fixin' to be married, and then we're leavin' this country."

That brought surprise even to Modock, who had never thought of the Bishops except as a cohesive unit. It hadn't occurred to him they might split away from each other in disagreement. "You meanin' to tell us you'd leave your daddy in the midst of a fight? I'm disappointed in you. You ain't a true Bishop after all. Givin' the devil his due, I'd say that Blair Bishop wouldn't never run out on *nobody*."

"I'm not runnin' out; I been *put* out. If it was up to me, I'd stay and fight you, Modock."

The tall gunman frowned, chewing quietly on something as his eyes dwelt on Allan. "Well, I'd say you got a good chance to do that right here, because I done made up my mind you ain't takin' that gal noplace."

"You got no hold on her."

Modock said, "Then I reckon I'll *put* one on her."

It came to Allan with sudden impact, a thought that had never quite reached him before. Modock had a hunger for this girl, just as Allan did. And he became certain this was as far up this road as he would get unless he could somehow beat Modock. He could see death in Modock's hard eyes.

Allan felt trapped like a fly in a spiderweb. His heart quickened. He tried to look around him without giving away his anxiety. They were moving to box him in, the red-bearded Owen Darby passing around to get behind him. But Jessie was still back a few feet, out of it. She could, if she would, spur clear. Then it would be a matter of a horserace whether they could catch her or not. Allan said to her, "Jessie, light out of here. Don't you stop till you get to Dad. You tell him—"

Modock broke in. "She ain't fixin' to tell him nothin'. And neither are you."

Allan sensed that Jessie wouldn't do what he told her; she wouldn't run off and leave him here. He could see the intention in Modock's eyes and knew at any second Modock would reach for the pistol at his hip. He tried to remember all his father had told him about keeping his head, but none of the admonitions seemed to hold for him now. He found himself drawing inexorably toward a contest. Even as he realized he couldn't win, he found himself easing his hand down toward the butt of his pistol. *Don't be a fool,* he told himself, *they'll kill you.* But then he told himself, *They'll kill you anyhow. At least, take Modock.* He ducked low in the saddle, his hand darting for the gun.

Modock moved so swiftly Allan barely saw. He caught the swift streak of the man's pistol coming up, saw the flash and heard the explosion before his own hand had more than grasped the butt of his weapon. The bullet smashed into him like the strike of a sledge, driving him backward out of his saddle. He felt the frightened jump of his horse and felt himself suspended a moment in midair before he knew the sensation of falling. He struck the ground almost beneath his horse's hoofs.

Modock grunted. "He ducked just as I fired. I didn't get me no clean shot. But I don't reckon he'll duck again." The excited horse was in his way as he leveled the gun toward the sprawled body on the ground. Modock shouted impatiently, "Hyahhhh! Get out of here!"

Jessie Cass was on the ground, screaming at him. Before the horse galloped off in panic, clearing the way, Jessie had thrown herself over the downed boy and was looking up at Modock with eyes ablaze. "No! Don't you shoot him again."

Impatient, Modock gestured with the gun barrel. "Git aside, girl."

"I won't move. To shoot him, you'll have to shoot me first."

Owen Darby coldly rode up on the other side. "I can get him from here, Macy. She can't cover him from both of us."

Jessie Cass glanced back in desperation, knowing Darby could and would.

Clarence Cass brought himself up to mild protest. "Macy, you don't really need to do it. He's old man Blair's boy. Folks'll raise hell. You can leave when you've finished what you come to do, but me, I got to live here."

Modock flashed him a look of disgust. "Old man, you ain't ever really seen *nothin'* clear, have you? I don't figure on leavin' here at all. And I won't be finished with what I come to do till all these Bishops are put away in a pine box. This one is just the first." He turned his back on the frightened old rancher and tried to see a way to aim past Jessie without hitting her.

Jessie saw he intended to do it. She straightened, got what control she could muster and told him: "Go ahead, then, if you have to do it, but you'd better shoot me too. If you don't, I'll get you, Modock. Somewhere, somehow, I'll get hold of a gun, and I'll kill you. If I can't get a gun, I'll get a knife, and someday you'll doze off and forget to watch me, or you'll look away a minute and I'll drive that knife into you to the hilt. I'll kill you, Macy Modock. I promise, I'll kill you!"

Modock blinked, unprepared for her savage response. A chill touched him; he hadn't guessed it was in her. Yet, he could tell she meant every word, and she would carry through if it cost her life. He lowered the pistol. "Hell, maybe he'd be worth more to us alive than dead anyway. Long's we got him laid up with a bullethole bigger than a bushel basket, he won't be goin' noplace, and neither will she. Could be he'll make us a hole card if we need it to use against old Blair Bishop. Catch that horse, somebody, and we'll throw him across the saddle."

Jessie pleaded, "He'll bleed to death."

"Let him bleed. Weaker he is, the less we got to worry."

They threw him roughly up onto his horse. Jessie had used a handkerchief to help stanch the blood, and now she rode close beside him to help hold him onto the saddle. Modock glared at her.

"All right, girl, you got him. Now you better remember this. *We* got him too. First bad move you make, we'll blow him out like a lamp. You listen to every word I tell you and you do what I say. Long's you pay attention, that's how long he stays alive. Now, let's git movin'."

{ TWELVE }

Blair Bishop drew rein in front of the Two Forks Livery & Grain, stepped down and limped heavily into the big open door. "Harley Mills, where you at? Harley, you git yourself out here! I come to talk to you!"

He caught a shadowy movement toward the end of the horse stalls and walked angrily in that direction, cursing a little in pent-up bitterness. He slowed as an old man stepped out into view. Blair broke off the profanity. "I took you for Harley. Where the hell is he at?"

The old man shrugged. "He ain't been here in two-three days. He just up and quit his job; said he had enough money he didn't have to shovel horse manure no more. Ain't seen him since."

Blair Bishop seethed in frustration but decided this was only a momentary setback. Depending upon how much money Harley had been given, he would be either in one of the saloons drinking his fill or out someplace sleeping like a man pistol-whipped. Harley was one of those bachelor cowboys who had never had a wife and didn't need one; whiskey was both his comfort and his personal hell.

"I'll find him quick enough," Bishop gritted, turning.

"I heard what he done," the old man said. "He was lyin', wasn't he?"

"He was lyin'."

"Don't think too harsh of him, Mister Blair. He can't control himself when it comes to whiskey. He'd do anything to get it."

"I don't plan to hurt him much; just bust his head if he don't tell the truth."

Followed by his son Billy, Blair tromped from one saloon to another, impatiently inquiring after Harley Mills. To his surprise, he found no one who had seen Harley in a couple of days. Harley had bought several bottles and dropped out of sight. A thought struck Blair, and he started back down the saloons, inquiring if anyone had bought any unusually large amounts of whiskey lately. At the third place, he found out Judge Quincy had bought a full case. That was strange, for Quincy was, at most, a light drinker. Whatever his shortcomings might have been, an affinity for alcohol was not one of them. His legal mind, if devious, stayed nevertheless sharp.

Blair stood outside the saloon door with young Billy, grinding his teeth. "He took Harley's deposition and then hid him out, that's what he done. He's hidin' him someplace to keep us from gettin' any chance to shake the truth out of him."

"Ain't many ranches around here would do that to you, Dad. By now they all know what Harley done. No friend of yours would help Macy Modock."

"No reason a friend of mine would have to. Ten to one they got Harley at the Cass place where Modock can keep an eye on him till he needs him in court."

"Well, then, let's go out there and git him."

Blair shook his head. "This mornin' the odds were on our side. If we was to ride out there, they'd be on Modock's side, and don't you think for a minute he wouldn't use them. He'd cut us both to pieces. And he'd have a legal leg, because we'd be the trespassers, not him."

"Then we can't touch Harley Mills?"

"Not unless he runs out of whiskey and comes to town. I'm goin' to leave word around with some friends to keep an eye out for him."

"Modock'll figure that. He won't let Harley run out of whiskey till he's through with him."

"Which only leaves Judge Quincy."

Billy grinned humorlessly and rubbed his knuckles. "Come right down to it, he's the cause of all this trouble. Without him, Modock couldn't of done a thing, hardly. Let's go work on him."

"We'll go *talk* to him," Blair corrected his eager son. "And I'll do all the talkin'."

The moment Blair Bishop's shadow fell across his door Quincy was on his feet. He hurried behind a long table spread with papers and law books and turned defensively. "Blair Bishop, I been promised the sheriff's protection. You lay one hand on me and I'll sue you for every acre you got, every cow . . ."

"Settle down, Judge." Blair's voice was dry. "I come friendly. No, I take that back . . . not friendly. But I come peaceful. All I want to do is talk."

"We've done our talking. Anything else you have to say to me you can say it in court."

Blair eyed him thoughtfully. "I ain't no lawyer, Judge, but through the years I've picked up a legal word here and there. One of them is *perjury.* Another is *disbarment.*"

"You'll not get away with threatening me. Intimidation is against the law . . ."

"I ain't threatenin', and I ain't intimidatin'. Let's say I'm askin' for a little bit of legal information, and I'm willin' to pay the goin' fee for it. My question is this: how does a man go about filin' for disbarment of a lawyer who knowingly builds up a case based on perjury . . . who maybe even personally bribes a witness to give false testimony?"

"You're still trying to intimidate a legally licensed attorney into defaulting on a client, Blair Bishop. The bar will not hold still for it."

"I never mentioned your name; never mentioned nobody's name. I just asked for a piece of legal information. If you don't care to answer it, I can go to somebody else who knows law. Maybe the district judge . . ."

Blair's leg hurt; he'd slept little, and he had done a lot of riding. He shifted his weight. Quincy took that for a move forward, and he cringed. "Bishop, don't you come any closer. I have a gun in here. I'll use it."

Blair heard footsteps scrape across the threshold, and he saw relief flush over Quincy's face. Quincy said, "Sheriff, you sure took your time getting here."

Blair glanced back at Erly Greenwood. "Howdy, Erly. Seems like a man runs into you almost everyplace these days, except when he needs you."

"Maybe you do need me right now, Blair. Maybe you was about to do somethin' that could cost you more than you could afford to pay."

"I wasn't goin' to do anything to him. I'm as close right now as I ever care to be. The smell of him would kill cotton at forty paces."

Erly studied Blair Bishop gravely. "Blair, you got trouble enough without makin' it worse. Why don't you go on home and get some sleep? Then maybe you'll be in a better position to think things through. Better yet, you come on over to my house and bunk down awhile. You'll see things clearer."

"I'm tired, but I ain't blind. I see things clear enough. Quincy bribed Harley Mills into makin' a deposition that he homesteaded his place through fraud and that I was the one put him up to it, so I could buy the land from him. You know it's a lie; Quincy knows it's a lie. But some visitin' judge from another part of the state won't know it's a lie unless Harley or Quincy owns up to it. I come to talk sense to Quincy."

"And I come to talk sense to you, Blair. A mistake right now could cost you your case."

"I ain't fixin' to lose my land, Erly, not to a set of lies told by a crooked lawyer and a whiskey-soaked stable sweeper."

"You *could* lose it. You got to walk easy till this thing has come to a head. You got to keep your distance from Judge Quincy. It's my job to give him protection."

"Seems to me like you been takin' your job awful seriously here of late."

"I always did, Blair." Erly shook his head, taking a hard, long look at Quincy. "And there's never been a time I ever hated it till now."

Quincy watched the sheriff until he found confidence in himself. "You're letting your personal feelings influence you, Greenwood. A peace officer cannot afford to do that."

"A peace officer cannot afford to let his personal feelings be an influence in what he does," Erly corrected him. "There's no law can keep an officer from havin' them. You know mine. Somethin' for you to keep in mind if ever I catch you steppin' over the line."

The sheriff followed Blair and Billy out into the street. Blair stood slumped, exhausted in body and spirit. "Seems like every way I turn, they got me boxed, Erly."

"I'm sorry they've made me a party to it. Only way I could change it would be to resign, and that wouldn't help anything. The next man couldn't do no different, not and live up to his oath."

"Don't resign, Erly. Maybe they'll make a mistake. Then we'll need you behind that badge."

"And if they don't make any mistakes?"

Blair thought awhile. "Then I'll need you to keep me from makin' one and killin' them all."

Erly walked along with him. He didn't have to move very fast, for Blair was dragging some. He said, "Blair, I still wish you'd come out to the house and rest awhile. You need it."

"I got a lot of thinkin' to do. I think better at home." It occurred to him to ask, "You never have found any sign of Joe Little?"

Erly shook his head. "None at all. He's plumb left the country."

"I don't agree with you. I still believe he was the first mistake Macy Modock made."

"You keep thinkin' that, Blair, if it'll make you feel any better."

"It don't help my feelin'. But it helps keep me convinced that one way or another, I got to stop Macy Modock. Only thing bothers me is, how many more men will he kill before I get *him?*"

Harley Mills was well into his second bottle for the day, but his vision wasn't so foggy he couldn't see that one of the horses was bringing somebody wounded. The thought filtered through his brain that he could've told them old Blair Bishop would fight like a mountain lion with its tail in a steel trap, that they wouldn't come home in one piece. But they hadn't asked him. They hadn't asked him much of anything, come to think of it.

Well, it wasn't going to be any bother to him one way or the other. The hell with them. Soon as they got that court hearing over with and paid him off, Harley Mills was going to be long gone out of this country. He didn't give a damn then if Modock and all of his bunch got shot into pieces too little for chili. In fact, he almost hoped they would. He found it impossible ever to feel easy in the presence of Modock or Owen Darby. He never got over the feeling that Darby would shoot a man just for the fun of seeing him jump and fall, and that Modock had some devil chewing on him all the time. Mills would be glad to get the money in his hands and run. It had occurred to him more than once that for the amount promised him, Modock probably wouldn't hesitate to kill a man.

I'll be sober that day, Mills pledged himself, *and I'll have eyes in the back of my head. Once I get paid off, all they'll see of Harley Mills is a blue streak and a little cloud of dust.*

He didn't care enough to get up and go see who was wounded; he didn't know any of these Modock men anyway, and if it was old man Clarence the world would be that much better off, in Mills' view. But his interest was aroused a little when he saw Cass' girl, Jessie, jump down from her sidesaddle. The way he had seen her ride away from here earlier with that young Bishop, he had figured she was gone for good. Mills blinked as they led the wounded man's horse up to the shed where he lay with the bottle. To his surprise he recognized Allan Bishop. Mills staggered to his feet, stumbled over a pitchfork and got up again. His first thought was, *He'll tell old Blair where I'm at and he'll come after me with a bullwhip or a gun.* Then he realized that the shape Allan appeared to be in, he wouldn't be going anywhere. Mills tried to figure out how come they had brought young Bishop here, but liquor had left him no chance with logic. Nothing came very clear to him except that an uncomfortable situation was becoming increasingly bad.

"Move over, Mills," Macy Modock said curtly. "We got to have that cot you been lyin' on."

Mills stared in confusion at the unconscious Allan Bishop. "How come him to be here?" He was too puzzled even to feel resentment over being done out of his cot. He would have to sleep on the hay now.

"We shot him," Modock said.

"Old man Blair'll come huntin' him, and there'll be hell to pay."

"Bishop figures he run off with the Cass girl," Modock said. "He won't be lookin' for him."

Mills stared down at the blood-streaked face. "He goin' to die?" He had punched cows with Allan, back when Allan was just a kid. He had been a good-enough kind of a button, Mills had always thought, considering that he was the son of a big cowman like Blair Bishop. A little humility wouldn't have hurt him none, but Mills wouldn't have wished him a bullet. "Somebody better fetch him a doctor."

"No doctor," said Modock. "The less Blair Bishop knows, the better. I'll tell him myself if I think the time is right."

"What if that boy was to die?"

"Then I'd give you a shovel and tell you to go bury

him, since you're a friend of his. And if you said a word to anybody about it, I'd see that you was buried right next to him. Do you get that through your head, Mills?"

Harley nodded, fearing the man. But he had another fear too. "If Blair finds out about this, I sure don't want him thinkin' I had anything to do with it."

Modock snarled. "You and old Clarence . . . neither one of you has got sense enough to see daylight. Time I get through, Blair Bishop won't trouble *nobody*."

Harley Mills sat on the ground and silently pulled at the bottle as he watched tearful Jessie Cass and her father dig the bullet out of Allan and wrap clean cloth around the wound. He listened to Clarence Cass complaining. "I didn't noways figure on nothin' like this. I ain't a-goin' to stand for it. One of these days I'm goin' to walk up to Macy Modock and I'm goin' to tell him . . ."

Mills snorted to himself, feeling better in the knowledge that he wasn't the only coward on the place. *You ain't goin' to tell him nothin', Clarence, same as I ain't goin' to tell him nothin'. You're goin' to listen and say yes, sir. Difference is, I'm goin' to get my money and ride out of here. What're you goin' to get, Clarence?*

{ THIRTEEN }

B lair Bishop lay down for a fitful nap when he got home, but he arose for a supper quickly cooked by Chaco Martinez. Mostly he drank coffee. It didn't make him feel any easier, but it woke him up. He stayed awake long past his accustomed bedtime, bolstered by a notion that Allan would get over his anger and come on home. He didn't really believe his son would leave here at a time like this, angry or not. And Blair had cooled too, in the face of so many other problems. He could remember how strongly the tides of young manhood had surged in him when he was Allan's age and could, now that he was calmer, understand why the boy would turn his back on father and home in favor of a girl. Blair sat on the porch a long time, sometimes rocking, sometimes still, listening vainly for hoofbeats. He fell asleep finally and woke up with a crick in his neck. Sadly he made his way to bed, knowing Allan wasn't coming.

Next morning he was up early, problems still unresolved. He knew what he had to do about one of them, and he had to do it quick. He had to get a lot of cattle off of his land in a hurry or he wouldn't have anything left except their sun-whitened bones.

He ate his breakfast at the bunkhouse with the men.

"Bad as I hate to," he told them, "we got to take a deep cut into the cow herd. We can't sell them at home. It's so dry that most people here are more of a mind to sell than to buy. We'll make a drag on our oldest cows and drive them over to the railroad. Maybe we can get a decent price for them in Kansas City."

Billy Blair put in, "Seems like an awful pity to have to sell off them good Double B cows."

"Be a worse pity to watch them die for water. If we can save the young cows, we'll at least have seed."

"There was a time," Billy said, "when you wouldn't have done it this way. You'd have took care of Macy Modock and everything would've been all right."

Blair frowned. It surprised him, the quick-fighting spirit Billy was showing these days. Blair wondered where his son had gotten this sudden contrariness from; certainly not from his father. "Times change, boy. There was a time years ago when I could've killed Modock and nobody would've said a word."

"You sorry now you didn't?"

Blair thought about it a minute. "Maybe. For some things in this world, there's no cure as dependable as a good old-fashioned funeral."

He took the small crew to the Black Bull pasture where yesterday's trouble had been. There the water problem was most immediate, and most acute. The cattle had been watered yesterday. Today there wouldn't be enough. The cowboys made a broad sweep of the pasture, pushing all the cattle before them. As they moved, Blair Bishop rode back and forth among them, cutting out the younger cows carefully as he could without disrupting the herd. No use walking them extra miles for nothing. He kept the big steers in the herd, and the older cows, and the steer calves and yearlings. These were expendable. These would walk the better part of two days to the railroad.

When he had finished cutting the herd, Blair looked back for sign of Chaco Martinez. He had told Chaco to load the chuck wagon and bring it, for cowboys had to eat along the trail. They had to have changes of horses, too. He sent Hez Northcutt to round up the remuda. Then Blair took the point and let Billy and the rest of the riders string the herd out behind him. Some of the cattle were bawling, for they already had walked miles in the roundup and were showing thirst. They would have to skirt around Clarence Cass' land, for they would find no welcome there, Blair knew. But beyond Clarence lay the Finley ranch, and John Finley would spare water for a neighbor's passing herd as long as a drop was left.

They walked the cattle through the heat of the afternoon, thirst cracking Blair's dry lips as he rode along watching the dancing dust devils and peering toward the shimmering horizon line that changed but slowly in the deliberate pace of the herd. Chaco rode ahead and off to the right, keeping the wagon out of the herd's dust, for cowboys who ate dust all day didn't want to find it in their supper at night. Along late in the afternoon Blair called Billy up to take his place on the point and loped ahead to find John Finley and get permission to water the herd.

Blair's conscience hurt him as he watched his cattle watering by twilight, the stronger cows hooking impatiently at the weaker ones, fighting their way down to the deeper water. John had only a surface tank, much like Blair's own Black Bull Tank had been. When it emptied, that would be all of it until rain came again. But John hadn't had the heart to turn down Blair Bishop in his time of trouble. Blair shouted at the men, "Let's keep them movin'. Let them get enough water, but don't let them stay too long." Normally he would have bedded the cattle for the night near water, but this was not a normal situation. Soon as they had slaked their thirst, Blair moved out on point and had the cowboys push them a couple more miles to get them away from John's dwindling tank. Maybe they hadn't had all the water they wanted, but they had had enough to see them through another day's drive. There would be water again at the railroad.

The cowboys strung the cattle out in the cool of the morning and walked them steadily, pushing for all the miles they could get without hurting the stock. As the day wore on and the heat came up, the cattle slowed, bawling in distress. Blair plodded along, matching his pace to that of the cattle. He had water in a canteen, but he used it sparingly. Somehow it didn't seem right for a man to drink when his stock was suffering. Blair rode steadily and suffered with them.

Sometime after noon he began noticing the clouds change. Up to then, they had been the same puffy white clouds he had watched drift aimlessly across the sky all the dry spring and summer, leaving no benefit other than a brief respite from the sun's burning heat as they passed over the land. Now, however, the clouds seemed to thicken and turn darker.

Could it be that a summertime rain was coming up? Blair felt his pulse quicken a little at the thought. It wasn't often that a drought broke in this country in August, but sometimes a man got lucky and caught enough hard, pounding rain to run the draws and fill his tanks, to revive the grass and keep its roots alive until the more generous fall rains gave it one last chance before winter.

As the clouds became a leaden gray in the north, excitement built in Blair Bishop. He was tempted to stop the herd. If it would just come one of those old-timey chip floaters and fill his tanks, his cattle would have water enough. He wouldn't have to sell them.

But he knew that since he had gone this far, he had as well go the whole way to the railroad. The grass would revive better and the land would hair over sooner if he got some of the excess cattle off of it.

Riding point, he came to the creekbed where a flash flood had swept the cowboy named Abernathy to his death years ago. The creek was bone dry, as Blair had known it would be. Watching the clouds, he had a feeling it was a good thing the crew would have time enough to get the herd across before the rain started.

He was tired, and he was still desperately thirsty, but it didn't bother him now. He didn't seem to feel it. All he could feel was a faintly cooler wind coming out of the north, out from under those beautiful clouds. *Any minute now, she's going to start,* he thought. *Any minute now, we're goin' to get ourselves soaked.*

A drop of water struck his hat brim, and he turned his face up to the sky. A couple more drops splattered across his nose and his mouth. He turned in the saddle and gave a loud holler that would carry all the way to the drag end of the herd.

But something happened. Even as he watched, the cloud began to split almost directly overhead. He could see blue sky through a rift. As quickly as they had made up, the clouds broke apart and began drifting away. Blair watched dry-mouthed and stunned.

He had seen clouds break up like this more times than he could ever count. But he had never seen a time he had so desperately wanted it to rain.

The sun broke through, as hot as it had ever been. Blair pulled his hat down low to protect his eyes from it. His eyes were burning a little, somehow; must have gotten dust in them. His throat was tight. All of a sudden he realized anew how thirsty he was, and how far it still was to the railroad. He slumped in the saddle and rode along in silent misery.

Late in the afternoon he summoned Billy. "Looks to me like we ought to make it to the shippin' pens about dark. I was thinkin' me and you would ride in and make arrangements with the agent for water and hay. Ain't likely they can spot cars for us till tomorrow sometime."

Billy nodded and went back with orders for someone else to take the point. Then he reined in beside his father, his dusty face proud. This was a sign he was coming of age; this was the sharing of a man's job. Any kid could drive cattle; it took somebody responsible to handle the business end of a ranch.

Blair studied his youngest son as they rode and he liked what he saw. Give the boy a couple-three more years and he would be the man Allan was. Maybe if Blair was lucky, Billy wouldn't fall in love with the wrong woman, either. Time had come, Blair guessed, to talk to him straight-out about things like responsibility, and women and such as that. Maybe that had been the trouble with Allan; maybe Blair hadn't talked to him enough.

I won't make that mistake with Billy, Blair thought. *I'll sure talk to him. But not today; I'm too dry. I'll get around to it one of these days, when the right time comes.*

Blair saw dust rising from the railroad shipping pens and knew another herd was there ahead of him. Late as it was already, he figured it unlikely that herd would load out tonight.

"That's too bad," he said. "I'd figured we could turn them cattle into the pens on hay and water. Then we wouldn't have to fool with them."

Curiosity would normally have carried him by the pens to look at the cattle, but he had too much on his mind now to spend time on idle things. He rode straight to the depot. Every bone in him ached as he handed his reins to Billy and limped up the plank steps. Billy tied the horses and followed him. First thing Blair did was to find the water bucket and empty the dipper three times . . . twice down his throat and once over his head. Handing it to Billy, he turned and sought the railroad agent. The agent was a fairly new man, for Blair didn't recognize him. He said, "I got a herd of cattle comin' in directly. Blair Bishop, from over at Two Forks. Need cars to take them to Kansas City. Tonight we'll need hay and water."

The agent explained what Blair had already seen, that another herd had preceded him and had occupied the corrals. "However, we have a large water lot with troughs in it. You can bring the cattle, water them good, then take them back out and herd them on the prairie till the train comes tomorrow."

"That'll have to do," Blair said. The agent sat down and began filling out the papers. "Bishop," he murmured. "Blair Bishop. I believe I've shipped cattle for you before, Mister Bishop. What's that brand again?"

"A Double B."

The agent looked up in surprise. "Perhaps I misunderstood you, Mister Blair. You talked as if your cattle were still to come in."

"They are. They'll be here in an hour, give or take a little."

"But most of those cattle down there waiting for shipment are Double B too. Let me see." He riffled through a sheaf of papers and came up with one. "Yes, it says right here: Double B. Bishop ranch. They were signed for by one of your cowboys."

Blair looked incredulously at Billy, then back at the agent. He reached for the paper. "Let me have a look at that." His gaze went quickly down the paper till he reached the signature at the bottom. "That's no cowboy of mine. I never heard of this man."

The agent blinked. "But those cattle carry your brand, and your name . . ." He stood up solemnly. "We've got a deputy sheriff here. I think I'd better get him."

Blair nodded, suddenly grim. "I think you'd better. We'll go with you."

They found the deputy relaxed in the shade at a livery barn. This was a different county than Erly Greenwood's, and Blair didn't know the lawman. But he thought by the look in the man's eyes that he probably savvied his line of work, for he had a riot-stopping stare. The deputy had heard of Blair Bishop. He shook hands. "My name's Hawk. Family name. Folks around here nicknamed me Bird. I'd still rather it was Hawk."

"Hawk," Blair said, "the agent tells me there's cattle in them shippin' pens carryin' my brand. There oughtn't to be. I'd like you to go with me to investigate."

The deputy was immediately all business. "I'll saddle my old pony and be right with you."

It didn't take him a minute. Blair turned to his son. "Billy, if I'd had any thought of trouble, I wouldn't of brought you. I want you to stay here."

Billy's reply wasn't argumentative; it was a plain statement of fact. "Like hell I will. I stayed home the last time."

Momentarily inclined to raise Cain with him, Blair decided against it. At Billy's age he had taken on all of a man's responsibilities and was the veteran of two Indian fights. "All right, boy, but you watch yourself."

They rode to the shipping pens in an easy trot. Blair took the shotgun out of his scabbard, painfully loaded it with an aching hand and laid it across his lap to be ready. Hawk eyed him warily. "Mister Bishop, we'll talk first."

"That," Blair said, "depends on them."

Two cowboys were in a corral spreading hay. Blair needed only a glance to know that the cattle in the pen were his. They carried the Double B and his earmark. He told the deputy so.

The deputy said, "I know them two hands, Mister Bishop. They been around town here lookin' for work. I didn't figure them for thieves."

"Can't always tell by looks. Damn few cow rustlers go around carryin' a sign."

Without dismounting, the deputy hailed the two cowboys over to the fence. They came without apparent suspicion, until they spotted Blair's shotgun casually aimed in their direction. That stopped them in consternation. "Boys," the deputy spoke, "we come to talk to you. We want to know whose cows them are yonder."

One of the cowboys moved up cautiously, his eyes never leaving the shotgun. "They belong to a feller name of Bishop. Lives over at Two Forks."

The deputy asked, "Do you know Bishop?"

"No, sir, never met him."

Blair demanded, "Then what're you doin' with them cows?"

"We was hired to help drive them up here and see they got shipped all right."

Blair eased off with the shotgun, for he began to suspect these men were the inevitable innocent bystanders who get hurt in every fight. "Who hired you?"

"His foreman. Leastways, he said he was." The two cowboys were beginning to sense the way the wind blew. "Said he'd pay us ten dollars apiece to help make the drive and stay till the shippin' was done."

"He paid you yet?" Blair asked.

"Not yet."

"Then you've likely lost ten dollars apiece. I'm Blair Bishop."

The cowboys gave each other a sick look. One of them tried a weak smile that didn't work. "Somehow, I was startin' to suspect that. Last we seen of that foreman, him and a pal of his was over in the Legal Tender havin' a snort and waitin' for the train."

The deputy motioned. "You-all come with us. You'll have to point them out."

The cowboys were eager, for by now nobody had to explain the situation any further to them. They might come out of this broke, but they wanted to be sure they came out of it clean. There had been a time not too long before when a man caught with somebody else's cattle stood a good chance of looking up a rope at a nice, sturdy tree limb. Climbing into his saddle, one of the cowboys studied Blair the way a jackrabbit might study a wolf. "Mister Bishop, I bet you ain't even *got* a fore-man." Blair said, "I did have. He was killed."

The cowboy pleaded, "We didn't know. We needed work, and we took him for what he said he was. We sure don't want no trouble."

Blair said, "You just point him out, and you won't be in no trouble."

They reined up a few doors from the Legal Tender and went on afoot. All but Billy. Blair told him to ride around to the back door. If anybody came running out, Billy was to detain him. Blair figured it would be much safer out there than in the saloon.

The front doors stood wide open, and all the windows were up, for the heat still lingered here into the dusk. The cowboys walked in front of Blair and the deputy. They paused at the door. One pointed. "That's him, the one yonder with the ventilation holes punched in his hat." Blair squinted. Two men sat at a small table, a bottle half emptied in front of them. They had both been with Macy Modock at the Harley Mills fence.

He realized he had never thought to count the cattle Modock had pushed out of that pasture. Other things had seemed far more important at the time. Now he knew Modock had probably shorted him, depending upon there being no count. And he realized where some of the other cattle he had been missing must have gone.

The cowboys stepped back out of the way. Blair moved into the saloon, flanked by the deputy. The two men looked up. Recognition was instantaneous. Both jumped to their feet.

Other men in the saloon dived for cover as the one who had posed as foreman whipped a pistol out of his waistband, his eyes on Blair. *He'll take me first,* Blair thought, bringing the shotgun up into line and stiff-handedly pulling the trigger. Even as the weapon boomed, he knew he had jerked too hard and had missed. But the reaction to the blast threw off the cow thief's aim. His shot went astray. He never got a chance for a second one. The deputy's pistol roared, and the man staggered back.

The second man never made a move toward his pistol. He ran for the open back door. Blair leveled the shotgun at him, but he had no time to reload. The deputy was too engrossed in seeing that the first man didn't fire again to do more than glance at the second. The man hit the door in a dead run.

Blair heard Billy cry out for him to stop. Shots were fired, and Blair could hear horses' hoofs as he limped toward the door, feverishly trying to reload the shotgun and fumbling it. He hit the back step and saw Billy Blair running toward a fallen man. A horse galloped away in panic, stirrups flopping.

Billy stood over the man, smoking pistol in his hand. Blair rushed to him, followed by the deputy and the two cowboys. Other men from the saloon trailed in curiosity.

The deputy looked at the man, who lay sprawled on his stomach. He turned him over, puzzled. "Where'd you hit him, son?"

"I didn't," Billy said, barely above a whisper. "I missed him." He trembled from shock. "He grabbed a horse and tried to run off. He was lookin' back at me. He didn't see that clothesline."

The deputy felt for a pulse, then laid his ear to the man's chest. "You can tell by the way his head lays that he broke his neck. See that rope burn? Done the same as if he'd dropped through a trapdoor with a hemp necktie on."

Blair Bishop placed his hand on Billy's shoulder. "Good thing it turned out this way, boy. You're a shade too young to have a man on your conscience."

"In a way," Billy said regretfully, "I did do it."

"He wasn't runnin' from you, really. He was runnin' from a hangrope. He missed one and found another." Blair turned back to the deputy. "The other one . . . he dead too?"

The deputy nodded. "Been a poor day for cow thieves."

Bishop scowled. "And for me too. I wish we could've got them alive . . . one of them, anyway. Now we got no way to prove Macy Modock was behind them. Far as any court can tell, they was workin' for themselves."

He had explained a little about Modock to the deputy as they had ridden in from the shipping pens. The deputy shook his head sympathetically. "Sorry, Mister Bishop."

"Can't be helped. At least we all still got our health." He rubbed his hurting hand. "Most of it, anyway."

The deputy said, "I reckon now you'll want to claim your cattle."

Blair nodded. "Long as they're already here, I'd just as well ship them with the others I got comin' in. No point in drivin' them back to a dried-out range." He turned to the two cowboys. "You said they promised you ten dollars apiece. I got a herd out yonder. I'll pay you ten dollars if you'll meet them and help bring them on in."

"Fair enough, Mister Bishop." The cowboys rode off in the direction Blair pointed, glad they hadn't found themselves neck deep in trouble.

Blair and Billy rode to the pens again. Blair sat outside the fence on his horse, looking across at some young heifers he wished he could save. Billy rode on around to look at the rest of the cattle. Presently he came back. "Dad," he said urgently, "these ain't all yours."

Blair was a little surprised, though he realized he shouldn't be. A cow thief was not likely to be particular. "Whose are the rest of them?"

"There's a bunch of C Bars in there, too. Clarence Cass."

That *did* surprise Blair, till he had time to think about it a little. Gradually, though, it all began to fit. He laughed dryly when the full irony of the situation came to him. Cass was offering sanctuary to Macy Modock, hoping to see Modock break Blair Bishop, and all the time Modock was stealing from the old man too.

"Cast thy bread upon the waters . . ." Blair Bishop mused. "I reckon old Clarence's bread must've been a little moldy."

{ FOURTEEN }

Macy Modock was napping out the afternoon heat when Owen Darby gripped his shoulder and shook him. "Somebody's comin' yonder," Darby said. "Can't tell yet who it is, but I'm pretty sure it ain't Jim and Charlie back from the railroad."

Macy Modock got to his feet and wiped the sweat from his face. He strode out into the yard, softly cursing the interruption and looking down the wagon road. Recognition was slow in coming, but when it came he was suddenly wide awake. "It's Blair Bishop. And he's got the sheriff with him." Modock turned quickly, barking orders. "Owen, you put one of the boys out in the shed to watch that girl and the Bishop boy. No . . . come to think of it . . . you better do it yourself. Tell that girl if she makes as much as a howdydo you'll blow that boy's brains out. And keep Harley Mills out of sight too. Old Bishop'd just love to see him here."

Darby strode to the nearby shed. The rest of Modock's tough crew strayed up from one place and another. Clarence Cass shuffled out of the house sleepy-eyed. "What's goin' on?"

Modock spat, "You just stand back and keep your

mouth shut, Clarence. One wrong word and I'll bust out what few teeth you still got left."

Cass stood blinking, trying to figure what he had said wrong.

Modock didn't trust even Darby to do a job without supervision. He looked into the shed. He found Harley Mills seated on the hay-strewn floor, his back to the wall, a near-empty bottle in his hands and an empty look in his eyes. Allan Bishop lay in a fever, half out of his head. The girl sat in a rawhide chair beside the cot, placing wet cloths over Allan's face every now and then. Her eyes hated Modock as she looked up. Owen Darby stood with his back to the wall, pistol pointed at Allan.

"I told her like you said, Macy. If they see her, or hear a sound out of this shed, the boy's dead." Argument showed in his eyes. "But hell, Macy, there ain't but the two of them. You been wantin' to kill Blair Bishop all this time. It'd be easy now."

"Too quick. I ain't got him to his knees yet. Anyway, we'd have to kill the sheriff too. I don't want to run no more. I want to do this in a way that when it's over, I can stay here and enjoy what I've got." He looked at Jessie.

Darby shrugged. "However you want it, Macy. Just seems to me sometimes like you sure go about things the hard way."

"But it's my way. Don't you mess it up."

Modock checked his pistol to be sure it was fully loaded, then walked out into the yard. He didn't plan to use it, but a man never could tell. He stood waiting beside a nervous Clarence Cass while the sheriff and Blair Bishop took their own sweet time about riding in.

The sheriff spoke first. "Howdy, Clarence. Modock."

Blair Bishop looked at Modock, but he spoke to Cass. "Clarence."

Ranch country custom called for a man to invite any visitor to light and hitch, whether he be friend or enemy. But Modock had never been one to concern himself over any custom but his own. "Sheriff, you're welcome here any time." He pointedly left out Bishop.

Blair Bishop observed with a touch of sarcasm, "I'd always thought this was Clarence Cass' place." He glanced at Cass in a way that was like rubbing salt into an open sore.

"Me and Clarence is partners," Modock said.

Bishop grunted. "I'm glad to hear that. I thought you'd taken plumb over." He was still looking at Cass, making sure the point wasn't lost. It wasn't.

Modock growled, "You didn't come over here to say howdy."

The sheriff shook his head. "No, we didn't." He looked at the men gathered loosely around Modock. "Seems to me like you had a couple or three more men when you throwed Blair's cattle out of that pasture."

Suspiciously Modock said, "A couple. Does that make any difference?"

Blair Bishop braced his hands against the saddle horn and leaned forward, shifting his weight to one side to ease an aching leg. "We was over at the railroad yesterday. Drove a bunch of cattle there to ship. We found another herd had got there ahead of us. Funny thing about them cattle. Big part of them was wearin' the Double B brand."

Modock frowned. "I wouldn't know nothin' about that."

"There was a couple of your friends over there with

them. One was shippin' the cattle and signin' himself as a sales agent for me. The money was supposed to come back to him."

The sheriff said, "To've got them cattle to the railroad yesterday, they had to be gone from here two or three days. Don't a thing like that make you suspicious, Modock?"

"A couple of my boys quit me after that set-to over at the fence. They was nervous about all them guns. Maybe they decided to take a little somethin' with them as they went."

"Maybe so," said Bishop. "Now, Macy, you'll be glad to know that the money for them cattle will all come to me."

"Always tickled to see the right thing done." Modock's dark eyes were a-glitter with anger. "What did you do with them two boys?"

The sheriff said, "They're buryin' them today."

Modock's eyes momentarily flashed a fury he was helpless to hide. He had figured on that money . . . had counted on getting it. Losing it threw a monkey wrench into a bunch of things, but he said, "I reckon they had it comin'. If there's anything I got no use for, it's a thief."

Bishop glanced at the sheriff. "Well, Erly, since Macy wasn't noway involved, I reckon we got no more business here." He started to pull away, then looked at Clarence Cass. "Clarence, I was wonderin' about that daughter of yours. I don't see her noplace around."

Cass shook his head, trembling. "No, you don't."

Bishop nodded solemnly. "Then I take it she's gone. My boy Allan, he said he was goin' to come get her. I hoped maybe he'd come to his senses." Bishop showed disappointment, and he looked a moment at the ground.

Then he brought his gaze back to Cass. "One other thing, Clarence. You took any count on your cattle lately?"

Cass' mouth came open in puzzlement. "No, why?"

"Because all them cattle over at the railroad wasn't mine. A big bunch of them was yours." Bishop paused, watching an explosive reaction in Cass' whiskered face. "Since they was already in the shippin' pens and since you're overstocked anyway, I told the station agent to go ahead and load them out for Kansas City along with mine. The payment will come to you."

Clarence Cass' face was flushed. He looked sharply at Modock, then away. Bishop added with an evident touch of malice, "The station agent told me them wasn't the first of your cattle *or* mine that've been shipped lately. Been several other loads gone out. Naturally my first thought was that Macy Modock done it. But from what he tells us, I guess he didn't . . . seein' as you're such good partners." His voice went bitter. "Surely Macy wouldn't have no call to be stealin' from himself." Bishop pulled his horse away. "*Adiós,* Clarence."

Clarence Cass seethed, and Modock knew it, but he didn't give a damn. He stood simmering in his own frustration over loss of that herd, and over the fact that Bishop and the sheriff were wise to him, even if they lacked evidence to make a legal move. He would have the devil's own time getting any more Bishop cattle out from under old Blair's nose. And Modock wanted that money.

Owen Darby walked over from the shed, squinting after the departing riders and making it plain he had rather have seen them lying here on the ground. "How come Bishop bring the sheriff, since he didn't make no move against us?"

"Protection. Knew we wouldn't do nothin' long as the sheriff was here."

"But I don't see what he come for in the first place."

"Sniffin'. He's an old bloodhound, that Bishop. Lookin' for that boy of his, for one thing. Lookin' for anything he might be able to use against us. And lookin' for a chance to stir up trouble between us and Clarence."

Cass could contain himself no longer. "You been stealin' from me, Macy. We made a deal, and then you turned around and went to takin' my cattle."

"Shut up, Clarence."

"Damn you, Macy . . ." Cass' fury had momentarily overcome his fear. "Damn you for a double-crossin' thief!"

Modock's short fuse went up in smoke. He brought his fist around and struck the old man square in the face, hitting him so hard that Clarence went down on his back. Nose bloodied, the rancher raised up onto one elbow. "Damn you all to hell, Macy! I'm goin' to ride after the sheriff and tell him . . ."

Modock reached down and grabbed Cass' shirtfront, savagely hauling the old man to his feet and striking him down again. His voice dropped to almost a whisper—a deadly one. "If I thought you would— If I thought there was even a chance you would do that, Clarence, I'd wring your scrawny neck the way I'd kill a rooster."

Cass tried to crawl away, and Modock kicked him hard enough to have caved in his ribs if he had hit him right. "But you ain't goin' to do it, old man. You got too much blood on your own hands. You ain't goin' to say a word . . . not one little bitty word. You was there when we killed Joe Little. You was with us when we broke into the bank to make it look like he done it and ran off."

"You forced me to go with you to the bank. And I didn't have nothin' to do with that killin'. You-all done it."

"You was there. You was an accessory. The court that hangs us hangs *you*. So you'll keep your mouth shut, Clarence, or I'll shut it for you. And when I shut it, it'll stay shut for good." He grabbed the old man again and pulled him up, taking such a grip on the shirtfront that Clarence nearly choked. "Anything you don't understand, Clarence?"

The old man sobbed in fear. "No, Macy, no."

Macy dropped him. Clarence lay on the ground at Modock's feet. Modock's anger led him to say the rest of it. "Sure, we was stealin' your cattle. You was too lazy to get out and look, and too stupid to've seen if you'd been out. I was goin' to steal you blind and buy you out with the money from your own cattle. I already had Judge Quincy draw up the papers for you to sign when the time come. You'd of took your money and left this country, and this ranch would be mine. This ranch first, then Blair Bishop's. And all the people that stood around and rubbed their hands when Macy Modock went to prison, I'd have them sweatin' blood."

Cass murmured, "Blair Bishop'll stop you now."

"There ain't nobody stoppin' me. I was goin' to pay you for this ranch, but now I'll have it without payin' you, Clarence. You'll sign them papers for nothin'. You'll sign them because you know I'll kill you if you don't."

"This ranch is all I got."

"Not anymore it ain't. I'm takin' it."

"But what'll me and Jessie do? Take this away and we got nothin'."

"I'm takin' Jessie away from you too, old man. I been

wantin' her since the first day I ever seen her. I've held off with her till I could have it all. Now I'm *takin'* it all." He leaned down. "Get up, Clarence. You got papers to sign."

The old man wept. "You'll kill me when I do."

"I'll kill you if you don't."

"I won't sign them, Macy. I won't sign them."

Modock hauled him to his feet. "You will. I'll put you out in that shed and let you look at that Bishop boy awhile. You figure how you'd like to be in the shape he is. You'll sign." Modock shoved him toward the shed. The old man stumbled and went to his knees. Roughly Modock picked him up and shoved him again. "Git in there, Clarence. You'll git in there till you've made up your mind. I ain't foolin' with you no more; I ain't goin' to soft-talk with you. I'll come in ever' so often and stomp on you a little bit to help make up your mind."

In the shed, Modock looked a moment at the girl, and he felt a strong urge to grab her by the hand and drag her over to the house. But he would wait; she wouldn't try to go anywhere as long as that Bishop boy was there and helpless. Taking her now might cause old Clarence to do something foolish and not ever get around to signing those papers. Moreover, he still had Harley Mills here, and he depended upon Mills' testimony to help him wrest that land away from Blair Bishop. Mills was a man of no particular character, but even a bottle bum might climb out over the fence if he saw Modock use force on the girl.

"Keep an eye on them, Owen," Modock said to Darby. "Old Clarence has got some thinkin' to do."

Darby nodded. "Want me to help him?"

"I'll take care of that, Owen. You might overdo things, and a dead man don't write very good."

Clarence Cass withered up into a huddle of misery. He sat hunched on the floor, tears running down his cheeks and into his beard, his thin shoulders shaking as he wept in helplessness.

Jessie looked at him in a mixture of disappointment and pity. "You're dead if you sign them papers."

"I'm dead if I don't."

"I heard what you was sayin'. What's this about you bein' there when they killed somebody, and about the bank?"

Cass told her, his voice broken in despair. "I didn't go to do it. I been an honest man all my life; you know that. It was Modock; he forced me into it."

"You don't think for a minute that he can let you leave here alive, knowin' what you do? He knows sooner or later you'd break down and tell somebody, then they'd come after him. Once he gets your name on them papers he wants, you're dead. We're all dead."

"Not you. He wants you."

"I'd as soon be dead. Anyway, he'd get tired of me, and then he'd have to kill me too because I know the whole story now."

The old man buried his face in his hands. "I never knowed it would end thisaway. I was so filled with hate for Blair Bishop, I'd of done anything Modock wanted me to." In a minute he looked up, a little hope in his eyes. "Maybe if we promised him we wouldn't ever say nothin' . . . maybe if we promised we'd leave this country and not ever come back within three hundred miles . . ."

"He won't let you leave here, or me," she said gravely.

"He'll kill Allan first, and then you . . . and eventually me. The minute you sign them papers, it's over for all of us." She looked at Harley Mills, who slacked against the wall on the far side of the shed. Mills was drunk, but he had heard enough that alarm was beginning to reach him. He kept trying to focus his eyes on Owen Darby, who sat with pistol in his hand, listening and smiling to himself. Sunlight kept striking Mills in the face through one of the several big holes in the west wall. He would blink and move a little, but in a minute he would sag a little and the sun would hit him again.

The expression in Darby's face showed plainly that every word the girl said was true. Jessie spoke to Mills. "If you're not stupid drunk, Harley Mills, you better think a little bit about your own situation. Sooner or later Modock's goin' to decide maybe you've heard too much and seen too much too. Once he's got what he needs from you, you'll be in the same fix as the rest of us."

Darby snarled at her. "Shut up."

Jessie took a cloth from Allan's head and soaked it in a pan of water while she put a fresh wet cloth in its place. "And if I don't?"

"You may've got into Macy's blood, but you ain't got into mine."

Old Clarence looked fearfully at Darby. "You'd kill a woman?"

Darby raised the pistol a little, then lowered it. "Takes one bullet for a woman, same as for a man. I can buy all the woman I need in town for five dollars. This one wouldn't be no loss to me."

Clarence buried his face again. "Oh, God, little girl, what did I get you into?"

* * *

Macy Modock waited a long while before he came back into the shed. He had calculated on the wait to shatter Clarence Cass' nerves. He stood in the door, the afternoon sun ominously casting the shadow of his tall frame across the shed floor. "I got the papers laid out on the kitchen table. You ready, Clarence?"

From somewhere, Cass summoned strength to say, "Go to hell, Macy."

Macy Modock gave him a kick that sent him backward, arms flailing. Modock took a long stride and stood over him. "Sometimes I get awful short of patience, Clarence."

Clarence Cass drew up in pain, shaking his head. "I ain't signin'. I ain't signin'."

Darby stood up. "Why don't you go take yourself a drink, Macy? Let me argue with him a little."

Angrily Modock said, "Just don't kill him . . . quite." He turned on his heel.

Darby enjoyed his work. He kept it up until Jessie jumped from the unconscious boy's side and threw herself against Darby, striking at him with her fists and cursing him in language a girl wasn't supposed to know. Darby grabbed her shoulders and flung her roughly into the hay.

Harley Mills had sat bleary-eyed and fearful during the beating of the old ranchman. At the manhandling of the girl, he pushed to a wobbly stand and took a halting step forward. "Now you just looky here . . ."

Darby turned on him. "Sit down and shut up, drunk. Take another slug of whiskey and don't pay no attention to what don't concern you."

Modock came back presently. He saw the girl first, disheveled, the hay clinging. His angry eyes cut dangerously toward Darby.

Darby said, "She come at me a-fightin'. I just shook a little sense into her, is all."

"She's mine, Owen, and you damn well better remember it." Modock leaned over and grasped the old ranchman's shirtfront. "Clarence . . ." He shook Cass, but he got little response. He let go, and the ranchman fell back. Modock straightened, speaking sharply to Darby. "I told you not to kill him. He ain't no good to me if he ain't in shape to sign his name."

"He ain't hurt. He's just a cowardly old man playin' possum on you."

Modock towered over Cass, hands on his hips. "Listen to me, Clarence. Don't pretend you can't hear me. I'll be back in a little while, and you better be ready to sign. Else I'll take a horse and a rope and I'll drag you up and down that brushy flat yonder."

Three of Modock's hands confronted him as he stepped out of the shed. Modock could see trouble in the way they looked at him. One had elected himself spokesman. "Macy, we don't like the way things is shapin' up."

Modock stiffened. "What's the matter with them?"

"First thing, you oughtn't to've sent Jim and Charlie out by theirselves with that herd the way you done. Maybe they wouldn't of gotten killed. And besides that, takin' land and cattle away from a big man like Blair Bishop is one thing. Beatin' the life out of a weak-backed old man like Clarence is somethin' else; we don't like the smell of it. And we don't like what you got in mind for that girl either. When you can buy more women than you'd know what to do with, we don't like you misusin' one."

Modock's hand was near the butt of his pistol. "Any one of you feel like he's man enough to stop me?"

The men looked at each other, then at Modock. "Maybe we can't stop you, but we sure don't aim to stay around and help you. We're goin' on, Macy."

Macy Modock boiled in frustration. He wanted to draw and shoot them like the slinking dogs that they were. But he knew it was unlikely he could beat all three. "Then go on, damn you. Run like a pack of rabbits. Ain't nobody needs you around here."

But as he watched them saddling their horses to leave, he felt the whole thing beginning to trickle away between his fingers. He *did* need them. He needed the force they represented. He couldn't do this thing alone, just him and Darby. Damn them for cowards! Damn them for quitters! He watched them leave and trembled in helpless fury. He drew his pistol and nearly gave way to an urge to kill them all. But as the men rode, they were all turned in their saddles, watching him until they were well out of range.

Modock stared after them, the fierce anger burning unchecked. When they were beyond recall, he turned sharply and strode back into the shed. Roughly he yanked Cass to his feet. "I've pussyfooted all I'm goin' to. We're goin' into that house, Clarence, and you're signin' them papers if you do it with your last dyin' breath!" He flung Cass through the door. The old man went down on his knees, but Modock didn't let him stay there. Modock half carried, half dragged him to the house while Jessie Cass stood in the shed door and watched, her hands to her mouth. Harley Mills swayed with one hand braced back against the wall, sobering under the impact of violence. Owen Darby walked to the door and shoved the girl back. "Sit down!" he said roughly, and then stood in the doorway, a hard smile across his face as he watched the house and imagined what Modock was doing in there.

Modock pushed Clarence Cass toward the kitchen table where he had the deeds spread out. A pen lay atop the papers, and an ink bottle beside them. "Sign, Clarence. Sign them papers or I'll kill you where you stand!"

Clarence Cass sobbed aloud, because he could see death in Modock's fury . . . death whether he signed or whether he didn't. Modock struck him. "Sign!"

Cass sank into a chair. He reached for the pen, jabbing the point at the ink bottle without realizing he had to unscrew the top.

"Open it first, you stupid . . ."

Cass fumbled with the bottle, got the top off, then let the whole thing slip through his fingers. The bottle hit the floor rolling, the ink spilling. Before Modock could outrun it and pick it up, it was empty. It didn't have ink enough left to wet the pen. Modock hurled it against a wall, then turned and struck Cass again. "You'll sign if you have to do it in your own damned blood!"

Cass huddled in the chair, trembling like a cottonwood leaf. He said, "I think I know where there's another bottle."

"Get it!"

Cass pushed shakily to his feet. He walked into the room where he customarily slept and swayed forward, catching himself on a battered old chest of drawers. He paused a moment, summoning strength, then pulled out the drawer. He reached into it, his hand hidden momentarily from Modock. When he turned, he held an old pistol in his hands. His eyes were desperate. He shrilled, "Die, Modock!" and pulled the trigger.

It clicked.

Modock couldn't risk the next one doing the same. His own pistol came up and leveled swiftly. Even as he squeezed the trigger, he knew he had lost this ranch.

The gun thundered. Clarence Cass was driven backward against the window. He fell through it and out in a shower of glass. He lay hanging, his knees bent across the windowsill, his arms slacked, his limp hands touching the ground outside.

Modock picked up the fallen pistol. He flipped open the cylinder and shouted aloud. "Empty!" He hurled it through the broken window, knowing Cass was dead, knowing that by grabbing up an empty gun he had wiped away all Modock's hopes of taking this land. Modock leaned out the window and cursed him and emptied his gun into the frail body.

At the shed, Owen Darby stood transfixed. He had heard the commotion in the house, heard the shot and saw Cass fall backward through the window. He watched hypnotized as Modock fired again and again in fury and frustration.

Jessie Cass had known when her father went into that house he had little chance of leaving it alive. To her he was dead before she ever heard the first shot. She flinched, and she cried out, but she had already given up.

"It's Allan next," she rasped to Harley Mills, "and then you, and then me."

She pushed to her feet as the other shots began. Outside the shed, she could see Darby standing frozen, forgetting about the people in the shed because of his fascination in the scene at the house. He held the pistol loosely in his hand, forgotten in the excitement.

Her blood like ice, she stared at the pistol. Her hands flexed, and she considered her chances of running out and grabbing it. They were nil, for Darby's strength would be too much.

Harley Mills was sobering fast. From the pile of hay he took the pitchfork and staggered forward. Jessie saw what he was trying and knew he was in no condition to carry through. She wrested the fork from his hands, took a firm grip and rushed.

Darby heard. He turned, bringing up the pistol. She speared his hand with one of the sharp tines, and he let the weapon drop. She kicked it aside. Holding the bleeding hand, he stared at her a moment in rage, then rushed her. She dropped the butt end of the fork to the ground to brace it. The force of his rush carried him headlong into the tines.

Darby screamed and fought against the embedded fork. He managed somehow to pull it free. He staggered, holding his arms tight against his belly as he cried to Macy Modock for help. Jessie grabbed up the fallen pistol and rushed back into the shed.

Modock ran out of the house, eyes wide in confusion. He saw the staggering Darby and started toward him. In panic, holding the pistol in both hands, Jessie fired. She missed him by a long way, but she stopped him. He ran back around the house.

Darby kept crying out, staggering until loss of blood brought him to his knees. He called to Modock for help, but Modock was in no position to assist him.

Mills was cold sober now. Darby's cries chilled him.

"For God's sake, girl, shoot him. Put him out of his misery."

Milk-pale, Jessie shook her head. "I've used up one bullet. We may need all that's left."

In blind agony, Darby crawled up the tank dam and over toward the water that lay beyond the deep mud. Presently he went quiet. Jessie shuddered. "You watch that side of the shed and I'll watch this one," she told Mills. "We can't let Modock slip up on us."

Modock waited awhile before he showed himself, calling from the corner of the house. "Girl, you can't hold out in there by yourself. That boy's no help to you, or that drunk. You throw the pistol out here where I can see it. There won't no harm come to you. Wouldn't be no reason for it anymore."

Her throat was dry and tight, and her heart throbbed in fear. She didn't answer. She held the pistol in both hands and braced it against the doorframe, sighting down the barrel.

Emboldened, Modock stepped out a little farther. "Girl, you better listen to me. I got more time and patience than you have."

She squeezed the trigger. Through the smoke she saw splinters fly from the corner of the house. Modock rushed back out of sight.

"Would've been better," Mills said, "if Darby had died here in the door. We could've got the cartridges out of his belt."

Jessie nodded, her hands trembling as she lowered the smoking pistol. This was a six-shooter. She had fired two shots. Provided that Darby had kept it fully loaded—which she was sure he would—she had four shots left.

Modock leaned out from the corner of the house and

fired deliberately at the shed. Jessie dropped to the floor as the bullets smacked into the wall over her head. When she had time to think, she realized Modock must have purposely aimed high.

He still wanted her alive, she knew. He was trying to scare her, and he was doing a good job of it.

She raised up, her instinct to fire back at him, but she knew the shot would be wasted. He was probably trying to lure her into doing just that. She sank to her knees, the pistol across her lap. Warm tears ran down her face.

"Girl," Harley Mills said, "you better let me have that gun."

She looked up at him and saw he was shaking. "No," she said, "you got way too much whiskey in you. You'd wind up killin' us instead of Modock."

Presently Modock fired again, still aiming high. Jessie ducked involuntarily and cried out as splinters showered down. She heard a horse running excitedly in a corral behind the shed. Through a crack in the wall she looked at the house, and a fresh hope began to rise.

"Mister Mills, he's still behind the house, or in it. He can't get away from it very well without me seein' him. That's his horse behind the shed makin' all the commotion. You could catch that horse and saddle it without exposin' yourself to Modock none. There's a wagon behind the shed too. You could go down into the draw, fetch up the team, and we could hitch it to the wagon. We could load Allan into the wagon and light out of here in a dead run. Modock bein' afoot, there wouldn't be no way he could stop us once we started."

Mills shook his head fearfully. "I don't know. If he was to ever get a clear shot at me . . ."

"He won't, if you watch how you handle yourself. Anyway, I'll keep the house covered."

"Girl, you can't even hit that house, much less hit Modock."

She flung all her anger at him. "Have you got a drop of red blood left in your veins, or has it all gone to whiskey?"

He dropped his chin. The violence had largely cleared his mind, though his reflexes were still not coordinated. "I didn't come out here to get killed."

"You came out here to lie your way into some whiskey money. Maybe you've learned now you don't get nothin' you don't pay for. Are you goin' out there and catch that horse?"

Slump-shouldered, Mills took a bridle from a hook and a rope from a saddle that had belonged to Darby. Jessie went back to watching the house. She could hear the horse running around and around the pen and could hear the swish of the loop as Mills tried several times to catch him and missed. But finally from the sounds she knew he had caught the horse and was saddling him. She stepped to the shed's corral door long enough to see Mills swing into the saddle. She called, "You bring back that team, do you hear?"

Mills bare-heeled the horse into a lope and bent low over the saddle as he left the pen. He angled in such a way that he kept the shed between him and the house until he was out of range. Jessie went back to her vigil by the front door and waited for Mills to return. She felt of Allan's forehead and found it hot. Allan mumbled feverishly, unaware of what was going on.

"We'll be out of here directly," she murmured. "Just as soon as Mills gets back with that team."

Time moved rapidly enough at first as in her mind she followed Mills down into the draw. She knew where the wagon team usually grazed, and how long it would take Mills to get down there. She visualized his picking them up and starting back toward the barn. She followed his progress all the way.

"He ought to be comin' just about now," she said to the unconscious boy. "We'll hear him any minute."

The minutes ticked by slowly then, no sound coming. Maybe the team had grazed farther than usual, she tried to tell herself. Even a horse doesn't do the same thing every day; even a horse likes variety. She allowed the extra time, mentally beginning over, giving Mills a fresh start back from the draw. Still he didn't come.

For a long time she resisted the obvious: he wasn't coming back. But finally the realization forced itself upon her against her will. For the first time she broke down and openly cried.

{ FIFTEEN }

It was dusk now. Jessie knew that only so long as there was still light could she keep Modock pinned behind that house. Even then, there was no way to be absolutely sure. He could walk away, carefully keeping the house between him and the shed, and she would not see him. If he walked far enough to lose himself in the brush, he could get completely away, or he could circle back and come up on her from behind.

But Modock was still at the house. She heard him call. "Mills is gone now, girl. That boy can't help you, so it's just me and you."

She didn't answer him. He waited a little, then said, "You can't hold out. Sooner or later you got to give up. Do it now and I promise I won't do that boy no more harm. You and me, we'll ride out of here together."

She knew he was lying. For a while there had been some possible advantage to him in keeping Allan alive. Now there was none. She knew his hatred for Blair Bishop was so intense that he would kill Allan simply for revenge on Allan's father. And when he was done, he would still carry Jessie away with him. There was no bargaining with a man who knew no honor.

"You stay away, Modock," she cried. "You stay away from us."

He showed himself, and in a moment of desperation she fired again. Instantly she realized she had made a mistake.

That was it: he was trying to lure her into using up her cartridges. Once she had done that, all he had to do was walk in and take her.

He waited a time, then called to her again. "It's up to you, girl. I ain't goin' to put up with this all night. If I have to, I'll kill that boy."

To make his point, he fired at the shed. She saw the thin wood wall crack where the bullet struck, very little above Allan's cot. Modock knew the position where Allan lay. If he made up his mind to it, he could fire through the wall and kill him. And if a pistol wouldn't do it, there were a couple of rifles in the house at Modock's disposal.

Jessie took Allan's feverish hand and stared at him. She ran her fingers through his tousled hair. "If I move you," she said, "that wound is liable to break open and bleed some more. If I don't move you, he'll kill you sure. I got to do it, Allan. Try to help me if you can. I got to do it."

She didn't think her words ever got through to him. She reached under his shoulders and tried to lift him. He was too heavy. She could drag him off the cot, but then she wouldn't be able to keep him from falling, and that would hurt him for certain. The big problem was to ease him somehow to the floor. She mulled over it a moment, then reached across him with both hands, lifting the far edge of the cot, tipping it gradually toward her, pressing her body against his to keep him from falling. The lifting was heavy till she had the cot tipped halfway up; then the problem was to prevent the cot from falling too fast and Allan from tumbling. She held the cot most of the way. By the time it became too heavy for her, Allan was almost in her lap. He slid gently, and she had him. She cradled him in her arms a moment, pressing her cheek against him. He mumbled fevered words that had no meaning.

Modock fired again, and she saw a ragged hole appear in the wall where Allan had been. Modock had a rifle now. He had given up fooling around. Jessie lay on the ground, her arms around Allan, and began laboriously dragging him away. She crawled a few inches at a time toward the back of the shed, while Macy Modock methodically sent slug after slug tearing through the wall.

If she hadn't moved Allan, he would be dead by now.

She didn't stop dragging until she had him almost to the back wall. She looked around for anything she could pile up between him and the wall that faced the house. She flung down Darby's saddle and one of her father's and also her own, knowing all of them together might not be enough to stop a rifle bullet. She piled up the horse collars and the harness and several sacks of grain that had been bought for the chickens.

"He's dead now, girl," Modock shouted. "No point in you tryin' to protect him anymore. You come on out here and throw that gun away."

The clapboard walls were shoddily constructed, like everything else on the Cass place. Jessie could watch the house through spaces between the boards. She saw Modock step out experimentally in the dusk, inviting her to fire at him. She wanted to, but she resisted. She held her breath, taking in a gasp of air once in a while, then holding while she watched Modock. He waited a while for her to fire then moved a few feet forward and stopped again.

"Girl," he called, "do you hear me?"

She made no reply. He took a few more steps, and she could see his face clearly. In his changing expressions she could almost read his mind. He was suddenly becoming fearful he had hit her with some of those shots intended for Allan Bishop. He came forward again, halting occasionally, still not sure.

"Girl, are you all right? I want you to answer me."

The closer he came, the surer he seemed to be that she had been hit, and the less caution he showed. Jessie sat up, holding the pistol firmly in both hands, arms extended stiffly. She aimed at the doorframe, waiting for the moment he would step through into full sight.

She couldn't see him now, but she could hear the slow tread of his boots. She caught a deep breath and held it.

He came through the door, pistol ready. "Girl?"

He couldn't see her immediately, not in the darkness at the back of the shed. His gaze went to the overturned cot and the blankets.

Jessie saw him over the sights, took a firm grip on the pistol and pulled the trigger. Modock jerked, and she fired again. Black smoke billowed, hiding him from her view.

She heard him cry out in surprise and pain, and she heard his footsteps running again across the yard. She dropped onto her stomach and peered out through the spaces. She saw him half running, half hopping as he disappeared behind the house.

She hadn't killed him, but she had drawn blood. He would think a long time before he came again.

And Jessie knew she would have to think a long time

before she fired at him, for the next shot would be her last. She had but one bullet left.

Allan whispered, "Jessie." She turned quickly to him and saw his eyelids flicker a little. The gunfire had stirred him at last. She put her arms around him and lay against him and put her cheek to his burning forehead. "Lie easy," she said, "just lie easy. Everything will be all right."

Then it was dark and she could see no more. All she could do now was lie here by Allan and listen fearfully. With the darkness came all the night sounds of the crickets and the night birds and the far-off bawling of a cow in search of its calf. But no noise came from the house. Jessie listened intently, trying to separate each sound and analyze it, looking for menace in the light summer wind that rustled the leaves, chilling at the sudden yip of a roaming coyote far out on the prairie.

The dark hours dragged by. She had cried some at first, but now the tears were dried. Hands that had been cold-sweaty against the gunbutt held it now as firmly as ever, but they too were dry. She no longer stirred at every sound; she had listened to them so long that she knew now which ones were natural.

When Modock came—and she was still sure he would—he wouldn't find her in panic again. He would find her ready. With the one bullet she had left, she would kill him if she could. And if she didn't kill him, she would force him to kill her. He wasn't going to have her . . . not alive.

She had no way of keeping up with time. She didn't particularly want to, for she felt sure Modock would make his move before daylight came again, and she was not eager to see the night end. But she knew midnight must have come and gone when she heard the sounds. She pushed to her elbows, listening, trying to pin down their source.

She doubted Modock would try the front door again. Perhaps not the back one, either, for he would not want to be as plain a target as he had been before. She expected him to slip up to the wall, for it had plenty of holes and cracks that he could see through without unnecessarily exposing himself to fire. Probably he would try to wound her just enough to put her out of the fight. A wounded girl was better than a dead one, he would probably figure. She lay holding her breath, listening.

The sounds were louder. He must be easing closer. She took a deep breath and then held it again.

Where was he? For God's sake, where was he?

Then she recognized the sounds: horses, running. It wasn't Modock! It was somebody else, somebody coming.

"Allan," she cried, "do you hear it? They're comin' to help us."

She judged that the horses were in the draw now. They would be here in minutes.

She heard something else, too—a man afoot, hurrying across the yard. Modock was coming. This was his last chance, and he was going to use it. He wasn't making any effort to slip up on her. He didn't have time. She knew he was coming straight for the door. She sat up, bringing the pistol into line, both hands gripping it steady. When he came through that door she would get him. This time she wouldn't miss.

The dark shape suddenly hurled itself at her. Crying out involuntarily, she squeezed the trigger. The flash seemed to light up the whole shed, and she saw the shape fall.

But it didn't fall like a man. It fell limp and lay flat.

In anguish, Jessie realized Modock had tricked her out of her last shot. He had flung a blanket through that door, and in the darkness she had thrown away her last chance. He stood now where the blanket had appeared.

"That's all of it, girl."

Not quite all. She threw the empty pistol at him in desperation and pushed to her feet. She didn't wait for him to come to her; she rushed at him, pummeling him with her fists, crying out in her hatred of him. He put his pistol away, grabbed her hands and pushed her back. When she came at him again, he lashed out with his fist and caught her chin. She fell to her knees, stunned.

"You're a fighter," he rasped, "I'll admit that. I just wish I'd of thought about that blanket trick hours ago. Then I'd of had some time with you. Now I got no time left, and no patience. You've caused me all the grief I'm goin' to take." He drew the pistol and shoved it at her. "Give me one more bit of trouble and I'll kill that boy yonder. Then, if I decide to—and I may—I'll kill you too."

The horses loped into the yard. A deep voice called out.

"Allan! Allan, boy, where you at?"

Helpless to resist anymore, Jessie crawled to Allan and put her arms around him. His eyes were open, and he was trying to clear them. "Jessie?" he said, his voice only a whisper.

"Yes, Allan, it's me."

"Jessie, what's goin' on?"

"Your dad is here. He's outside. But Modock is in here with us, and he's got a gun."

From the sounds, Jessie could tell the men were dismounting in the yard and spreading out. She recognized

Blair Bishop's voice calling again. "Allan! Jessie! Are you-all here?"

Jessie cried, "Stay away, Mister Bishop! It's Modock!"

Modock pulled back into the shadows, nearer Jessie and Allan. "Like she says, Bishop, we're all in here together. Why don't you come on in . . . if you want this boy killed?"

There was silence for a moment, then Bishop said, "Modock, whatever quarrel you got, it's with me, not with my boy or that girl."

"That's right, Bishop, it's you and me. It's always been you and me."

"Well, then," Bishop called, "what do you want?"

"Just you, Bishop, just you."

"You got me, if you'll let them kids go. What do you want me to do?"

"Make them men of yours git away . . . plumb away. Just you is all I want to see out there. Just you and two horses . . . one for you and one for me."

Jessie could hear Blair Bishop quietly giving orders and the men pulling back.

Modock said: "You give them orders that I get to ride out of here clean. And you're goin' with me."

"They heard you," Bishop said. "It's the same as an order from me."

Modock moved closer to the door, satisfying himself that the other riders had remounted and moved back. "All right, Bishop, you come closer where I can look at you."

Jessie could hear Bishop's footsteps and made out the heavy shape of him, dark against the open door. Modock gloated. "Well, it didn't turn out the way I figured on, but I got this one thing I was after. You did come to *me*. Drop your pistol."

Bishop raised his hands a little. "Ain't got one, Macy. These old hands, I couldn't use one if I carried it, so I don't bother myself packin' the weight."

Jessie became aware of a slight scurrying noise at the back wall. She looked around, mouth open in wonder. She saw the barrel of a shotgun poke through a knothole a little above her head. She saw it move up and down, its holder outside trying vainly to draw a bead on Modock.

At the bottom of the wall was a hole big enough for a cat to move through. Quietly she leaned forward and eased her hand out. The shotgun muzzle quickly disappeared. She felt the touch of cold steel, and then the touch of fingers, gently pressing the shotgun into her hand. Carefully, her eyes on Modock, she began pulling the shotgun into the barn.

Modock was busy glorying over getting Blair Bishop into a trap. He had his back turned to her. She kept pulling the shotgun until it was clearly inside, then cautiously brought it up. She almost had a bead on Modock when Blair Bishop stepped fully into the barn.

Her heart sank. She couldn't fire without Bishop sharing the blast.

Bishop was saying: "I'll go with you, Macy. But first I got to see about my boy. I got to be sure he's alive."

Modock backed away, giving Bishop room to pass by. But it wasn't enough room that Jessie could get a clear shot. And she knew that when he turned to let his gaze follow Bishop, he would see the shotgun in her hands. She lowered it, laying it lengthwise beside Allan Bishop, hoping Modock wouldn't spot it in the darkness.

"He's alive," Modock said. "That girl has kept him

alive in spite of all I could do. But go see for yourself. Then you and me are ridin' out of here, Bishop. You're my ticket for a free passage."

Blair Bishop limped over and dropped to one knee. "Allan?"

Allan whispered, "Dad." Bishop rasped, "Thank God." He raised his eyes to Jessie and looked at her a minute. "And thank you, girl."

He reached out for her hand. She caught his fingers and gently guided them down to the shotgun. She saw the surprise show for a second in his face before he covered it. Bishop bent over as if to hug his son.

"You've seen him," Modock said. "Now come on."

"I'm comin'," Blair replied, his back turned to Modock as he slowly arose, holding the shotgun against his body.

Jessie flattened herself beside Allan. Blair turned, getting as good a grip on the shotgun as his stiff hands would let him.

Confident of Blair's helplessness, Modock had let his pistol sag. He saw the shotgun too late. Giving a startled cry, he tried to bring up the pistol. Bishop didn't give him time. The blast knocked Modock to the floor. He rolled halfway through the door, gathered one knee up as if to push again to his feet, then slumped forward and died there.

Blair Bishop said, "Harley Mills didn't have it in him to go back with the team, once he got clear of the place. But he did work up enough courage to come and tell me. I reckon that took some guts just in itself."

He stood at the foot of Allan's bed in the Bishop house, looking at a weary Jessie Cass, who ought to have been off somewhere asleep but wouldn't leave Allan's side. She sat in a chair by the bed and watched Allan.

"I don't know what these boys are comin' to, this day and time," Blair went on. "There wouldn't none of this of wound up the way it did if my two boys had listened to what I told them. I tried to raise them different, but they're just plain contrary. Got it from their mother, God bless her. Allan first. I told him to stay home and not be runnin' off to you, but he went anyway, and you see what become of him for it. Then Billy . . . when Harley Mills come by, I told Billy to stay home. He was too young to get into a fight like this, and I didn't want to lose *two* boys. He come anyhow. And when I told him to move out of the way with the others, he took the shotgun and run for the back of the shed instead.

"No, seems like I can't tell them boys nothin' anymore. And it's probably a good thing."

Jessie nodded wearily, agreeing with him, though she was plainly too tired to know half of what he said. It looked to Blair as if she would drop off to sleep in that chair, and maybe he ought to go away and let her. But he had one more thing he wanted to say. "I never been wrong but very few times in my life, and I hope I ain't never wrong again. But I was wrong about you, girl. I'll make it up to you, any way an old man can find to do it."

"You just give me Allan, Mister Bishop, and that's all the makin' up you'll ever have to do."

"He's yours. He ought to be up and goin' again pretty soon. September's just around the corner. I feel like we'll get a good rain then, and everything'll look better.

How would you like a nice big September weddin',
girl?"

She smiled. "I'd *like* a September weddin'. In the
rain."

SIX BITS A DAY

{ ONE }

Hewey Calloway's stomach growled like an angry bear. He had not been so hungry in all his twenty-two years. Yesterday he and his year-younger brother, Walter, had eaten their last chunk of hog belly. It was so fat that he had had to force it down. Now he would trade almost anything he owned for another piece of it, not that he owned much. Everything he had was either on his back or tied to his saddle.

Walter had been riding in moody silence. He pulled up beside Hewey after passing around the far side of a mesquite whose thorns threatened to reach out and grab him. He said, "Even the trees here try to tear off a strip of hide. How far do you reckon we've traveled?"

Hewey grunted. "A good ways." He wanted to keep a cheerful face, even if doubts were weighing on him.

Walter said, "We ain't seen a human bein' in two days, and no game bigger than a jackrabbit. My belly is flatter than a stove lid."

"Mine ain't no better."

There had been a few jackrabbits, and Hewey had shot at them with an old wooden-handled six-shooter he carried in his saddlebags. But he was no marksman.

Each bullet kicked up dirt several feet from the target and set the rabbit into startled flight.

Walter said, "Some cowboys we are. I ain't got a pistol, and you'd just as well've left yours behind. I never saw such a poor shot."

Hewey tried not to appear testy. "Had you rather be choppin' cotton and sloppin' hogs? That's all we'd have if we went back to East Texas."

"Maybe we'd have a job and somethin' to eat."

Hewey saw one saving grace. "At least we're a long ways west of the cotton fields, and it's been a week since we've seen a hog."

The 1880s were nearing an end, and most Texas land still open for new settlement was in the semiarid western region beyond the Conchos. Short, sparse grass shared ground with desert plants such as greasewood and mesquite and a dozen kinds of thorny cactuses that lay in ambush for the careless or the unlucky.

Hewey and Walter's mother had died when they were boys. Over the next few years their restless father had led them in a fruitless circle from the East Texas blacklands to Oklahoma and Kansas, searching for an ideal home he would see only in his dreams. After his death the brothers had wandered about, laboring at whatever they could find to ward off the wolves that had been at the Calloway door as far back as Hewey could remember.

They struggled through a numbing variety of pick-and-shovel jobs before joining a trail outfit driving cattle to the Kansas railroad. Horseback work had fitted Hewey like kid gloves. Now, however, the trails north were mostly closed. Farms and barbed wire had blocked them off. Long cattle drives were being rendered unnecessary by the extension of railroads across Texas.

He had heard that large ranches were building up west of the farming country and needed men willing to work. He had no objection to work if he could do it in the saddle. Unlike Walter, he had never been able to fit his hands properly around a plow handle.

"Our luck is bound to change," he said. He usually accepted the vagaries of life without getting his underwear in a twist. "We'll find work out here somewhere."

Walter preferred a sparrow in the hand to a hawk on the wing. "If we don't starve to death first. I can imagine somebody findin' us five or ten years from now, two little dried-up husks layin' out on the prairie. Kind of like a pair of old corncobs with the shucks still on."

"The coyotes would chew us up long before that." Hewey toyed with the mental image. "I wish a coyote *would* show hisself. I'd eat him before he could eat me."

"Not if you had to shoot him."

The brothers had set out on this trip three weeks ago with hope and youthful high spirits. Like Pa, Hewey fantasized about the far hills and what might lie beyond. He envisioned a horseback life of freedom and adventure, excitement and glory. The trouble was that he was more than ten years too late to share the fighting against Comanches and Kiowas, and the buffalo were gone. Most of the famous outlaws were dead, too, like Billy the Kid and Sam Bass and Jesse James. So far as he could see, the cowboy life was about all that remained to him. He meant to carve out a piece of it somewhere in western Texas.

Walter did not share Hewey's longing for adventure. He was comfortable with what he could see and hear and touch. He would be content with a solid job where pay and meals came regularly, where tomorrow was no more of a mystery than yesterday. Hewey enjoyed reading blood-stirring novels about cowboys and pirates and knights of old. Walter found satisfaction in guiding a plow and keeping a straight row. He would have been happy to spend his life as a farmer somewhere back in the blacklands.

In Hewey's view, East Texas had been cottoned out. It offered no future that interested him, while West Texas promised a fresh beginning. But his shining hopes had gradually diminished along with the supplies he and Walter had brought on the trip. At the moment, he would trade a month of tomorrows for a plate of beans.

Walter said, "Neither one of us would make a meal for a coyote. Even the buzzards don't pay us any mind."

They had come across an occasional scattering of cattle, which usually hoisted their tails and clattered off into the nearest thicket. Hewey grasped at the tattered shreds of his optimism. "Where there's cows there's bound to be a ranch. And where there's a ranch, they're bound to need cowboys."

The animals were of all colors and ran more to horn than to flesh. Hewey said, "Takes a tough breed to make it in this western country."

"You sure *we're* tough enough?"

Hewey set his jaw. "Our name's Calloway, ain't it? Pa carried a Yankee bullet in him for twenty years, right up to the day he died. We've just got to take another hitch in our belts."

He would have to punch a new hole to make his any tighter.

Sundown came with no sign of a dwelling or watering place. But at dusk Hewey saw the flicker of a campfire. Walter said, "Maybe they'll give us somethin' to eat."

Hewey said, "We ain't goin' to ride in there and beg. Us Calloways have never begged for nothin'."

Walter said, "Maybe they'll hear our stomachs growl."

Hewey assumed the lead as he usually did, being a year or so older. He put his horse into an easy lope and did not slow until he was within rock-throwing distance of the fire. He saw nobody.

A stern voice spoke from behind a bush. "You-all lift them hands to where I can see them."

Hewey did not spot the man at first, or the gun, but his gut told him they were there in the dusk. "Friend," he said shakily, "we ain't out for no trouble."

A tall, lanky man walked into the open, holding a pistol. He said, "You must be pilgrims, or you'd know not to charge into a camp like that. You always holler first to find out if you're welcome."

A shiny badge reflected firelight. Law officers made Hewey uneasy. Back where they came from he had had a couple of run-ins with old Sheriff Noonan, a man with a stern commitment to the letter of the law. There was, for instance, the time Hewey had slipped over to Old Man Babcock's farm one night and whacked off all the pigs' tails. A penful of bobtailed pigs looked funny to Hewey, but Babcock and the sheriff had not seen the humor in it. The jail cot was the hardest bed Hewey had ever tried to sleep on.

He said, "Don't shoot, mister. We'll ride on and not bother you no more."

Moving closer, the man gave each brother a moment's study, then slipped the pistol back into a holster on his hip. The frown slowly left his thin face. "I had to be certain of your intentions. Name's Len Tanner."

"Ours is Calloway. I'm Hewey, and he's Walter. Pleased

to make your acquaintance." Hewey kept looking at the badge. It was circular with a star in the center. "You a sheriff?"

"Texas Ranger." Tanner touched his forefinger to the badge. "Pretty, ain't it? Had it made out of a Mexican peso."

Hewey judged that Tanner was well into middle age. Firelight exaggerated the facial creases and the roughness of a skin weathered by sun and wind. It crossed Hewey's mind that a ranger must lead an exciting life, maybe better even than a cowboy's. But he did not dwell on the notion long, for he knew he was too poor a marksman to be accepted into such a demanding organization. He could not hit a barn from the inside.

The campfire drew his attention. A small coffeepot sat on the coals. A half-cooked slice of beef lay in a skillet on the ground. Tanner had probably set it off to one side when he heard the horses coming. Hewey said, "I'd trade you a good pocketknife for some of that."

Tanner shook his head. "Already got a knife." Seeing Hewey's disappointment, he added, "But you're welcome to share my supper. Didn't cost me nothin' anyway. It's contraband."

"Contraband?" Hewey thought that was some kind of illegal whiskey.

"I was trailin' a pair of thieves that butchered another man's beef. They ran off and left the meat behind."

"You didn't catch them?"

"I know where they'll light. Most criminals ain't weighted down with brains." He fetched a tin cup out of a canvas bag and tapped it on his knee to dislodge a scorpion or anything else that might be in it. He handed it to Hewey. "Help yourselves to the coffee. I'll heat the skillet again."

Hewey filled the cup. The rim burned his lips. He handed the cup to Walter. "Hot. Needs to be blowed a little."

Hewey had no compunctions about sharing a cup. He was used to drinking from cisterns and wells that had a community cup for use by anyone who came along. He said, "I remember a story about some yahoo that dragged into town starvin' to death for water. They asked him why he didn't drink at one of the wells he passed along the way, and he said, 'I couldn't. I had no cup.'"

Tanner chuckled at the story and told a couple of his own while he waited for the steaks to get done. He watched bemused as Hewey and Walter wolfed down the meat, which was sizzling hot from the skillet. "Sorry I got no gravy." He fried a second helping, then sat back while the brothers finished that, too.

He asked, "How long since you boys left the cotton patch?"

Hewey said, "Does it show?"

"You've both got lint in your ears. What brings you out so far from water? There ain't a decent farm in a hundred miles."

Hewey said, "That's the way we want it. We're lookin' for cowboy work."

Tanner grunted. "Cowboy life ain't exactly like the storybooks tell it. You're up before daylight and out till dark. You sweat for thirty days to earn a piddlin' wage that you can blow in thirty minutes."

Walter asked, "Does rangerin' pay better?"

"Not always, but a ranger don't have to put up with a

bunch of bawlin' cows. Ain't nothin' dumber than a cow unless it's a sheep."

Hewey said, "We know. We've done some cow work ourselves."

Tanner responded, "A horse is a little smarter, but not much. I've been throwed off and stomped on more times than I've ever been shot at, even bein' a ranger."

Hewey nodded. "I notice you've got to look quick if you want to see these cattle around here. They're up and gone before you can say scat."

"They ain't housebroke. Some'll run you ragged, then try to put a horn through your gizzard. But if you're bound and determined to chase cows, good luck to you. I do better chasin' outlaws."

Hewey's imagination ran free as he pictured the adventures this lawman might have experienced. "How long you been a ranger?"

"I started in the Indian times before the big war. Wasn't much more than a skinny button then."

He was still skinny, Hewey thought, but long past being a button.

The talkative Tanner related stories about chasing and being chased by Comanches, and about long searches for criminals of every stripe. He said, "For a while of late I was down on the Ryo Grandy, chasin' after border jumpers from both sides of the river. Big state, Texas is, and I've crossed every river in it just about. Got the scars to prove it."

He rolled up his sleeve to show a raised mark about five inches long. "That's one of the littlest. A knife blade done that."

Hewey chilled at the thought of cold steel.

Tanner asked, "Ever hear of Rusty Shannon and Andy Pickard?"

Hewey had not.

Tanner said, "Good men, both of them. Me and them rode many a mile together. They're out of the rangers now. Old Rusty's married and got two young'uns. Andy took him a pretty young wife, too."

Hewey asked, "You ever been married?"

"Naw, horses and dogs like me, but I don't shine in the womenfolks' eyes. The Lord didn't choose to make me handsome. He just made me lucky instead."

After breakfast Tanner gave the brothers most of the meat that remained. He ignored their polite objections. He said, "It don't take much for a skinny old hull like me. You two need it to keep your strength up in this big dry country."

Hewey regretted parting company with the ranger, but Tanner was headed southward. Watching him ride away, Walter said, "He's a great talker. You reckon half of what he told us really happened?"

"If it didn't, it ought to have." Hewey touched spurs to his horse and started west. "We ain't findin' work settin' here."

At the middle of the afternoon he saw dust ahead, stirred by a herd of cattle. "Maybe somebody can point us to a job of work." He moved his horse into a lope. He was halfway there before Walter caught up with him.

Two horsemen appeared from within a clump of mesquite brush, brandishing pistols. A scowling rider with two weeks' growth of mottled whiskers demanded, "Who are you, and what's your business here?"

Staring into two formidable-looking muzzles, Hewey

felt a chill. He had never been drawn to guns. He stammered, "Nothin'. We don't even rightly know where we're at."

The man's belligerence slowly subsided. "You-all ain't nothin' but a pair of punkin' rollers. We thought you might be cattle rustlers. In this country we got to be careful." He holstered the pistol and gave a silent signal to his younger partner to do the same. The second man had not used a razor in a while either, but his stubble was more like fuzz than whiskers. "Just lookin' over the country, are you?"

Hewey's voice steadied. "What we're really lookin' for is a job."

"Cowboys, are you?"

"We've been up the trail once."

The man considered for a minute. "Me and Chum here could use a little help. How about six bits a day and found?"

"Found?"

"Grub and all the ground you need to roll out your beddin'."

Six bits wasn't much, Hewey thought, but it beat what they had been doing. The thought of regular grub made up for a lot. "Just tell us what you want done."

"Fall in behind them cows and help us keep them movin'. Me and Chum ain't been makin' good time by ourselves."

Hewey said, "We can do that." He started to ride up but paused. "What do we call you, mister?"

"Call me Mr. Smith. You don't have to *mister* my partner. Just call him Chum."

Hewey rough-counted about a hundred cows in this bunch, and most had calves. He could not see that driving them offered much challenge. They appeared to have been driven far and hard already. Heads down, they drooled and dragged their feet. Many calves had fallen to the dusty rear, unable to keep up with their mothers. Cows kept stopping and turning back, bawling for their offspring. The smell of their saliva and fresh, warm manure was strong in Hewey's nostrils.

Smith and Chum left Hewey and Walter in the dust and took positions farther ahead. After a while Smith turned back, agitated. "You're lettin' the drags fall behind. Punch them up."

Hewey said, "These calves ain't got much left in them to punch. How much farther do they have to go?"

The answer was curt. "I'll let you know when we get there. Keep pushin'."

Walter rode over beside Hewey. "He's goin' to walk the hooves plumb off of them."

Hewey shrugged. "They're his, so it's none of our worry as long as we get paid." Nevertheless, he disliked seeing animals punished, especially small calves. "I don't see where it'd make much difference if it took a little longer. Cows don't know what time it is."

He noticed that most of the cows were branded CC and earmarked with a swallow fork. Several bore a J Bar brand and a different mark.

Walter started to speak. "You don't suppose . . ." He broke off in mid-sentence. "No, they wouldn't be."

"Be what?" Hewey asked.

"Nothin'. I don't know why I said anything."

Hewey puzzled over what Walter might have been thinking, but he did not dwell on it long. "We've got what we came for, a payin' job that'll feed us."

Smith did not stop the drive until after sundown.

Chum built a small fire to boil coffee and fry just enough bacon to neutralize the hunger pangs. He took the bacon away from the heat while it was a little raw. "We got to put this fire out. They can see it for a long ways in the dark."

Hewey knew it was best not to question the boss, but he asked anyway. "Who is *they?*"

Smith said, "Indians."

"I thought all the Indians were on the reservation."

"Never can tell when some of them bucks may bust out. A herd like this would be easy pickin's."

Hewey thought Smith was overcautious. It had been years since he had heard of any Indian trouble. "All the Indians I ever saw was tame ones."

Smith studied their back trail, his eyes narrowed. "You boys are too young to remember the old days. Once you've heard a war whoop, you never forget it."

Hewey looked in all directions. "I don't see anything."

"It's when you don't see anything that you'd better be extra careful."

Hewey hoped Smith would tell about some of his adventures with Indians, but unlike Tanner he was not a talker. He held his cards close to the vest. As he poured a second cup of coffee he said, "You boys take the first watch. Me and Chum will relieve you after midnight."

The cattle were so leg-weary that they bedded down easily once the cows and calves had paired up. Hewey saw little danger that they would stampede in the night.

The moon was full. He rode a slow circle around the herd and met Walter coming from the other direction.

Walter said, "I ain't heard you singin' to them."

"With my voice, they'd jump and run."

"Yeah, I've heard you in church. You ain't no night-ingale."

Pa had taught Hewey how to tell time in a general way by the position of the stars as they made a slow circle in the night sky. He judged it was considerably past midnight when Smith rode up to him and asked, "See or hear anything?"

"Nothin' but a cow with the croup. No Indians."

"There's other things to worry about besides Indians. It'd be a shame if cattle rustlers was to take this herd before we can get it to the ranch."

"Where's that?"

"Other side of the Rio Grande." Smith jerked his head in a southward direction. "Better get a little sleep. We'll be drivin' them hard again tomorrow."

"The pace is tough on the calves."

Smith's voice was sharp. "I'll worry about the stock. You just do what I hired you for."

Hewey shrugged. Though he felt sorry for the cattle, it was none of his business if the boss worked them down to hide and bone. It just didn't seem logical for an owner to mistreat his property. This herd was worth money.

He met Walter before reaching camp. Hewey said, "I could use a cup of coffee."

Walter said, "Chum told me not to start that fire again. He's worried about cow thieves seein' it."

"No self-respectin' cattle thief would be out stirrin' around at this time of the night," Hewey said. But orders were orders, and they hadn't earned but six bits apiece so far.

In the dark Hewey had a hard time finding a place smooth enough to spread his blanket. Something kept poking him in the back. He finally got sleepy enough to ignore it. By the time he came fully awake, the sun was rising. He saw that Walter was sitting up, listening.

Walter said, "I hear horses runnin'."

Hewey flung the blanket aside and stood up. He saw two horsemen moving south in a long lope, leaving the herd behind.

"That's Smith and Chum," he said. "Must be chasin' a runaway cow."

"Looks more like they're *bein'* chased." Walter pointed to horsemen approaching rapidly from the north. Four men split off in pursuit of Smith and Chum; four others came toward the herd.

Hewey felt sudden apprehension. "They may be the cattle thieves Smith was worried about."

Walter's expression was grave. "Or maybe the real thieves are them two we hired on with."

Hewey's eyes widened as the suggestion soaked in. "You think we been drivin' stolen cattle?"

"It crossed my mind."

"Then we're in a mess of trouble." Hewey expelled a long breath. "I wish you'd told me what you was thinkin'."

"You're the oldest. You're supposed to be the smartest."

"I ought to've suspicioned them myself. I was just too anxious about gettin' a job and somethin' to eat."

Walter's voice was shaky. "Those people look pretty mad."

"Just try to appear innocent, like we don't know nothin'. That ought to come natural."

The four riders seemed to bristle with guns. Hewey assumed the oldest was the leader. He was a smallish, skinny man of middle age or perhaps a little past. It was hard to tell through several days' growth of whiskers. He pointed a pistol that appeared from Hewey's angle to be larger than he was. The man wore a dusty, misshapen old felt hat with deep grease stains and a wide brim tattered along its edges. He looked as if he might have crawled out from under a freight car. He gave Hewey and Walter a blistering look and declared, "Thought you got my cows cheap, did you? Two Cs beef comes awful high."

A young man with a round, chubby face grinned with anticipation. "Let's hang them, Mr. Tarpley."

Tarpley's reply was curt. "Use your head. There ain't a tree around here big enough to hang a man on."

"Just thought it'd be a good lesson to them."

"In the old days we could take thieves like these and give their necks a stretchin' without havin' to go to the courthouse. Now it'd stir up a narrow-minded sheriff and a dozen swivel-jawed lawyers."

Hewey struggled for voice. "We ain't thieves."

"We caught you red-handed with my cows. I'd call that thievin'."

"But we didn't know they was stolen. Me and Walter, we just hired out yesterday. The man said they was his."

"What man was that? What was his name?"

"Smith."

"We seen two run off. Who was the other one?"

"The only name we heard was Chum."

Tarpley snorted. "Smith! I reckon you-all are named Jones?"

"No sir, I'm Hewey Calloway, and this is my brother Walter. We just come from over in East Texas."

The chubby boy said, "If we can't hang them, can we shoot them?"

Tarpley snapped, "Shut up, Fat."

Another cowboy put in, "I kind of believe them, C.C. They look too green to be cow thieves. Probably a couple of farm boys fresh off of the plow."

"What would you know about farm boys, Grady Welch?"

"I was one myself, greener than a gourd vine when I came out here. I was a lot like these two."

Tarpley seemed to give at least some consideration to what this cowboy said. "We'll have to let the sheriff sort it all out." He looked back at Hewey. "You boys got any guns?"

Hewey pointed to his saddle lying on the ground. "Walter don't. I got a six-shooter in my saddlebags, but I can't hit anything with it."

"Damned few cowboys can. Fat, go fetch it to me. Then you boys saddle up. You're goin' to help us drive these cows and calves back to where they come from."

Hewey thought about asking him if they would be paid for the work, but Tarpley did not appear in a mood to discuss wages.

The four riders who had pursued Smith and Chum returned empty-handed. "Sorry, C.C.," one said, "but their horses was faster than ours. One of them was that half Thoroughbred you used to match races with."

Tarpley scowled. "Ain't but one thing lower than a cow thief, and that's a man that'd steal your best horse." He jerked his head as a signal. "Let's take them cows home."

{ TWO }

Tarpley grumbled about the condition of the cattle. "They're drawed pretty bad. You boys been runnin' them, looks like."

Hewey said, "I told Mr. Smith we was pushin' them too hard. He said he was afraid cattle rustlers might catch up to us."

"Wasn't rustlers he was afraid of, it was me. There was a time when cow thieves shivered at the name of C.C. Tarpley. They ain't forgot my reputation. I'm surprised you didn't recognize my brand."

"Like I told you, me and Walter are strangers here. We just hired out yesterday."

"I got to have more than your word about that."

Hewey watched, puzzled, as Tarpley moved away. The rancher hardly fitted his vision of a big, important cowman. Instead of boots he wore a pair of old lace-up shoes crusted with dirt. His saddle could have been a veteran of the first drive up the Chisholm Trail, and his clothes looked as if they might have been cast off by some passing tramp.

The cowboy named Grady pulled up beside Hewey. He sat in his saddle with the ease of a man who knew his way around a horse. Though he wore a loose shirt with a ripped sleeve clumsily repaired, his broad-brimmed felt hat was carefully shaped. His boots appeared to be custom made. His leather chaps bore silver conchas, which hadn't come cheaply, and inlaid silver hearts decorated his spurs. In contrast to Tarpley, he looked as if he were trying to live up to an image shaped by the penny-dreadful magazines.

Hewey said, "Mr. Tarpley don't look like a cattle baron to me. I'd expect to see him swampin' out a saloon."

Grady smiled. "He may not look like much, but when he shows up at the bank, they call out a brass band." He rolled and lighted a cigarette and offered the sack to Hewey. "What part of East Texas are you boys from?"

Nervous, Hewey spilled more tobacco than went onto the paper. He passed the sack back to Grady without offering it to Walter. He was trying to shield his kid brother from bad habits. "Our pa sharecropped over in the blacklands."

"I'm from the piney woods myself. Came out here four years ago."

"Been a cowboy all that time?"

"That's about all there is to do unless you want to herd sheep. That's left mostly to the Mexicans."

Tarpley hollered, "Grady, I wouldn't get too sociable with them boys. They're liable to contaminate you."

"They've got honest faces."

"So did Billy the Kid."

The cattle were allowed to set their own slow pace, grazing as they went. By late afternoon Hewey guessed they had not traveled more than five or six miles. They came to a large pool where runoff from a recent rain had gathered in a depression. The cows and calves picked up the pace as they smelled the water. They eagerly crowded into it, some standing belly deep while they drank.

Hewey was feeling dry himself. He was not sure he wanted to drink where the mud had been stirred, but he changed his mind when he saw Grady kneel and scoop up water in his cupped hands where no cattle or horses had been. Grady said, "I'm thinkin' about growin' me a mustache. It'd serve as a strainer."

Hewey tried to do as Grady did. After a couple of tries he managed to hold enough water in his hands that he could get a decent mouthful. As he expected, it tasted of mud.

Grady said, "This beats drinkin' out of a cow track. Done that a few times."

Hewey looked back toward C. C. Tarpley. "Ain't you afraid I'll contaminate you?"

Grady smiled. "C.C. barks loud, but he ain't got any teeth, hardly. He's a damned good cowman, even if he has got the soul of an old pirate."

"Pirate?"

"He's big and intends to get bigger no matter what it takes. He's a dried-up, skinny little feller, but he's tied together with rawhide."

Hewey grimaced. That did not bode well for him and Walter.

Tarpley decided to make camp so the cattle could water again when they wanted to. He did not feed much better than Smith had. Pursuit of the cattle thieves had been undertaken too quickly to allow for much preparation. Somebody had thrown a bag of Arbuckle's coffee and a smoked ham into a canvas sack. That had been dinner. Now it was supper, and it would be tomorrow's breakfast if it lasted that long. In the pressure of the moment no one had thought to pick up the little food that had remained in Smith's camp. That had probably become some coyote's supper by now.

Hewey noted that everybody in the outfit was on the lean side except for the one called Fat. It occurred to him that cowboy life might not be the best choice for somebody who loved to eat.

Grady warmed a slice of smoked ham on a stick, holding it over a small fire. He offered it to Hewey, who cut off half and handed the rest back. He said, "I'd think a cow outfit would be eatin' beef."

Grady said, "Only if it's a stray. C.C. thinks too much of his cattle to eat them."

Fat glared at Grady. "It ain't right to feed them cow thieves when the rest of us ain't got enough."

Grady retorted, "A wagonload of groceries wouldn't be enough for you, Fat."

Fat said something under his breath and stalked away. Grady said in a low voice, "Don't pay no attention to Fat Gervin. He was born on the wrong side of the bed and been gettin' up that way ever since."

"At least he's got a job."

"The only place he makes a hand is at the table. I think C.C. keeps him on just so he's got somebody to holler at that's afraid to holler back."

"Right now Mr. Tarpley scares me a little, too."

"Don't let him. He's stubborn as a mule and tight as the bark on a tree, but you never saw anybody gentler when it comes to his livestock. He don't wear spurs because he don't want to hurt a horse. He won't hardly even cuss a cow, not out loud."

A hawk soared overhead and screamed a warning as

the riders approached its nest. Hewey envied the bird. He wished he had its wings and could simply fly away from here. "I don't know what he's liable to do to me and Walter."

"I wouldn't worry too much. They don't hang cow thieves anymore. For a first offense they just send them up for five to ten years."

Grady made a thin smile, but his comment sounded too much like the truth to be funny.

Toward noon the next day Hewey saw a couple of windmills ahead, towering over the scrub mesquite and greasewood. Beyond lay a long, flat-topped desert mountain. Grady said, "We're comin' to the ranch headquarters."

Fat Gervin drew in close, smiling wickedly at Hewey and Walter. "We're short of trees, but we could hang them inside a windmill tower."

Grady said, "Don't bedevil the boys, Fat."

Gervin's face flushed. "You know I don't like anybody to call me that. My name is Frank."

"C.C. calls you Fat."

"Mr. Tarpley ain't just anybody. He's the one that pays me."

"I'll try to remember that, Fat."

Tarpley rode back from the point of the herd. "We'll turn them loose on the water and let them scatter on their own. First, though, there's a few Jessup cows in the bunch. We'll cut them out."

He did the cutting himself. The rancher quietly worked his horse in and out of the herd with an ease that came from long years' experience. Grady had lauded Tarpley's abilities as a cowman. Hewey could see what he meant.

Tarpley removed about a dozen cows from the herd.

They bore a J Bar brand. Several had calves not yet branded. He said, "Shorty, you and Baker drive them back onto Eli Jessup's land. *Way* back. Be damned if I'll let that old land hog fatten his cows on my grass."

Hewey said, "Doesn't sound like he's got much use for this feller Jessup."

Grady replied, "He'd ride bareback a hundred miles to attend old Eli's funeral."

A spotted dog came trotting out to meet the horsemen. It barked a welcome, then trotted alongside Tarpley's horse, escorting his owner in.

The headquarters was utilitarian. The only natural trees were a few large "granddaddy" mesquites with thick, gnarly trunks shielded by dry, rough bark. Evidently no one had taken time or trouble to plant domestic varieties. Hewey counted three frame structures, unpainted but not yet old enough to have turned the gray of weathered lumber. One was obviously a barn. He assumed a long, narrow building to be a bunkhouse. A small, square one appeared to be a family residence. A woman and a girl stood on the narrow front porch, watching the riders approach.

Grady said, "That's C.C.'s wife and daughter."

"It don't look like much of a house for an owner."

"C.C. says there'll be time to build a big house when he's got enough land and cows to suit him. With his ambition, that ain't likely to be soon. Jessup's ranch is bigger than his, and it plagues him like a case of hives."

Hewey noticed that Fat kept staring toward the house, probably at Tarpley's daughter. From here he would guess her to be sixteen or so, just ripening. She was no great shakes for looks, however.

The dog separated itself from the riders and moved into the shade of the Tarpley house.

Tarpley's gaze lighted upon Hewey and Walter. "Over yonder is a dugout that I lived in when I first come here. It ain't got but one door. We'll put you boys in there till we can get the sheriff to come out." He nodded at Grady. "Bar the door from the outside and keep watch on it. Fat'll relieve you after a while."

The pudgy cowboy turned red in the face at the use of his uncomplimentary nickname. Hewey had noticed that no one except Fat called the boss "Mr. Tarpley." Everybody else said "C.C."

Grady jerked his head as a signal for Hewey and Walter to follow him. The dugout had been built into a low, gravelly bank. Its roof was of mesquite branches and bear grass clumps weighted down with dirt. The door was of rough lumber, dry and splitting. Grady opened it and looked inside.

He said, "Ain't exactly the Menger Hotel, but it's probably cooler than the bunkhouse. You might want to look it over to be sure you ain't got company. There's somethin' about dugouts that just naturally draws rattlesnakes."

Dismounting, Hewey untied his blanket from behind the cantle of his saddle and paused at the door. The place smelled musty. "What about our horses?"

"I'll take care of them, and I'll see to it that the cook feeds you after a while. Make yourselves to home."

Walter said, "Right now I wish we *had* a home."

Grady shooed a couple of chickens outside, then pushed the door shut. Hewey flinched at the sound of a wooden bar falling into place. The interior seemed gloomy and dark at first. As his eyes adjusted, he saw light streaming in from wide cracks in the door and holes in the roof where the dirt covering had thinned and either washed or blown away from the dry branches that supported it.

He said, "Kind of like bein' in jail."

Walter said, "I wouldn't know. Never been there."

"I have, by invitation of Sheriff Noonan. The old reprobate always took things too serious." Hewey looked up at the low roof. He could see blue sky in places. "A man could probably dig through there in a little while."

"And then what? We're out in the middle of nowhere."

"Every place is somewhere, and there's always someplace to the west of it. Come dark we could catch our horses and git."

"And get chased all the way to El Paso? I say we keep tellin' them what really happened. Pa always said the truth'll come out if you wait long enough."

"Like after five to ten years in the pen?"

"We ought to be able to get some character references from back home."

Hewey shook his head. "Not from Sheriff Noonan. He's had it in for me ever since the night I took his paint horse from in front of the jailhouse and tied it at Big Bessie's. Everybody in town knew that horse."

"You never was one to think much about consequences."

Despite the gloomy situation, the memory made Hewey smile. "His wife wouldn't even speak to him."

Walter said, "The truth finally came out. The truth'll come out for me and you, too."

"I always knew I might have to pay the fiddler when I pulled that stunt on old Noonan. But gettin' in this mess wasn't my fault."

"I'm not blamin' you for it." Walter spread his blanket on the dirt floor and stretched out. "The fact is, I always wished I had a little of your recklessness. But every time I felt tempted I stopped and thought about it first, and then I didn't do it."

"Thinkin' too much spoils the fun."

"Are you havin' fun now?"

Hewey admitted, "Not much." He looked up again at the roof and thought how easy it might be to dig out. Maybe after dark. . . .

Sometime in the late afternoon he heard the bar slide away and the bottom of the door drag against the hard-packed earth. The bright light hurt his eyes. Grady Welch motioned for him and Walter to come out. "Supper's ready at the kitchen. C.C. says it's all right for you-all to come down."

Hewey asked, "And risk contaminatin' the crew?"

"He's startin' to lean a little in your direction, so don't do anything to abuse his hospitality."

Hewey promised, "We'll even try to be nice to Fat Gervin."

He and Walter followed Grady to the bunkhouse. The kitchen took up one end of it, sharing its space with two plain dining tables and four wooden benches. Grady showed the brothers where to wash. He said, "The cook's kind of contrary. Old Soapy always wants you to wash your hands whether they need it or not. He'll think better of you if you'll comb your hair, too. There's a comb layin' by the washpan."

A cracked mirror was attached to a post. Hewey looked at himself and rubbed his rough chin. He saw that he needed to shave. He tried to do that every week or two.

Grady washed first. Drying his hands on a community towel, he said, "You never want to get the cook mad at you. The worst a boss can do is fire you, but a contrary cook can starve you to death."

The cowboys were already at the tables, their plates filled. A couple slid down the bench to make room for Hewey, Walter, and Grady. Fat Gervin got up and moved to the other table.

Grady passed Hewey a platter containing several slabs of fried steak. He said, "Here, have some of Old Man Jessup's stray beef. And you'll be wantin' some whistle berries, too." He handed over a bowl of red beans.

Hewey was heartened to see that most of the men evidenced no hostile feelings, though he and Walter remained under suspicion. Fat was an exception. Hewey heard him mutter something about bad company, but it seemed to have no adverse effect upon his appetite.

Tarpley was not there.

Grady said, "C.C. don't often eat with the hands except when we're out with the wagon. It hurts him to watch cowpunchers puttin' away so much high-priced grub. The missus fixes for him up at the big house."

If that was Grady's idea of a big house, Hewey thought, it would be interesting to see what he called a little one.

The cook leaned against the doorjamb, watching with satisfaction as the men devoured the results of his labor. He was a wizened little fellow built on lines similar to Tarpley, except that his stomach stuck out like a pregnant woman's. He wore a flour-dusted sugar sack tied around his belt as an apron. The brand name showed through in reverse.

Hewey ate until his stomach hurt. He could not remember when he had had such a good meal, or as big a meal. He told the cook, "These sure are good fixin's."

Soapy replied dryly, "That's what C.C. pays me such a big salary for."

Walter said, "It's mighty generous of Mr. Tarpley to feed us like this."

Gervin gave the Calloways a narrow look from the other table and said, "It's customary to give condemned men a good last meal."

Hewey tried to think of an appropriate retort. He decided it might be wise to keep his mouth shut, though it was a strain.

Grady spoke for him. "Fat, it ain't etiquette to talk with your mouth plumb full and your head plumb empty."

A few snickers around both tables indicated that the other cowboys agreed with Grady. Face coloring, Fat bowed his head and shoveled a big chunk of steak into his mouth. Gravy trickled from his lower lip and down his broad chin.

Hewey made up his mind that if the opportunity ever came, he would set fire to Fat's shirttail.

The cook walked to the open door and peered out. "We got company comin'. Three men." Flour and dried dough stuck to the hand he raised to shade his eyes. "Looks to me like one of them is that ranger."

Grady got up from the bench and joined Soapy at the door. "Damned if it ain't. I better go tell C.C." He trotted away.

Fat grinned at Hewey, his eyes mocking. "The rangers been known to make short work of cow thieves."

Hewey felt fresh hope. He said, "If it's the same ranger me and Walter met the other evenin', he can vouch for us." He reached with his fork and speared another slice of steak from the platter. "I believe I feel like eatin' a little more." He glanced toward the other table. "If it's all the same to you, Fat."

He heard a commotion out in the yard, a voice raised in sharp command and a sullen response. A tall, lanky man stepped into the open doorway and said, "You-all got any supper left? Me and my prisoners are as lank as gutted snowbirds."

Hewey heard hurried footsteps and Tarpley's voice. "Who you got here, Len?"

Len Tanner turned back to respond. "A couple of boys that taken a likin' to other folks' cattle. Recognize them, C.C.?"

Tarpley said, "Can't say that I do, but they don't look like Sunday schoolteachers." He exploded, "By damn, that's my good Thoroughbred he's ridin'!"

Hewey left the table and went outside. There, hand-cuffed to their saddles, he saw the pair who had left him and Walter with the stolen cattle. He declared, "That's the ginks I was tellin' you about, the ones that called theirselves Smith and Chum."

Smith looked daggers at him. Chum trembled a little and stared at the ground.

The ranger said, "Smith ain't the name his mother gave him." He took a small notebook from his pocket. "They're both here on the fugitive list." He took a better look at Hewey, then at Walter, who had come out to stand at his brother's side. "Well, I see you boys found yourselves a job."

Hewey nodded toward the prisoners. "We did, with them. We didn't know they was drivin' stolen cattle."

Tarpley jerked his thumb at Hewey and Walter. "Do you know these boys, Len?"

"Yeah, we shared a camp a few nights ago. They was lookin' for work. I'm glad they found your place."

"They didn't. I brought them here as prisoners." Tarpley walked up to the older thief, who sat on the Thoroughbred. "Are these boys tellin' it straight, that you hired them without lettin' them know those cows was stolen?"

Sullenly the thief said, "I don't admit to nothin'."

Hewey told him, "You owe us six bits apiece. We won't charge you for that second day."

Smith growled, "You'll keep your mouth shut if you know what's good for you, farm boy."

Tarpley gave Hewey a look of regret. "I ought to've known you were tellin' the truth. Nobody would make up an excuse as dumb as yours. You'll have to admit, though, you boys looked suspicious."

Walter spoke. "Like I told you, Hewey, the truth always comes out."

Tanner had sized up the situation. "C.C., wasn't you tellin' me you've been shorthanded? These boys are lookin' for a job."

Tarpley gave Hewey and Walter a solemn appraisal. "Most of the cowpunchers that drift through here have got too high an opinion of theirselves. The price of cattle bein' what it is, a man can't afford to pay what they think they're worth."

Hewey said, "We figure a dollar a day wouldn't be too much."

Tarpley raised one eyebrow. "I heard you say you hired on to these thieves for six bits a day. Would you charge an honest man more than you'd charge a thief?"

Hewey considered. "Money ain't the only thing in life. It's just that when you don't have any it can be sort of inconvenient. Six bits will do." He turned to his brother as an afterthought. "Won't it?"

"I reckon."

Tarpley said, "Money is wasted on cowboys anyway. They blow it every time they get to town. Better it stays with a man who knows how to invest it."

Tanner said, "Would you mind, C.C., if I took the Calloway boys to town with me? I'd like them to swear out a deposition against these two renegades."

C.C. nodded. "Sure, take them. I ain't put them on the payroll yet anyway. Time enough to do that when they get to work."

Tanner said it was too late to escort the prisoners to town and asked if Tarpley had a place where they might be kept overnight. "Otherwise I'll have to handcuff them to a wagon wheel or somethin'. Not that they don't deserve it."

The rancher said, "Use that old dugout over yonder. That's where I put these boys."

Hewey declared, "Maybe it ain't my place to speak up, but that roof ain't too sturdy. I was figurin' on bustin' through it tonight so me and Walter could get away from here. These two could do the same."

Smith gave Hewey a look that could have withered cotton. His lips moved in silent threat.

Tarpley said, "Maybe cuffin' them to a wagon wheel is the best idea after all. That old dugout always did leak."

While Tanner led the rustlers toward a wagon, Walter said in a subdued voice, "You ought to've kept your mouth shut, Hewey. That Smith will hate you from now on."

"That's all right. I don't like him, either."

{ THREE }

Whoever named the town Upton City must have been a reckless optimist, Hewey thought. But at least it had the bare essentials of urban civilization. He saw a modest stone courthouse and adjacent jail, a general store, and a blacksmith shop. Tanner pointed to a boarding house where transient drummers, lawyers, and the like could bunk and get a decent meal. "They'll even feed cowboys if they're washed and curried," he said. "It doesn't cost so much that you have to sell your horse to eat there."

Hewey was more interested in a square-fronted frame building that sported a sign reading SPIRITOUS LIQUORS AND BILLIARDS. "That means saloon, don't it?"

Tanner grunted. "I didn't figure you farm boys would have much use for a place like that."

Hewey said, "Walter don't, but he's just barely come of age."

Walter declared, "I'm old enough. I'm just not crazy about the taste of whiskey."

Pa had never held with whiskey except for medicinal purposes. However, he had been sick a lot after Ma was buried.

At the moment the saloon might as well be a hundred

miles away. Hewey was too broke to buy a drink. Smith hadn't paid the six bits he owed, and it seemed unlikely he ever would. He had been surly as a chained dog all the way to town.

Chum was mournfully quiet, his eyes downcast. Now he looked at the courthouse and adjacent jail with palpable fear. He murmured, "I hear they got a gallows in there."

Tanner replied, "No such of a thing. See that big mesquite in the courtyard? They use that. It's cheaper." He winked at Hewey. "But if you was to decide to turn state's evidence, I think they might let you bust rocks instead of stretchin' rope."

Smith growled to his accomplice, "You'll keep your mouth shut if you know what's good for you."

Tanner said, "If he knew what's good for him he wouldn't have gone with you in the first place. But I guess he's a slow learner. I remember an old horse I had once. . . ." He launched into a tale about a mount that never could learn to stop eating when he was full. He kept foundering himself until finally one day his stomach exploded and he died. "It was such a mess that they finally decided just to burn the barn down."

Chum looked ill.

Tanner said, "I expect you buzzards have been in better jails than this, but you got to remember that this is ranchin' country, and ranchers hate to pay taxes. If you want a nicer jail you'll need to do your stealin' in a rich county."

Holding the pistol, Tanner started to dismount. Smith suddenly lunged at him. He caught the ranger off balance and pushed him out of the saddle. Tanner landed on his back. Smith whirled his horse around and bumped violently into Hewey's.

The impact jerked Hewey's foot out of the stirrup and twisted it. His spur jabbed into the flank of Smith's mount. The horse squealed and made a high jump. Smith sailed from the saddle and flopped on his stomach. Tanner pushed up onto hands and knees and grabbed him before he could get to his feet. Smith wrestled and cursed but could not break loose from the ranger's determined grip.

A gray-haired man with bent shoulders and a look of dyspepsia had stepped out of the jail to meet the riders. A star shone prominently on his vest. He quietly thrust the muzzle of a pistol against Smith's chin and said, "How do, Tanner. You want me to shoot him?"

"No, it'd cause me too much paperwork." Breathing hard, Tanner roughly pulled Smith back to his feet. He gave Hewey a look of gratitude. "Thanks, cowboy."

Hewey's heart was still thumping from the unexpected action. "I didn't do nothin'. He bumped into my horse."

Smith flashed Hewey a look of hatred.

Probably thinks I got him throwed off on purpose, Hewey thought. *If I'd had time I'd have gotten out of his way.*

The sheriff resembled old Noonan back in East Texas. He said, "Tanner, I ain't got bunks enough for four prisoners. A couple of them got to sleep on the floor."

Tanner dusted himself off. "Just two prisoners, Jed. The other two are witnesses."

The sheriff frowned. "They all look like outlaws to me." He gave Walter a closer study. "Except maybe that youngest one."

Walter grinned at Hewey.

The sheriff asked Tanner, "What's the charges?"

"Cow theft here, and there's paper on them back East for considerable worse."

"Stealin' beef, hunh? Well, they'll see mighty little beef in my jail. They'll get corn bread and beans."

Tanner said, "If the judge is around, I'd like him to take these two cowpunchers' deposition."

"Far as I know, he's in his office."

Tanner said, "I'll help you get these prisoners stoppered up good and tight. Then I'll take these boys over to the courthouse and have them tell the judge all they know."

Smith glowered at Hewey. "I'll remember you. I'll come lookin' for you when I get out."

Tanner said, "Hell, feller, you ain't *gettin'* out."

He saw to it that the pair were placed in separate cells. Smith might intimidate his partner with shouted threats, but he would be unable to get his hands on him. Hewey figured Chum for the type to break down and confess all.

From behind the bars Smith demanded, "When do we get somethin' to eat? That ranger ain't let us have nothin' since breakfast."

The sheriff said sourly, "You'll eat when I get in the mood, and right now I ain't in the mood." He turned to Hewey and Walter. "Have I got to feed these two as well?"

Tanner shook his head. "They've earned a good supper over at Mrs. Pearson's boardin' house."

Hewey pointed out, "Me and Walter are flat broke."

"I expect the judge will authorize the county to pay for it since you're here as witnesses."

The sheriff said, "Just see that it ain't charged up to jail expenses. The commissioner's court has been ridin' me about the high cost of upkeep over here."

As had been the case with the sheriff, the silver-haired

judge's first impression was that Hewey and Walter were Tanner's prisoners. His severe countenance softened when the ranger explained why he had brought them. He summoned a clerk to take dictation while Hewey and Walter described their experience with the rustlers.

Tanner read the two men's true names from his fugitive book. "Let the record show that the one who calls hisself Smith is Olin Trumble, wanted in San Saba County for horse theft, armed robbery, and murder." He glanced at Hewey. "He's accused of murderin' the man who testified against him in the horse stealin' case." He flipped several pages. "The other one is Chumley Barringer, wanted in Tarrant County for armed robbery, assault with intent to do bodily injury, and stealin' a hog." He shook his head. "Looks like a man who commits armed robbery and assault ought to have more ambition than to steal a hog."

Hewey barely heard the last part about the hog. His mind was on the part about Smith-Trumble murdering a man who testified against him. It shook him a little. "Sounds like he don't turn loose of a grudge."

The ranger assured him, "You don't need to fret about him comin' to get you. When them people over at San Saba get done, he'll have a permanent rope burn right under his jaw."

"I'm not worried." Hewey swallowed, for he could still see in his mind's eye the look of hatred the thief had shown him. "But if you're goin' to send them somewhere else, what do you need statements from me and Walter for?"

The judge said, "You're cowboys. If the courts back East don't do their duty, we'll bring those two back here for trial on charges of cow theft. We want your words on paper, signed and notarized, because cowhands drift. By the time we needed you, you might be anywhere from Mexico to Montana."

Tanner said, "Let's put our horses away, then go eat."

Hewey was uncertain about his appetite after hearing Smith's threat.

The livery stable was nothing more than a modest wooden barn with several corrals out back. The owner leaned against the doorframe and nodded what passed for a welcome. He was dressed like a cowboy, and a broke one at that. Hewey would not have taken him to be a businessman.

Tanner said, "Sandy, we'd like to put our horses up for the night."

The stableman gave Hewey and Walter a quick looking over. "I seen you come in to town a while ago. Looked like you had some prisoners."

Tanner said, "Couple of fellers got careless with other people's stock. These boys ain't them."

"Just two is all there was?"

"Two is all I caught, but coyotes sometimes run in packs."

Hewey guessed the stableman's nickname came from the color of his shaggy hair. The man opened a corral gate for the horses. "Throw them in there. You can stow the saddles in the barn. You want me to feed them, I guess?"

Tanner said, "Naturally. I'll need you to write me out a receipt so I can turn my expenses in to the state."

"It won't be but a couple of dollars."

"Without a receipt they won't pay me back. They'll complain if I ask for an extra two bits. For a dollar, they'll holler like a stuck pig."

"You'll get your receipt. Just seems like a lot of fuss over a little of nothin'."

Hewey tended to agree with the stableman. Money had never been of primary concern to him. So long as he had enough to put a little jingle in his pocket, he felt rich. At the moment, however, if a dollar would buy a whole saloon, he couldn't afford a bar rag.

Tanner asked the stable owner, "How's cow business, Sandy?"

"Slow. My kids would go hungry if I didn't have this stable. The little man has got an uphill battle, but I ain't goin' to be a little man forever. I'll have a herd as big as Tarpley's and Jessup's someday."

Tanner looked back as they walked away. "You've got to give Sandy credit for ambition. He's tryin' to build a herd of his own, but he's squeezed between C.C. and Eli. Wherever a blade of grass comes up, there's a Two Cs or a J Bar cow waitin' to graze it."

Hewey said, "That's why I'd rather be a cow*boy* than a cow*man*. I don't have to worry about things like that."

Walter said, "I think Sandy has got the right idea. A man ought to try to build somethin' of his own."

They turned toward the boardinghouse. Tanner said, "It'll be good for a change to have a meal cooked by womenfolks. A man gets awful tired of fixin' for himself wherever the night catches him."

He explained that the boardinghouse served the town in lieu of a hotel. "Better watch your manners. Old Lady Pearson don't like the smell of whiskey, and she don't stand for monkeyshines. She's been known to grab a cowpuncher by the scruff of his neck and throw him plumb off of the porch. She's a woman of powerful opinions."

Mrs. Pearson met the three as they ascended the

steps. Her greeting was civil but hardly warm. "Mr. Tanner, I do not fancy feeding prisoners at my table."

The ranger had to explain to her as he had explained to the sheriff and the judge. "These ain't prisoners, ma'am, they're witnesses. They've been of help to me on a case."

She continued to give the brothers a stern appraisal, especially Hewey. "Well then, maybe." Barely more than five feet tall, she was built for strength rather than speed. Hewey guessed she would tip the scales at close to two hundred pounds, much of it pure muscle. Tanner had said she had been married twice, burying one husband and running the other out of town. She was not looking for a third.

She asked suspiciously, "You-all been at the saloon?"

Tanner assured her, "We've come directly from the courthouse. These boys are sober as old Judge Stone."

"I've seen Judge Stone when he couldn't make it up onto the porch. But you-all come on in. We'll be ringin' the supper bell directly. You know where to wash."

Tanner said, "Thank you kindly, ma'am."

Strong women made Hewey uneasy. He had a feeling it was their intention to take over the world, if they had not already done so. Some reckless politicians were even talking about letting women vote, a radical notion from Europe or some other foreign country.

Walter made it a point to wipe his boots on an old piece of rug that lay just outside the door. Mrs. Pearson noticed and nodded approval. She said, "Sometimes when I see a cowboy with good manners I get to hopin' this old world may survive its tribulations after all."

"Yes, ma'am," Walter said, hat in his hands.

Hewey wiped his feet, too.

Several men stood on the back porch, awaiting the

call to supper. Hewey tried to guess at their occupations. It was difficult to tell which might be a lawyer and which a whiskey drummer. He decided it didn't matter much. They were all peddling something.

A young woman stepped out onto the porch and rang a small bell. Hewey guessed that she was not Mrs. Pearson's daughter, for he saw no resemblance. She was taller but probably weighed little more than half as much. Her face was pleasant enough, even a little shy. He would not regard her as pretty, but she was not really plain, either. She was hard to classify. He might not have given her a second look except that the only women he had seen in a while had been Tarpley's wife and daughter, and then only at some little distance. The daughter was definitely what he would call plain. Being C. C.'s offspring, she could not help it.

Some of the men made a rush toward the long dining table. Hewey started, but Walter caught his arm and said, "Let's show them that cowboys do have manners."

Hewey grunted. "More than lawyers and drummers, anyway." He watched two men grab for the same chair and try to glare one another down.

Hewey noticed that Walter was looking at the young woman. It occurred to him that his brother's show of manners was not altogether for Mrs. Pearson.

The landlady held onto one chair at the head of the table. "Judge Stone is comin'. This seat is his."

The judge walked in, leaving his derby hat on a rack in the parlor. Mrs. Pearson held the chair out for him. She glanced at Hewey, Walter, and Tanner, then nodded toward the far end of the table, away from the judge and away from the meat and potatoes.

If he had had any doubt, Hewey knew now what she

thought about cowboys. She seemed to have doubts about rangers, too.

She stood back from the table, watching the men eat. At length she called, "Eve, you'd better fetch another platter of biscuits. I don't suppose any of these gentlemen have noticed the high cost of flour."

The young woman appeared, holding a pan from which she replenished the biscuit platter. Walter said shyly, "They're mighty tasty, ma'am." He broke a biscuit in two and slathered butter on half of it. Watching the young woman instead of the biscuit, he spread some of the butter on the heel of his hand. She noticed and smiled. Walter blushed and started to lick the butter from his hand, then thought better of it. When the woman looked away, he wiped his hand on the underside of the cotton tablecloth.

Mrs. Pearson brought out a pan of cobbler pie, giving the judge the first helping, then letting the pan work its way down to the cowboy end of the table. By the time it reached Hewey it was empty. He poured molasses into his plate, mixed butter in it with a table knife, then swabbed it up with a biscuit. That was his notion of a sensible cowboy dessert anyway.

The boarders began leaving the table. Hewey grabbed another biscuit to take with him.

Walter said, "That was an awful good supper, Mrs. Pearson." Though he spoke to the older woman, his gaze was on the younger one.

Mrs. Pearson turned away but said over her shoulder, "Even a cowboy deserves a decent meal once in a while. God knows they don't get many in a cow camp." She followed the judge to the door, complimenting him on his dignified appearance. He was a steady customer. Cowboys just dropped in occasionally and could not be depended upon for repeat business.

The young woman smiled at Walter. "Come again."

"I will. What time do you serve breakfast?"

"At seven in the mornin'."

"I'll be here at six, settin' on the porch and waitin'." Walter started to leave, but turned back. "I heard Mrs. Pearson call you Eve. You kin to her?"

She said, "No kin. I just work here."

"I'm Walter Calloway. It's a real pleasure to make your acquaintance." As an afterthought he said, "I guess you know Mr. Tanner. And this other one here, he's my brother Hewey."

"Howdy," Hewey said.

He stooped to retrieve his hat, which he had tossed at the rack on his way in but missed. It lay on the floor. He waited until he was on the porch before he put it on. Mrs. Pearson stood there, watching the judge's departure. She said nothing to the cowboys or Tanner.

Out of earshot, Hewey said, "The old lady wasn't real tickled about us bein' here, but I don't reckon she has any compunctions about takin' the county's money."

Walter said, "Eve was awful sweet, though."

Hewey frowned. "Kind of forward with her, wasn't you?"

Walter looked puzzled. "I'm generally a little uneasy around womenfolks, young ones especially. But there was somethin' about Eve . . ."

"You look like you got gas on your stomach. What you need is a strong shot of whiskey."

Tanner grinned. "I'll set you-all up to a drink."

Hewey took only one. He knew this was coming out of Tanner's pocket, not the county treasury. He doubted that the ranger had much of a bank account.

They slept on a pile of hay in the wagon yard and had breakfast at the boardinghouse on the county's dollar. Eve stood on the porch and watched as Hewey and Walter rode away toward the ranch. Walter kept looking back.

The cowboys had a bronc hemmed against the fence in a round corral. Grady Welch took a firm grip on the horse's ears. "Throw the saddle on him, Fat."

Resentful at the use of the nickname, Fat lifted the saddle from the ground. He dropped it and ran for the fence when the bronc jumped in his direction. For a man of his weight, he moved with alacrity. Grady grumbled under his breath. "Help me here, Shorty."

The bronc tried to kick and pitch, but Grady did not lose his hold on the ears as Shorty fought to put the saddle into place. When the cinch was tight, Grady said, "All right, Hewey, he's yours."

Watching the pony's efforts to fight, Hewey had second thoughts about being so quick to volunteer. "Kind of wiggly, ain't he?"

Grady said, "Playful, is all. There ain't nothin' to it. You just plant yourself in the middle and keep one leg on each side. Anybody can do it. Except maybe Fat."

Hewey was well aware that close to a dozen men were watching him, including Tarpley and Walter. He clamped his teeth together in determination and reached for the saddle horn. He swung up and firmly planted both feet in the stirrups. "Turn him aloose."

Grady released his hold on the bronc's ears and

stepped quickly out of the way. The horse kicked at him in passing, but missed. Grady shouted, "Show him who's boss."

The bronc made several ineffective crow hops. Hewey's confidence came back in a rush. He turned his head in a search for Walter and saw his brother sitting on the fence. He shouted, "Like Grady said, there ain't nothin' to it."

He was unprepared when the bronc suddenly twisted back and seemed to turn himself wrongside out. Hewey's neck felt as if it had snapped in two. He was aware of two high jumps, both ending with a jarring impact as all four hooves struck the hard ground at one time. For a moment he was suspended in the air with nothing under him. The horse was gone. Hewey's rump struck first. The back of his head thumped solidly against the packed earth. His teeth came together with an audible click and bit his tongue.

He lay stunned, aware that the bronc was still pitching, empty stirrups slapping against its sides.

Grady leaned over and extended his hand to help Hewey to his feet. "You can't just lay there and let him get away with that," he said. "If he thinks he's run his bluff on you, he'll try it every time."

It took Hewey a minute to regain enough breath to answer. He rubbed the back of his aching neck. The bronc had stopped pitching but still circled the pen in a run. "You sure he was bluffin'? I had a notion he meant business."

"A colt like that has always got some play in him. You don't want to let him get the idea that you're afraid of him, do you?"

"No, I wouldn't want him thinkin' that." Hewey

waited in vain for someone to volunteer to take over for him. "All right, catch him. As long as I've still got a chip to play, I don't quit a losin' game."

Grady grinned. "All this fun and gettin' paid for it, too. What man wouldn't love this kind of a job?"

Hewey lasted longer the next time. He expected the quick reversal and leaned into it. He managed to survive several jumps before he lost one stirrup and then the other. He struck the ground feetfirst. It was not as painful as before.

Grady said, "You're gettin' the hang of it."

The tiring bronc was dripping sweat as Hewey got on him again. This time the reversal was slower, and the jumps were not so high. Hewey gripped hard with his knees and remained in the saddle until the horse wore itself down and quit, heaving for breath.

Grady walked out to hold the animal while Hewey dismounted, his legs quivering from fatigue. "You done good, Hewey," he said. "You're beginnin' to look like an honest-to-God west-of-the-Pecos cowpuncher."

Beaming, Hewey looked toward his brother. "Told you, Walter. We've about got this cowboy thing whipped."

Tarpley had been watching from the other side of the fence. He said, "Someday you're liable to be worth a whole dollar a day. Maybe in a year or two."

{ FOUR }

B y the next spring's branding time, Hewey and Walter had diminished C. C. Tarpley's fortune by about two hundred dollars apiece at seventy-five cents a day. Walter still had most of his earnings stuffed in the toe of a sock under the cornshuck mattress that covered his cot. Hewey had barely enough left to buy tobacco. He contended that money was meant to be spent so the poor folks could get their share. He did not consider himself poor folks, not at six bits a day.

He had invested in a new saddle at twenty-seven dollars, boots like Grady Welch's, a wide-brimmed hat, and a pair of leather chaps to turn away mesquite thorns. To replace his cheap OK spurs he had bought a pair with silver-plated shanks shaped like a woman's leg. He considered that he made a handsome shadow on horseback.

Walter had inherited Hewey's OK spurs. He said the horses couldn't tell the difference.

Tarpley had not wasted his assets on unnecessary equipment or by building a lot of corrals, which would have made the cowboys' work easier. His position was that if they didn't want to work, they shouldn't have hired on. Most of the branding was done in the open. A skeleton crew held the gathered herd in check while the calves were roped and dragged out to a fire where the branding irons were heated. Flankers threw them down and held them while the animals were branded and ear-marked, the bull calves castrated.

It was an honor of sorts to be chosen to do the roping. The job was usually assigned to the most accomplished in use of the loop. Among the Tarpley crew, that meant Grady Welch. Grady had been in the saddle a couple of hours, catching smaller calves around the neck, larger ones around the hind feet, and dragging them out to flankers, including Hewey and Walter.

One mark of an experienced roper was hands scarred by rope burns or missing parts of one or more fingers, pinched off between rope and saddle horn.

Grady bent over in pain, hugging his right arm tightly against his chest. He rode back toward the fire, his face twisted. Hewey saw that his sleeve was torn, his arm an angry red.

"Rope got twisted around my wrist. Like to've burned my arm off."

Tarpley walked over to look. He was conservative with sympathy, as with all else. "Better go to the wagon and get some of Soapy's bacon grease. Rub it in real good."

Walter said, "Maybe he'd better go to a doctor."

Tarpley replied, "It's too far to town. Bacon grease'll fix about anything except a broken leg." He waved away any further discussion and went to what he saw as his larger and more immediate problem. "Just lost my best heeler. Hewey, I've noticed that you're gettin' handy with a rope."

"Been practicin' with Grady."

"Then climb aboard Grady's horse and get at it. Can't

have flankers idlin' around here drawin' a wage and not doin' nothin' to earn it."

Hewey's elation at being trusted with such a responsibility was compromised by guilt inasmuch as it had come at Grady's expense. He said, "Find you another flankin' partner, Walter," and mounted Grady's horse.

Under Grady's instruction Hewey had roped at anything that would move and much that would not. The chickens had learned to run at the sight of him. A tomcat that headquartered in the barn was missing some of its fur. A hoe handle had never fit Hewey's hands, but a rope felt just right.

For a while he caught every unbranded calf at which he aimed. He had not missed a loop. He hoped Tarpley was paying attention, but he doubted that he was. Tarpley took it for granted that his men could do any job to which he assigned them. If they couldn't, they didn't belong with the Two Cs. The only exception was Fat Gervin. Hewey often wondered why Tarpley tolerated him. When it came to cowboy work, he was as useless as teats on a boar hog.

Hewey's arm eventually began to tire, and he started missing a loop now and again. Fat, working as a flanker, began offering unwanted advice. "Try ropin' left-handed. You couldn't do no worse." Then, "You goin' blind? I could do better with a sack over my head."

Hewey was tempted to step down and *put* a sack over Fat's head. Following Grady's lead, he had been roping the larger calves by the hind feet because they could put up less of a fight than if caught around the neck. He made his way slowly through the herd and picked the biggest unbranded bull calf he could find. It was probably close to being a yearling. He dropped a small loop around its neck and began drawing the animal toward the branding fire. It kicked and pitched and bawled in anger and fear. Hewey said, "Caught him first loop, Fat. He's all yours."

Fat didn't want him, but pride would not let him back away with everybody watching and hoping to see him make a fool of himself. Tentatively he reached to grab a leg. The calf kicked him in the belly with a lightning-fast hind foot. Fat reeled. The cowboys began shouting advice, most of it bad.

Fat grabbed the agitated animal around the neck and bounced about like a ball on the end of a string. The calf shook him off and stepped on him. Walter and Shorty moved in to bring the animal down. Fat was on his knees, wheezing, trying to suck breath back into his lungs.

Hewey was tempted to taunt him, but seeing a scarlet hue in Fat's round face was enough.

After a time he saw Grady trotting from the chuck wagon toward the branding fire, a distance of two hundred yards. The branding was always done far enough away from the wagon to keep dust from settling on the food. He assumed Grady was ready to resume heeling calves, so he rode partway to meet him. Grady was almost out of breath as he hurried up to Tarpley.

"Trouble comin', C.C." He turned and pointed.

Four horsemen approached from the north. Squinting, Tarpley cursed under his breath. "Eli Jessup. Can't be lookin' for much of a fight, only bringin' three men with him."

Grady argued, "He can do a right smart of damage without help. Folks tell me he charged a Comanche camp once all by himself."

Tarpley grunted. "Wasn't but two Indians in it, and

one of them was crippled. If he could fight like he can brag, ain't no tellin' how much mischief he could do."

Hewey had been hearing the Jessup name for months, but he had never seen the man until now. He knew only that bad blood had existed between Jessup and Tarpley for years. Both men wanted to become the biggest rancher in West Texas. It was not a distinction that could be shared.

Jessup was no taller than Tarpley but outweighed him by forty or fifty pounds. On windy days Hewey thought Tarpley needed to carry rocks in his pockets to keep from blowing away. In contrast to Tarpley, Jessup dressed more like a banker than a dust-eating rancher. He wore a vest and a string tie, and his hat looked new. His saddle bore the marks of an expert saddlemaker. It was evident that he had money, and he liked to spend it, at least on himself. His principal facial feature was a bushy but well-combed mustache, mixed gray and black. He had a broad nose, perhaps broken in some long-ago fight, and sharp eyes that tried to burn a hole in whatever they looked upon.

He paid no attention to anyone except Tarpley. He rode up so close that Tarpley could have touched the horse's nose. Though a blind man could see what was going on, he asked, "Are you brandin'?"

Tarpley met the question with contempt. "Of course we're brandin'. Did you think we was throwin' a dance?"

"Thought I ought to come over and be sure you wasn't losin' your eyesight in your old age, maybe puttin' your brand on calves that rightfully ought to carry a J Bar."

"If I was goin' to steal cattle, I'd steal better than that scrub stock you raise."

Hewey looked for a reaction in Jessup's face. The

rancher never changed expression as he said, "How would you know? You couldn't tell a cull heifer from a high-grade bull. Mind if we ride through your herd and look for any stray J Bars?"

Tarpley frowned. "Nobody cuts my herd but me. But if it'll ease your mind, the first thing we done was to cut out the J Bar cows and their calves. They wasn't hard to spot. I got two men right now drivin' the sorry specimens back onto your range and off of my grass."

"*Your* grass? Most of this land still belongs to the state of Texas. As a taxpayer, I'm a part owner. I got as much right to use it as you do."

"The same goes for your place. We're both just squatters if you come right down to it. But I don't aim to be a squatter forever. I buy every acre I can as soon as it comes on the market."

"Well, don't you get any notions about buyin' anything out from under me. I moved in when the Comanches moved out, and I got a shotgun claim on every acre of it."

Jessup jerked his head as a signal for his three cowboys to leave with him. But one lanky, lazy-looking rider hung back. He grinned at Grady Welch, a gold tooth shining. "How do, Grady. Why don't you come over and work for a *good* outfit again?"

Grady grinned back. "Howdy, Snort. How long since you threw a real fumble, stumble, and fall-down drunk?"

"Too long. We'll get together one day and see which of us can soak up the most brave-maker without fallin' over dead."

"You'd have the advantage. You've had a lot more practice than me."

"Like hell. If me and you was to both quit drinkin',
the whole state of Kentucky would go bust." Snort saw
that his boss was fifty yards on his way. "Got to go before
he fires me again. He's already done it twice this month.
See you in town, Grady." He rode off with a careless ease,
letting his shoulders sag.

Hewey observed that the animosity between the two
owners was not shared by their hands. He felt drawn to
the Jessup cowboy on first sight. He asked Grady, "Who's
your friend?"

"Snort Yarnell. He's a top hand and a good old boy,
but he don't give a damn whether school keeps or not.
Been fired off of nearly every ranch on the Pecos River.
He acts like he's still just twelve years old."

Tarpley growled, "A man with any gumption about
him had rather herd sheep than hire out to Eli Jessup.
Let's get back to work before the irons go cold."

Tarpley's cattle were scattered over more than three
hundred square miles fronting on the Pecos. It was not
fenced—fencing cost money—so Tarpley and his crew
worked twenty or so square miles at a time, rounding up
all the cattle within a rough circle. After the calves were
branded, the herd was turned loose, the wagon was moved,
and the next circle was worked. Each lapped over the
edges of those adjoining it to pick up any unworked cattle
that might drift. It took all spring to get the branding done.
Not until the wagon was ready to return to headquarters
did Tarpley reluctantly pay off the cowboys and allow
them time to go to town.

He told them, "Now, don't you-all do anything to cause
me shame. Upton City is a nice quiet little place, and folks

there have got a lot of respect for C. C. Tarpley. I'm even thinkin' of startin' a bank there one of these days, when I've got a little spare money saved up. It'll be a place where you boys can put your earnin's and see them grow."

Hewey did not say so, but the thought came to him that Tarpley would probably charge his borrowers a lot more interest than he would pay to his depositors. Besides, if a man put his money in a bank, there was always a risk of it being robbed. If he invested it in a rousing good time, nobody could take that away from him.

Walter said, "I'm leavin' the biggest part of my money here so I don't spend it in town."

Hewey argued, "Mine can't do me any good if it's here and I'm there. What if a bronc was to throw me off and break my neck? I'd rather go to my rest rememberin' the fun I had instead of thinkin' about the money I left layin' here goin' to waste."

"C.C. Tarpley didn't get where he is by spendin' all his money on fun and frolic."

"And where is he? Does he own this ranch, or does it own him? I'll bet he lays awake half the night worryin' about losin' it. I don't own nothin', so I got no worries."

Walter said, "The time'll come when you'll want to get married and settle down. You'll be glad if you saved somethin'."

"Get married and take on all that responsibility? I remember how hard Pa worked to keep Ma and us fed and a roof over our heads. What good did it do him? Ma died, and we set out on the drift. Pa went to his grave a tired old man with nothin' to show for all that work."

"He went knowin' he'd tried his best. He felt justified in the sight of the Lord."

Hewey frowned. "The Lord ought not to've worked

him so hard. He ought to've let him have more pleasure along the way."

"Pa had his own idea of pleasure. Even with all his troubles, he never gave up his dreams. He was a happy man."

"I'm a *happier* one, not havin' any troubles."

Grady and Hewey led the cowboy procession. Walter and the others were strung out behind for fifty yards. They all spurred up when the town came into view. Fat shouted, "Look out, Upton City, here comes the Two Cs. Bring out the women and the whiskey."

Grady told Hewey, "The women in Upton City are mostly too young, too old, or too married. Anyway, Fat wouldn't know what to do with one even if he could catch her."

Hewey had noticed the lack of women on his previous visit. The only ones he had seen close up were Eve and Mrs. Pearson. "If it wasn't for the saloon, they could call this place Saint's Roost."

Walter pulled up beside Hewey. "I'm hungry enough to eat a side of beef by myself. I'm goin' to the boardin' house and see if supper's ready."

Hewey frowned. He knew supper was not the primary reason Walter was interested in going to the boarding-house. "It's been months since we was here last. Like as not, she's married some dry-goods drummer by now."

"Then again, maybe she hasn't."

It would not do to let their horses stand all night tied to a hitching post. Grady led the Two Cs men to the stable so their mounts could be freed of the saddles and receive the unaccustomed luxury of being fed oats.

Hewey said, "If we deserve a holiday in town, so do they."

A boy of twelve or so met the horsemen at the stable's front door. Grady said, "Where's Sandy at?"

The boy said, "Dad is out lookin' after his cattle. Left me to watch things."

"Pretty big responsibility for a boy your size."

"I can handle it. He always lets me do it when he's gone from town. And he's gone a lot."

Grady accepted that. "Give them a good bait of oats, but watch that none of them kick the others out of the way and founder theirselves. When it comes to feed, these Two Cs horses ain't got good manners."

The boardinghouse would not have been Hewey's next choice of a place to go, but his stomach was talking to him. So was Walter.

Hewey gave in to his brother's argument. "All right. I doubt that the boys can soak it all up before we get there. Ain't good to drink on an empty stomach anyway. You get drunk too fast, and then you're through."

Grady warned, "Remember now, you've got to sidle up to Mrs. Pearson on her good side, or she won't let you in the house."

Hewey said, "If she has a good side, she kept it turned away from me."

The landlady met the three on the porch. Grady removed his hat and made a wide sweep with it as he bowed. "Mrs. Pearson, there's three lank and hungry cowpokes here who can't wait to be blessed by your wonderful cookin'. My old mother back in the piney woods couldn't match the fixin's that you lay on your table."

A tiny smile managed to escape before she covered it

with a frown. "Save your sweet talk for them too young to know better. I can recognize blarney when I hear it." She gave Hewey and Walter a second examination. "Seems I remember you two. Wasn't you here once with that ranger Tanner?"

Hewey said, "Yes, ma'am, we was."

"Too bad what happened to Tanner afterwards."

Hewey blinked. "I didn't know anything had. Out at the ranch, we don't hear much."

"He was deliverin' two prisoners from here to somewhere back East. One of them managed to hit him over the head, then shoot him with his own pistol."

Hewey sucked in a sharp breath. "Kill him?"

"No, just bunged him up some from what I heard. He might've bled to death, but the other prisoner stayed and took him where he could get help."

Walter asked, "Do you know who the prisoners were?"

She shook her head. "All I know is that they were in jail here for cattle rustlin'. They were wanted somewhere else for worse."

Hewey said, "Smith and Chum. It'd be Smith that done the shootin'." Remembering Smith's threat, he felt cold. "So now he's on the loose. No tellin' where at."

Walter said, "I wouldn't think he's mad enough to come back here lookin' for you. Too much risk. He probably rode for Mexico as fast as his horse could carry him."

"I guess." Hewey tried to dismiss the thought, but it would not leave him. He felt that he needed a drink more than he needed supper.

Walter followed Mrs. Pearson through the door and said, "Are you comin'?"

"Go ahead on. I'll be along." Hewey stood on the

porch a minute, staring into the distance. He knew the notion was foolish, but he could not help feeling that Smith-Trumble might be out there somewhere right now, drawing a bead on him.

Grady clapped him on the shoulder. "Don't worry, nobody's goin' to hurt a Two Cs cowhand. C.C. Tarpley wouldn't stand for it."

Hewey's reply held a touch of sarcasm. "That sure makes me feel better."

Several men waited in the parlor. For all Hewey could tell, they might have been the same ones he saw the last time, though they probably were not. He just did not pay a lot of attention to drummers and lawyers.

Judge Stone came in and placed his derby hat carefully on the rack. He recognized Hewey and moved toward him. "You've heard what happened to your friend Len Tanner?"

"Just now, from Mrs. Pearson."

"He should have retired from the Rangers a long time ago. Instead, he's back on the job, chasing outlaws again."

"Maybe that's all he knows to do."

"Age must be making him careless, or he wouldn't have let a criminal seize the advantage."

"I hear the other prisoner helped Len."

"That helped lighten his sentence when he went to trial," the judge said. "Meanwhile, Trumble is back in every Ranger's fugitive book."

"I just hope he's not out here somewhere lookin' for me."

"I am sure he has more pressing matters on his mind than going after revenge on some dollar-a-day cowboy."

"Six bits," Hewey said.

Eve came out of the kitchen, carrying a platter of sliced roast to the table. She glanced toward the men in the parlor, her gaze lighting upon Walter. He gave her a quick bow. "How do, Miss Eve. It is still *Miss,* I hope."

"Certainly," she said, staring at him, evidently trying to remember who he was. "Oh yes, you were in here a few months ago with your brother. I remember you sittin' on the porch the next mornin', waitin' for breakfast."

"Yes'm, that was me. And a good breakfast it was."

"We do our best to please." She went back to the kitchen.

Walter turned to Hewey, beaming. "Told you she wouldn't be married."

"I don't see where that makes any difference. You're too young to think about marryin'. You couldn't afford it in the first place."

"I won't always be workin' for six bits a day."

"No, the time may come when you're makin' a dollar. That still won't be enough."

The saloon was as plain as every other commercial building in town, constructed of rough-sawed lumber that had never been blessed by a coat of paint. A dozen or so horses were tied to hitch racks and posts up and down the street. Approaching the open doors, Hewey could hear several voices raised in what was meant to be song. He would classify it as noise.

He said, "The boys have got a head start on us."

Grady responded, "We'll catch up."

Fat Gervin sat at a table alone, his head bent forward. He was singing something completely different from the rest of the men. The words were so slurred and the tune so off-key that Hewey had no idea what song it was supposed to be.

Grady said, "It don't take much for Fat. He can get drunk just sniffin' the cork." He led the Calloways to the bar. The bartender did not bother to ask what they wanted. He poured whiskey into three glasses and shoved them forward. His only greeting was, "Two bits apiece."

Hewey dug into his pocket for the bankroll that had been resurrected from near death when Tarpley had paid his hands. Two bits for a larruping good supper and two bits for a shot of whiskey. A sound investment, he thought.

Grady remarked to the bartender, "The boys couldn't carry a tune in a washtub. You ought to get a piano in here."

The man wiped up a few drops of whiskey with a dirty rag. "There ain't two people in town could play it. Anyway, the music I like best is the sound of coins ringin' on this bar."

A loud, whiskey-tinged voice shouted from a back corner, "Hey, Grady, about time you got yourself in here." Snort Yarnell lifted a bottle for him to see, then tipped it over when he set it back on the round table in front of him. "Bring us a fresh bottle. This soldier is dead."

Grady asked the bartender, "How long has Snort been here?"

"Long enough to drink up more money than he could earn in a month. I can't seem to get him full."

"I'll try." Grady reached across the bar and grasped a bottle, then nodded for Hewey and Walter to follow him. Snort arose to extend his hand and almost overturned the table. "You boys light and squat. I want you to meet some of my J Bar compadres." He called the names of three punchers who shared the table with him. They all shook hands. Hewey knew he would not remember the names for five minutes.

Grady uncorked his bottle and poured seven drinks. "How come you in town, Snort? Did Jessup finish his brandin'?"

"Nope, still at it. Brandin' camp is just a little ways out of town. But my nose got sore from all that burnin' hair, and my ears were ringin' from all them bawlin' cattle. Decided it was time me and my compadres took ourselves a little vacation."

"You left before the brandin' was done? You're liable to get fired again."

"Already been, but it don't matter. I got to countin' and found I had more than fifty dollars in my pocket. Why should I keep workin' when I'm damned near rich?" Snort drained his glass without stopping for breath.

Grady said, "You won't be rich long, not at this rate."

"Then I'll go back to work. There's always more work out there than a man can get done, but there ain't that many good times. I figure I better enjoy myself before I get stomped to death by some outlawed bronc." He winked. "Or shot by some jealous husband."

Dryly, Grady said, "Yeah, a handsome feller like you is always a big threat around the womenfolks."

Hewey thought Snort was about as homely a cowboy as he had seen yet. His nose was large and his ears stuck out. The gold tooth called attention to the fact that the rest were crooked. When the Lord had passed out looks, Snort was probably asleep behind the barn. Drunk, maybe.

Snort said, "Drink up, boys. Next bottle is on me and Old Man Jessup. I'm squanderin' his wealth one drink at a time."

The seven had just about polished off Grady's bottle when Hewey heard spurs jingling and footsteps thumping on the wooden sidewalk outside. Four men strode in. One he recognized as rancher Eli Jessup. The others' clothing and boots proclaimed them to be cowpunchers. He thought he remembered seeing one with Jessup the day the neighboring rancher had shown up at Tarpley's branding. He stood better than six feet tall and ax-handle broad in the shoulders.

In a voice that rattled glassware, Jessup declared, "Yonder they are," and led the others toward the corner where Snort sat.

Snort raised his glass. "The J Bars have arrived. You boys set yourselves down and have a drink."

Jessup's eyes crackled. "Drink hell! You-all are goin' back to work right now." He jerked his head toward the door. Three J Bar men quickly stood up and weaved their way outside. He did not have to tell them twice.

Snort just sat there. Jessup demanded, "What about you?"

Snort showed no reaction. "You fired me."

"Well, you're unfired. Damn you, you gutted my brandin' crew. Now get up from there and find your horse."

Snort grinned and poured another drink.

Jessup turned to the big cowboy. "Bring him, Mitch. Get him back to the wagon. Alive if you can." He strode across the room and out the door, shouting orders at the men who had already retreated outside.

Mitch seemed to tower over Snort. "You look like you've had enough. Mr. Jessup said fetch you."

Snort's jovial grin soured. "I ain't ready to be fetched. The night's still young, and so am I."

"It ain't polite to ride off before the work's done.

Mr. Jessup got his feelin's hurt. When his feelin's are hurt, he sees to it that the rest of us hurt too." The cowboy extended a muscled arm that would do credit to a blacksmith. "I'll help you up."

Snort gripped the edge of the table with both hands. "I ain't goin'. Old Eli fired me."

"You heard him say he's unfired you. Now come on."

"I'm a free-born citizen of the sovereign state of Texas. Go tell him I'll stay fired as long as I want to."

Mitch grabbed Snort's arm and tried to pull him away from the table. Two of the newly arrived Jessup cowhands moved to help.

Grady pushed quickly to his feet. "Snort ain't goin' anyplace he don't want to. Turn him aloose."

Mitch struck Grady in the face. Hewey jumped up and grabbed Mitch, shoving him against the wall. "Ain't nobody hits a friend of mine." He punched the cowboy in the stomach. It felt as hard as a cedar stump. Hewey knew he had hurt himself more than he hurt Mitch.

Somebody grabbed Hewey's shoulder and jerked him backward. Hewey tripped over a chair and fell. He came up swinging, only to meet Mitch's fist. It jarred him like the kick of a mule. Two men immediately piled on him, knocking him flat on the floor. Mitch and one other became heavily involved with Grady.

Snort Yarnell continued to sit in the corner, happily watching the fight as if he had bought a ticket. He grabbed the bottle when one of the combatants fell against the table. The glasses all rolled to the floor. "Sure has got noisy in here," he said.

Hewey was in a bad way, the two men holding him down and punching him about the head. Walter joined the fray, pulling one of the men off and driving a fist into his face. The other Two Cs punchers gathered around, shouting encouragement but not joining in. Like Snort, they remained enthusiastic spectators.

Hewey half hoped the sheriff would show up and stop the fight, for he was getting the worst of it. Instead it was Snort who brought the fracas to an end. He tugged at Grady's shoulder, then reached down and got hold of Hewey's shirt. "Grady, Hewey, you've had fun enough. Now stop whuppin' up on friends of mine. Hell, you're *all* friends of mine. Ain't no use in friends fightin' friends."

Grady felt of a bruised jaw and mumbled, "We done it to help you, Snort."

Hewey rubbed bleeding knuckles against a trousers leg.

Snort told Mitch, "I'll go back to camp with you in the mornin'. I'll be broke by then anyhow. Now all you boys have a drink. Ain't no use in anybody carryin' a grudge. We're all friends here."

The J Bar hands and the Two Cs men eyed each other warily. Snort put one arm around Mitch and the other around Hewey. "You-all shake and let's uncork another bottle."

Hesitantly Hewey extended his hand. Pain shot through him when Mitch gripped it. He managed a half-hearted smile, though his lower lip was split.

Snort said, "Let's drink to Eli Jessup. And to C.C. Tarpley—the two biggest skinflints on the Pecos River. May they live long, and die of the piles."

The cowboys took kindly to the toast.

Hewey heard a thump. Fat had slumped forward, his head striking the table where he sat alone. His bottle rolled off onto the floor, but Fat made no effort to retrieve it. He did not know it was gone.

Jessup reentered the saloon and did not appear pleased

to see that the combatants had made peace. He placed his knotted fists on his hips and shouted, "Any man of mine not back at the wagon by mornin' don't need to come back at all." He stomped out.

There was a man, Hewey thought, who ought to be an officer in the army. Or at least a fancy-house bouncer in Hell's Half Acre.

Snort said, "Don't worry, boys. He needs us to get the brandin' done. Come mornin' he'll be his natural self. Still mad as hell."

In a little while a stranger walking in would not have been able to tell the J Bars from the Two Cs. They were mixed up together, all trying to sing at the same time but in three or four different keys.

The proprietor smiled, counting the change spread across his bar.

{ FIVE }

Awakening, Hewey found himself lying on a pool table in the back of the saloon. He did not remember how he got there. Rising up on one elbow, he thought every muscle in his body had declared war on him.

Walter lay on the floor, half covered by his blanket. His eyes were open. Hewey could not see a mark on him. His part in the fight had been minimal.

Walter said, "You all in one piece, Hewey?"

"I don't know. Feels like I'm scattered a little."

Grady was sitting up, leaning against a back wall. Snort lay under a table, snoring. The rest of the Two Cs and J Bar hands were lying here, there, and yonder.

The front door opened. The bartender walked in, stopping to survey his domain. He said, "Looks like the walls are still standin'. You boys get up. I need to swamp out in here."

Hewey vaguely remembered the bartender leaving about midnight, admonishing the cowboys to keep track of their drinks so everybody could settle in the morning. It would have been easy for the men to have left early without squaring up what they owed, but few would have considered doing that. It was accepted as holy writ that they paid for what they drank and settled for what they broke.

Hewey looked around for some notion of the damage. Beyond a few smashed glasses, the only casualty he saw of last night's little wrestling match was a broken chair.

The bartender built a fire in a fat-bellied, flat-topped stove and set a large coffeepot on to boil. "If you boys want the hair of the dog, come over to the bar. If you'd rather have coffee, it'll be ready directly."

Most of the punchers elected to wait for the coffee, though Snort and Grady stumbled to the bar and leaned on it for support.

Walter said, "I'm for havin' breakfast over at the boardin'house. What about you, Hewey?"

Hewey started to shake his head, but it hurt too much. "How do I look?"

"If you feel as bad as you look, you've got one foot in the grave."

"Then go by yourself. That old lady'd probably take a broom and sweep me out into the street."

After Walter left, Hewey made his way by stages to the stove to listen to the coffee boil. The bartender brought a glass of water and poured it in to settle the grounds. "Help yourselves, boys."

Hewey's joints hurt, and his cheek and nose were sore to the touch. His knuckles were skinned and bruised. He poured a cup of coffee and sat down to hold it between his hands, hoping its warmth might draw out some of the ache. It struck him strange that the J Bar men he had fought with last night sat at the table with him, as friendly as if nothing had happened. They looked to be in about as bad a shape as he was. There was probably a lesson in this somewhere, he thought. He would study on it when he felt better.

Grady asked him, "Where's Walter?"

"Said he was goin' to the boardin' house for breakfast. I think mainly he wanted another look at that young woman."

"Eve? I ain't surprised. She's a nice girl, and pleasant to the eyes."

"Sort of skinny, I thought."

"She comes from good folks, but poor as church mice. They've had a hard time keepin' groceries on the table. That's why she works for Mrs. Pearson."

Hewey thought about Pa. The problem in East Texas hadn't been dryness so much as used-up soil and ravenous insects, poor markets and high interest. A farmer's life was seldom peaches and cream. It was more often skim milk and clabber. "Walter's too young to be thinkin' about women. Ain't nothin' but a kid."

"You're not payin' attention. He's twenty-one at least. If he wasn't thinkin' about women there'd be somethin' wrong with him." Grady arched an eyebrow. "Anything wrong with *you*, Hewey?"

"Nothin' except bein' dumb enough to get into somebody else's fight." Hewey gave Snort a critical glance. "I don't see no bruises on you."

"They're friends of mine."

"I wish you'd told us that before."

"I started to, but then it turned into a dandy scrap. Broke up the monotony."

"And like to've broke my jaw."

After partaking of the bartender's coffee, the J Bar cowboys started riding off in the direction of their branding camp. Mitch said, "I wish I could invite you fellers out to the wagon for breakfast, but Old Eli would paw and beller about feedin' C.C. Tarpley's hands. Even if the beef is C.C.'s."

Snort grunted. "Bellerin' don't hurt him. A little aggravation helps keep his blood from clottin' up."

Grady demurred. "Thanks anyway, but if we was to go to your wagon, C.C. might think we was swappin' sides."

Mitch said, "There ought not to be any sides, but I guess that's the way it is when you get two old mossy-horns buttin' heads. Let's just try to see that none of us hands gets caught up in their feud."

Grady looked regretful. "Old men start the wars and send young men off to fight them."

Mitch put his horse into an easy lope to catch up to the other J Bar cowboys. Snort held back a minute. He said, "I thank you, Grady, for takin' my part last night." His big hand was heavy on Hewey's shoulder. "And Hewey Calloway, you're a good old boy. Hell, we're *all* good old boys."

Slouching in the saddle, he rode after his friends.

The Two Cs hands made their way to the general store. They breakfasted on crackers, sardines, and canned tomatoes. None wanted to visit Mrs. Pearson's boardinghouse. She probably would not let them in, and even if she did, they would not want to hear her lecture on abstinence and clean living. After last night, they were already convinced anyway.

Walter wandered back after a while, picking his teeth and looking much too contented. Hewey said, "I can tell you've been talkin' to that girl."

Walter smiled. "Eve told me about her folks, and I told her about ours. She said there's a dance tonight in

Shelby's barn. Since we don't have to be back at the ranch yet, I thought I'd go."

"You don't know how to dance."

"I've watched it done. Ain't nothin' to it. You just walk in a circle and drag your feet."

"You want to get your arms around that girl, is all. That's dangerous. Women are always out to hook you for whatever they can get."

"What would you know? The only women you've ever spent time with were at Big Bessie's, and places like hers."

Hewey's cheeks stung. "That ain't so." He knew it was.

"You weren't near as sneaky as you thought you were. I always knew where you went."

Hewey could not think of a good response. "Anyway, what do you want with a skinny farm girl? First thing you know, she'll be sweet-talkin' you about gettin' married. You'll end up workin' in a store or pushin' a plow because there ain't no cowboy can support a wife."

"Who's talkin' about gettin' married? I don't hardly know her yet."

"Be careful, or you may get to know her a lot more than you intended to. She'll have one ring on her finger and another one in your nose."

Hewey knew he had to nip this thing in the bud. He just didn't know how.

Shelby was a horse trader who had built a barn at the edge of town. Part of it had a wooden floor fit for dancing. It bore the strong smell of horses and horse liniment, hay, and old leather. That was little hindrance to the citizens of Upton City. It was a ranch town, and they were used to such things.

Hewey was hesitant about going to the dance. He would rather spend the evening in the saloon, quietly contemplating life's deeper meaning, but he felt that Walter needed a chaperone. He might be past twenty-one, as Grady had pointed out, but to Hewey he was still a kid whose inexperience made him vulnerable. He could be manipulated by people who might have their own interests in mind rather than his.

He still felt sore in most of his joints, and he knew without looking in a mirror that his face was swollen. He asked Walter, "Reckon anybody'll notice?"

Walter studied him critically. "Not if you stay in the dark end of the barn. If you're worried about what people might think, you don't need to go over there. I'm old enough to take care of myself."

"I wish I was as sure as you are." Hewey ran a comb through his hair and found another tender spot he had not known about. "I promised Pa I'd look out for you."

"What could happen to me here? Bein' in this town is like bein' in church, almost."

"I've been to funerals in church." Hewey paused. "And a weddin' or two."

Word had gone out that Shelby did not want any drinking in his barn, which had indicated to Hewey that this dance would be about as much fun as a memorial service. But as he and Walter walked toward the sound of fiddle music he saw that though the letter of the law might be observed, its spirit was being broken like a barroom mirror. He observed men stashing bottles in wagons and buggies and in a couple of bushes just outside the door.

He said, "Maybe the night ain't lost after all."

Walter frowned. "You ain't goin' to get drunk, I hope."

"Me? You know I wouldn't do such as that and embarrass you in front of your girl." The idea suddenly seemed to have a lot of merit.

Walter said, "She's not my girl. Yet."

A goodly crowd was already in the lantern-lit barn when Hewey and Walter arrived. Besides town folk, many had come from ranches for miles around. Hewey found himself looking at the faces, searching for the cattle thief named Smith-Trumble. He realized how foolish that was. In this town where he was known, and in a crowd like this, was surely the last place Smith would want to be.

He recognized a couple of the J Bar cowboys he had seen the previous evening. They evidently had sneaked in from Eli Jessup's branding camp. A few of the Two Cs cowboys were there, too. One was Fat Gervin. His belly stretched a clean new shirt that was still wrinkled from being folded in a stack at the general store.

Hewey found a dark corner where his bruises and contusions would not be so obvious. He watched the dancers stepping with enthusiasm to an Irish jig played loudly, if not quite in tune, on a fiddle and a banjo. He picked up the rhythm and tapped his foot. This was his kind of music.

He hoped Eve would arrive with some man, which might discourage Walter from pursuing her. He was disappointed, for she and Mrs. Pearson came through the door together. Fat Gervin immediately hurried toward her, but Walter got there first. She curtsied, and he shook her hand as he would shake with any cowboy he met.

Mrs. Pearson gave Walter a critical study. He looked well-brushed and combed, but it was obvious that her suspicions were not allayed. The music and the sound of dancers' feet sliding across rough pine prevented Hewey from hearing what she said. Walter took Eve in his arms and moved awkwardly onto the floor with her. Mrs. Pearson watched like a mother hen concerned about a wayward chick.

Hewey had been right about Walter not knowing how to dance, but he made a creditable effort. Eve offered him guidance. After a few tunes he had improved considerably.

Walter danced Eve over to where Hewey stood. He said, "Look at her, Hewey. She's the prettiest girl here."

Hewey could not argue with that, but the competition was not substantial.

Eve scrutinized Hewey's bruised face. "What happened to you?"

"Horse," he said, hoping that was enough.

Her smile broadened. "I heard that the horse had a J Bar brand on him." She danced away with Walter.

A gruff voice demanded, "Ain't you dancin', Hewey Calloway?" Snort Yarnell had walked up behind him.

Hewey asked, "You been fired again?"

"Naw, me and Old Man Jessup have come to an understandin'. He goes where he wants to, and I go where I want to. A lot less aggravation that way. Looks like your little brother's havin' hisself a time."

"Too good a time. Look at that grin on his face. Like a possum lickin' cream."

"Yeah." Snort nodded gravely. "If he ain't careful, his cowboy days are numbered. That'd be a waste of good talent. What you goin' to do about it, Hewey?"

"Damned if I know. Somethin'."

"I know what *I'm* goin' to do. There's several bottles of good drinkin' whiskey out yonder in a bush, not doin' nobody any good. Join me?"

"Don't mind if I do." Hewey looked back. Fat Gervin was watching Walter and Eve with envy in his eyes. Hewey said, "Wait a minute, Snort. I believe I just gave birth to an idea." He walked to where Fat stood, his gaze wistfully following the pair. "Howdy, Fat."

Fat flashed him a resentful look. "Frank's the name."

"I was wonderin' if you'd do me a favor, Fat. That girl has been dancin' with my brother ever since she came. Won't let him dance with anybody else. Him and me would both take it as a favor if you'd go out there and cut in."

Fat instantly shed his resentment. "It'd be a pleasure. Thanks, Hewey."

"It's you that deserves the thanks." Hewey watched with satisfaction as Fat worked his way through the dancers and tapped Walter on the shoulder. Hewey could not hear the words, but he saw the look of surprise on Eve's face and dismay on Walter's. Fat danced away with Eve, leaving Walter standing in the midst of the dancers. He weaved through the crowd to where Hewey waited.

He looked puzzled. "I don't understand. What's this cuttin'-in business?"

"You ain't been to many dances. Generally the girl lets somebody know she'd like to change partners. Like as not, she gave Fat a signal."

"She wouldn't do that. We were havin' a good time."

"*You* were, anyway. She probably got tired of you

steppin' on her feet. Come on. Me and Snort were fixin' to have a drink."

Outside, Snort was talking to a lanky rancher whose shirttail was halfway out and whose string tie was undone, dangling beneath a prominent Adam's apple. Snort hailed Hewey. "Come over here and meet somebody."

The rancher extended a bottle toward the brothers. "You fellers look like you could stand a little drop of kindness."

Walter hung back, turning so he could watch the open barn door. Hewey accepted the offer and took a long drink. He was no connoisseur, but he knew this was not ordinary over-the-bar whiskey. "Prime stuff."

The rancher nodded, pleased. "Kentucky's finest. You can taste the bluegrass. You-all friends of Snort Yarnell?"

Hewey said, "Like we'd known him all our lives."

Snort grinned. "This here is Alvin Lawdermilk. Got him a ranch out yonder way." He waved his hand vaguely. "Yonder way" could have been in any direction.

Lawdermilk said, "It ain't near as big as C. C.'s or Old Man Jessup's, but it's mine."

A woman came out of the barn and stood in the doorway, peering into the darkness. Lawdermilk quickly moved behind a wagon. "My wife Cora," he said. "She don't hold with strong drink." He watched until the woman went back inside. "I've got to take a chaw of tobacco to cover up my breath."

Hewey said, "You sure she'd rather smell chewin' tobacco than whiskey?"

"She don't like either one, but she can't holler much

about the tobacco. Her old mother dips snuff. Boys, that woman's breath would knock a skunk into the ditch."

Walter declined Lawdermilk's offer of the bottle. "I still can't believe it," he lamented. "I didn't take Eve to be the fickle type."

Hewey said, "Just shows that a cowboy ought to stick to horses. With a horse, he's either gentle or he throws you off. He don't leave you wonderin' where you stand."

Lawdermilk nodded. "I love my Cora dearly, but there's days when I wonder if we're both speakin' the same language. There's times when I almost wish I'd never got married. Of course I always get over that notion when I set myself down to the table."

Walter looked inside the barn again. Fat was waltzing with Eve, clumsily bumping against other dancers. He said, "It beats me what she can see in him."

Hewey shrugged. "Some women like them chunky. There's more to get ahold of. I know this has got your goat, but you'll be a better man for knowin' the truth. Now, let's go over to the saloon. They've got the right medicine to treat what ails you."

Lawdermilk said, "That's a dandy idea. I believe I'll go with you. The first round is on me."

Hewey asked, "What about your wife?"

"She's already mad anyway. She'll be over it in two or three days."

Snort laid a big hand on Lawdermilk's shoulder. "Alvin, you're a good old boy."

Walter was still nursing his first drink at the bar when Hewey, Snort, and Lawdermilk were working on their third. Grady Welch had joined them, breathing heavily after dancing with most of the younger women. He seemed unaware of Walter's distress. He said, "You ought to be out at Shelby's barn, Walter. Fat Gervin is beatin' your time."

That was spark enough to light Walter's fuse. He turned toward the door. "I'm fixin' to go see about that."

Hewey grabbed at him but missed. He apologized to the other men. "I'd better try to keep my little brother from gettin' himself in trouble." He followed Walter out into the night and down toward the barn, where the fiddle and banjo continued to play in lively rhythm. He shouted, "Hey, Walter, hold up!"

Walter slowed but did not stop. Hewey trotted to catch up to him and said, "You oughtn't to do anything that'll make you look foolish. Accept it, you ain't no ladies' man."

Walter kept walking, not attempting a reply. As they neared the barn they saw two men escorting Fat out the door, holding firmly to his arms. They gave him a shove and ordered, "Don't you be comin' back."

Fat seemed bewildered. Hewey asked, "What's the trouble, Fat?"

Fat looked back. "All she had to do was to say no. Her bein' just a waitress, I thought . . ." He fixed a baleful gaze on Hewey. "Next time you want somebody to take over a gal, don't pick on me." He trudged off in the direction of the saloon.

Walter turned on Hewey. "What did he mean, take over a gal?"

Hewey feigned innocence. "Damned if I know. Fat don't always make sense."

Mrs. Pearson came out, Eve at her side. She spotted Walter and made straight for him, her face severe. "It's your fault. You left me with that awful Fat Gervin."

Walter sputtered, "What happened?"

Mrs. Pearson answered, "He made an indecent proposal to Eve, that's what, and she slapped him. It was his good luck that a couple of gentlemen hustled him out of the barn quick. Some of the young men were gettin' ready to stomp on him."

Eve demanded, "Why didn't you cut back in?"

Walter said, "I thought you wanted to dance with him. I thought . . ."

Eve said, "I don't know where you got such a fool idea."

Walter stammered. "But Hewey said . . ."

Now both Walter and Eve turned their anger on Hewey. Defensively he raised his hands and backed up a step. "I must've made a mistake. I never was good at readin' women's minds."

Eve declared, "I'll bet you can read my mind now."

He thought for a few seconds that she was going to strike him. He would not know how to handle that.

Walter said, "Eve, I did enjoy dancin' with you. I'd be pleasured to dance with you again if you'll go back in there with me."

She shook her head. "I'm too mad to face that crowd anymore tonight. And I'm too mad to stand here talkin' to you. Next time you think about askin' me to dance, don't."

Walter looked as if he had been knocked down by a runaway wagon he had not seen coming. "Eve . . ."

Eve turned away toward the boardinghouse. Mrs. Pearson gave both brothers a withering glance. "Good night, *gentlemen*."

As the women moved away, Walter called after them. "I'll be over for breakfast. Maybe we can talk."

Mrs. Pearson said, "There won't be any empty chairs."

Hewey tried to measure his words. "Someday you'll look back on this and be glad it turned out like it did. You could've got yourself trapped, and she'd pretty soon have you hooked up to a plow. You're too good a cowboy to waste your life like that."

Walter snapped, "The next time you feel like buttin' into my business, don't." He strode away, making it clear that he did not want Hewey to walk with him.

Hewey thought, *I'm just tryin' to keep him out of trouble. It's a good thing Pa ain't here to see this.*

Lying on the pool table, he slept fitfully. He was assaulted by dreams of Eve and Mrs. Pearson beating him with broom handles, of Eve driving away in a wagon with Walter. When that nightmare faded, he was certain he saw the rustler Smith-Trumble coming after him with a pistol. As he awakened for the tenth time, fighting his blanket, he gave up any attempt at sleep. Walter was lying on the floor, awake. He turned away when he saw that Hewey was looking at him.

Hewey said, "I'm thinkin' about goin' over to the boardin'house and apologizin' to that girl."

Walter's voice was crisp. "You've caused trouble enough already. Stay away from her."

Hewey fished for the right words. "I never had no thought of hurtin' you. I've always looked out for you the best I could, like a big brother is supposed to."

"I'm not as little a brother as you think I am. I'm a grown man, and I can handle myself pretty good, thank you."

"I reckon you're right. It ain't my place to do the thinkin' for you anymore."

He lay back down on his blanket and began trying to figure out the best way to keep Walter and Eve apart.

{ SIX }

C. C. Tarpley poked his head in the bunkhouse door after the crew returned to the ranch from their holiday in town. "Anybody here sober?"

Grady feigned innocence. "C.C., you know nobody in this outfit ever drinks."

"Only when they get the chance." Tarpley beckoned Hewey, Walter, and Grady outside. "You-all come and go with me. I've got somethin' to talk to you about." Looking around to be sure no one else could hear, he led them to a corral fence and leaned his bony shoulder against it. "Boys," he said, "I hope you-all will do somethin' for me."

That sounded as if they had a choice. They didn't if they wanted to keep working for the Two Cs.

Tarpley said, "I been tallyin' the figures. Our brandin' came up a mite short. The way it looks to me, somebody's been skimmin' off part of the crop. I see the fine hand of Eli Jessup in this."

Grady suggested, "It was dry last year. Maybe the cows didn't breed up like they ought to."

"Ain't nothin' wrong with our cows, or our bulls, either. They know their job." Tarpley's eyes narrowed. "Old Eli's still brandin'. Now, I ain't exactly sayin' he's a thief, but on the other hand there's no bounds to his ambition."

Hewey doubted that Tarpley's ambition knew any bounds, either, but the boss wouldn't want to hear that.

Tarpley lowered his voice as if he were divulging a military secret. "I'd like for you boys to sneak out of here and scout around over Eli's country. I've got a hunch you might find some J Bar–branded calves suckin' on Two Cs cows. If you do, I'll put the sheriff onto that old reprobate like I'd sic a dog onto a coyote."

Grady frowned. "I know most of the boys that work for Eli, and they're good folks. They'd quit before they'd be a party to such as that."

Tarpley looked annoyed at having his judgment questioned. "Maybe you don't know them as well as you think. There's many a man will forget about his conscience if there's enough profit to be had."

Grady argued, "But every once in a while Eli gathers up Two Cs strays and sends them back here where they belong. He could just as easy keep them."

Tarpley sniffed. "Maybe he does that just so I don't suspicion him."

Hewey said, "If he catches us pokin' around over there, he'll be the one that calls for the sheriff."

"See to it that you don't get caught. Stay away from where he's still gatherin' and brandin'. Scout around where he's already moved on."

Grady reluctantly nodded acceptance. "Eli's got a lot of country. How long do you want us to keep lookin'?"

"Till you're plumb satisfied one way or the other."

Hewey glanced at Walter. One good thing about this assignment: it would keep him away from town and that girl. He said, "This might take a right smart while. We'll need to pack plenty of grub."

Tarpley's face pinched at the thought. "Go easy on the expenses. Money don't come easy around here."

Hewey already knew that.

Tarpley added, "Don't tell anybody where you're goin'. I wouldn't want the word getting' to Eli. I'd wager ten dollars—well, maybe five—that he's got a spy or two on this place. On my payroll!" The idea that some of his money might be going to an enemy spy appeared to cause him considerable pain.

Hewey immediately thought of Fat Gervin but rejected the idea. Not that Fat was above such a thing, but he didn't seem to have that much ambition.

Tarpley added another bit of advice. "Don't you boys flash any firearms. That'd just give Eli's crew an excuse to shoot you. If you do happen to get caught, just say you were drunk and got lost. That'll sound logical."

Grady looked as if he had bitten into a sour apple. When Tarpley was gone, he said, "Me, get lost? I know every cow trail and rabbit track from here to Pontoon Crossin'. We won't find any Two Cs calves over there. Old Eli ain't no cow thief, even if he is as ornery as a sore-footed badger."

Walter shrugged. "The boss may not always be right, but he's the one that pays us."

Grady started for the kitchen. "Let's go jaw with Soapy."

They tried to get supplies without letting Soapy in on the secret, but the cook was a step ahead of them. He said, "C.C. has always suspicioned that Eli is stealin' from him, but I think you boys are off on a snipe hunt. When it's over you'll be holdin' an empty sack."

Hewey said, "It's C.C.'s sack. We'll be drawin' our six bits a day, regardless."

"Six bits? I'm gettin' a dollar and a quarter and don't even have to climb on a horse."

Grady impatiently turned toward the door. "Throw the stuff in a couple of sacks, Soapy. We'll saddle up and come back for it."

Hewey objected, "Just a couple of sacks? That'll be lean pickin's if we're out for very long."

Soapy asked, "Ain't you ever et jackrabbit?"

"Never did."

"No matter. With you-all doin' your own cookin', most of it won't be fit to eat noway."

Hewey was inclined to agree with Grady and Soapy about the futility of the mission Tarpley had assigned. They seemed confident that however numerous his faults might be, Eli Jessup was not one to steal cattle from his neighbors beyond the common practice of slaughtering strays for beef. On the other hand, the saving grace might be that the trip would keep Walter occupied. Hewey's brother had spoken to him but little since the incident at the dance. Perhaps a change of scenery would have healing powers.

Hewey had envied Len Tanner as he listened to stories about adventures the ranger had known. Crossing over onto Jessup's range provided a tingling sense of adventure and risk. Maybe he had not been born too late after all.

"Eli has got a good bunch of boys workin' for him," Grady said, "but it's best we don't stumble into any of them. They might feel duty bound to tell him they saw us. Eli's got the same suspicious mind as C.C. He'd figure we're out to steal from him."

Hewey asked, "How do we know where to go, and where not to?"

"I worked for Eli my first year out here. I know his country and the way he works. Wherever we find the calves already branded, we can be satisfied that he's finished workin' that part of the place."

It did not take long to find the first J Bar cattle. Hewey's limited experience told him Jessup's range was stocked more heavily than Tarpley's. Jessup probably figured Tarpley received more rain—just another reason to resent him—but the fact was that he had more cattle searching after a limited amount of grass. No wonder Jessup was always looking for more land and allowing his stock to push over Tarpley's outer perimeter.

It was not easy to see the J Bar cattle close up. Worked recently, they were leery of horseback riders. Hewey, Walter, and Grady had to circle around and hold them up for a good look at the brands.

The first group set the pattern. Grady checked them over and said, "Not a Two Cs amongst them."

Near nightfall Grady pointed to a distant windmill. "Pretty good water there. It'll be a place to camp for the night and rest the horses."

Hewey said, "We could rest them for a week, no more good than we're doin'."

Walter said, "We're followin' orders and earnin' our time."

Soapy had wrapped some beef and put it in one of the sacks. Grady said, "We'd just as well eat hearty. It won't keep long anyway. After this it'll be sowbelly and whatever we can find. We might manage to kill us a javelina hog."

Hewey frowned. "They don't look fit to eat, with those long teeth and all that bristly hair."

"You don't eat the hair. Javelinas are fair to middlin' if they ain't too scrawny."

Hewey had seen several of the wild pigs. Scared up by the horses, they would go clattering away into the nearest brush, snorting and grunting in alarm. They were a far cry from the domestic hogs Hewey remembered on the farm. It had not occurred to him that they might make a decent supper.

Frying steak in a small skillet over a cow-chip fire, Grady said, "Ain't far from here to the old Butterfield Trail. There was thousands of immigrants passed over it, goin' and comin'. You could tell which ones was headin' west, full of faith and hope. They left ham bones and tin cans behind them. Comin' back east, they was usually wore out and draggin' their feet. All you found in their camps was rabbit fur and quail bones."

Hewey said, "I expect when they got to this part of the country it looked like the jumpin' off place to hell."

"Charles Goodnight called the Pecos River the grave of a cowman's hopes. But it's not as poor as it sometimes looks. A man has just got to know how to manage it. C.C. does pretty good. Eli tries to wring more out of it than it can give."

His stomach full, Hewey stretched out on his blanket and watched the evening star brighten in the darkening sky. The night birds tuned up for their evening concert, and somewhere in the distance a cow bawled for her strayed calf. He felt contented with the world.

"Grady," he said, "is there anything you'd rather do than be a cowpuncher?"

"I've studied on it some. Never came up with anything better."

"Me neither." Hewey looked at Walter, but Walter had nothing to say.

After four days of hunting they still had not found any Two Cs calves except a few following Two Cs mothers. These had simply strayed onto Jessup's land after branding. Even a cow ought to have more judgment, Hewey thought. The grass was better on the Tarpley range.

Riding away from the last bunch they had inspected, Grady declared, "I told C.C. this was a wild goose chase. If Jessup was goin' to steal, he's too big a man to mess around with penny-ante stuff like this. He'd do it in a big way. I've got a good mind to give up this foolishness and go home. If C.C. doesn't like it, he can fire me. There's always other jobs."

That might be so for a top hand of Grady's caliber, Hewey thought, but he and Walter did not yet qualify.

He had enjoyed this little adventure for its own sake, whether anything came of it or not.

Grady said, "We've still got grub. If nothin' else, we could go over to the river and fish for a few days. C.C. doesn't expect us back so soon."

Walter had not talked much during the trip, especially to Hewey. He rode most of the time in brooding silence. Now he protested, "That wouldn't be playin' the game square with C.C."

"The game we're playin' ain't exactly square either," Hewey replied, "trespassin' on another man's land, stirrin' up his stock."

Grady said, "I was just lettin' off a little steam. No, I wouldn't shortchange C.C. We'll keep lookin'."

The next day they found about twenty cattle shaded up in a mesquite thicket where a shallow depression held water after a rain. They started pushing them out into the open for yet another perfunctory look at brands. The cattle balked at first, reluctant to give up the shade.

Grady made a pass around the bunched cows and calves, giving the brands little more than a glance. Then he pulled up short and took a second look at a heifer calf. He turned back to examine more closely another calf that had recently been rendered a steer. A remnant of dried blood still clung to its hind legs. He dropped a small loop over the calf's neck to hold it.

"Hewey, Walter, come look at this."

Hewey and Walter drew in closer. Hewey saw nothing remarkable. "It's a J Bar, and the cows are J Bars. Just like all the others we've seen."

"Look again. That brand don't go all the way to the hide. It's just a hair brand."

Hewey did not grasp the significance. "Somebody didn't take the time to do a good job."

"Somebody knew damned well what he was doin'. The hair'll grow out after a while, and then there won't be any brand. Soon as its mammy's milk dries up and this calf weans off, it'll be a maverick. Anybody can burn his own brand on it. Chances are Eli would never know."

Walter looked puzzled. "How did they manage to do this under Jessup's nose?"

Grady explained, "Whoever done it worked out ahead of Eli's brandin' crew. He was smart enough not to be greedy about it. Just sleepered a few here, there, and yonder. Eli's boys would be too busy for a close look.

They'd see the fresh brands and figure these calves just drifted over from an earlier gather."

Hewey got the picture. "Next fall or winter somebody'll gather up the mavericks and brand them for their own."

Grady said, "He put Eli's earmarks on them, but a sharp knife can alter those."

Walter mused, "Who would think of such a thing?"

"It's an old trick. Probably started with the vaqueros in Mexico, like most everything else we do."

Hewey said, "Kind of odd. We came over here tryin' to prove that Eli is a thief, and instead we find out he's the victim."

Grady frowned. "Maybe not the only one. Our brandin' count came up short. I'll bet somebody's been doin' the same thing to us."

Walter said, "We'd better go by town and tell the sheriff."

Hewey suspected Walter had another motive for a trip to Upton City. He said, "No, the sheriff would ask why we were on Jessup's land in the first place. He might even figure it was us that did the hair brands. And if he didn't, Jessup would."

Grady agreed. "We'd best not say anything to the sheriff, and we sure don't want to tell Eli. But if I get the chance I'll whisper in Mitch's ear, or Snort's."

They had not ridden more than a mile when Hewey saw the chance coming. He looked back and saw two riders. He said, "Somebody's catchin' up to us from behind."

"Hell," Grady wheezed. "We better think of somethin' quick."

As the horsemen neared, Hewey recognized Snort Yarnell and the foreman Mitch. Snort gave a loud yell from fifty yards away.

Mitch seemed to suppress a grin as he reined up. "Howdy, Grady. Ain't you a long ways from where you belong? I thought Eli fired you off of this place three or four years ago."

Grady said, "Eli never got the chance to fire me. I quit."

"He'll want to know what you-all are up to, sashayin' around over his country."

Grady struggled for a reply. Hewey spoke up, saying the first thing that popped into his head. "We're trailin' after some horses that strayed or got stolen."

Mitch shifted his attention to Hewey. "Name's Calloway, ain't it? Seems like me and you had a slight disagreement in town."

"It didn't amount to much. We had a drink together afterwards. Several of them, the best I recall."

Mitch asked, "What kind of horses was they?"

"Horses?"

"The ones you're trailin'."

Hewey said, "Oh, them. One was a roan, kind of between a gray and a blue, thirteen hands high, stockin' on his right forefoot. And there was a black with a blaze face, carries some kind of a Mexican brand on the left hip. Walks a little paddle-footed." He amazed himself at the ease with which he picked the descriptions out of thin air. He could only hope that Mitch did not ask him to repeat them.

Mitch studied the ground. "You say you've been trailin' them. I don't see no tracks here."

Hewey said, "We lost the trail back yonder a ways. We're tryin' to pick it up again."

Mitch sniffed. "Except maybe for Grady, I never saw a Two Cs hand who could track a steer herd through a cornfield. You boys had better give it up and go back home before Eli puts the law on you for trespass."

Hewey tried to sound plaintive. "What about those horses?"

"We'll scout around. If we find them we'll send them home. If we don't, C.C. can afford a little loss. He's got more cows than old Abraham."

Hewey nodded regretfully. "He'll be awful disappointed."

Snort moved up beside Hewey. He grinned, his gold tooth shining. "What color did you say them horses was, Hewey?"

Hewey realized Snort hadn't believed a word of it. He said, "Don't you remember?"

Snort shook his head. "I thought I wore the crown as the best liar in this part of the country, but after listenin' to you I'm afraid that crown don't set easy on my head anymore."

Grady shrugged. "Hell, Mitch, there ain't no horses. Hewey just made that up."

Mitch nodded. "I figured that."

Grady said, "C.C. sent us over here to hunt for Two Cs calves carryin' the J Bar brand. We didn't find any, but we found somethin' else you ought to know about." He described the hair-branded calves. "Don't let Eli know we told you. He'd lay it onto us."

Mitch frowned. "He'd blame you, anyway. He's got a suspicious mind when it comes to Tarpley and the Two Cs." He was deep in thought while he rolled a cigarette, then offered the sack to the others. "Best thing to do is for us to hunt down those sleepered calves and brand them on the sly. The less Eli knows about it, the better." Another thought came to him. "Whoever done this to us has probably done the same thing to the Two Cs."

Grady said, "If they have, C.C. would probably blame it on Eli. We'd best find them and brand them without makin' any noise about it."

Mitch agreed. "I wish the two knotheads would get together. They could fix this problem. But they'd probably go at one another like two old bulls and get somebody hurt. Somebody like us."

Grady said, "Kind of makes me homesick for the piney woods. But we had a lot of knotheads there, too. The whole world's infested with them. Come on, we'll show you them calves we found."

The calves were with their mothers, back in the shade of a thicket. Mitch dropped a loop over the neck of one and dragged it into the open. "Would you-all build a fire? I've got a cinch ring."

The two cows pawed dirt and threatened while Mitch used the heated ring to burn a proper J Bar on their bawling calves' hides. As soon as their offspring were released they led them back into the thicket in a long trot.

Snort had been staring off into the distance as if he had little interest in the proceedings. He said, "Eli would want us to escort you three off of his property. It wouldn't be much out of the way for us to go by town."

It would be considerably out of the way. Mitch said, "Not me. Every time Eli fires you, he hires you back. With me he might make it permanent."

Hewey saw a hopeful gleam in Walter's eyes. He quickly headed it off. "Great idea, Snort, but we'd better get back to the Two Cs and start lookin' for hair-branded calves of our own."

Without thinking about it, Hewey had adopted a typical cowboy's sense of commitment to the outfit for which he worked. So long as he drew its pay, it would be *our* ranch, *our* cattle.

Snort said, "You can do what you want to, Mitch. I'm goin' to town. If Eli asks about me, just tell him the last time you seen me I was headed straight up and anglin' a little to the west."

Watching Snort move away, Mitch shook his head. "There goes the best-natured old boy I ever knew, only he hasn't got a lick of judgment."

Hewey said, "I like a man who goes his own way, sunshine or rain. I wish I could be like that."

Walter said, "You're closer to it than you know."

They rode half a mile before Mitch reined to a stop, worry in his eyes. "You boys don't need me to guide you back to the Two Cs. I'd better trail after Snort and try to keep him out of trouble. If I can get him to the ranch before daylight, Eli won't ever have to know."

Walter offered, "If you need any help with him, I'll go along."

To Hewey's relief, Mitch said, "I can usually handle Snort, but thanks anyway."

Walter looked disappointed. Hewey knew he was thinking about that girl in town.

He said, "You're a cowboy. You can't afford a woman anyway."

"I may not always be a cowboy."

Hewey was not prepared for that. "A man couldn't want a better life than what we've got right here."

"Yes he could," Walter said.

No fence divided the two ranches. There was only a reluctant and unspoken understanding between Tarpley and Jessup regarding the boundary. In truth, neither actually owned all the land he claimed. Much still belonged to the state of Texas but was too far from Austin for authorities to come and measure each man's use and collect for it. The two ranchers simply paid lease on enough acreage to make a show of legality. They did not acknowledge that they had cattle on the rest.

Anyone else would have had a legal right to turn cattle loose on the unleased land, but few dared. Tarpley and Jessup had reputations that intimidated all but the most determined. Both men had a nagging fear that some interloper would come along and buy the state land out from under them. For that reason, each had bought selected tracts that offered water. Neither was yet willing to make the investment that would give him full title to all the land his cattle grazed.

After reaching the Two Cs, Hewey, Walter, and Grady rode through several bunches of cattle, carefully looking over the calves. Hewey saw the first of the hair brands and pointed. "There's one." It was not obvious. He would easily have overlooked the fraud had he not specifically been looking for it. The ranch's branding crew had innocently passed over these calves because they appeared to have been branded already.

Walter said, "And here's another."

The rest of the calves bore normal brands.

Grady said, "Let's brand them here and now."

They built a small fire and heated a cinch ring. Hewey and Walter held the calves down while Grady laboriously burned the brands.

Hewey said, "There's apt to be more."

Grady nodded. "C.C. ain't expectin' us back yet. We've got enough grub to keep us for several more days. What say we three stay out and hunt for hair brands? C.C. don't need to know."

Hewey said, "Whatever you say. I wonder who done this?"

"Some small owner, tryin' to get bigger."

Hewey tried to remember the small owners he had met. "What about that feller Lawdermilk? Alvin Lawdermilk."

Grady said, "I don't want to believe it could be Alvin. He seems like a good old boy. But you never can be sure about people."

Hewey said, "We ought to let the rest of the crew know what's happened so they can be on the lookout, too."

Grady agreed. "All except Fat Gervin. He'd run to C.C. like a schoolboy tattlin' to the teacher. Then C.C. might go gunnin' for Eli. There's a good chance we'd have to bury two stubborn old men, and maybe some of ourselves."

{ SEVEN }

The sheriff was waiting with Tarpley when Hewey rode up to the corrals on a young horse he was training. *Oh, hell!* Hewey thought. *C.C. has found out about those hair brands.* The Two Cs crew had found and quietly rebranded more than a hundred calves in the weeks since the discovery was made. Hewey gripped the hackamore rein tightly and stepped down as far from the saddle as his legs would reach. The bronc had a worrisome habit of pawing at a dismounting rider.

Trouble showed in Tarpley's face. "The sheriff's got somethin' to talk to you about, Hewey."

Hewey felt an anxious moment, though he could not remember that he had committed any serious breach of the peace. He had not even been to town lately. *Those damned calves. They're going to cause a war between C.C. and Eli Jessup yet,* he thought.

The sheriff's expression was as dark as Tarpley's. "Calloway, you remember the two fellers you testified against?"

The subject was not what Hewey expected. "Seems to me like I do." He tried not to be infected by the older men's mood, but it made him feel cold.

"You probably heard that Trumble—you called him

Smith—got away from Ranger Tanner some time back. He swore he would come back someday and get you."

"Seems to me like I remember that, too." Hewey had thought about it every day.

"There's a rumor that he's been seen. I don't know that I believe it. If I was him I'd be in California by now, or maybe sailin' to China. It don't make sense that he'd risk his neck just to get even with an ordinary cowpuncher like you. But criminals don't think like normal folks. Their brains are set in their heads sideways."

Walter had ridden up behind Hewey. He had heard most of it. Worriedly he said, "Maybe you'd better get away from here for a while."

Hewey appreciated his concern, especially because Walter had not been talking to him much.

"Where? I hate to just ride off and leave a good job. C.C. has been talkin' about givin' us a raise."

Tarpley spoke quickly, "I ain't said when that'll be."

The sheriff asked, "How good a shot are you, Calloway?"

Hewey twisted the hackamore rein. "I couldn't hit a bull in the butt with a shotgun."

"Too bad. You've got to figure that Trumble is right peart with a firearm. That's one of the few things most criminals are good at."

Hewey tried to rationalize. "If he was hell-bent on it, he could've found me easy before now."

The sheriff agreed. "It's probably a false rumor, but we'd better not forget that he cussed you every day he spent in my jail. He blamed you as much as he blamed Tanner. And you heard what he done to Tanner."

Hewey said, "I testified because I was sore about him

leavin' me and Walter to take the punishment for him. Besides, Tanner told me it was my bounden duty."

Tarpley said, "It happens I've got a job that'll take you away from here for a while. And you'll still draw your wages. By the time you get back, maybe Trumble will be on cornbread and beans again. Or smellin' flowers from the underside."

Hewey said, "I'm listenin' with both ears."

"I had figured on sendin' Grady, but you'll have to do. An old cowboy named Jerome Padgett wrote that he's located a herd of cows for me. They're somewhere south of San Antonio. He wouldn't tell me just where. I guess he was afraid I'd go around him and do him out of a commission."

Hewey said, "Surely you wouldn't do that."

"I thought about it, but I might need him again sometime. Anyway, I'm buyin' out the brand and eight hundred head that go with it. I'd like you to receive them for me, then help Jerome drive them out here."

Hewey grinned at Walter. This was the kind of work he liked. Despite bad weather, indifferent food, and several wild and wet river crossings, he had enjoyed the trip he and Walter made up the trail to Kansas with a herd out of central Texas. He told Tarpley, "If I get started, I can travel a good ways before sundown."

"Tomorrow mornin' will be soon enough. I doubt that Trumble will get to you before dark."

"I'm not afraid of Trumble. Well, not a lot."

"Come over to the house after supper. I'll give you directions and write a letter for you to carry."

Hewey recognized that if he left here alone, Walter would be without his supervision and counsel. There was no telling what mess his brother might get himself into. He asked, "Can I take Walter with me? I may need his help."

Walter made a quick objection, but Tarpley seemed not to hear it. He said, "I figured on Jerome Padgett hirin' whatever extra men he thinks he'll need. Down there they're mostly Mexicans, and they work cheap. But go ahead and take Walter if you want to. He's not costin' me much more than a Mexican would."

"I'm much obliged."

Walter was not, but he said nothing. His sour expression indicated that he would have much to say later.

Tarpley appeared ready to turn away, then paused. "One more thing. I'd like you to take Fat Gervin with you."

Hewey's jaw dropped. Fat would be about as much help as a broken leg. "What do we need with Fat?"

"I'd like to be shed of him for a while."

"Why don't you just fire him?"

"Can't. For some reason my wife and daughter have got attached to him. There's enough things botherin' my life without two naggin' women addin' to the load."

The last thing Hewey needed was Fat Gervin like a two-hundred-pound weight on his shoulders. But it was Tarpley's ranch, and his call. "Whatever you say. I just wish you'd tell him that I'm the boss till Jerome Padgett takes over."

"If he gives you any trouble, go off and leave him. You'd be doin' me a favor, and the womenfolks would blame you instead of me."

Hewey found little consolation in that. He said, "Maybe Padgett will run him off, and neither one of us will get blamed. What kind of feller is this Padgett?"

"He's had as many birthdays as I have. There ain't

much cow country that he hasn't left tracks in. As a young'un he drove herds all the way to New Orleans before the Yankee war. But don't worry about his age. He's forgotten more than you'll ever know about punchin' cattle."

That satisfied Hewey. "Maybe me and Walter can learn some things from him."

"Just watch and listen. Sober, he's a better hand than even Grady Welch. But he's got the same weakness as Snort Yarnell. It'll be up to you to keep him away from whiskey."

"How can we tell him what to do if he's bossin' the drive?"

"Figure it out as you go along. It's part of what I'm payin' you for."

Tarpley and the sheriff retreated toward Tarpley's house. Walter turned on Hewey, his voice sharp. "You had no call to volunteer me. You're just tryin' to keep me away from Eve."

"The last I saw, she was doin' that for herself."

"Only because you put me in a bad light with her. I've got a good notion to tell C.C. that I ain't goin'."

"Bosses don't like bein' told what a man won't do. The trip'll be good for you. I'll bet by the time we get back you'll forget all about that farm girl."

"I'll take you up on that bet. Twenty dollars. No, better make it ten."

Fat Gervin was unsaddling his horse. Walter asked, "Are you fixin' to tell Fat that he's goin' with us?"

"Not me. He'll take orders better if they come from C.C."

After putting away a healthy feed of red beans and Jessup beef, Hewey told Walter, "Let's go over to the big house and get our instructions." He used the term *big house* with a touch of irony.

Walter said curtly, "You go. You dragged me into this."

"Pa would be disappointed if he could see the way you're actin'. Our ma wouldn't be proud, either."

"If Pa had had you for a brother, he never would've got to marry Ma in the first place. Then where would me and you be?"

Fat Gervin sat on the edge of the narrow porch, talking to C.C.'s daughter. She seemed to be hanging on every word. Poor girl, Hewey thought. Even if she *was* plain as a board fence, she could do better than Fat if she lived in a town where she had a chance to meet more young men. As it was, she seldom saw anyone other than the Two Cs cowboys. Even among those, he thought, any would be a better catch than Fat.

He tipped his hat. "Evenin', Doreen. Is your daddy in the house?"

Tarpley hollered from inside. "The door's open."

Hewey hoped for Doreen's sake that Tarpley was keeping one eye on her and Fat, but the rancher was hunched at a battered rolltop desk. It appeared old enough and battered enough to have fallen out of an immigrant wagon on the Butterfield Trail. Tarpley looked up over a pair of black-rimmed reading glasses and nodded toward a rawhide-bottomed chair. "Set yourself down. I'm finishin' a letter for you to give to the seller, along with a draft on a San Antonio bank. You'll have to write in the figure after you and Jerome have done countin' the cattle. He could count a herd of jackrabbits, but he don't read and write very good." His eyebrows raised. "You *can* read and write, can't you?"

"Sure. I went plumb through the fourth grade. Our pa was real particular about us gettin' an education."

"Fourth grade is plenty for a cowboy. All he needs is to know more than the cows. Now looky here." He spread a map across the desk and traced with his forefinger. "Best thing is for you to go east and strike the head of the Middle Concho. Follow it to San Angelo. From there an old military road will take you down through the hills to Friedrichsburg and on to San Antone. That's where you'll find Jerome Padgett. He'll take you to where the cattle are at. I gather that they're a ways south of San Antone."

"How come he lives in San Antone but the cattle are someplace else?"

"He doesn't *live* anywhere. Home is wherever he happens to drop his bedroll of an evenin'. When you get to San Antone, hunt up a feller name of Patrick Appleby. Lives a couple blocks east of the Alamo. He can help you find Jerome."

"Do we follow the same route comin' back?"

"That'll be up to Jerome. He knows how to travel through the settled country without a bunch of mad farmers gettin' the whole outfit throwed in jail. He'll likely go around the towns. He wouldn't want a bunch of town dogs stampedin' the cattle through somebody's front parlor."

Tarpley told Hewey he could draw on the San Antonio bank for necessary supplies. "Go easy, though. I ain't fattenin' up a bunch of lean and hungry cowhands."

Mrs. Tarpley came out from the kitchen and offered Hewey a cup of coffee. She was a dainty little woman with a subdued voice she probably didn't get to use much when her husband was around. Tarpley told her sternly,

"He's just et." She retreated back into the kitchen before Hewey could accept the offer. Tarpley said, "Too much coffee can addle the brain near as bad as whiskey."

Hewey arose. Tarpley held up a finger. "Now listen good. I don't want everybody to know about this till we get the cattle home and situated. I got my eye on some land for sale on the other side of the river. If Eli gets wind of what I'm doin', that greedy old devil will bust a gut tryin' to buy it out from under me."

"He won't find out from me and Walter."

"If you run into any J Bar hands and they ask, tell them you're goin' back East to visit your folks."

"Ma died years ago. Pa just lasted a few years longer. Me and Walter ain't got any folks."

"Well then, just lie to them. Those J Bar hands will believe anything."

"Have you told Fat that he's goin' with us?"

Tarpley looked toward the front door. Fat still sat on the porch with Tarpley's daughter. "Nope. As you leave, tell him to come in here. I'll spoil his evenin' for him."

Hewey was pleased to comply.

Hewey and Walter saddled their horses soon after sunrise. Fat lingered at the breakfast table, throwing them late in getting started. He was puffed up like a toad when he finally appeared at the barn. He avoided speaking, but it was clear that he did not relish the prospect of a long ride to South Texas and an even slower cattle drive back. He mumbled to himself as he dragged his rigging out of the saddle shed.

Hewey was not eager for his company. He said, "We're startin'. You can catch up when you're ready." He led a packhorse carrying enough supplies to last through the trip. Tarpley did not trust merchants along the way because they tended to take advantage of travelers who had no other recourse. He owned half interest in the Upton City mercantile and got his goods at wholesale.

Walter did not speak half a dozen words the first couple of miles. Hewey tried several times to get him to break his silence, but to no avail. Then Walter veered off to the west.

Hewey pointed eastward. "San Angelo's thataway."

"Upton City is this way. I ain't goin' anyplace till I get things straight with Eve. Go by yourself if you don't like it."

Hewey did not like it, but he saw that Walter was going to be stubborn. He never had been able to understand stubborn people. "You don't know if she'll even talk to you."

"I'll do the talkin' if she won't."

"C.C. will count the days we're gone."

"I don't figure on marryin' C.C., but one of these days I'm goin' to marry Eve."

Walter's jaw was set like Ma's used to be when she made up her mind to something. Once she went that far, Hewey had never seen her back off. He saw nothing more to be said or done for now. Maybe while they were gone Eve would attach herself to some other poor cowpuncher or some Fort Worth drummer and let Walter go on being free like a man was supposed to be, the way Hewey was.

Fat had been trailing behind, his mood morose. He brightened as he realized they were headed for town. He caught up and stayed up.

They reached the boardinghouse before midday. The

noon dinner crowd had not begun to gather. Walter dismounted and boldly walked up the steps and onto the porch. He rapped his knuckles on the doorframe.

Mrs. Pearson appeared, carrying a dish towel. She placed both hands on her broad hips. "Well?"

Walter declared, "I've come to see Eve."

"We're busy fixin' dinner. Anyway, she's already said about all there was to say to you."

"Maybe so, but I've got something to say even if she ain't." He pushed past a flustered Mrs. Pearson and entered the house.

Hewey had never seen Walter be so assertive. It seemed a pity to waste all that newfound boldness on some farm girl so thin she hardly threw a decent shadow. He tied the horses and followed. He hoped Eve might throw a pan of dishwater at Walter and prove that Hewey had been right all along. Such a show would be worth seeing.

Eve was sliding a tray of biscuits into the oven when Walter spoke her name. Startled, she burned her hand and lifted it to her lips.

Walter blurted, "I've got somethin' to say to you."

She stared at him with wide eyes, the hand still against her mouth.

"Eve, I tried to tell you before, but you wouldn't listen. I thought you wanted to dance with Fat Gervin. I ought to've known it was all Hewey's doin'. I wouldn't hurt you for the world. I'm willin' to hurt Hewey, though, if it'll make you feel better. I'll beat him to a pulp."

Hewey backed up a step.

Eve shook off her surprise and offered Walter the slightest hint of a smile. "You'd whip your own brother? For me?"

"If you say so. He's not much of a fighter."

The look she gave Hewey indicated that she was thinking about it. He backed up a little more.

She asked, "Why? You don't know me, hardly."

"But I'm goin' to know you a lot better. One of these days I'm goin' to marry you."

She blinked a couple of times. "How do you know I'll marry *you?*"

"You will when you get to know me. And I'm goin' to see that you get to know me a lot better."

She seemed too stunned to reply.

Walter said, "Me and Hewey are goin' off on a trip for C.C. Tarpley. When we get back, I'll come callin'."

Eve recovered her voice. "I'm still provoked at you. I'm not promisin' you anything."

"I wouldn't expect you to, yet. I just want you to know I'm serious, and I've got honorable intentions."

She cast a disapproving glance at Hewey. "What about *him?*"

Walter said, "He don't count. It's just me and you."

Mrs. Pearson had been taken aback. Now she intervened. "If you men want dinner, you'll have to get out and let us finish cookin'."

Walter said, "Yes, ma'am. We'll be on the porch." He jerked his head at Hewey.

Hewey spoke to Mrs. Pearson. "Fat Gervin's outside. Would you feed him, too?"

Mrs. Pearson looked at Eve, posing a silent question. Eve said, "If he'll act the gentleman, I'll try to overlook his past behavior."

Outside, Hewey told Walter, "You've split your britches now."

"You already split them for me. I'm just tryin' to get them mended."

After dinner, Fat complained loudly about leaving town without a drink. Hewey gave in. "Just one, and then we're leavin'."

Walter hung back to talk to Eve some more. Hewey entered the saloon with Fat. He saw a face he remembered from the night of the dance. Rancher Alvin Lawdermilk leaned on the bar. "Howdy, cowboys. You-all come over and have one with me."

It was evident that he had already had one, or perhaps three.

Hewey was hesitant, for he suspected Lawdermilk might be the man hair-branding Two Cs and J Bar calves. But Lawdermilk was insistent, declaring, "I don't get to come to town every day, but my mother-in-law has run us plumb out of flour and sugar and stuff. I never seen a woman who could eat so much. Keeps one man busy all day choppin' enough firewood for the stove."

The bartender placed two glasses on the bar, and Lawdermilk filled them. "Belly up, cowboys. Ain't no use puttin' off till tomorrow what you can drink today."

Hewey asked, "How's your calf crop this year?"

"Best I ever saw. Even some of my bulls are havin' twins."

It may not be as good as he expects, Hewey thought. *We found most of those hair-branded calves.*

They rode at a leisurely pace that would not tax the horses, though Fat griped as if it taxed him considerably. Toward sundown Hewey saw a windmill against the skyline, its cypress-vaned fan turning lazily in a light wind. Though not yet plentiful, mills like this were beginning to spread across dry West Texas to bring water from underground in places where nature had not placed it on the surface. They allowed livestock to graze neglected areas formerly too far from water for animals to walk. They, along with barbed wire, were making it possible for settlement to survive in a desertlike environment.

Hewey said, "That'll be a good place to make camp. The horses need water."

They had left Upton City miles behind, but Walter's mind was still there. Hewey tried to pry some conversation out of him. "I'm not sure where the Middle Concho commences. If we follow this wagon trail east, we ought to find it in fifty or sixty miles. What do you think?"

Walter just grunted.

Fat had been trailing again, hunched in the saddle. Hewey had ignored his frequent requests that they stop and rest.

The windmill pumped water into a man-made shallow depression gouged into the ground. Elsewhere it would be called a pond. Out here it was called a tank. Though the facility was not yet old, small mesquites had already taken root around the edge of the water. Hewey had been told that cattle scattered the seed in their droppings. Several J Bar cows and calves loafed around the surface tank. They retreated fifty yards and turned to watch uneasily as the three men dismounted to let their horses drink.

Fat warned, "This is a J Bar windmill. Old Eli might get us throwed in the calaboose for trespassin'."

Hewey said, "It's a public road, and the Lord furnished the water."

"The Lord didn't put up the mill."

The site was devoid of firewood. Hewey told Walter, "If you'll unpack the chuck, me and Fat will gather some cow chips and get a little fire started."

Walter went about his task in silence. Fat was more vocal. Hewey pulled several handfuls of old grass and stuffed them beneath a small stack of dry chips. He struck a match and set the grass to smoldering, blowing on the blaze to help it take hold. In a little while the chips were glowing and throwing off heat enough to boil coffee and fry bacon. That and a couple of Soapy's cold biscuits made up what passed for a meal.

Hewey leaned back and savored a second cup of coffee. "This is the life we was born for," he said. "Breathin' the clean outdoor air, eatin' from the fat of the land. We've got good horses to ride and nobody around to boss us. Paradise couldn't be no better."

Fat whimpered, "Sand blew into my plate. The bacon was burned, and the water has got gyp in it."

Hewey said, "You'd complain if they hung you with a new rope."

Walter said, "Fat was born complainin'."

That was as many words as he had spoken since they had left Upton City. Hewey began to hope his brother was finally coming around.

He said, "The way I figure it, the pace we're settin' ought to have us in San Angelo the day after tomorrow. I don't reckon C.C. would begrudge us spendin' a night there and seein' the sights."

Fat braced up. Hopefully he said, "I hear San Angelo is a wide-open town."

Walter frowned. "C.C. wouldn't want us spendin' his money on such as that."

Hewey said, "It wouldn't be his money. I brought some of my own."

"I swear, Hewey, when you die you won't have enough money left to bury you. They'll just drag you off away from the house and throw a little brush on top of you."

"That's how I'd like to go. Spend my last dollar just before I take my last breath, and die with a smile on my face. That way I won't have a bunch of kinfolks fightin' over what I leave behind."

"You don't have any kinfolks except me."

"That's enough. As long as me and you stick together, ain't nothin' can throw us."

He heard hooves and the rattle of a vehicle on the rutted trail. A buggy approached, drawn by two horses. Another horse with a rider trotted alongside. "Somebody's travelin' kind of late."

Fat declared, "Oh Lord, that's Eli Jessup comin' yonder. Told you we might wind up in the calaboose."

Hewey said, "Don't worry. If he says anything, I'll give him back his water."

Jessup drew on the reins and stared at the three cowboys. Hewey recognized the rider as Jessup's foreman, Mitch. He said, "Light and hitch, Mr. Jessup, Mitch. Have some coffee."

Jessup climbed down, his legs stiff, his face weary. His heavy mustache seemed to droop. "Seems to me I know you boys. Work for C.C. Tarpley, don't you?"

Hewey said, "Yes, sir, that's a fact."

"I guess you realize you're on my land."

"Just this little bit of it. We couldn't hardly camp in the middle of the county road."

Jessup shrugged his broad shoulders. "I don't reckon you're hurtin' anything if you don't stay long. What you doin' here, anyway?"

Fat started to answer. "We're goin' . . ." Hewey poked him with his elbow and shut him up.

C. C. had told Hewey to lie if pressed. Hewey said, "We're on our way to San Angelo to see if it's all the town that we heard it is." That was not a lie, just something less than the whole truth.

Jessup seemed to find something mildly humorous. He winked at his foreman. "It's enough of a place to give you all the trouble you can handle if you don't keep one hand on your gun and the other on your purse. Ain't I right, Mitch?"

The big cowboy smiled. "It's Snort Yarnell's favorite town. That tells you somethin'."

Jessup looked toward the little campfire. "I believe you mentioned coffee?"

Hewey said, "We'll fix you a fresh pot. It'll just take a jiffy."

While the coffee boiled, Hewey watched the sun sink below the western horizon behind a thin curtain of red and purple clouds. "You-all are welcome to camp the night with us if you'd like to."

Jessup said dryly, "That's kind of you, seein' as it's my land. But me and Mitch have got to get back to headquarters. Got some cows comin' in tomorrow from over on the Concho." He frowned. "I'd as soon C.C. didn't hear about it till we get them settled."

Hewey said, "We won't be seein' C.C. for a while."

"Good. He used to be a reasonable feller before he got old and cranky. Bet you didn't know we was partners once."

Hewey had not known that.

Jessup said, "It came to a point that we was arguin' all the time, so we decided to split everything before one of us got killed. Things rocked along all right till we got to one old roan horse we both wanted. He wasn't worth fightin' over, but C.C. got so belligerent that I had to stand up for my rights. Mighty opinionated, C.C. is. He'd fight a dog over a bone. It's hard to understand a man who'd let a friendship die over one old horse."

Hewey nodded as if he agreed, though it seemed to him there had been two mighty opinionated men in the dispute.

Jessup said, "C.C. ain't spoke a civil word to me since, nor me to him. I've got no use for a man that damned contrary."

Hewey asked, "What ever became of the horse?"

Jessup scowled. "Some horse thief run off with him. I mortally hate a thief."

Jessup drank his coffee and motioned to Mitch. "We'd better be movin' on if we want to get home before the rooster wakes up." He climbed into the buggy and called, "You boys watch out for yourselves. They got sharpers in San Angelo that can steal your underwear without takin' your pants off."

Fat asked innocently, "How can they do that?"

As the buggy departed, Hewey said, "He ain't got horns and a tail after all. At least, I didn't see them."

Walter nodded. "But if C.C. and him ever lock horns, we don't want to be standin' in the way."

{ EIGHT }

The route to San Angelo was marked by two small round mountains side by side on an undulating plain.

Fat asked, "You know what those make me think of?"

Hewey said, "I can imagine. Don't you ever think about anything except women?"

"Women, whiskey, and good eats. What else is there?"

Walter said curtly, "You do all right with the whiskey and the eats, Fat, but you don't know how to treat a decent woman."

Hewey felt encouraged. Walter was finally beginning to open up.

As the town came into sight, Fat said, "I vote that we spend a little of C.C.'s money and get us a hotel room. He can afford it."

Hewey and Walter had never slept in a hotel room. Hewey could only imagine how it would be to bask in such luxury. "I'll bet even C.C. never stays in a hotel. Sleep in a wagonyard, maybe, but not a hotel. That's for rich businessmen and whiskey drummers." He looked at Walter. "What do you think? Should we camp on the river and stake the horses out to grass, or put them in a livery barn and get them some oats?"

Walter frowned. "Why ask for my opinion? You'll do what you want to anyway."

"I always like to know what you're thinkin', even when you're wrong."

"C.C. would never pay us back for the stable bill. Whatever we spend, it'll be our own money."

Hewey shrugged. "Then we'll stake them out and spend our money for whiskey."

He had never been to San Angelo. He knew from conversation that it owed its birth to the confluence of the three Concho rivers and to a frontier army post established some twenty years earlier to protect westbound freighters, immigrants, and a stagecoach line from Comanches and Kiowas. Now Indian troubles were over in this part of the country. Gossips were saying the army's days here were numbered. The military had the same outlook as C. C. Tarpley: never spend a dollar until it has been squeezed like a lemon.

Following the river, Hewey saw a large tent. He said, "Reckon there's a circus in town? I'd sure admire to see an elephant."

Walter said, "It appears to be a camp meetin'. I believe I'll go tonight. I'd like to hear a little preachin' from somebody besides you."

"I wonder what kind of church it is, one that sprinkles you or one that tries to drown you?"

"I was baptized a long time ago. So were you, only you've probably forgotten about it."

"I remember. I must've swallowed a gallon of muddy water. I've shied away from preachers ever since."

They found a place along the river where the grass had not been grazed off. Hewey asked a passing rider if there would be any objection to their camping there.

"Not from me," the passerby said, "but it ain't mine. It's part of the town site, so I reckon it's open to whoever comes."

The three unsaddled and took the load from the pack-horse. The rider, appearing to be in no hurry, watched them stake the animals on long ropes that allowed plenty of grazing room.

Hewey asked, "Where can we buy a decent supper?"

The horseman pointed. "Cheapest is a little hole in the wall over on Concho Avenue. The Dutchman'll sell you a big bowl of chili for ten cents. Then there's a Greek place a ways up the street. It'll cost you more, but it's easier on the stomach."

Hewey said, "Greek sounds foreign to me. I reckon we'll take the Dutchman's chili."

Fat had grown fidgety like a horse wanting to be on the go. "You-all suit yourselves. I been told there's a fancy house here where all the women are good-lookin' and ready to play."

Hewey said, "You better not forget where this camp is at. We'll be travelin' about daylight. If you're not here, we'll leave without you."

Fat hurried away at a pace Hewey had seldom seen him achieve unless a cow was chasing him.

The chili joint was easily found, but not before Hewey had located three saloons and mentally filed away their locations for future reference. By the time he and Walter finished the chili and two cups of coffee, they had spent fifteen cents apiece.

To the southeast, across the river, Hewey could see the stone buildings of the sprawling fort. A bugle's notes drifted softly on a light southern breeze as the flag was lowered for the day. He had thought once about joining the army but decided it imposed too many rules for a free spirit. He saw several soldiers and realized they were black. This was a buffalo soldier post.

A large man walked up beside Hewey and pointed with a glowing cigar. "I wisht you'd look at them burr-heads tryin' to act like soldiers. Put a uniform on them and they think they're as good as white folks. It's high time the army pulled them out of here. We don't need them anymore."

Walter always sided with the underdog, for he had been one much of his life. He said, "I'll bet when you *did* need them you were glad they were here."

"It was different then. But we ain't seen an Indian in years. We need them darkies to be gathered up and gone."

Hewey said, "What would become of this town if the army was to close the post? It must put a pretty penny in people's pockets."

"We hear the railroad is comin' in. Give us the rail-road and we won't need Grierson's brunettes."

Hewey recalled hearing that Grierson was the post commandant's name. He shrugged. What happened to San Angelo or to the military was somebody else's worry. He was just passing through.

He and Walter returned to camp to check on the horses and found them contentedly cropping grass at the ends of their tethers. Hewey said, "Walter, I'm ready for a drink. You comin'?"

Walter shook his head. "I'm goin' to the meetin'. I don't want to have whiskey on my breath."

"Suit yourself. I guarantee I'll have more fun than you will." He walked back down Chadbourne Street and stood on the corner at Concho Avenue, trying to decide which saloon to try. The first proved to be a little fancy for his taste, but he went in anyway. It offered a shiny mahogany bar and a large mirror with a hand-carved frame. On one end of the bar was a free lunch of bread, sausages, and boiled eggs. It struck him that he could have eaten here and saved fifteen cents for a better use.

He ordered a whiskey and stood at the bar alone. He counted a dozen customers, but none paid any attention to him. They looked like bankers and lawyers and drummers, for the most part, not the kind of people eager to strike up a conversation with a dusty cowpuncher just in from the trail. Not even the bartender spoke to him beyond asking his pleasure and telling him the price. The whiskey was first-rate, but the company was cold. As darkness came and the stars began to show, he walked outside to hunt for a friendlier place.

He found it farther down on Concho. It was a plain-looking joint with a simple bar of pine lumber. Instead of a mirror it featured a painting of a woman lounging on a bed with nothing to hide her several charms except a strategically placed wisp of cloth. It was the kind of art he could appreciate. He gave it a careful scrutiny while he sipped at his drink, thinking that Fat would probably appreciate it, too, if he were not entangled with the real thing. The whiskey was not as good as at the other place, but he liked the atmosphere.

Two black soldiers came in and stood a little way down the bar. The bartender poured drinks and said, "Payday at the fort, ain't it?"

"Sure is," one replied. "Our pockets are jinglin'."

The bartender said, "Apt to be a busy night, then."

Hewey heard a low growl. A customer sitting alone at a table glowered at the soldiers through a spiral of cigar smoke. Hewey realized this was the man who had spoken to him at the river.

The soldiers caught the hostile look and did not linger long. Uncomfortable, they left without ordering another drink.

The bartender complained, "Arlow, payday don't come but once a month. I wish you wouldn't spoil it for me by chasing off my customers."

"Time was when niggers wasn't allowed where white men were drinkin'."

"You've got to understand that I'm in business. I need every dollar I can put together."

"I never could see a man sellin' out his principles for a handful of silver."

An old man at another table impatiently tapped his cane against the floor. "I remember a time when the Comanches had me surrounded. I was mighty glad to see them black boys come ridin' over the hill. I'd've been pleasured to stand and drink with them, and I'd've paid for the whiskey."

Arlow glared. "You old fart, ain't it time you was home in bed?" He went back to his drink.

Another black walked in. He was not wearing a uniform. The bartender looked him over, then nodded in recognition. "I didn't hardly know you in them town clothes, boy. What went with the soldier outfit?"

"Finished my enlistment. I ain't leavin' nothin' here but my tracks. First, though, I'll have some of the best whiskey you got."

"The best? You sure?"

"I can afford it. I got my musterin'-out money."

The barman reached down and fetched a bottle with a

label brighter than the one from which Hewey's drink had come.

Hewey felt the change in his pocket and said, "I believe I'll have a little of the same." The bartender poured it. Hewey raised it in salute. "Here's to the United States Army."

Arlow pushed up from his table, face reddening. "What kind of a white man are you, drinkin' with a darky?"

Hewey's face warmed. "I'm a free-born citizen of the sovereign state of Texas, and I'll drink with whoever I want to."

Arlow declared, "Maybe you've got a little tar in your blood, too." He turned, jabbing his cigar in the soldier's direction. "You've had your drink. Now get your black butt out of here."

The soldier straightened as if standing at attention on the parade ground. "I was born in bondage, but now I'm as free as any man. I'll leave when it suits me."

Arlow grabbed the cane from the old man's hand and struck the soldier across the side of the head. "I don't take sass from no uppity nigger."

The sudden move took Hewey by surprise. He saw the soldier hunch down, then bring his fist up like a hammer. Arlow's head jerked under the blow. He grabbed at the bar but landed heavily on his shoulder. He came roaring to his feet and drew a pistol from his boot. As he charged past, Hewey stuck out his foot. Arlow tripped and fell forward, striking his head against the brass rail at the foot of the bar. He lay too stunned to move. Blood trickled from a gash on his forehead.

The soldier held his hand against the place where the cane had struck him. His ear was bleeding. The bartender

said, "There's hell to pay now, boy. You'd better git before Arlow gets up. He's got a streak of mean in him a
yard wide. He's apt to kill you."

"He hit me first."

"But he's white, and you ain't."

The soldier replied, "I said I'd leave when I'm ready.
Well, I reckon I'm ready." He nodded a silent *thank you*
to Hewey and disappeared out the door.

The old man picked up his cane. It had a little blood on
it. He wiped it off on Arlow's trousers leg, then swung it
and gave Arlow a smart lick across the rump. He dropped
the big man's fallen pistol into a tobacco-stained spittoon.
"Old fart, am I?"

The bartender turned a baleful gaze in Hewey's direction. "You tripped Arlow, didn't you?"

"He just ran into my foot, is all. Some big men are
clumsy."

"He ain't much on forgiveness. If I was you, I'd be as
smart as that darky and make myself scarce, too. I'd get
plumb out of town."

Hewey saw that Arlow was beginning to stir. He said,
"Sometimes you got to choose between bein' brave and
bein' smart." He gulped the rest of his drink, took a lin-
gering look at the painting, and walked out into the street.
He tried to look nonchalant, but he glanced back toward
the saloon for any sign of pursuit.

He considered going to one of the other whiskey
joints but decided that Arlow might come looking for him.
He thought of the camp meeting. Arlow would not expect
to find him there. For that matter, Hewey surprised himself a little. He wondered how the camp-meeting idea had
come to him.

He heard the crowd singing an old gospel song. He

remembered the melody but not the words. Something about salvation.

The tent was lit by lanterns. Its sides were rolled up to let fresh air circulate. Hewey walked slowly around it until he saw his brother sitting on a bench, sharing a hymn book with an elderly woman. *At least,* Hewey thought, *he doesn't have his mind on romance.* He edged into the tent and made his way to Walter's side.

Walter's eyes widened as if he had seen the dead come to life. He whispered, "How come you suddenly got religion?"

Hewey wondered if Walter could smell his breath. "Don't you think it's about time?"

"It's considerable overdue."

The woman looked over her glasses at them and frowned her disapproval of their talking during the service. Walter went back to singing. Hewey could not see the hymnbook from where he stood, but he figured it was just as well. His voice might break up the proceedings.

Men came down the aisle with a collection plate. *I would get here just in time for that,* Hewey thought. He dug two bits from his pocket, changed his mind, and increased his contribution to four bits. He would have spent that on drink anyway had it not been for Arlow. Walter smiled at Hewey's show of generosity.

It's worth it if he finally gets over being mad at me, Hewey thought.

As the preacher wound down a strong sermon against sin and extolled the virtues of tithing, movement outside the tent caught Hewey's eye. Arlow and two friends were studying the crowd. Hewey turned his head away, hoping Arlow would not see him.

The service broke up after a closing hymn. Hewey

motioned for Walter to lead the exit on the opposite side of the tent from where Arlow had been. But Arlow had moved. He accosted Hewey in the edge of the lantern light and tapped him with his forefinger. His head was bandaged.

"Ain't you the punkin' roller that tripped me in the saloon?"

Hewey put on his most innocent face. "A saloon? I'm a church-goin' man." He feared his breath would betray him, but Arlow's was so strong that he could not have smelled anyone else's.

Arlow shoved his face close to Hewey's. "I'd swear you're the same bird. Maybe if the light was better . . ." He seemed inclined after a moment to give Hewey the benefit of the doubt. "We're lookin' for a nigger that attacked me. I don't reckon you've seen him?"

"How would I know him, seein' as I was here at the meetin'?" Hewey had noticed a number of black people standing just outside the tent, listening to the service but remaining apart from the whites. He doubted the one Arlow sought was among them. For his own safety the soldier had probably put some distance behind him by now.

Arlow said, "If we find him, me and my friends are goin' to skin him out and hang his hide on the saloon door. And if I find the son of a bitch that tripped me, I'll cut off a strip of his hide and make me a quirt."

He gave Hewey another suspicious looking-over before he and his friends melted away into the darkness.

Walter faced Hewey with his mouth hanging open. "What kind of trouble have you got yourself into now?"

Hewey shrugged. "He must've mistaken me for some other handsome feller."

"If you wasn't in trouble you wouldn't have joined back up with me so soon. I wouldn't have seen you till you came draggin' in about daylight."

As they walked toward camp Hewey decided to tell Walter what had led to Arlow's fall. "Wasn't my fault he didn't see my foot. He ought not to drink so much."

"I never would've thought you'd get yourself in Dutch over a darky."

"It wasn't all that much. You'd have done the same if you'd been there."

"I guess you did right. But we might be smart to break camp early in case he comes huntin' for you in the mornin'."

"Yeah, he's cost San Angelo our business."

{ NINE }

H ewey and Walter broke camp at the first good light. As they had anticipated, Fat had not shown up.

Hewey said, "We warned him he'd better be here."

Walter finished tying their load on the packhorse. "He knows we're takin' the San Antonio road. He can catch up to us if he wants to. Otherwise . . ."

Hewey completed the sentence. "To hell with him."

The military road from Fort Concho to Fort McKavett led southeastward through rolling grassland and broad flats dotted with dense mottes and scattered big live-oak trees whose heavy branches reached out far enough to shade a goodly number of cattle. Hewey judged it to be good cow country, for those he saw looked fleshier than those out on the Pecos.

They had traveled about two miles when he heard a horse loping up behind them. His first thought was of Arlow. He turned in the saddle to look back. He was unsure whether to feel relieved or not. "I hoped Fat would stay in San Angelo."

Fat Gervin's face was flushed, and he was almost out of breath as he reined up beside the brothers. "How come you-all didn't wait on me? I ain't even had any breakfast."

Hewey said, "Ain't that a shame. You're liable to waste away."

Walter said, "We told you this trip is strictly business. Where were you all night? No, don't tell me. I don't think I want to hear about it."

Fat broke into a broad grin. "There was this girl. Red hair and the bluest eyes you ever seen. It was all I could do to get up this mornin' and leave her."

Hewey asked, "Have you got any money left?"

"Just a little. But I'm tellin' you, boys, she was worth it."

Walter frowned. "What would C.C.'s daughter think?"

Fat's grin slipped away. "You ain't goin' to say anything about it, are you?"

"Not if you hold up your end on the rest of this trip."

They passed a band of sheep scattered over an open prairie. A Mexican herder watched them but showed no reaction until Hewey waved. The herder made a small and tentative gesture in response. Hewey supposed that Mexicans hereabouts, badly outnumbered, adhered to a cautious policy of speaking only if spoken to when dealing with Anglos. The Alamo was not yet forgotten.

Fat's face twisted in distaste. "Sheep! Ain't nothin' stinks worse."

Walter said, "They ain't that bad. A bunch of cows don't smell like flowers either, especially if they been on green feed and their bowels are loose. Folks say sheep are good money makers. When I get a place of my own someday, I'll have me a little flock."

Hewey asked, "How do you think you'll ever get a place of your own at six bits a day?"

"By savin' six bits a day. It'll add up after a while."

"You can have my share of sheep, and the land, too.

Any time I take a notion to get up and go, I don't want nothin' holdin' me back."

"What'll you do when you get old?"

"I don't expect I'll live that long."

Hewey caught a glimpse of someone partially hidden in the dark protection of a motte. He thought again of Arlow, but it seemed unreasonable that the man carried a heavy enough grudge to set up an ambush miles from town.

As the horsemen neared the motte, the man warily stepped out into the open.

Fat exclaimed, "A nigger. Probably goin' to try to bum some money off of us."

Hewey recognized the retired soldier whose retort to Arlow had set off a brief tempest in the saloon. He told Walter, "That's the darky Arlow was lookin' for. If he ain't got a horse, he must've walked all night."

The black man approached with his hat in his hand. "I don't reckon you gentlemen would have some water I could borry?"

Hewey lifted a canteen from the horn of his saddle. The soldier clutched it eagerly and took several long swallows without pausing for breath. "I'm much obliged. There's a good spring farther on a ways, but I ain't sure I could've made it there." He looked closer at Hewey. "You're the gentlemen that helped me last night."

Hewey was unaccustomed to being called a gentle-man. "It wasn't much. I just stuck my foot out, and be danged if that clumsy Arlow didn't fall over it."

"I thank you kindly. He was cocked and primed to shoot me." The soldier looked back apprehensively. "You don't reckon he might be trailin' me?"

"I wouldn't think so. Most likely he's got his head under his wing this mornin'. Probably can't even remember what you look like. Where are you headed afoot?"

The soldier shrugged. "Someplace where there ain't no trouble. You reckon there *is* such a place?"

"I never found one."

The soldier handed the canteen back to Hewey. "You-all mind if I travel along with you a ways? I know this trail. Been up and down it a good many times."

"Think you can keep up, walkin'?"

"I was infantry."

Hewey said, "Sure, come along." He had neglected to ask Walter, and he looked to him now for belated approval. Fat's opinion did not matter.

Walter said, "Why not? He knows the trail. Me and you might come to a fork and not know which way to go."

The soldier said, "There's a stagecoach stand up ahead. Feller calls it Toenail Station. Says he ain't got nothin' but a toenail hold."

Hewey said, "That's all me and Walter have had most of our lives. By the way, what'll we call you?"

"My old mama named me Gabriel. She said when I was born I squalled louder than old Gabriel's horn. Friends just call me Gabe. That don't sound so high-falutin, and it's easier to write."

Hewey was a little surprised. "You can read and write?" It was his impression that most black folks couldn't.

"Army chaplain taught me. Said just because I chanced to be born a slave wasn't no reason for me to stay ignorant."

"I'm Hewey, and this is my brother Walter." Almost as an afterthought, he added, "That there is Fat Gervin."

Sullenly Fat said, "The name is Frank."

Gabe nodded. "Mr. Hewey. Mr. Walter. Mr. Fat."

Walter shook his head. "*Mister* is what they used to call our daddy, but he was old. You don't have to use it for us."

Hewey suspected he would anyway. The racial divide was still formidable. Blacks and Mexicans were expected to feign deference whether they felt it or not.

Gabe fetched a blanket roll he had dropped at the edge of the motte. It was tied with a rope and had a loop so he could hang it over his shoulder.

Hewey said, "You travel light."

"A foot soldier can't afford to own more than he can tote. Every mile you walk, it gets heavier. How far you-all goin'?"

Hewey said, "San Antonio, then south a ways."

"We been marched all the way down to San Antonio and back several times. They got a big army post there named for Mr. Sam Houston. He must've been a mighty man to get his name put on so much stuff. I don't reckon there'll ever be anything marked with my name on it unless it's a tombstone."

Fat edged up close to Hewey. "I don't see why we're lettin' him come along. Ain't nothin' good'll come of it, travelin' with a nigger. Like as not he'll steal what he can get his hands on and slip away when we're not watchin'."

Hewey winked at Walter. "Then maybe you'd better keep an eye on him for us."

Fat said, "I'll do that. I'll damn sure do that."

They might have reached Fort McKavett in a day if they had pushed, but Hewey saw no reason to do so. Tarpley had given them no specific date by which they must be back at the ranch. There were the horses to consider, and Gabe. Hewey was a little surprised that the soldier kept up as well as he did. A couple of miles would have finished Hewey, for it was the cowboy way to ride horseback if the distance was as much as a hundred yards. Used to walking, Gabe often moved out in front of the horses.

They did not find a convenient spring or creek late in the afternoon, so they made a dry camp. They had water enough in canteens for making coffee, and the horses had drunk their fill a little earlier as they came upon a small natural basin holding water from a recent rain. Supper was three squirrels Gabe had shot with Hewey's pistol. Hewey had tried but had managed only to splinter bark from the trees and send the squirrels scurrying for cover.

He considered giving the weapon to Gabe but decided he might need it in a pinch someday. It could serve as collateral for a small loan if his pockets were empty.

In answer to a question from Walter, Gabe said he had been born in Mississippi to a mother who was a house slave. After emancipation she had continued to work in the same house but drew a small wage that gave her a tentative sense of independence.

He said, "She couldn't read the scriptures, but she would walk ten miles to hear a preacher talk about them. She named all us children after them old fellers in the Bible. She wouldn't name none of us Judas, though. That's where she drawed the line."

Walter said, "Give a dog a bad name and you hang him."

"I never was keen on workin' in the cotton fields, but there wasn't much else I knowed how to do," Gabe said. "Soon as I got my growth I lit out. Went down to New

Orleans because folks said you could pick up money right off of the street. I found out folks lied. Wasn't no easy money anyplace."

Walter said, "A man is supposed to sweat for what he gets. Otherwise he can't take pride in it."

"Pride is for them that can afford it. One day a man come along talkin' about the army, and how we could make twelve dollars a month and never set foot in a cotton patch. All we had to do was march a little and shoot a gun." He frowned, remembering. "Oh, how that man lied! He'll get a scorchin' when Gabriel blows that horn."

Hewey did a quick mental calculation. What Tarpley paid him wasn't much, but it beat army wages. Seemed like the meaner the job, the less it paid.

Gabe said, "If all the walkin' I done in the army had been in a straight line, I'd've fell right off the edge of the earth. At least we et regular most of the time."

Hewey said, "Havin' enough to eat and a place to sleep is worth more than money. Ain't that so, Walter?"

Walter replied, "If you have money, them things just naturally come to you. I don't aim to be poor all my life."

Hewey said, "A man ain't poor for not havin' money. He's poor from wantin' too much."

They washed their faces and watered their horses in the San Saba River before riding into Fort McKavett.

Gabe said, "We'd all better drink up. It's a ways to the next water."

Hewey replied, "I'm ready for somethin' stronger than water."

Fat said, "Me too."

Fort McKavett was a ragtag town smaller than San Angelo. Citizens had taken advantage of the abandoned fort, using some of the rock buildings for dwellings, barns, and storage, dismantling others for the roofing lumber and window and doorframes. Though limited in size, the place did not lack for enterprises catering to the drinking man.

Walter said, "Ain't much to it, but I guess it's big enough for somebody to get in trouble if he really tried."

Gabe showed a disliking for the place. "If it's all the same, I'd like to stick close by you-all. They've got a reputation here for siccin' the dogs on black folks. The only time us soldiers felt safe was when we stayed in bunches."

Walter said, "I don't see that we need to stop. We've got all the supplies we need."

Hewey said, "We left Angelo quicker than we figured on. Wouldn't hurt to clear the dust out of our throats. There's still aplenty of miles ahead of us."

Fat added, "Thirsty miles."

Hewey picked a small frame structure that might have been thrown together by a drunken carpenter. Some of the nails were bent over, and dents in the wood indicated many false hammer strikes. Uneven red letters painted on a board declared that it served the finest liquors south of St. Louis.

"That takes in a lot of territory," Hewey observed. "Sounds like my kind of place."

Walter looked dubious, but he tied his horse alongside Hewey's. Only a handful of people were on the streets. They seemed to be staring at the newcomers, or perhaps only at Gabe. Nervously Gabe said, "I ain't stayin' out here by myself. I'm comin' in with you."

Hewey's eyes were slow in adjusting to the poor light.

There were no customers. He saw a huge man get up from a table and move ponderously behind the crude plank bar. His voice sounded as if it came from the bottom of a barrel. "What'll it be, gents?"

Hewey laid a few coins on the bar, and the barman picked them up with a hand that was as big as a satchel. He seemed to notice Gabe for the first time. He demanded, "Did that boy come in here with you-all?"

Hewey felt his pulse picking up. "He did. We're all in need of a drink."

The barman frowned. "He'll have to get his from the cistern. And he'd better have his own cup, because he ain't drinkin' from the one out there."

Walter said, "We don't none of us really need a drink, Hewey. Let's get out of here." He took a couple of steps. Gabe was two paces ahead of him.

Hewey wanted to make for the door, but he was too provoked to move. He could hardly believe he heard himself say, "He already took our money. We got drinks comin'. Four of them."

Gabe said, "I ain't much given to drink. A sip of water from the cistern would suit me fine."

The proprietor slid several coins across the bar. "Here's your money back. I could whip you in a minute, cowboy, but if we was to fight, we'd bust up this place. I'd as soon not have to do the fixin' afterwards."

Hewey saw that the man was giving him a chance to back away with minimum compromise to dignity. As a boy he had avoided schoolyard fights when he could. Even on the few occasions when he had won, he still hurt. Boyhood bruises and contusions had convinced him it was better to be embarrassed for retreating in haste than to be embarrassed for getting the whey knocked out of him.

He said, "I'd hate to see this joint wrecked any worse than it already is." The saloon looked as if someone had turned a bull loose inside. He counted the money to be sure the bartender was not cheating him.

The barman looked relieved. It would not require much violence to bring the flimsy walls crashing down. "You three are welcome, but next time, leave that darky outside."

Hewey said, "There ain't goin' to be a next time." Fort McKavett would have to get along without their financial support.

Outside, Hewey was torn between anger over the barman's attitude and relief that he had been given a way out of a fight that could have had but one outcome.

Fat was frustrated. "I told you this nigger was liable to be trouble. Now we didn't get nothin' to drink."

Gabe said, "I'm afraid I been a trial to you gentlemen. On account of me, you're leavin' thirsty."

Walter said, "We're lucky we're not leavin' bloody. I swear, Hewey, sometimes your mouth runs a mile ahead of your brain. That barkeep could've cracked us like eggshells. All of us."

"He backed down."

"No, he gave *you* a chance to back down. I was scared you wasn't goin' to take it."

Hewey said, "I wasn't all that thirsty anyhow."

Fat protested, "Well, I was." His eyes were red, his sweaty face flushed from the effects of a long night and little sleep. His shirt was wet under the armpits and along his back.

Several people on the streets stopped what they were doing to watch with curiosity as the four trailed out, a black man walking ahead of three white cowboys on horseback. Hewey looked back in regret. He had not drunk from the river, anticipating something better in town. Now he was thirsty. Walter would probably chide him if he mentioned it, so he did not.

He even felt a brief resentment against Gabe. Had the ex-soldier not been there, they would probably still be in the saloon, enjoying a respite from travel. He realized the feeling was not justified. The problem had not been Gabe himself; it had been the bartender's unjustified reaction to him.

The wagon road became rougher, snaking its stony way between limestone hills and around heavy live-oak mottes. Though Gabe had been strong early in the trip, the uneven ground was wearing him down. Instead of walking ahead of the horses much of the time, he began falling behind. More than once the riders stopped to let their horses "blow" while Gabe caught up.

Walter said, "I'm kind of saddle-weary. Let's get down and set a spell."

Hewey knew that was more for Gabe's sake than Walter's own. "Been hopin' you'd say that."

Fat said, "It's about time. I'm gettin' tired of all this scenery." Sweat trickled from beneath his hat and into his eyes. He wiped a sleeve across his flushed face.

Gabe seated himself on a rock and removed one shoe. He rubbed his foot. "Looks like this sole is goin' to wear plumb through before we get to San Antonio."

Hewey considered letting Gabe ride the packhorse, but they could not afford to jettison any supplies. He said, "We got to see about gettin' you somethin' to ride. You *can* ride a horse, can't you?"

"Fair to middlin', but I ain't no bronc rider. Any old skate would do for me as long as it's got four legs and can walk."

"Maybe we'll come upon somethin' along the way."

They rested a while, then resumed the journey. After a time they came upon a moving set of goats whose long hair shone white in the sun. Hewey said, "What you reckon those are? I never seen the like of them before."

Walter could only shrug.

Fat said, "A goat is a goat."

The animals were driven by a young black woman riding bareback on a dun horse. Gabe exclaimed, "Lordy, would you look at that." He stared, his mouth sagging open. As she approached, he exclaimed, "Young missy, are you real?"

She looked back at him as if she did not believe *he* was real. Crisply she said, "What do you think I am, a ghost? You see me, don't you?"

"But what're you doin' out here in the middle of nowhere?"

"This ain't nowhere. It's somewhere, and I live here. What I'm doin' is, I'm drivin' these goats to the pen so Mr. Hickson can look them over for wormies."

"Them's funny-lookin' critters."

She said, "They're Angoras. Folks say they come from far off, some place called Turkey."

Gabe said, "Never heared of it. Must be back East, in Yankee country."

Fat mused, "Why would anybody want to turn goats loose on good cow range? I'd as soon keep hogs."

The girl said, "These ain't no ordinary goats. Mr. Hickson cuts their hair off, and people weave it into rugs and such. Mohair, they call it."

Fat said, "They're still goats."

Gabe stood as if paralyzed, staring at the girl. She said impatiently, "Would you move yourself out of the way? I'm tryin' to drive these goats."

The riders had already given her room. Gabe quickly stepped aside. As she rode past him she said, "What're you doin' without a horse anyway? A man afoot out here is as helpless as a newborn baby, and you look to me like you done been weaned."

She went on, following the bleating goats. Gabe stared after her. "Who'd've thought I'd see somethin' like her in a place like this?"

Fat commented, "She's a little dark-complected for me."

Ahead, Hewey saw a ranch house built of chiseled limestone blocks. It lay just off the road a hundred yards or so. Beyond it sprawled several corrals formed of upright cedar stakes set tightly against one another and tied with rawhide. Most of the bark had been stripped off. A gate swung open, and the girl drove the goats through it.

Hewey licked his dry lips. "Maybe we can get a drink of water from that windmill yonder."

A gray-bearded man about as skinny as C. C. Tarpley walked among the long-haired Angoras the girl had just brought in. She slipped the bridle from her horse and started toward the house after giving Gabe a long look. The rancher grabbed a goat by its leg. It let out a plaintive cry as if it were being butchered. It had blood on its forehead. The rancher smeared a black liquid over the wound and turned the goat loose. It bounded across the pen, ramming its way into a mass of animals in a corner.

The three riders went to a nearby windmill and drank their fill of water from an open pipe that drained into a surface tank. Gabe waited until they were done, then cupped his hands beneath the pipe and sipped. The goat man walked over to the picket fence and waited, wiping his face with a red bandanna. "Got to keep watch on these crazy billies," he explained. "They get to buttin' heads and don't know when to stop. If they draw blood, first thing you know they've got a case of screwworms."

Hewey knew about screwworms. Hatched from blowfly eggs in animal wounds, they were a summertime scourge that could cripple or kill livestock and wildlife.

The rancher wore a shapeless hat that should be black but was gray with imbedded dirt and spotted with dried animal blood. His clothes were dusty, stained, and patched in several places. Streaks in his beard revealed him to be a tobacco chewer. Squinting one heavily browed eye, he said, "Hickson's my name. You fellers look like cowpunchers to me, except for that dark-complected boy. What's the matter, he lose his horse?"

Hewey said, "He never had one. I don't suppose you might have one for sale?"

The rancher gave Gabe a speculative study. "Belinda told me about you, boy. Said you looked her over like she was a filly you was thinkin' of buyin'."

"I didn't mean no harm."

"She's my cook's daughter. Just because she's colored, don't get the notion she's somebody you can play around with. She don't have any truck with drifters that come ramblin' through here."

Gabe said, "I had no such notion. Didn't have a notion of no kind."

"Good. Now, about a horse. Might be I have one for sale if you ain't lookin' for a show animal." The rancher jerked his head as a signal for the travelers to follow him to the barn. He opened a gate into another pen and pointed at one of the droopiest-looking animals Hewey had ever seen. It was a bay with rough hair badly in need of a curry comb. A few burrs clung to its long black tail.

The rancher said, "I kind of hate to sell Old Belcher. My wife and kids was all partial to him, but the kids've grown up and left the nest, and my wife died. I don't get much use out of him anymore."

Hewey said, "He looks kind of old."

"Experienced," the man responded. "There ain't much he don't know about handlin' stock." The rancher whistled. The old horse showed no response. "He's been well broke. You don't have to worry about him throwin' you off."

Or running away with you, Hewey thought. He said, "He ain't much for pretty."

"Like I said, he don't look very good. But he'll get you there and bring you back."

If you don't go very far, Hewey thought. But anything beat walking. At any rate the choice was not his to make. He turned to Gabe. "What do you think?"

Gabe appeared less than impressed. "He's got four legs, though I ain't seen any of them move."

The rancher walked up to the horse and slapped it on the rump, raising a little dust and making it take a few steps. "See there? Sound of wind and limb."

Fat said, "I'd hate for any of my friends to see me ridin' an old wreck like that."

Hewey fought down a temptation to ask him how many friends he had.

Gabe said, "I ain't exactly flush with money. What'll you take for him?"

"Like I told you, I kind of hate to part with Old Belcher. He's been like part of the family. But seein' as you need him pretty bad and I don't, I think a fair price would be . . ." He paused to consider. "Say, fifty dollars."

Fifty dollars ought to buy a racehorse, Hewey thought.

Gabe said, "Say, ten dollars."

"Say, forty."

"Say, fifteen."

The rancher made a deep frown. "Boy, you must like walkin'. Say twenty."

"Only if you got a saddle you can throw in. His backbone looks sharp enough to cut a man where it would hurt the worst."

"Done. I got a saddle in the barn. Feller worked here a while and left owin' me money. Consider that you got the horse for twenty dollars and the saddle throwed in free. *Pilón,* the Mexicans call it. You can have his bridle and blanket, too."

The saddle appeared to predate the war. Hewey told Gabe, "I wouldn't trust that cinch too far. If that horse was to jump, it'd likely snap in two."

Gabe shook his head. "I doubt this old horse has got a jump left in him."

Gabe counted twenty dollars from his mustering-out pay. The rancher smiled as he counted again for himself. Satisfied, he asked, "Any of you-all interested in a job?"

Nobody answered.

The rancher said, "I'm in bad need of help. I don't normally send a girl out to do a man's work, but my last hired hand decided to go to San Antone. I pay a fair wage, and I've got a good cook."

Hewey said, "Thank you kindly, but we're workin' for Mr. C.C. Tarpley. I reckon we'll be goin' on."

Hickson looked at Gabe. Gabe said, "I'm with these fellers."

He saddled the horse and mounted him. The stirrups were set short for his long legs, but they could be adjusted if the leather strings weren't too rotten to unlace. Starting through the gate, the horse bumped its head against a post. Gabe dismounted and made a close examination.

He declared, "I do believe this horse is blind."

"Not altogether," Hickson said. "He's still got some sight in his right eye. I told you he don't *look* good."

Hewey's face warmed with indignation, but Gabe seemed to accept the deceit without much surprise. Perhaps he was used to white men taking advantage of him. He said only, "I reckon I'll have to do the seein' for him."

Hewey told the rancher, "You ought to be ashamed, foistin' a blind horse off on somebody."

"I am. Nearly as ashamed as I was when I let a horse trader palm that skate off on me a while back." The rancher shoved the money deep into his pocket. "At least now I'm even again."

"Then you lied about this bein' an old family pet."

"Son, nobody ever lies when they're swappin' or sellin' horses. They just don't let facts get in the way of a trade. I expect when that boy gets to where he's goin' he can sell the horse and get most of his money back. In the meantime he's got transportation cheaper than the stagecoach, even if they'd let him on, him bein' black."

The girl stood on the porch watching as they left. She was grinning.

Gabe said, "She laughed at me for walkin'. Now she's laughin' at me for ridin'. But at least I ain't walkin' no more."

Hewey said, "Yet. You may be walkin' again when that old plug wears out. You may wind up carryin' *him*."

"I feel kind of sorry for the poor thing."

Hewey grumbled, "It'd serve that old scoundrel right if one of them goats butted him plumb over the fence."

Walter said, "You didn't do anything to stop him."

"It was Gabe's trade. Come to think of it, he got the horse and the whole outfit for less than half of what the old man first asked."

Walter said, "So maybe it wasn't such a bad deal after all."

"Still, I wouldn't be surprised to see the old liar's mother crawl out from under the porch and bite him on the leg."

{ TEN }

Old Belcher had more stamina than Hewey would have guessed. The bay horse plodded along and kept up with the younger animals, showing little evident strain. It even exhibited an unexpected burst of speed when a startled deer bounded out of a thicket almost under its nose. Caught off guard, Gabe wound up sitting on the ground. Hewey had to chase the frightened horse more than two hundred yards. He caught it only when it ran into a grove of trees and stopped, confused because it could not see where to go.

He led it back and handed the reins to Gabe. "I'm surprised he had it in him," he said.

Gabe rubbed his backside. "You ain't near as surprised as I am. Like to've busted my tailbone."

Fat was the only one who laughed.

Gabe felt better when he saw a town ahead. "That's Friedrichsburg," he said. "Mostly Germans there. They don't mind black folks the way lots of others do."

Hewey suggested, "Might be a good place to pick up a few supplies."

Walter disagreed. "I can't think of anything we need."

"Maybe we'll think of somethin' when we get there."

Fat said, "I can think of somethin'."

Walter gave him a hard look. "You had enough in San Angelo."

Many of the signs were not in English, and Hewey couldn't say *scat* in German. He saw one, however, that contained the word *Bier*. He was pretty sure he knew what that meant. "Might be a good place to stop and think about what we need."

Walter said, "You know what this trip is for. We're supposed to take care of business."

"I can't take care of business unless I take care of *me*."

"Just one beer, then." Walter turned to Fat. "One, do you hear?"

"Who the hell put you in charge?"

They walked into the stone structure, which seemed oppressively dark until Hewey's eyes adjusted. Nobody paid much attention, even to Gabe. Hewey took that for a good omen. Several men stood at the bar or sat at tables, some sipping beer, some drinking stronger stuff. By their dress many appeared to be cowboys, yet they were talking in a language Hewey could not understand. That struck him as strange. He had never run across a cowboy he could not talk to, outside of a few Mexicans.

"I'd better have a second one," he said. "Maybe then I'll savvy what they're talkin' about."

Walter objected. "We agreed on just havin' one."

"You agreed. I didn't. What do you think, Gabe?"

Gabe shrugged. "One is enough. Else I might go to thinkin' I'm white. That could get me killed."

Hewey gave in. "Just one, then." He did not ask Fat's opinion. He knew what it would be, and he did not want to hear it.

Outside, he saw two men walking along speaking

English. He hailed them. "How long will it take us to get to San Antonio?"

One of the men looked toward the four tied horses. "Does that old bay belong to one of you?"

Hewey pointed his thumb at Gabe. "Him."

"Most people can make it from here in two days without pushin'. With that old nag, you better figure four."

Gabe watched the men enter the saloon. He asked, "How come everybody makes sport of my horse? He can't help it that he don't look good."

Hewey said, "Maybe they're jealous. They're afoot and you're not."

They had not ridden far when they had to turn aside to make way for two racers thundering along a flat stretch of the road toward them. A couple of dozen men were lined up along the edge of the impromptu track, cheering. A clod of dirt struck Hewey on the cheek as the horses pounded past him. A long-legged brown won the race by a length.

Fat said, "Too bad we didn't get here in time to place a bet. That's the one I would've put my money on."

Walter said, "It's easy to pick the winner after the race is over."

Hewey wiped the dirt from his face. "We ain't in so big a hurry we can't stop to watch a little. Let's wait and see if they match another one."

He pulled in close so he could hear the bystanders' animated conversation. Much was in German and therefore gibberish to him, but some was in English. The gist was that the crowd wanted another run for their money. A tall man in farmer overalls spotted the four newcomers and ambled up. He asked, "Did you-all come out for the races?"

Hewey said, "We just happened to be passin' by."

The man said, "We're lookin' for another race. That horse you're ridin' looks like it could run."

"No, he's long on looks but short on doin'." But the question made Hewey remember how fast Old Belcher had run when the deer startled him. "We might match this bay if you've got somethin' about his caliber. Maybe somethin' a little lame."

Several men looked over Gabe's mount. Some could not keep from grinning. The man in overalls said, "We've got a little black snide that's been beat by everything in town. But even at that he might peel the hide off of that broken-down nag of yours. To make things fair we could put a heavy rider on him, somebody like Anse there."

The man called Anse was walking proof of beer's fattening qualities. He appeared to weigh well over two hundred pounds. Looking around, Hewey saw a sleepy-eyed little black horse whose forelegs both appeared to grow out of the same place. One hock was slightly swollen.

Emboldened, he said, "That ain't necessary. We wouldn't want to take advantage."

Walter said, speaking with alarm in his voice, "Hewey, what do you think you're doin'? In the first place, Belcher ain't yours to run. He belongs to Gabe. In the second place, what're you figurin' to bet with?"

"We got the expense money C.C. gave us."

"That's meant to get us through the rest of the trip, not to blow on a horse race."

Hewey pulled Walter and Gabe off to one side so no one else could hear. Fat joined without invitation. Hewey argued, "You saw how Old Belcher ran when that deer

spooked him. I'll bet my life's savin's that he'll leave
that sorry-lookin' little black standin' still."

Walter retorted, "Your life savin's wouldn't fill a tobacco sack. You're talkin' about C.C.'s money."

"C.C. won't mind, not if we double it."

"I swear, Hewey, that reckless streak of yours scares
the hell out of me."

"Ain't nothin' reckless about it when you've got a
cinch bet." Hewey looked at Gabe. "What do you say?"

Gabe rubbed his chin, pondering. "Old Belcher's liable
to die of heart failure halfway down the track. But my
life's been a gamble ever since my old mammy birthed
me in a cotton patch. I might even put up a little of my
musterin'-out pay."

Satisfied, Hewey returned to the cluster of men. From
his saddlebag he fetched up the money Tarpley had ad-
vanced and turned it over to the stakes holder. "Bring
out that black horse you were talkin' about."

Gabe contributed ten dollars. Fat examined the little
he had left after San Angelo and stuck it back into his
pocket. "Druther buy whiskey," he said.

Walter stood to one side, offering only silent rebuke.

Hewey immediately had second thoughts when one
of the men led the animal forward. This was not the little black he had assumed it would be. This horse was
taller. Its trim legs and the proud arch of its neck showed
a healthy amount of Thoroughbred blood.

He protested, "You boys have run a ringer on me."

The man in overalls smiled wickedly. "We never done
no such of a thing. We just said it was a black horse. We
didn't say which one."

Walter stood with his hands on his hips, a stance Pa

had often taken when he was about to give Hewey a good chewing-out. "Hewey, you've done it again."

The spokesman asked, "Who's your jockey?"

Hewey looked at Gabe. Dubiously Gabe said, "Belcher left me on the ground the last time."

To call on Fat was out of the question. Hewey said, "You're the lightest of us. You got to do it."

Gabe reluctantly agreed. He dropped the blanket and small pack that had been tied behind the saddle.

Hewey said, "Too bad there ain't any deer to booger him."

Gabe blinked. "I just thought of somethin' that might do just as much good." He lowered his voice. "Give me the borry of that pistol you got."

Hewey hesitated. "I hope you ain't figurin' on shootin' the other horse."

"No, nor mine neither." Gabe held out his hand.

Puzzled, Hewey dug the pistol from his saddlebag, turning away to hide what he was doing. He checked to be sure a cartridge was in the chamber, then handed the weapon over.

Gabe shoved it into a trousers pocket and said, "Me and Old Belcher are as ready as we're goin' to get."

Most of the observers remained at the finish line, a simple mark scratched across the road with a broken live-oak limb. Hewey accompanied the starter, Gabe, and the rider of the black horse down the road to the starting place.

The starter scraped a fresh mark across the road and saw that the two horses stood with their forefeet against it. He raised his arm as a get-ready signal, looked expectantly at the riders, then dropped his arm. Gabe spurred vigorously. Belcher barely moved into a trot. The black horse galloped off ahead of him.

Hewey started thinking about writing Tarpley a letter saying he had been called to South America.

He was startled by a pistol shot. The old bay horse bolted in fright. The sudden surge forward almost drove Gabe back over its rump.

The shot that so frightened the old bay had a different effect on the black. Spooked, it crow-hopped several jumps before it broke into a run at a tangent, leaving the road. Belcher moved well ahead. Gabe leaned forward, shouting in the bay's ear.

Hewey hollered, "Run, you buzzard bait, run."

Maybe he wouldn't have to write C. C. a letter after all.

Gabe lost his hat but did not look back. The black's rider managed to pull his mount into the road and begin catching up. Hewey spurred into a lope, following the racers. He tried to gauge the distance to the finish line, but the wind made his eyes water.

He began to hear the crowd cheering at the finish line. He could see that the black horse was pushing up close behind the bay. Gabe leaned farther forward, drumming his heels against Belcher's ribs.

Something prodded Belcher to greater speed. Hewey reasoned that the bay had glimpsed the other horse crowding him on the right side. Given his limited sight, Belcher probably saw the black as a potential booger coming after him. The frightened old bay moved back in front by a length.

The cheering died as the horses neared the finish line, for the crowd's money had been on the black one. Hewey heard Gabe shouting encouragement.

Even Walter gave a holler as Belcher crossed the mark. Fat looked solemn, probably regretting that he had not bet. Gabe let Belcher run on another hundred yards, gradually slowing him down. He turned around and let him trot back to where the crowd waited. As Gabe dismounted, breathing heavily, Hewey stepped forward and grabbed the bridle just above the bits. He patted the horse on its sweaty neck. "You done good, old feller. You may be ugly as a mud fence, but you sure looked pretty crossin' that line."

The old bay danced nervously and rolled its eyes, for it was still a little frightened.

Walter said, "You got away with it again, Hewey. I never saw anybody with so much pure dumb luck."

"Wasn't no luck to it. Belcher's a better horse than he looks to be." He turned his attention to Gabe. "Had him a good rider, too."

The stakes holder came forward, his hands full of money, his face creased in a deep frown. "What was that shot we heard just as the race started?"

Admitting what Hewey knew might cause an unpleasant commotion. "Must've been some hunter shootin' at a deer." The other rider might tell about it later, but by then the money would have changed hands, and Hewey intended to be farther down the road.

The man in overalls looked Belcher over from the tips of his ears to his fetlocks. "You boys been doin' this a long time?"

"Doin' what?" Hewey asked.

"Suckerin' people into bettin' against this old skate. He don't look like much, but his daddy must have been part antelope."

"This is the first time we've raced him."

The farmer grunted in disbelief. "Sure, and my name is Ulysses S. Grant. What'll you take for him?"

"He's not mine to sell. He belongs to Gabe."

The man turned to Gabe. "I think me and my friends could clean up, takin' this old horse around to tracks where nobody's seen him. I'll give you fifty dollars for him."

Gabe swallowed. "Fifty dollars? I just give . . ."

Hewey cut him off with a frown.

Gabe caught his breath. "No, sir, him and me have got kind of attached. He ain't for sellin'."

"I'll make it sixty, boy. That's my best offer."

"Thank you kindly, sir, but I reckon I'll keep him." Gabe looked at the black horse that Belcher had just beaten. "But tell you what, I might be in a buyin' mood. That black of yours can't run much, but he'd do for plain ridin'. What'll you take for him?"

"I'd make you an even swap." Seeing no reaction, the farmer said, "And twenty dollars to boot."

Gabe counted on his fingers. "I don't want to trade, but I'd pay you twenty dollars for him, cash money."

"Twenty?" The farmer looked insulted and turned away. Then he turned again. "He's given me about all the disappointment I can stand. He's lost every race I put him in, but I was sure he could win this one. You couldn't give thirty?"

"No, sir, just twenty."

"Take him. Get him out of my sight."

Gabe had bet ten and won ten. Hewey counted out twenty dollars and handed the bills to him. Gabe in turn gave them to the seller. Gleefully he said, "I got me a horse for free."

Hewey started to remind him that ten dollars had

been his in the first place, but he did not want to throw cold water on Gabe's moment of triumph. Later he would give Gabe part of the winnings gained on Tarpley's money. It might upset some of these sports to see a black man with so much money in his hands, especially *their* money. He would wait until they were down the road.

Leaving, Gabe rode the black horse and led the tired bay. When they had traveled a while he returned the pistol to Hewey. He said, "Belcher would never make a war horse. He's gun-shy."

Fat demanded, "What's the matter with you, boy? The man offered you sixty. You just paid twenty for Belcher. You throwed away forty dollars clear profit."

Hewey argued, "Money ain't any account by itself. You can't eat it or drink it. All it's good for is to spend on somethin' you want. A horse, for instance."

Gabe said, "I was afeered they might mistreat him, draggin' him around to races, runnin' him till his poor old legs went out from under him. I figured he had more comin' to him than that."

Walter smiled. "You've got a good heart, Gabe."

Gabe shrugged. "I been wooled around a lot in my life. I couldn't let it happen to that horse just so I could make a few dollars. The money'd leak out of my pockets anyway, the first town I come to. He can't help it that he's old."

Fat grumbled, "Forty dollars passed up is forty dollars lost."

They rode through what Hewey considered some of the prettiest country he had ever seen, green rolling hills with narrow, fertile valleys and small creeks fed by bubbling seeps and springs. The four riders stopped beside one of the springs to make camp. The grass was taller than Hewey's boot tops.

Gabe stood in awed silence, surveying the valley. He said, "If we was horses, this here is the kind of place we'd be lookin' for. Water, shade, and all the grazin' we could ever want."

Hewey said, "But we ain't horses."

Gabe rubbed Belcher's neck. "When I see a sight like this, I almost wisht we was." He slipped the lead rope from around the bay's neck and gave the horse a gentle slap on the rump. "Get along, old man. From now on, this is your home."

The horse walked off a few steps, then turned its head to look back. Gabe motioned with his hand. "I got me another horse now. Go on. I done emancipated you." The horse walked a short way, then moved into an easy trot.

Fat said reprovingly, "That's sixty dollars goin' to waste."

Gabe said, "Abraham Lincoln freed the slaves. All I done was free one tired old horse."

San Antonio was the largest town Hewey had seen, and he felt a tingle of apprehension. Nothing he had encountered on the trail to Kansas or the long trip out to the Pecos River had quite prepared him. It appeared to him that a man could get lost in its narrow, winding streets and never be found. All he knew was that he needed to locate a man named Patrick Appleby who lived somewhere east of the Alamo.

He was not sure he could even find the Alamo.

Ahead he saw a man driving a heavily laden freight

wagon. He said, "He acts like he knows where he's goin'. Let's follow him."

As they approached the city's center they were caught up in considerable horse, wagon, and even some oxcart traffic.

"Sure a lot of busy people in this place," Hewey said. "Makes me tired just watchin' them stir around." He began watching for a saloon.

Walter said, "Business first. Drink afterwards."

"I never said nothin' about wantin' a drink."

"But it's on your mind. I can tell by lookin' at you."

Hewey had moments when he regretted bringing Walter along. Without his brother he could have had a lot more fun on this trip, though he would probably still be a few days short of San Antonio.

Gabe said, "The streets are laid out like a wagon wheel and all lead to the middle. They say it started with the Spaniards' oxcarts comin' in from all directions. If we follow this here street, it'll take us to the Alamo."

Walter asked, "What you goin' to do now, Gabe? You got somewhere to go?"

"No, sir, got no folks anyplace that I know of. I just figured to stick with you fellers if you'll let me. Never have punched cows, but I reckon I could learn."

Hewey said, "Hirin' and firin' for the drive will be up to Jerome Padgett, but you're welcome to stay with us till he says yes or no."

"Thank you kindly. My musterin' out pay ain't apt to last me long."

Fat said, "Not when you throw away sixty dollars at a time."

Hewey was filled with curiosity about the old mission

where so many had died fighting for Texas freedom from Mexico, or in the case of Santa Anna's troops, against it. He said, "Been a heap of blood soaked into these streets."

Gabe agreed. "Spanish first, then Mexican and American. Some black folks, too. Comanches killed and scalped people right here between these houses. If I was afeered of ghosts, I wouldn't come to this town at all."

Walter said, "I hope nobody's goin' to cause you trouble on account of you bein' . . . different."

Gabe pointed to a black couple walking along a narrow alley. "There's a good many folks of color here. You never seen the like of mixed-up people: Mexicans, Germans, Polanders, Frenchmen, Chinamen, and some I got no idea what breed they are. Half the time you can't tell what they're sayin'. I wonder if *they* do."

They came into a plaza. Hewey saw a low stone building whose scars and weathered front made it look as if it could have been there for ages.

Gabe said, "That's the Alamo. That's where they fit so hard against old Santy Anna."

Hewey felt let down. "Kind of small. I figured it'd be a lot bigger."

"You're just lookin' at what used to be the church. There was more to it, but most of it got torn down. They're usin' the old church for a warehouse now."

Walter voiced his indignation. "A warehouse? It ought to be a monument."

Fat said, "You can't blame folks for wantin' to make a dollar."

Hewey pointed. "Accordin' to C.C., that feller Appletree ought to live somewhere yonderway."

Walter corrected him. "Appleby."

"That's what I said."

They turned east after passing the Alamo. Hewey hailed an elderly Mexican. He used the few Spanish words he knew. "Amigo, you know where an hombre named Applegate lives?"

"No entiendo."

Hewey grimaced. "I think he said he don't intend to tell us."

Gabe said, "No, he's sayin' he don't understand you."

Hewey had not expected Gabe to know Spanish. "You speak their lingo?"

"Just enough to get myself in trouble. But maybe I can help a little." He spoke to the Mexican. The only word Hewey got out of it was *Appleby.*

The Mexican launched into a long answer, punctuated with lively hand gestures.

Gabe shook his head. "The best I can figure, he don't know anybody by that name. But if we want to buy some apples, his brother has got a store down the street yonder."

They came across a middle-aged woman carrying fresh produce in a canvas sack. Hewey guessed she had come from an open-air market they had passed. She was Anglo, so maybe he could talk to her. He asked, "Do you know a man around here by the name of Applewhite?"

Anger flashed in the woman's face. "I think you mean Appleby. Are you tryin' to say, young man, that I am a loose woman?"

Flustered, Hewey tried to decide how to rephrase the question. "No, ma'am, we've got business with him. Just thought you might know where he lives."

"Sir, I am a respectable married woman. I cross the street to avoid sharing a sidewalk with Mr. Appleby, or anyone else of his ilk. And I will not stand here and bandy words with anyone who does business with him. Good day."

"Good night," Hewey said as she walked away, her back rigid and her head high. "Mr. Applegate must be a ring-tailed rounder. Kind of like you, Fat."

A thin, brown-faced boy of perhaps ten came skipping down the street, kicking a tin can ahead of him and singing a song in Spanish. Hewey raised a hand to get his attention. "Young'un, do you speak English?"

"Damn betcha," the boy replied. "Soldiers come to see my sister. Teach me many English."

Gabe grinned. "Sounds like the kind of soldiers I know."

Hewey said, "We're lookin' for a man named Apple. Can you tell us where he lives?"

"*Señor* Appleby? Damn betcha. For two bits I show you."

Hewey dug the money from his pocket. "Deal."

The boy kicked the can up against an adobe wall and motioned for the riders to follow him. He cut between two houses and down an alley, then into another narrow dirt street. He pointed to a flat-topped stone house. "*Aquí,*" he said. "Mama and Papa get mad if I go closer. He got no wife, but he got plenty women. Better you knock."

Hewey handed him the two bits. "What you goin' to spend it on?"

"Tortillas and beans." The boy skipped away.

Walter said, "At least it's goin' for a good cause. The kid doesn't look like he gets enough to eat."

Fat said, "I don't either."

Gabe said, "There's a wolf hangin' around just about every door in this part of town."

Walter glanced at Hewey. "Like you say, money's not everything. But it looks like everything when you're hungry."

The doorstep was covered with dirt blown up from the street. Hewey suspected that the only sweeping it ever got was by the wind. He rapped his knuckles against the wooden door and listened. He heard nothing until he rapped a second time. From inside came a rough voice. "What the hell do you want?"

"We come to see you. C.C. Tarpley sent us."

"Come back later. I'm busy."

"We've traveled a long ways. We'll wait."

It was a long wait, at least half an hour, though Hewey had no watch by which to time it. Finally the door opened. A short, fat, balding man scowled at Hewey. Beyond him Hewey saw a woman slipping out a back door. Though he could not see her face, he noticed she had long, black hair that fell to a slender, youthful waist.

The man's scowl deepened. "Who the hell are you, and what've you come botherin' me for? I got better things to do."

Hewey had seen her. He said, "We need to talk to you, Mr. Applewhite."

"You said C.C. Tarpley sent you. Is that old warthog still alive?"

"And kickin'. He said you can help us find Jerome Padgett."

"I don't help nobody for nothin', and I sure ain't travelin' anywhere to help you find Jerome Padgett. He's done wore out his welcome with me."

Hewey jingled his pocket without drawing out any

money. "It'd be worth somethin' if we could locate him."

The sound of loose coin caught Appleby's attention. "I do hate to turn down somebody who's in real need. You-all come on in." He seemed to notice Gabe for the first time and have reservations. But he said, "You can come in, too, I reckon."

Gabe said, "Much obliged," and removed his hat before he stepped through the door. Hewey had kept his hat on until he was inside.

Appleby motioned for everybody to sit down. There were not enough seats, so Gabe sat on the floor, against the wall. A woman's black shawl lay across the back of the chair that Hewey took. She had left in a hurry and evidently forgot it.

Appleby said, "Now, about Jerome. If he owes you money, there ain't a damned thing I can do about it."

Hewey said, "No, sir, nothin' like that. He located some cattle for Mr. Tarpley. We need him to show us where they're at and to help us drive them out west."

That seemed to please Appleby. "West? How far?"

"To the Pecos River."

"That'd keep him gone from here for a long while, wouldn't it?"

"A few weeks at least. He might even decide to stay on with Mr. Tarpley. He ain't bad to work for, only a little cheap."

Appleby traded his frown for a broad smile. "So I wouldn't be pestered with Jerome for a time. That calls for a drink. I suppose you boys do drink?"

Hewey nodded. "We've been known to."

Fat could not contain his eagerness. "We don't understand when they talk Mexican around this town, but we understand that."

Appleby poured a glass for Gabe, but he and Hewey and Fat drank from the bottle. Walter declined. The chubby Appleby became more expansive after a second drink. "Well, sir, I can tell you where Jerome was the last time I heard, and I doubt they've turned him loose. He's in jail."

Hewey was only mildly surprised. Tarpley had told him that Padgett was not given to living by the rules.

Appleby turned the bottle in his hands, studying the label. "You've got to take Jerome the way he is. He ain't goin' to change for me or you or anybody. He's sober most of the time, and he's all business. But when he gets too much of that old kill-me-dead under his belt, you never know what he's liable to do. He may try to hug your neck, or he may try to break it. He can change moods quicker than I can change shirts."

Hewey realized Tarpley had not told him everything.

Appleby said, "He knows the inside of the San Antonio jail like it was his home. The local laws make allowances for him, but he's got himself in Dutch with a sheriff south of here who wouldn't make allowances for his own mother. You may have to wait till he's served out whatever sentence they laid on him."

He finished giving directions, then opened the front door. "You boys will have to excuse me now. I'm lookin' for a lady to drop in."

Hewey shook his hand. "Much obliged, Mr. Applewhite."

"Take Jerome away for a while and I'll be obliged to *you*."

Walter stopped in the dirt street. "Looks like we may have to get along without Mr. Padgett."

"We got to have him, no matter what it takes." Hewey turned to get his bearings. "Whichaway is south?"

{ ELEVEN }

The stone courthouse was boxy and plain, without the ornate cupolas and clocks and gargoyles popular in so many towns given to boasting about their prospects. The conservative structure bespoke a county where tax-hating citizens voted down civic projects that might cost them money. The jail, hunkered beside it on the square, was a small fortress with thick stone walls and heavy bars. It appeared that the county expected its prisoners to be bent on breaking out and was determined to thwart them.

Hewey said, "It'd be tough to bust him out of there."

Walter said, "It'd be stupid to try. We'd end up in there with him. Or dead."

Hewey eyed the courthouse with apprehension. He always dreaded meeting a sheriff. He stopped a passerby and asked, "What kind of sheriff you got in this town?"

The farmer hooked his thumbs in the straps of his overalls and looked Hewey over before he answered. "Depends. If you're a quiet, honest, law-abidin' citizen, and you like a quiet, honest, law-abidin' town, then Old Quincy is your man. But if you ain't, you'll hate to see him comin'."

Must be kin to Sheriff Noonan back home, Hewey thought.

Walter asked, "You want me to talk to him?"

Hewey was tempted, but he said, "Naw, C.C. put me in charge. It's up to me to do it. I just ain't got the least notion what to say to him."

He turned to Gabe, but Gabe was no help. "I always go way around any white man with a badge on. They'd rap me up 'side the head for just lookin' at them. I'll stay out here and watch the horses."

Fat said, "Me too. I ain't paid enough to butt heads with no officer of the law."

Maybe the sheriff won't be there, Hewey thought hopefully. If he wasn't, they could put this off for a time. But he had found that the longer he stood back and looked at a bad horse, the tougher the ride when it finally came. He said, "Walter, at least *you* can come along and back me up."

Walter trailed a couple of steps behind Hewey as they entered the courthouse. The various offices were identified by small signs standing out at right angles to the door-frames. At the end of a short hall a sign read SHERIFF.

A middle-aged man with sleeves partially rolled up and glasses perched halfway down his nose was hunched over a desk, laboriously writing a letter. The steel-tipped pen scratched audibly against the paper. He raised his graying head to peer at Hewey over the rims of the glasses. His dark eyes seemed to bore through Hewey and fasten on Walter behind him. He had heavy eyebrows and a salt-and-pepper mustache almost as large as Eli Jessup's. He declared, "You two look like you've been whipped about the shoulders with a wet rope. You come to report a murder or somethin'?"

Hewey asked, "Are you the sheriff?"

The man laid down the pen and tapped thick fingers against a star-shaped badge on his shirt. "That's what it says on here. Name's Quincy Ames."

Hewey couldn't read the lettering that far, but he recognized the attitude. It was just like Sheriff Noonan's. "We come to see you about a man named Jerome Padgett. We're told you've got him locked up."

The answer was firm. "Just as tight as I can. You got a grievance against him?"

"No, sir, nothin' like that. We got business. Can we see him?"

"When I let him out of jail."

"How soon'll that be?"

The sheriff stood up and moved to a calendar on the wall. "This shows he's been in here for ten days. He'll be out in another fifty, if I don't find some reason to keep him longer. Come back then, and we'll see."

"We can't wait that long."

The sheriff's brow took on several deep wrinkles. "If you're fixin' to make trouble, I've got some empty cells left. Then you can talk to him all you want."

"No, sir, we didn't come to make trouble. We were sent to see him about some cattle business. If we don't, we'll be in trouble with our boss."

"Who is your boss?"

"Name's C.C. Tarpley, out at Upton City."

The sheriff grunted. "I remember him. Little dried-up wart. Carries a dollar around till he's rubbed the writin' off before he'll spend it."

"That's him."

"If you boys are workin' for him, you've got my sympathy. Maybe you ought to just write him a letter sayin' you quit, then see if you can find a job around here. It'd probably pay better anyway."

Hewey and Walter looked at one another. Hewey had a feeling the sheriff was offering him good advice, but he said, "Our pa always preached that a man doesn't quit till he gets the job done."

Quincy gave Hewey a long stare that made him start to sweat. Finally he said, "Sounds like your pa had a good handle on things. Tell you what: out of the goodness of my heart I'll let you go and talk to him, but that's all. See how quick you can wrap up your business." He looked down at Hewey's waist. "Either of you packin' iron?"

"No, sir. Somethin' else Pa said was that the only thing a pistol is good for is to shoot yourself in the foot. I keep mine in my saddlebags."

"That's good. The only thing better would be to sell it or give it away." Quincy took his hat from a rack. It had a high, uncreased crown, a broad brim, and sweat stains around a band of rattlesnake skin. "Come on over to the jail with me."

Walking out of the courthouse, Quincy noticed Gabe and Fat sitting at some distance apart on the square's perimeter fence, near the tied horses. "I don't recognize that black boy," he said. "I better go check up on him."

Hewey spoke quickly. "He's with us."

"What's his name?"

"Gabe."

"Ain't he got any other name?"

"He ain't mentioned it, and we ain't asked him."

The sheriff growled, "Well, you better keep him out of trouble. Folks here can be touchy. Sooner you get him away from town, the better."

"That depends on what we find out from Mr. Padgett."

The jail walls were every bit as thick as Hewey had thought them to be. The door was heavy enough that it groaned against the hinges. The jailer sat napping, his straight chair leaning back, his feet propped on an old desk. The sheriff threw his hat, striking him in the face. The young man awakened with a cry of alarm. The front legs of his chair struck hard against the floor.

Quincy's voice crackled. "Damn you, Willy, you're paid to watch the jail. If every prisoner in the place was to bust out, you'd sleep right through it."

Defensively the jailer said, "We ain't got but one prisoner, Uncle Quincy, and he ain't goin' nowhere."

If the jailer was the sheriff's nephew, Hewey thought, he was in little danger of losing his job no matter how sound a sleeper he might be.

Quincy said, "Get your keys. These two cowpunchers want to talk to Jerome. They'll have to do it from the hallway. We ain't lettin' them into his cell."

Willy nodded and took a ring of heavy keys from the desk. He said, "About time for the widder Simpson to bring supper, ain't it? She's been mighty prompt since you've had Padgett in here."

"Never mind about Miz Ellie, or supper, either. You ain't missed many meals." Quincy explained to Hewey and Walter, "Ellie Simpson runs an eatin' joint across the street. She's got a contract to feed prisoners when we have any."

Hewey said, "Maybe we'll go there for supper."

"You'll have to leave that black boy behind or else feed him on the back step. There was a time when his kind wasn't even allowed here after sundown."

Hewey had never spent much time thinking about the

plight of black people, mainly because he had not been around many. No Calloway could ever afford to hire one to work, much less to own a slave in the times before the War of Yankee Aggression.

Walter mused, "Gabe can't help bein' the way he was born. That was the Lord's doin'."

Quincy grunted. "I wish the Lord had seen fit to leave them where they was in the first place. I hope the first white men that brought them to this country are roastin' in hell. There ain't no tellin' how much their cheap labor has cost us."

Hewey and Walter followed Quincy to the dark cells, where Hewey saw the shadowy form of a man lying on a cot, hands behind his head.

Quincy barked, "Rouse yourself, Jerome. You got company."

From the gloom a brusque voice answered, "If they're kinfolks, I don't want to see them. If they ain't, I don't want to see them, either."

Quincy said to Hewey, "You won't do any good tryin' to talk to that old rascal. He's spent his whole life with horses and cattle. He don't know how to act around human people."

The voice said sharply, "I'd know how to act if ever I caught you in some other county, without your badge on."

Quincy said, "That's the attitude that got him in here in the first place."

Hewey said, "Mr. Padgett, we came here for C.C. Tarpley."

"I wish he'd come himself, and bring money to bail me out. I know he's got it. Trouble is, he never wants to spend any of it."

"Maybe there's somethin' we can do to help."

"With Quincy runnin' the county courthouse? You'd just as well go back to C.C. and tell him the deal is off. I'll be in here a right good while."

Quincy nodded in the affirmative. "That's the truth if he ever told it."

Hewey asked, "What about bail?"

Quincy said, "That'd be up to the judge. He always does what I suggest when it comes to prisoners. I don't see Jerome gettin' out before the snow flies. And it don't fly often around here."

Hewey turned to Walter for advice, but Walter had none. "Looks like we're leavin' with an empty sack."

Hewey was not ready to give up, not after their long trip from the Pecos. "Look, Mr. Padgett, tell us where the cattle are at. Me and Walter can go ahead and make the deal for them, and we'll pay you a commission just like if you'd done it yourself. I believe that'd set all right with C.C."

Padgett swung his legs over the edge of the cot. He was barefoot, his high-topped boots and his socks lying on the floor. As he stood, Hewey saw that he was a lean, angular man. His hair was gray, his face deeply lined. His mustache showed signs of careful trimming in the past, though it had been neglected recently. He limped as he made his way across the narrow cell.

Been thrown off of too many horses, Hewey thought.

Gripping the bars with arthritis-knotted hands, Padgett asked, "How bad do you boys want them cattle?"

Hewey said, "Bad enough. C.C.'s countin' on us."

"What C. C. Tarpley wants don't bother me a particle. What *I* want, though, is another matter. I want out of this jail. You boys find some way to fix it, and I'll take you to the cattle. If you don't, them cattle stay right where they're at."

Hewey said, "We're liable to get fired."

"In this world, every man has got to take care of hisself. Ain't nobody else goin' to do it."

Hewey said, "Maybe if we talk to that judge . . ."

The sheriff put in, "Like I told you, the judge leaves things of this sort up to me. If you go botherin' him, I'm liable to have to lock you up for disturbin' the peace. Then you can sit behind these bars and play checkers with Jerome."

Damn stubborn people! Hewey thought. It was bad enough confronting them one at a time. Now he faced two. He turned to Walter. "Let's go outside and talk this over."

Quincy said, "Ain't nothin' to talk over, boys. Jerome stays right here till I'm ready to let him go."

The jailer poked his head through the door. "The widder Simpson's comin' with Jerome's supper."

Testily the sheriff said, "Well, don't stand there like a cigar-store Indian. Show her in."

A middle-aged woman entered as the jailer stepped out of the way. She carried a tray covered with a white cloth. Hewey caught the aroma of warm food and coffee. She paid no attention at first to the men standing outside the cell. She said, "Here you are, Jerome. Fried chicken and gravy and hot biscuits. Got to get your strength up so you can take me dancin' when Quincy makes up his mind to turn you loose."

She was forty years old if she was a day, but Hewey thought her an attractive woman, for her age. Her hair was a light brown with a few early signs of gray that were somehow becoming to her.

He caught a jealous look in the sheriff's eyes. Quincy said, "Maybe I better look under that cloth, Ellie, just to make sure nothin's there that oughtn't to be."

She made a show of indignation. "You know I wouldn't smuggle in a file, much less a six-shooter. You used to act like a gentleman. Now you're gettin' to be as cross as an old bear."

"Who wouldn't be cross, with you makin' a fuss over this worn-out old brush popper?"

"He's a cowboy. It's an honest profession."

Quincy motioned for the jailer to open the cell door. He reached for the tray. "I'll take it to him."

Mrs. Simpson spoke past him to Padgett. "You'll find an extra-big slice of chocolate cake there, Jerome. I know that's your favorite."

Quincy grumbled under his breath. Hewey thought he heard him say he hoped Padgett would choke on it.

The widow acknowledged Hewey's and Walter's presence for the first time. "Are you boys friends of Jerome's?"

Hewey said, "We'd like to be. We came a long way to do business with him, but it looks like there's no chance. He can't get out."

"Too bad. Well, if you-all come over to my restaurant for supper, I'll fix you somethin' nice."

"You can figure on it, ma'am."

She glanced at the sheriff. "I expect you'll be over after a while too, Quincy? Unless you're ready to poison yourself on your own cookin'."

His reply was curt. "I'll be along."

As she turned to leave, she shouted over her shoulder, "Eat hearty, Jerome. I'll see you at breakfast time."

Padgett answered, "Sure. I ain't goin' nowhere."

When she was gone he sat on the cot with the tray on his lap and dug into the fried chicken. Quincy gave him a look of resentment and turned away. Gruffly he said to Hewey, "You boys had just as well move on. Ain't nothin' more for you here."

Hewey admitted, "I reckon not." He hesitated. "Sheriff, supposin' we could raise money for his bail, how much would it be?"

"More than you cowpunchers can get ahold of."

"What did he do to get himself in so much trouble?"

The sheriff extended the fingers of his left hand and began counting them. "There was drunk and disorderly. There was destruction of property and cussin' in public. There was disrespect to an officer of the law. There was assault on an officer of the law. There was resistance to arrest. Then there was just bein' Jerome. That in itself is good for thirty days."

"In other words, you just plain don't like him."

"Now, where would you get an idea like that?"

Hewey and Walter walked across the courthouse square to where Gabe and Fat were waiting. Hewey said, "The lady that runs the restaurant asked us over for supper. At least the day ain't a total failure."

Gabe asked, "Does that include me?"

"We'll find out."

The restaurant was simple, four tables and a counter with a few stools. A large iron range stood along the back wall, and to the left of it a set of shelves on which plates, saucers, and porcelain cups were stacked. A closed door indicated that another room or two existed beyond that, possibly a pantry and living quarters.

Mrs. Simpson smiled as the four entered. "Welcome, boys. You-all set yourselves down at a table." The smile faltered as she noticed Gabe.

He caught her reaction and said, "You got a place somewhere for me, ma'am?"

She thought about it. "Right now I've got no other customers. Sit with your friends if you want to. If somebody comes in, you can move back into the kitchen."

Hewey failed to see the difference. Her kitchen was separated from the rest of the room only by the short counter. But that was the way things were, and he saw no gain in starting another Civil War he was certain to lose. He said, "Ma'am, we appreciated your invitation, but we expect to pay."

"And I expect you to. A woman's got to live, and there ain't too many ways for a respectable widow to do it these days." She shoved a couple of sticks of wood into the stove. "I took the last of my chicken to Jerome. Beefsteak suit you? It's cheaper than chicken anyhow."

"Beef sounds just fine." Eli Jessup's beef had always tasted good on the Two Cs table, dinner, supper, and sometimes for breakfast. There were usually enough J Bar strays that Tarpley's own beef was seldom needed. Even when it was, nobody told Tarpley.

She dipped the steaks in flour, then dropped them into sizzling lard in a deep cast-iron skillet. After they were fried she made gravy with flour and part of the leftover grease. She brought it out in four plates, following up with coffee.

Hewey asked her, "You known the sheriff long?"

"Long enough."

"He's got us in an awful bind. Is there a soft side to him anywhere?"

She stared out the window toward the courthouse. "He's a better man than most folks know, only he's kin to a Missouri mule. Everything has got to be his own idea or it's no good. What's your trouble with him?"

Hewey explained about their need to get Jerome Padgett out of jail. She listened thoughtfully, then said, "By rights Jerome ought not to be there. It was all on account of Quincy bein' jealous that he got in trouble. Some of the fault is mine."

"How do you figure that?"

She pulled up a chair and sat at a corner of the table. "You might think me and Quincy are too old for romance, but that's not so. He's been about halfway courtin' me for a couple of years now. The trouble is, he starts shyin' away whenever it looks like we're fixin' to get serious. Every time I think I'm gettin' him in a marryin' notion, he draws back. Jerome showed up here and acted like he was takin' a shine to me. So I started tryin' to make Quincy think I was interested."

"Was you?"

"Not really, and I don't think Jerome was, either. I was just tryin' to build a fire under Quincy. Guess I overdid it a little. He picked a fight with Jerome, a real head and knuckle buster. Quincy filed charges, and the judge ordered Jerome to jail. I feel bad about it because it wasn't none of Jerome's fault. It was mine. But he's the one payin' for it."

Hewey grimaced. "And us. Without him, we're rimfired."

"I wish I could help you. I've tried tellin' Quincy that

Jerome doesn't mean anything to me. It's like he's gone deaf in both ears."

Hewey found a piece of gristle in his steak. Grass beef was sometimes tough, but it could be chewed if one was determined. Most other problems could be worked out too if one chewed on them hard enough, he thought. He had run into what looked like a stone wall with Appleby in San Antonio, but that had been resolved. Appleby was happy to tell him how to find Padgett once he realized this cattle venture would take the old cowman away for a while.

He said, "Maybe we've been goin' about this backwards. We tried to get the sheriff to sympathize with us, and there ain't much sympathy in him. But if he was to realize we'd be takin' Padgett off to West Texas and out of his way, he might see things different."

The widow pursed her lips as she considered. "Might not work. I think it warms his heart to see Jerome behind those bars."

"But what if he decided it'd make his heart even warmer not to see him at all?"

"What would make him decide that?"

"Maybe the notion that feelin' sorry for Jerome was makin' you get more and more interested in him."

"I played that game already. You see what came of it."

"This time might be different. Maybe it hasn't soaked in on Quincy yet that as long as Jerome is in jail and you're feedin' him, you'll be seein' him three times a day."

Walter argued, "Hewey, I don't know where you got such a sneaky way of thinkin'."

"Bein' straightforward hasn't got us anywhere. It's time to try a little innocent dishonesty."

The widow brought the steaming coffeepot to refill the cups. "I don't guess things could get much worse. With Quincy, though, you've got to haze him along careful and make him believe it's his own idea."

Hewey looked out the window. "Now's a good time to start. I see him comin'."

Gabe got up from the table and carried his supper behind the counter, near the big range.

Quincy entered, speaking first to Mrs. Simpson. "Howdy, Ellie. Got anything left?"

"Not much. I gave the best to Jerome. Looked to me like he deserved it."

"He don't deserve nothin'." The sheriff turned his attention to the three cowboys at the table. "When are you-all leavin'?" It sounded like an invitation to go, and soon.

Hewey said, "We need to rest our horses a day or two before we head back to the Pecos. It's a long ways."

"How long?"

"It'll take us a couple of weeks if we don't want to wear down the horses. It'd take a lot longer if we was drivin' cattle. Might take a month on account of the calves."

Mrs. Simpson said, "I for one am glad Jerome won't be makin' such a long trip at his age. I enjoy feedin' a man that likes my cookin' the way he does."

The sheriff growled, "He likes it too much. You're spoilin' him."

"Where's the harm in that? Maybe it'll fatten him up a bit. I like to see a man with some flesh on his bones."

"Have you looked at him real good? He's as ugly as an old rail fence."

"You're not seein' him with a woman's eyes. A woman looks past the outside. She sees what's in his heart."

She brought the sheriff a fried steak with potatoes, biscuits, and coffee. "Sorry I don't have any cake left for you. I gave the last of it to Jerome."

Quincy grumbled, "Looks to me like Jerome gets the best of everything."

"Just tryin' to keep him as happy as I can. My heart goes out to him, wastin' away in that awful jail."

Quincy picked at his food, showing no pleasure in it. Finally he dropped his fork. "Dammit, Ellie, I wish you'd quit comin' over there."

"A single woman has got to make a livin'. I have a contract with the county to feed the prisoners as long as there are any."

Quincy stared so hard at the three cowboys that Hewey began to fear he was about to arrest them for something. Being sheriff, he could always find a reason. "You say it'd take you a month or more to drive them cattle out to the Pecos?"

"Likely. And we'd have to buy and gather them first. That might take another week or two."

"Are you sure Jerome would be goin' with you?"

"That's the agreement he had with C.C. Tarpley."

Quincy glanced back and forth between Hewey and Ellie Simpson, his face in a twist. "I'll go talk to the judge. Might be he'd see his way clear to suspend Jerome's sentence. But he'd want to be promised that Jerome wouldn't be comin' back and causin' trouble anytime soon."

Hewey said, "He might even decide to stay out on the Pecos."

Quincy told Mrs. Simpson, "This means you'd lose a customer."

She feigned disappointment. "I'll sure miss him."

Jerome Padgett looked over his shoulder at the courthouse receding in the distance. "I don't know what you boys done to Quincy, but I'm almighty glad to be out in the fresh air and sunshine. A man can get moldy layin' around a stuffy old jailhouse."

Hewey said, "We just appealed to his good nature."

"I didn't know he had one." Padgett looked at the riders on either side of him. "Is this the crew C.C. sent?"

"All but Gabe. We picked him up on the trail."

"What does he know about cows?"

"He knows where the feed goes in and where it comes out. That's about all. But I'm bettin' he can learn."

"I've seen some black boys that was good hands. They can bring trouble to you, though. There's always people that don't like them."

"We've already found that out. But he's got no kin and no place in particular to go. We figure he can hold up his end of the work."

"It's up to you to see that he does. I ain't got the time or patience to be schoolin' any greenhorns."

As soon as they were clear of town, Padgett reached into his saddlebag and drew out a pint whiskey bottle less than half full. Hewey watched worriedly as Padgett flipped the cork out and let it fall to the ground, for he remembered Tarpley's warning. Padgett tilted the bottle up and did not lower it until it was empty. He coughed, wiped a sleeve across his mouth, then threw the bottle off to the side of the trail.

He cleared his throat with a mighty noise. "Had to get the taste of the jailhouse out of my mouth. That's my last drink till we deliver the herd." He made a crooked grin that exposed a gap in his teeth. "Bet Old Quincy told you I'm a hard-drinkin' man. I don't know where folks get such a notion. I only get drunk four or five times a year. Ain't never killed anybody, even when I felt like it."

Fat stared wistfully at the empty bottle, which cast a reflection in the sunlight. He complained, "Wouldn't have hurt him to share some of it."

Padgett heard. He said, "Fat boy, if you're goin' to bellyache through this whole trip, you'd better strike out for home right now. I don't tolerate malcontents when I boss an outfit."

Fat looked at the ground. "I didn't mean nothin'. Just a little thirsty, is all."

"Water and coffee'll have to do you. There's a time to drink and a time to work. They don't mix worth a damn." He turned to Gabe. "Are you a drinkin' man, boy?"

"Only when I can get it. That's been seldom."

"Let's keep it that way. If you've got any questions, ask Hewey or Walter. Don't come botherin' me with them. Do your job and I won't pay notice to what color you are."

"Does that mean I'm hired?"

"Four bits a day. Six when you show me you're a cowboy." Padgett asked Hewey, "You think that's all right with C.C.?"

Hewey nodded. "He's payin' me and Walter six."

"That ain't enough, but cowpunchers are in surplus supply. Cow*boys,* though, there ain't near enough of them."

"There's a difference between cowpunchers and cow-boys?"

"There is. We'll find out pretty soon which one you are."

{ TWELVE }

B ecause of a late start in leaving town, they did not
reach Karnes County until dusk the second day.
Padgett did not remain with the wagon road. Knowing his way, he cut across the sandy grassland through
mesquite and live oak.

He said, "Dark is fixin' to catch us. We'll make camp
on a little creek up ahead. I'd rather approach Old Man
Dodge in the daylight anyway. If we ride up on him in the
dark, he's liable to shoot first and then ask us who we are."

Hewey said, "Nervous, is he?"

"Karnes County is a nervous locality. Been a good
many men killed. Helena used to be the jumpin'-off place
to the coast, as well as to Mexico. It was a hell-roarin'
town till the railroad passed it by. It rolled over and died
after that."

"Just because it didn't get the railroad?"

"It's happened to lots of places. Most of the business
moved away. Folks called a new county-seat election.
Karnes City won, but it had to send an armed posse to
steal the records out of the old Helena courthouse in the
dead of night. You can still get killed if you cross the
wrong people. Old Man Dodge has crossed a good many
in his time."

Fat listened with growing apprehension. "I didn't figure on runnin' into any kind of danger."

"We won't run *from* any. A little danger flavors up your life, like salt flavors the beans. Just a pinch, though. Too much spoils the pot."

Hewey suspected Padgett was having a little fun at Fat's expense, but there was a chance he was serious. He said, "I'd better tell you now: if we run into trouble, I'm not a good shot."

"No matter. I'll do the shootin'. Me and the fat boy."

Fat looked as if he had swallowed a chew of tobacco.

Next morning they rode by several prosperous-looking farms and a small community with a steepled church. Padgett said, "There's good soil here. It doesn't always rain enough, but that's Texas for you. Before the war a bunch of Polanders came here from the old country. Poor as church mice they was. They come nigh starvin' the first winter till old Colonel Butler brought them a bunch of his own steers for beef. A good man, the colonel, if you was his friend. But you didn't want him for an enemy.

"That's the way with folks down here. They'll give you their last shirt if they see you need it, but they'll fight like bulldogs if somebody tries to take it away from them."

Hewey said, "Sounds like C.C. Tarpley and Eli Jessup."

"I bossed trail herds for them two mosshorns way back when they was partners. They was set in their ways like a pair of old maids. Quarreled like two snot-nose kids in a school yard. I had a gutful of it and quit."

Hewey said, "It hasn't got any better. I suspect that C.C. is havin' you buy these cattle just for spite. He's found some land for sale and wants to stock it before Jessup can beat him to it."

Padgett chewed on that a while. "This is the kind of childishness that made me quit them. I believe I'll make C.C. pay me an extra commission on this deal. He'll squeal like a stuck pig."

They left the farming community behind. Padgett pointed to an adobe house in the distance. "We're comin' up on Dodge's country now."

"Where's the fence?"

"He hasn't got one, except for a holdin' trap. Them's his cows yonder with the D Cross brand."

Hewey noted that they were in good flesh. He figured they were likely to lose some of that out on the Pecos, where they had to hunt harder to find grass. He asked, "How come Dodge is sellin' out? This looks like good cattle country."

"He's gettin' on in years, and stove up to where he can't take care of things like he wants to. He's got no kids, just a shiftless nephew he doesn't like much. He believes the boy would squander the whole shebang."

Walter declared, "If it was mine, I wouldn't squander it. When I get a place of my own I'll hold onto it, come hell or high water."

Hewey said, "With the money Dodge'll get for these cattle and the ranch, he could go to San Antonio and live high. I would if I was in his place."

Padgett said, "Dodge's not one for high livin'. All he needs is a good horse or two, a roof that don't leak, and a bed that won't make his bones ache. That'll keep him as content as a natural old grouch can ever be."

Nearing the adobe house, Hewey saw that it was but a

crumbling shell, its roof gone, its windows and doors removed. At one corner stood a small round wall that he took to be the top of a cistern.

Fat exclaimed, "I'm thirsty enough to drink the whole thing dry."

Padgett made a wry smile as Fat loped ahead. "He's a little late. The cistern dried up years ago."

The windlass leaned a little. A short length of rotted rope still clung to it. Fat cursed a short complaint as he dismounted and peered over the edge. He said, "I can't see no water." He dropped a stone. Hewey heard it strike bottom. He heard no splash.

Padgett said, "Used to be a Mexican settler here. Dodge bought him out."

Hewey had heard stories about Americans driving the original owners away and taking over their land. "You sure he bought him out, or maybe he just run him off?"

"Old Dodge is rougher than a dry cob. He'll drive a hard bargain, but he wouldn't cheat anybody, not even a Mexican."

They came after a time to a fence. The barbed wire still had some of its original shine. Padgett said, "This is the holdin' trap. Dodge fenced it off for those times when he needs to keep stock gathered for a few days like for sellin' or for doctorin'. Keeps a few horses in it, too."

Rising dust drew Hewey's attention to a small gather of cattle moving up the fence toward him. A rider loped out in front and stepped down to open a wire gate. Padgett said, "Looks like they're throwin' them into the trap." He spurred up to help. Hewey and the others followed.

A Mexican lad in his teens gave them a civil nod, then turned his attention to pointing the cattle through the opening. Reed-thin, he was mounted on a sorrel bronc, using a hackamore instead of bridle and bits. The horse eyed the newcomers nervously, ears flicking back and forth as he searched for something to booger at.

The cattle, bearing the D Cross brand, filed through the open gate, followed by three Mexican riders. The young man beckoned Padgett and the others through the gate, then got down and closed it.

"Hola, Juanito," Padgett said. "We come to see your *patrón*." He turned to Hewey. "In this part of the country it helps if you can speak Spanish."

Juanito said, "Señor Padgett, you are many days late. The *patrón* has looked a long time for you."

"Had a little trouble. Where's the old man?"

"*A casa*. Yesterday he fall from his horse. Today he hurts much. We gather his cattle."

Hewey guessed four or five hundred head were confined within sight. He assumed there were more that he could not see. It would not take long for them to graze off whatever grass the small enclosure could provide.

Padgett said, "We'll ride on to the house and talk to him."

Juanito winced. "He has much to say to you, I think."

"What kind of humor is he in?"

"Same as every day. He has much anger."

"Nothin' new about that." Padgett jerked his head at Hewey and the others. "Come on, we'd just as well let him get the cussin' over with so we can settle down to business."

Hewey had built a pleasant mental image of what the Dodge homeplace should look like, perhaps a nice two-story frame house with a cupola and ornate gingerbread trim around the eaves. The first sight of it disillusioned him. He had seen spartan dwellings, including the one in which he and Walter had grown up, but the Dodge ranch headquarters was only a few notches better than a coyote den. The house was a small, squat adobe with much of its original plaster fallen away, leaving the mud walls exposed and gradually deteriorating. Standing in sharp contrast were a sturdy barn and an expansive set of solidly built corrals. Two windmills stood tall against the sky, their fans turning slowly. He could almost taste the water. It was clear that Dodge's first priority was business. Comfort came later, if at all.

Hewey said, "His stock lives better than he does. From the looks of this place, he doesn't have a woman naggin' at him for somethin' better." He aimed the remark more at Walter than at Padgett.

Walter made no response. Padgett said, "As far as I know he's been a bachelor all his life. When he was younger he would sometimes bring a sportin' woman down from San Antone, but they never stayed long."

Walter declared, "I can understand why. I'd want to give a woman somethin' better than what I see here."

Hewey frowned. "And she'd keep you broke. You're better off like you are. You don't have to worry about anybody but yourself."

"And you, Hewey. Sometimes you worry me half to death."

Hewey developed several different mental images of Dodge. They had one thing in common: eyes that flashed fire.

Padgett said to Fat and Gabe, "You boys tie your horses and rest yourselves in the shade. Mr. Dodge don't like too much company at once. Me and Hewey and Walter will go talk to him."

Fat seemed grateful for a chance to get out of the sun. He dismounted and handed his reins to Gabe, silently letting him know he expected Gabe to tie his horse for him. Hewey considered telling Fat to do it himself, but at the moment he had more pressing business.

If Gabe harbored any resentment, he did not betray it. He was probably used to being treated like a servant.

Padgett cautioned, "You-all better let me do the talkin'. Old Man Dodge is kind of peculiar."

More peculiar than you? Hewey wondered.

Padgett knocked on the doorframe because the door itself was open. From inside, Hewey heard a groan of protest, then the creaking of bedsprings. In a moment a bent-shouldered little man came to the door in his sock feet, limping heavily, grumbling with every step. He had shrunk considerably from Hewey's mental images.

The rancher blinked against the outdoor brightness, trying to see. "Who the hell is it, and what the hell do you want?"

Padgett said, "It's me, Mr. Dodge. Sorry if I got you up from bed."

Dodge mumbled, "Hell, if it wasn't you it'd be some other son of a bitch. Come on in." He squinted, still having trouble seeing. "Who's that with you? I don't invite just any damned Meskin into this house."

Hewey realized why Padgett had told Gabe to stay out in the shade. And he probably assumed Fat would have nothing constructive to add to the conversation.

Padgett said, "These boys are here representin' C.C. Tarpley. Hewey Calloway is C.C.'s top hand."

That was a shameless stretch of the truth, but Hewey liked the sound of it.

Dodge's flinty eyes were not ablaze, though otherwise

they were much as Hewey had imagined them. They bored through him like a drill. Dodge said, "The hell. I've heard about Tarpley. He's too much of a tightwad to keep a top hand. These boys don't look very damned bright to me."

Hewey considered telling him he had been all the way through the fourth grade. He could even exaggerate a little and make it the fifth grade, but he decided Dodge wasn't interested in that much information. He said, "Me and Walter have been up the trail once."

Dodge was not impressed. "Hell, half the men in this county have been up the trail, and lots of them still don't know how to pour water out of a bucket."

Hewey couldn't come up with a good answer. Though he had run into cranky people all his life, Old Man Dodge might be the crankiest of them all. By all odds he was the most profane. The Calloway brothers would earn their wages, looked like, just putting up with his irascible nature for however long it would take to get the cattle gathered and onto the trail.

He wondered if he might have been better off waiting at the ranch and taking his chances with Smith or Trumble or whatever the cow thief's real name was.

Dodge motioned for the three to come all the way into the house. It was small, just one room with a stove, steel cot, table, and three well-aged hard wooden chairs. Shelves along one wall held dishes and canned foodstuff. Dodge braced himself on a chair, then sank with care onto the edge of the cot. He grunted painfully and pressed a hand against his hip.

Padgett mentioned that they had encountered the young vaquero Juanito turning cattle into the trap. "He told me you fell off of a horse."

Dodge loosed a short spurt of profanity. "Like hell. I

ain't so old that I fall off of horses. I got throwed off fair and square. That boy talks too damned much."

Padgett quickly tried to cover. "Maybe he did say throwed off. Age has made me smarter, but it ain't helped my memory much."

Dodge ignored the explanation. "Where the hell have you been all this time? You was supposed to've got these cattle three weeks ago."

"Had a little run-in with a narrow-minded sheriff. I'd be in the hoosegow yet if it wasn't for these boys."

"You put me in a hell of a damned bind. I got to move all my cattle off of this property inside of three days. Me and my vaqueros been roundin' them up and throwin' them into the trap. Since you didn't show up, I figured I'd have to drive them to San Antone and take whatever the hell I can get for them."

"Why the big hurry?"

"Any remnants that's left here past the day after tomorrow will go to the new owner. I didn't figure on it takin' so long for you to get here."

It was common practice in ranch sales that ungathered remnants of cattle went to the buyer.

Padgett said, "It ain't your fault I got delayed. Looks like your buyer would give you some slack."

"Slack hell! You ever met Sid Slocum?"

"Seen him. Never cared to meet him."

"I shot better men than him in the border wars, and they wasn't even white. This'd be a better world if his mammy had stuffed him in a sack and drowned him the day he was born. Damned if I know how he's got by this long without somebody killin' him."

"The meek ain't inherited the earth yet. How come you sold to him in the first place?"

"I didn't." Dodge dropped his chin and turned his face to the wall. "I lied to you. I didn't exactly sell this place. I lost it to the bank, and they sold the paper to Slocum, the thievin' son of a bitch."

"I had no idea things was that tough."

"All I'll get out of it is what the cattle bring. They wasn't mortgaged."

"Why couldn't you have sold just enough cattle to pay off what you owed?"

"Too much debt and not enough cattle."

"Looks like the bank would accept what you could pay them and extend the note on the rest."

"The bank might've, but Slocum wouldn't. He demanded all of it in cash. He knowed I couldn't raise that much." Dodge's face was flushed with rage. "I wish I could set the whole damned place afire when I leave. Leave that bastard nothin' but a pile of ashes."

Hewey intruded. "Who is this Slocum?"

Dodge said, "He's a highbinder who got his start runnin' whiskey up in the Indian Nations. When he got chased out of there, he came down into this country and swindled poor Meskins out of their land. Now he's buyin' up mortgages and foreclosin' on them. A scavenger, is what he is."

Padgett said, "At least you'll have the cattle money. You can start over."

"At my age? Damn it to hell, why have we got to get old, anyway?"

"There's only one way to prevent it, and that's to die young. Me and you are already past that."

Dodge's anger subsided. "The way I figure it, we got just today and tomorrow to finish the gather, then push

my cattle across the property line by the day after tomorrow. Any remnants we leave behind are Slocum's."

"Juanito and some of your Mexicans was pushin' cattle into the trap as we came along."

"They'll have time enough for one more sweep before
sundown. We'll work the southeast corner tomorrow."

Hewey thought he was using the word *we* too loosely.
Dodge appeared too stove up to get back on a horse.

Padgett said, "Me and these boys will throw in with
you. We'll round up everything but the jackrabbits."

Dodge nodded. "I'll be able to ride tomorrow."

Hewey doubted that.

Dodge asked, "What kind of horse was Juanito ridin'?"

Padgett told him, "A sorrel bronc, with a hackamore."

"So I thought. He favors that colt and neglects the
others he's supposed to break. I've got to give him a
damned good bawlin' out."

Hewey suspected Dodge was handy at doing that.

Padgett observed, "Juanito seems like a good hand."

Dodge shook his head. "If arthritis didn't have such a
choke hold on me, I'd be breakin' the horses myself instead of turnin' them over to a Meskin. That Juanito thinks
he's *puro jiñete,* but he's got a hell of a lot to learn about
bronc stompin'. How can you teach these Meskin boys
anything when they're too dumb to know the American
language?"

"He speaks American better than I speak Mexican."

"If they're goin' to live here, by God, they ought to
learn to talk American. The Bible is in American. Ain't
that good enough for them?"

Hewey caught a faint smile in Walter's eyes and

hoped he was not going to try to educate Dodge on the history of the scriptures. The old man would probably chase both of them out of the house, and maybe off the ranch.

Dodge made an effort to get up from the edge of the cot but fell back, one hand pressed against his hip again. He seemed to pale.

Padgett took a quick step toward him. "Are you all right?"

Dodge waved him away. "Ain't nothin' wrong with me. Just sore as hell from that hard landin' yesterday."

Hewey suspected it was more than that, and Padgett's expression indicated that he had the same feeling. Padgett said, "We'll get out of the way and let you rest. If it's all right, we'll set up camp in your barn."

"Camp anywhere that suits you. Burn it down for all I care. It ain't mine for much longer anyway."

Dodge did not try again to get up as the three visitors went out the door. Walter said, "He looks like there might be more wrong with him than just fallin' off of a horse."

"He's wore out," Padgett said. "One of these old ranches'll do that to you."

Hewey agreed. "That's why I never want to have one. How many rich men did you ever see that looked happy? Soon as they get somethin', they start layin' awake at night afraid they'll lose it. Ownin' a lot of property makes a man grow old before his time."

Walter argued, "It hasn't hurt C.C. Tarpley."

"Don't get any notions about competin' with the likes of C.C. When a little fish tries to swim with the big fish, they turn around and eat him."

At the barn they found an elderly Mexican loading a wagon to which a chuckbox was attached.

Padgett said, "I suppose you're the *cocinero?*"

"The cook? *Sí, señor. Me llama Sixto.*"

"Well, Sixto, you got five more mouths to feed."

Hewey saw a horseman approaching the adobe house in an easy jog trot, his spine straight, his head back. He was Anglo, not Mexican, so he was no employee of Dodge's. His ruddy face was twisted as if he smelled a skunk.

Padgett clenched his fists. "Son of a bitch, that's Sid Slocum. Come to rub salt into Old Man Dodge's wounds, I expect. Stand by me, boys. We ain't lettin' him into the house." Padgett led Hewey and Walter back to the adobe. Gabe and Fat followed.

The closer Slocum came, the less Hewey liked his looks. He was already prejudiced by what Dodge had said, and the man's stiff-backed, arrogant way of sitting in the saddle indicated that he had appointed himself the cock of the walk. People like that made Hewey think of a bloated steer. The cure for those was a puncture in the side to let the air out.

Slocum glared down at the newcomers without making any move to dismount. "Who are you people, and what is your business here?"

Padgett set his feet apart in a challenging stance. "Ain't none of your business who comes here or what they do. This place ain't yours for a few more days."

"At midnight Wednesday, to be exact. I came to see if Dodge has moved his cattle yet."

"He's thrown most of them in a holdin' trap out yonder. You can't see but a few from here."

Slocum turned to look northward. A narrow neck of the trap ran up to the headquarters so that cattle could come in for water. A handful loafed around the water lot. The rest were grazing toward the trap's far end, out of sight.

Slocum declared, "They had better be gone on time, or they will be mine. The contract firmly states . . ."

Padgett stopped him with a gesture of dismissal. "I know all about your contract, and how you're drivin' an old man out of his home. You ain't wanted here while the place is still Mr. Dodge's. You'd better git before the sky clouds up and rains on you."

Slocum involuntarily looked up before he caught himself. Not a cloud was in sight. "I have come to talk to Dodge. I intend to do so."

"You can't. He's ailin'."

"He will ail more severely if he does not vacate this ranch. I'll be back Thursday to take possession." He scowled. "Your name is Padgett, is it not?"

Padgett gave him only a low grunt.

Slocum edged his horse closer to the house. Hewey stepped in to block him. "Mr. Padgett says you ain't goin' in."

Slocum's scowl deepened. "Get out of the way, cowboy." He spoke the word *cowboy* as he might say *smallpox*.

For a moment Slocum appeared ready to try to ride over Hewey. Gabe grabbed Slocum's bridle reins just below the bits. Slocum said, "Turn loose, nigger." He roughly yanked the reins from Gabe's hand and jerked his horse around. He rode away, his chin high in anger.

Gabe rubbed his hand, for Slocum's leather reins had burned his fingers.

Walter said, "You've made an enemy of him, Hewey."

"He ain't anybody I'd want for a friend."

"From what I gather," Padgett said, "he doesn't have

many of those anyway. But he's got money, and a man with plenty of money can rent friends when he needs them." He pointed at the barn. "Let's unload our stuff. Then we'll ride out and see if we can help Juanito pick up some more cattle."

He asked Gabe, "How's your hand?"

"Just smarts a little, is all."

"Rub some axle grease on it when we get back. Axle grease and Epsom salts will cure almost anything."

{ THIRTEEN }

They gathered more than a hundred head the next day and turned them into the small trap. Hewey noted that the grass was disappearing under the weight of heavy grazing. It would be high time to get these cattle on the move even if Dodge was not facing a short deadline.

Dodge had dragged himself from the house, ignoring Padgett's insistence that they could handle the job without him. By standing his horse next to a corral fence, he managed to climb up and force his aching body into the saddle. He turned away offers of help. "Dammit to hell, I can do this by myself," he declared, his face pinched in pain. "I ain't no damned cripple."

As the last small set of cows and calves passed through the wire gate and he finished counting, Dodge said grudgingly, "Altogether we're just about twenty short of seven hundred head. I hope whatever's left come down with the bloody scours." He reconsidered. "Naw, I wouldn't wish that onto a bunch of poor dumb animals. I wish Slocum would get the scours instead."

Padgett said, "We'll have to commence movin' them in the mornin' to get across your property line by sundown."

"You can bet that graspin' son of a bitch will watch us all the way," Dodge grumbled.

Hewey could see a man on horseback, observing from a distance of several hundred yards. He said, "I believe he already is."

After supper the old man hobbled around the adobe house and made his slow way out to the barn, pausing often to stare at first one thing and then another. Walter told Hewey, "He's takin' a last look around. He hates leavin' here a lot worse than he lets on."

For a long while Dodge leaned against a corral fence, his gaze fixed far away in space, and perhaps also in time.

The young vaquero Juanito tentatively moved in Dodge's direction as if he sought to give him comfort. He stopped short and considered. He turned back reluctantly, leaving the old rancher's privacy undisturbed.

Walter said, "I reckon he sees Dodge as a substitute daddy."

Hewey said, "The old dickens doesn't treat him like a substitute son."

Padgett said, "To hear Dodge cuss you might think he's too tough for tears, but he's weepin' inside. He's put a big part of his life into this place, a lot of blood and sweat."

Hewey nodded toward Walter. "That's what bein' tied to a piece of property will do to you. I don't want to stay in one place so long that I grieve when I leave it. There's always somethin' better over the hill."

Walter said, "Even if there is, it won't mean as much if none of it belongs to you."

Watching the old man, Hewey felt a tightening in his throat. He thought it was probably something he ate for supper. Sixto's cooking had more pepper in it than he was used to.

Juanito and the other Mexican hands slept near the corrals in an adobe even smaller than Dodge's. Hewey awoke in the barn before good daylight, stirred out of sleep by excited voices speaking in Spanish. He laid his top blanket aside, putting on his hat and then his boots. In his underwear, he walked out into the first light of a pink dawn to see Juanito on the night horse, galloping toward Dodge's house.

Hewey shouted, "What's the matter? Who's dead?"

Juanito shouted back, "Most of the cattle, they are gone."

The youngster jumped to the ground, dropped the reins, and raced into Dodge's house. Hewey reentered the barn and shouted, "Somethin's gone haywire. Everybody better get up."

He took time to put on his britches but was still buttoning his shirt when he went outside and headed down toward the house. Juanito hurried past him, leading the horse back to the corrals. With one boot on and one in his hand, Dodge stood on the front step trying to holler in a hoarse voice. "Saddle my old dun. I'll be there in a minute."

Hewey followed Juanito. The young Mexican said, "I go to rustle horses for work today, but I don't see many cattle. What I see is the fence down, and the cattle gone."

Hewey found himself talking like Dodge. "How in the hell could that happen?"

"I think it was Slocum."

The ranch horses were accustomed to a morning feed and had not gone away with the cattle. Juanito had brought them in. Hewey saddled and was following Juanito out into the trap before the other men began catching their mounts. As the sun broke over the horizon, Juanito stopped to look at the ground. "Many cattle tracks," he said.

Hewey saw horse tracks as well. "Them cattle didn't stray out by theirselves. Somebody drove them."

Juanito showed him where the fence was down at the back side of the trap, some distance from headquarters. The wires had been cut, then pulled free of the posts for most of fifty yards. The cattle had been pushed out through the wide opening and scattered. Hewey saw a few grazing in the morning's early light, for some would stop when they were no longer driven. There were no-where near the seven hundred that had been in the trap.

He said, "Slocum's bunch did their dirty work far enough away that none of us would hear them. And we were supposed to get the cattle off of the property today."

The other men caught up to Hewey and Juanito. Fat Gervin, sleepy-eyed, brought up the rear.

Dodge's face was crimson. "That damned Slocum. I always knowed he was a rattlesnake, but I never would've thought of him doin' this."

Padgett said, "We'll get busy and bring back as many as we can."

Dodge cursed. "How many will that be? Everything we can't find today will be remnants tomorrow. They'll belong to that schemin' son of a bitch."

"We'll do our best and salvage all we can," Padgett said.

Fat complained that he hadn't had breakfast, but no one paid attention to him. Hewey struck out in a long trot toward the farthest group of cattle he could see. Walter followed. They gave the cows and calves a push back toward the trap, then set out to seek more. Gabe joined them. Juanito and the other hands set off in different directions. Hewey lost track of Dodge and Padgett.

By noon a rough count told him they had recovered more than four hundred. That was well short of the number originally confined in the trap.

Fat said, "Looks like that old man ain't goin' to have as much money as he figured on for his retirement." If he felt any sympathy, he did not show it.

Hewey said, "We ain't done yet. We'll go back and scout for some more."

Fat's shoulders drooped. "I wouldn't've taken this job if I'd known it'd starve me to death."

"Missin' a meal won't kill you. If they was to render you out they'd get a hundred pounds of pure lard."

By late afternoon the hands had gathered a couple of hundred more. Dodge counted them, too discouraged even to curse. "Close to a hundred short."

Padgett said, "We'd best settle for what we've got and start them to movin'."

Dodge's face was pinched. "Even if we push all night, I doubt we can make it across my line by mornin'."

Padgett said, "Let's try anyway. Slocum ain't gettin' this herd without he knows he's been in a horse race."

Hewey helped get the cattle started westward, then stopped. "I'm for goin' back to hunt some more."

Juanito said, "I go, too."

Padgett counseled against it. "We'll need all hands to hold what we've got and keep them movin' at a good clip." He glanced worriedly at Dodge. "I don't know how much longer he can hold on, the shape he's in."

Walter warned, "Our horses are about give out."

Padgett nodded at Juanito. "You'd best go back to headquarters and bring up the rest of the remuda. Take Fat with you. He won't hinder you too much. And tell Sixto to load the chuckwagon with everything he can lay his hands on."

Fat was willing. He said, "Maybe then we can get somethin' to eat." He and Juanito rode off in a long trot.

Padgett looked toward the afternoon sun. "We've still got a couple hours of daylight. We'll keep pushin' after dark even if we lose a few." He rode over to talk to Dodge. Dodge still lamented leaving close to a hundred head for Slocum.

Padgett said, "You know the old Bible story about the man who went lookin' for one lost sheep and forgot about the other ninety and nine?"

Dodge said, "I never read it. And these ain't sheep."

Juanito and Fat brought up the remuda just before dark so all the riders could change to fresh mounts. Sixto took the wagon on ahead. Later he would stop to build a fire. He would reheat last night's beans and boil coffee to be ready when the herd reached him. Another vaquero took charge of the extra horses. By their nature they wanted to move faster than the cowherd. Some played, biting at one another and pitching, squealing, breaking wind.

Hewey speculated, "If we travel all night, maybe we'll be gone before Slocum knows we've trumped him."

Juanito's eyes were cold. "What I would like to do to the Slocum . . ." He slid a finger across his throat.

Hewey said, "There's probably some fool law against it."

The cattle were allowed to water in the creek while the men ate a quick supper of coffee, beans, and dutch oven bread that had not been given time to bake all the way through. Hewey looked at the rising moon. "Lucky for us it's full. At least we can see better what we're doin'."

The skimpy supper gave him fresh energy for a while, but the effect began to wear off in the long hours after midnight. One of the Mexican hands went to sleep and fell out of the saddle. The cattle had slowed considerably despite the best efforts of the men at the rear to keep punching them up.

He did not know the country well enough to recognize landmarks even if he had seen them. He became aware that darkness was fading under a weak show of early light in the east. He made out the ruins of a house ahead. It was the old adobe with the dried-up cistern.

Dodge seemed enlivened. His back straighter, he rode alongside the strung-out herd, encouraging the men. "Keep them comin', compadres. We're damn near there. My property ends a mile or so past that old homestead."

Hewey rubbed his eyes. His tired body ached, and the lack of sleep made his stomach cramp. He knew that from a legal standpoint they were already past the contract time for Dodge's ranch to pass into Slocum's ownership, and with it any cattle remaining on the property. But possession still counted for something.

Not enough, though. Three men rode out from behind the adobe walls. Hewey's stomach cramped harder as he recognized Sid Slocum. Not until the three approached the herd did he see the badge on one rider's vest. He assumed the third man was either a deputy or a Slocum hired hand. Neither was good news.

Dodge slumped. Padgett rode up on one side of him, Juanito on the other, offering moral support. Hewey moved closer, his tired horse slow to respond to the light touch of his spurs.

Slocum wasted no time on talk. He declared, "Sheriff, you have a duty to perform. You had best be about it, wouldn't you say?"

The sheriff grumbled, "If I was to say what I'm thinkin', it'd blister your ears." Reluctantly the lawman moved half a length ahead of Slocum, drawing a folded paper from inside his vest. "Mr. Dodge, I hate to do this."

Slocum said, "Get on with it."

The sheriff snapped back at him, "Don't be tellin' me what to do. I'm the law here."

"And I am a taxpaying citizen of this county."

"Be careful, or you may find yourself payin' a lot more. I'll remind you that I'm also the county tax assessor and collector." He crumpled the paper in his fist. "Mr. Dodge, this is an order to turn over your land and whatever's on it to Sidney Slocum as of midnight last night."

Dodge nodded dully.

The sheriff said, "As an officer of the law I've got no choice, even though I consider Mr. Slocum to be first cousin to a javelina hog." He gave Slocum a poisonous look and reined his horse around. "Let's travel, deputy."

Slocum cried out, "Wait. Where are you going?"

"Back to town. I've served your damned paper. The rest is up to you."

"But I'll need help."

"You're rich. Hire some."

Slocum's haughty manner left him. Apprehension

took its place. "I forbid you to ride off and leave me here by myself."

"Adiós, Slocum."

"I will sue you for malfeasance of duty," Slocum yelled.

The sheriff and the deputy kept riding.

Hewey wondered what *malfeasance* meant. It sounded like some dread disease. He hoped Slocum would catch it.

In his view the sheriff had left an open invitation. He waited for a reaction from Dodge.

Slocum did not wait. He reached down to his hip and came up with a pistol. "Now be gone from here, all of you. Be gone before I start shooting."

Dodge's eyes turned dangerous. "You ain't got the guts of a turkey buzzard. You won't shoot a man who's lookin' you in the eye." He urged his horse forward.

He was wrong. The pistol fired. Dodge grabbed his arm and almost fell. With a cry of rage Juanito slammed his horse against Slocum's, almost knocking the man from the saddle. Slocum brought the pistol down against Juanito's head. Juanito went to the ground.

Slocum waved the gun wildly. "Everyone stay back!"

The sheriff and deputy returned in a gallop. The lawman demanded, "Slocum, you throw that pistol down."

Slocum hesitated. The sheriff wrenched the smoking weapon from his hand and hurled it away. He sucked air between his teeth and rubbed his hand where the hot barrel had burned it.

Padgett helped Dodge down from his horse. Dodge knelt by Juanito's side, ignoring the wound in his own arm to dab his neckerchief at blood running down the boy's face.

"You all right, *hijo?* Say somethin', boy."

The sheriff dismounted, looking at first one, then the other. He touched the old man's arm. "You're hit, Mr. Dodge."

Dodge waved him away. "A scratch is all. I've had mesquite thorns bite me deeper than that. But he didn't have to pistolwhip this boy."

Slocum complained, "I was under imminent threat."

Padgett said, "As you can see, sheriff, there ain't nobody packin' iron except Slocum."

Slocum argued, "I was compelled to defend myself."

The sheriff frowned. "Looks to me like you overdid it. You want me to send a doctor out, Mr. Dodge?"

Juanito blinked, trying to clear his eyes. Dodge sighed, relieved. "You'll be all right, boy. You just lay still a while." He looked up at the sheriff. "Don't send no doctor. We can take care of our own."

"How about charges?"

"No charges, either. You go on back to town and get your breakfast." He gave Slocum a hard look and repeated, "We can take care of our own."

The sheriff gripped the reins his deputy had been holding and got on his horse. *"Hasta luego."*

Padgett said, "Ain't you takin' Slocum with you?"

"He ain't charged with anything. He can find his own way home."

Slocum yelled after the sheriff but to no avail. He made a run for his horse. Hewey cut in front of him, waving his hat and shouting. Already nervous from the shot, the horse ran off, trailing the reins. Gabe followed in a long trot, pushing it farther away. Slocum ran after him, shouting, "You bring that horse back here, nigger."

Gabe returned, but without the horse.

Fear came into Slocum's eyes. His voice was shrill. "I am within my legal rights."

Padgett knotted his fists. "Sure you are. Was I you, I'd go catch my horse right now and start inspectin' your ranch way over on the far side. Else some of these boys may forget their gentle nature."

Slocum ran for his pistol, which lay where the sheriff had thrown it.

Padgett shouted, "Head him off. He'll shoot somebody else sure as hell."

With no time to think about it, Hewey spurred between Slocum and the pistol. He loosed the horn string and shook out his rope. He flipped the loop around Slocum and rode away, taking a quick wrap around the horn. The rope went taut and jerked Slocum off his feet. He landed hard. Hewey dragged him away from the pistol.

Slocum tried to worm his way out of the loop, but Hewey jerked it tight. Slocum fell again. He raised up on his hands and shouted for the sheriff to help him.

The wind was blowing. The sheriff did not seem to hear.

The shot had spooked the cattle into a trot. They slowed again but continued moving westward. Padgett turned to Walter and the others who had gathered around. "Long as they're bound to drift anyway, I don't see any reason to get in their way."

Gabe grinned. "We'll just foller to be sure they don't get lost."

"We got to be careful not to drive them, exactly," Padgett cautioned. "The sheriff might consider that cheatin'. Just kind of nudge them a little."

Fat complained, "We're fixin' to get in bad trouble."

Walter rode to Hewey's side. "How long you goin' to keep your rope on Mr. Slocum?"

"I don't see any hurry. His horse has run off. Looks like the poor feller has got to walk home."

Padgett said, "He might come back with some of his hired help. It'd be nice if he could be talked into stayin' right here for a while."

Hewey looked toward the old house. Perhaps he might find something to which he could tie Slocum. His gaze fell upon the cistern. As he remembered, it was at least twenty feet deep.

He said, "I'll entertain Mr. Slocum while you-all go see after the cattle. It'd be a shame if they was to stray across the property line."

Gabe's grin reached all the way across his dark face. His teeth shone white as ivory. "Sure would."

Walter helped the shaky Juanito back onto his horse. Dodge admonished, "You hold on tight, boy. Wouldn't want you to fall off and hurt yourself some more." The two rode away in the wake of the cattle.

Walter held back. "Hewey, I don't know what you're plannin' on, but you're fixin' to get in trouble. Again."

"You go on. They can't lay any blame on you if you ain't here."

Walter left, but he looked back a couple of times.

Slocum still sat on the ground. Hewey made two more wraps around his middle, pulling the rope tight. Slocum's mouth sagged open. "What are you going to do?"

"I'm still studyin' on it. Been lookin' at them mesquites yonder, but I ain't sure any of them are big enough to hold a man of your weight."

Slocum blustered, "You wouldn't hang me." He swallowed hard. "Would you?"

"The thing that troubles me is what will I do with you afterwards? The shovel is on the chuckwagon, and it's gone on ahead. Couldn't depend on the coyotes to clean everything up."

He retrieved Slocum's pistol. "Get up and start walkin'."

Slocum struggled to his feet. The morning was not yet warm, but he sweated heavily. He rasped, "Be careful. That pistol is still loaded."

Hewey made a show of examining it. "Sure enough." He let it point casually toward Slocum.

"Look, cowboy, I have money. I'll give you a hundred dollars. . . ."

Hewey snorted. "A hundred dollars? That ain't a month's pay, hardly." Actually, it was more than three months' pay, but details could be tiresome.

Slocum dragged his feet as Hewey pointed him toward the crumbling mud walls. He got as far as the cistern when Hewey said, "That'll do. Stop right there."

Sweat cut little trails down Slocum's dusty face. "My God. Surely you wouldn't shoot me and throw me down that well."

"It crossed my mind."

Slocum trembled. "I'll do anything you ask me to. I'll even sign the ranch back over to Dodge."

Hewey shook his head. "Can't trust you. Soon as you got free you'd welch on the deal. But tell you what I'll do: you climb over into that well and I won't shoot you. Maybe somebody'll come along and find you eventually."

"I might starve to death before that."

"A slim chance is better than no chance at all. Climb over." He waved the pistol.

Slocum put one leg across the cistern wall. "You won't let me drop, will you? I could break my back."

"I'll hold onto the rope. You go on down."

He dismounted and braced the rope against his hip, playing it out as Slocum descended. It slackened when the man reached the dry bottom. Hewey said, "I want my rope back. I'll leave it here so if somebody was to come by, they'll have somethin' to haul you out with."

"What if no one comes by?"

"Let's don't think about that. Any rattlesnakes down there?"

"Snakes? My God."

"Must not be any or they'd've let you know. But if any show up, they won't bite you. They recognize their kin."

He opened the cylinder and removed the cartridges that remained in Slocum's pistol. Tossing them away, he leaned over the well and said, "I don't want you claimin' I stole your pistol." He dropped it in. Slocum yelped as it bounced off of his shoulder.

Riding away, Hewey could hear Slocum shouting, but the sound was muffled. He rode out to where Slocum's horse was grazing and removed the saddle, blanket, and bridle. He flipped the leather reins gently across the horse's rump. "I reckon you can find your way home." He watched the horse trot away, then took his time catching up with the herd.

Walter rode out to meet him. "I hope you didn't do somethin' that'll get us all sent to the pen."

"Never touched a hair on his head."

"Where's he at?"

"I left him back yonder. He's takin' a long look at some of his property."

{ FOURTEEN }

The herd was well beyond what had been Dodge's property line when Padgett rode back from the point and said, "We're comin' up on the San Antonio road."

Dodge was riding along with the drags and seemed to be having a hard time keeping up. The flesh wound he had suffered at Slocum's hands was evidently causing a little fever. Padgett said, "There's a ranch house up ahead. Why don't you stop off and rest awhile? You can catch up to us when you feel better."

Dodge waved him away. "I'm stayin' with you to San Antone."

"We're not so far from your place that we can't send back for anything you want to take along."

"What little I need is in Sixto's wagon. I can buy whatever I might want, and it'll be new, not junk like I'm leavin' for Slocum." He looked behind him. "Where *is* Slocum? I figured he'd've caught up and be raisin' hell with us again by now."

Hewey had not told anyone what he had done. If trouble should come of it, he wanted nobody else to be blamed.

Padgett said, "After shootin' you and pistol-whippin' Juanito, he's probably keepin' his head down."

Hewey said, "Way down."

Padgett pointed the cattle onto the trail, though most trudged along on either side of it. After a while Hewey became aware of a horseman catching up from behind. Recognizing the sheriff, he felt uneasy. Maybe he should have left the herd and made himself scarce for a while.

The sheriff was alone. He greeted Dodge first and inquired about his wound. Dodge muttered, "I've done forgot about it."

The lawman said, "I see that your cattle have strayed past your old property line."

Dodge admitted, "They wasn't past it at midnight. This is Thursday."

"As far as I'm concerned, this is Wednesday. I believe Slocum read his calendar wrong."

Dodge straightened his shoulders as he realized the sheriff was opening a door for him. "Might be he did."

The sheriff continued, "If he hollers, it'll be his word against ours. The way most folks feel about him, I doubt that any court around here would give him much of a show. You sure you're feelin' all right?"

"Like I was twenty years old."

The sheriff smiled. "Then take care of yourself, kid." He started to turn away.

Hewey called to him. "Sheriff, hold up a minute. I need to talk to you."

Walter gave him a questioning look, but Hewey motioned for him to go on. He waited until the others had passed beyond hearing before he said, "It's about Slocum."

The sheriff's eyebrows lifted. "I hope you've done no violence to him."

"No, he's safe and sound where I left him, but he ain't

goin' noplace for a while. You know that old adobe ruin with the dry cistern?"

"I've been there."

"I was figurin' on goin' back and doin' it myself, but since you're here . . . you might ride by that cistern and take a look down inside. Not today though, maybe tomorrow. By then I expect Slocum will agree to anything that'll get him back up into the daylight."

"You dropped him down that well?"

"Didn't drop him, exactly. He climbed down of his own free will and accord. Somehow he took a silly notion I was fixin' to hang him."

The sheriff laughed. "I wonder who gave him such an idea? All right, I'll go by there tomorrow. The next day for sure."

"If any trouble comes of this, I done it all myself. Wasn't nobody else knew about it."

"I'm not sure I ever heard your name. How does Bill Jones suit you?"

Hewey nodded. "That'll do."

Juanito rode in the wagon the first day on the San Antonio trail. The second day he insisted upon riding his sorrel bronc again. Dodge warned him, "You'll work that pony into the ground."

Juanito said, "A bronc needs plenty work. Work is the best teacher."

Padgett called an early halt. Dodge argued, "There's still daylight left."

"But there's grass and water here. A man don't want to push cows and calves too hard."

Hewey suspected Padgett's real concern was not the

herd. Dodge looked pale and drawn. Both men had counted the cattle and come to an agreement on the number. All that remained from a business standpoint was the writing of a draft on C. C. Tarpley's bank account. Dodge said he was in no hurry about that. He could not spend the money until he got to San Antonio anyway, and he did not want to risk losing it by carrying it around. "I got in trouble that way one time," he said. "Didn't bank my check for most of a month. By that time the old boy who wrote it had gone flat busted."

Hewey said, "You don't need to worry about C.C. I suspect he's still got the first dollar he ever made. He sure ain't spent it payin' wages."

"Cowboys don't need much anyway," Dodge said. "Money leaks through their fingers like sand through a sieve."

Dodge sat on his rolled blankets and stared into the dying embers of Sixto's cooking fire. "That ranch back yonder ain't the first place I ever lost. Every cowman I know has gone broke two or three times. I just wish somebody had got it besides Sid Slocum."

Padgett said, "At least you got away with most of the cattle. We've crossed the county line, so I don't think Slocum is apt to send the sheriff after you. We're out of his jurisdiction."

"He might send a pack of damned lawyers."

Hewey itched to tell what he had done to Slocum, but now and then he suffered a spasm of good judgment. He said, "The sheriff told me if it went to court he'd swear that Slocum was lookin' at last year's calendar and we got the cattle off on Wednesday."

"And after all," Padgett told Dodge, "the boundary wasn't fenced. Slocum would have to get it surveyed to prove exactly where it lays. By that time this herd would be all the way out to the Pecos River. He'd never find it unless you told him where it went."

"I wouldn't tell that damned skinflint where to find a water bucket if his britches was on fire."

Fat spoke up. "I'll bet you could hire some Mexican to kill him for fifty dollars. Maybe less."

Dodge seemed to savor the thought for just a minute. "Wouldn't do no good. Everything would go to his sorry kin, and I wouldn't be no better off."

Padgett studied the old man's face in the firelight. "I'm wonderin' how long you can idle around the San Antonio hotel lobbies before you start itchin' to get back in the cattle business."

"I don't know. I was chasin' mavericks and burnin' my own brand on them before the big war. I've rode the market up and down so many times I've lost count, and watched my cows starve through more damned droughts than I want to think about. But there's somethin' about it that gets in the blood, like other people take to drinkin' or gamblin'. I guess ranchers and dirt farmers are about the worst gamblers in the world. The deck is stacked against them most of the time, but they keep playin' the game as long as they've got a chip left."

Almost from the first, Hewey had his eye on a wily-eyed spotted cow that kept looking around, seeking an opening for escape. It seemed that no matter how docile a herd might be, one or two incorrigible bunch-quitters were always awaiting their chance. He had chased her down and turned her back into the herd three times. His first thought was that she might have left a calf behind, but her udder was not swollen. She was just unsociable. Exiling her to short grazing in the Pecos River country seemed a reasonable punishment for her errant behavior.

Between watching for the cow to break out again and watching the back trail for a sign of Sid Slocum and the law, his time was fully occupied.

Dodge was closest to the cow the next time she decided to return to familiar range. The old man spurred after the fugitive, roundly cursing her and all her antecedents. Hewey turned to help him but saw that Dodge had managed to get around her, waving a coiled rope and yelling. She started back toward the herd, her head high and tail curled in a clear message that she had lost the round but not the fight. She would try again.

Dodge gave her a final angry shout as she rejoined the drag, then he slumped suddenly, gasping, and dropped the rope. He leaned to one side, grabbing at the horn. He looked toward Hewey with wide eyes, then slid to the ground. His startled horse snorted and jumped sideways, ears pointed forward. For a few seconds Hewey feared Dodge's foot was caught in the stirrup. If the horse panicked, the old man could be dragged. But his foot fell free before Hewey could reach him.

Hewey was down and at Dodge's side before anyone else got there. The rancher's face was drained, his hands trembling. He wheezed, "Ought to've left the old bitch for Slocum."

Dodge was having a seizure of some kind, but Hewey did not know what to do about it. Dodge strained to get up. He lacked the strength. Hewey said, "Lay easy, Mr. Dodge. Somethin' has happened to you."

The reply was a forced whisper. "Damned horse

throwed me off is what happened." Dodge clutched the front of his shirt in a knotted fist.

He had fallen off, but Hewey would not anger him by saying so. Being thrown off a horse was no disgrace, but only a town-raised pumpkin roller would admit to falling off.

Word passed quickly to the point. Juanito came first and anxiously jumped down to join Hewey. "Señor Dodge, you are all right?"

The answer was hard to hear. "I'm fine. Just fine."

Padgett galloped back and demanded, "Is he hurt?"

Hewey said, "It's his heart, I'm thinkin'."

Frowning darkly, Padgett leaned over the rancher. "I been arguin' with him to ride in the wagon. He's got no business tryin' to be a cowboy anymore."

Dodge struggled to bring out the words. "You callin' me old?"

Juanito looked ready to cry. Padgett told him, "Ride up and tell the hands to hold the herd. We'll make camp."

Dodge whispered, "It's too damned early."

"It may be later than you want to admit."

Reluctantly the boy rode off on the assigned mission. Padgett muttered, "Couldn't let him bust out bawlin'. Looked like he was fixin' to."

Dodge murmured, "If *he* don't cry for me, who will?"

Walter rode ahead to catch Sixto and tell him to bring the wagon back. Hewey and Padgett carried Dodge into the thin shade of a mesquite and smoothed out a place for him in the soft sand. The old man gradually recovered enough strength to rail at his luck. "I wonder if that damned Slocum hired some *brujo* to put a curse on me."

Padgett said, "You know you don't believe in witches.

This has been sneakin' up on you. You just wouldn't let yourself see it comin'."

When the wagon arrived, Hewey and Walter stretched a tarp out from one side of it to make a shade. Against Dodge's protest, Padgett dispatched a Mexican hand to the next town to fetch a doctor. Dodge argued, "Damned small-town pill pushers, the only thing they ever do is open up my purse."

Sixto had a bottle of dark patent medicine in the chuckbox. Hewey recognized the label. It was advertised to cure almost any ailment known to man, woman, child, or horse. When Sixto uncorked it, the smell was like that of an animal two weeks dead. He prevailed on Dodge to swallow a large spoonful. The rancher immediately spit it out. He said, "Dammit, Sixto, you tryin' to hurry me into my grave? I'll get there soon enough."

Dodge lapsed into sleep after a time. His breathing was irregular and so quiet that more than once Hewey feared he had slipped away. Just at dark the Mexican cowboy returned by himself, explaining that the town ahead had no doctor.

Padgett accepted the news with a fatalistic shrug. "I don't know if a doctor could do much for him anyway. I'm afraid he may've run out his string."

Dodge opened his eyes partway. He said, "I'm afraid you're right. Old Nick has got me caught by the hind foot."

Padgett said ruefully, "I didn't think you were awake."

"Awake and thinkin'. You ain't wrote me that draft yet for the cattle."

"I'll do it right now."

"No need to hurry. I don't think I'm goin' anyplace where I can spend it." Dodge coughed and clutched at his chest. He motioned for Padgett to bend closer. "If I cash in, I want you to pay my hands the wages they've got comin', and a little extry besides. They're a good bunch."

Padgett seemed resigned. "Whatever you say, Mr. Dodge."

"And that boy Juanito . . ." Dodge coughed again. "He's the nearest thing to a son that I ever had. Take him with you and watch over him."

"Don't you worry. I'll see to it."

Dodge took a long breath. "Whatever money is left, send it to my nephew."

"If that's what you want."

"He'll blow it all in, but I reckon that's what I was fixin' to do with it myself. Too damned old to do anything else."

Dodge drifted off to sleep. Hewey sat on the ground watching him in the dim light of the campfire. Life left the old man so gently that Hewey did not realize for a while that he was gone. Juanito reverently folded Dodge's arms and pulled the blanket over his face, then walked out into the darkness alone.

Hewey started to follow him, but Padgett said, "Leave him be. Some things a boy has to work through by himself. Once he does, he's not a boy anymore."

Hewey and the hands dug a grave a little way off of the trail. Padgett said, "He can hear the herds goin' past. I think he'll like that." Padgett placed a silver dollar in the rancher's gnarled hand. "He's been broke more than once in life, but he'll never be broke again."

Juanito sniffled while Sixto recited a prayer in Spanish and crossed himself. They filled in the grave and marked it temporarily with a board out of the chuckwagon's end gate. Padgett promised to send money to the sheriff for a proper stone.

Walter asked, "What do you reckon it ought to say?"

Hewey suggested, *"If I don't like it where I'm goin', I swear by damn I'm comin' back."*

Late the next day a rider caught up to them from behind. Hewey recognized the deputy who had been with the sheriff and Slocum. The man rode up to the drags and said, "I'm lookin' for a feller the sheriff called Bill Jones."

Walter said, "There's nobody here by that name."

Hewey broke in. "There might be. Depends on why you're lookin' for him."

"The sheriff sent me to warn him that Sid Slocum is comin' and bringin' a ranger with him. Said to tell Jones he might want to take a *pasear* out to the west and enjoy a change of scenery."

Walter asked, "What's this Jones feller done?"

"Seems he coaxed Sid Slocum down into a dry cistern and left him there. Mr. Slocum ain't happy."

Walter forced a frown at Hewey, but his eyes were laughing. "It didn't really hurt him, did it?"

"Just left him a little drawed is all. But he was mad enough to chew up horseshoes and spit them at somebody. Especially somebody named Jones." He gave Hewey a slight grin that said he knew. "If you come across anybody by that name, you might pass the word on to him."

Hewey said, "We will, if we come across him. Tell the sheriff we're sure Jones'll be much obliged."

The deputy declined an invitation to ride along and take supper when Sixto made camp. "Got orders to keep lookin' for Jones. I think I'll hunt around over east."

When he was gone, Walter said, "Hewey, I don't know

how you'll ever make it to thirty without gettin' shot or hung." He chuckled. "I wish I could've seen Slocum's face. I'll bet he was a pretty sight."

Hewey had to grin. "I saw it, and there wasn't nothin' pretty about him."

"What'll you do now?"

"Like he said, mosey off to the west a little ways, just far enough that I can't hear the cattle bawl. When Slocum gives up, I'll come back."

"We're already out of that county sheriff's jurisdiction, but Slocum's got a ranger with him. The rangers can go anywhere."

Hewey loped up to the point of the herd to tell Padgett what he was going to do. Padgett chuckled as Hewey told him about Slocum and the cistern. He said, "I figured you must've done somethin' like that. I wish I'd thought of it."

"I'm kind of proud of it myself."

"Get some grub from Sixto. Keep track of us. When we get to the outskirts of San Antonio we'll turn west so we don't stir up more housewives and dogs than we have to."

"I'll find you." Hewey shook Padgett's hand.

Hewey stopped in a clump of brush before sunset and built a small fire to make coffee with water from a canteen. He ate a cold biscuit Sixto had given him and some hog meat left from the noon meal. When the coffee had boiled enough he kicked dirt over the fire to kill it. Otherwise the flames could be seen for a considerable distance after dark.

A feeling of loneliness came over him, for he had

never spent much time by himself. Walter had always been around, and usually other people as well. He wondered if Slocum and the ranger had caught up with the herd. If they hadn't, they probably would by tomorrow.

He could visualize Slocum and the ranger questioning the crew. The hands would probably feign ignorance of the English language. Mexicans often employed that defense against those who tried to intimidate them. Walter would not lie. That was something he had never been able to do. He would simply avoid a direct answer.

Padgett would probably just tell them to go to hell.

The next day Hewey rode at about the pace he knew the herd would travel, covering seven or eight miles. By supper he had eaten all the bread Sixto had given him, but he still had bacon and coffee enough to get him by. He saw a ranch house to the west and considered riding there for a meal. It was ranch custom to feed solitary drifters so long as they did not stay too long and abuse the hospitality. He decided against it, for if the ranger was serious about looking for him, he would probably visit the ranch and ask questions.

By the following day he had finished the bacon, and the sack of coffee was almost empty. He drew close enough to the herd that he could recognize the riders. He saw no strangers among them. He decided it was worth the risk to circle around and visit Sixto's wagon. It was a mile or so ahead of the cattle.

Putting a line of brush between him and the drive, he loped ahead. He sat at the edge of a thicket, watching as Sixto approached.

He had found the Mexican interesting. Sixto, well into middle age, had whiskers black as pitch, belying his age. He minded his own business and rarely talked beyond whatever was absolutely necessary. His black eyes seemed to see everything but hid whatever was behind them. He seemed always to be thinking. Hewey wondered if he thought in Spanish, or if he thought in words at all. He suspected the cook had come out of Mexico rather than South Texas. He liked to think Sixto had been a revolutionary and had killed some brutal hacendado for revenge. More likely, though, he had simply been a bandit.

Hewey rode out to intercept him. "I'm out of grub," he said. "Seen anything of Slocum?"

Sixto stood up and looked back toward the cattle. "Sí, the Slocum and a *rinche*. They come to find you, but they don't find nothing. Nobody tells them nothing."

"Where are they at now?"

Sixto shrugged. "*Quién sabe?* They go away, but two times they come back. They think maybe they catch you."

"They ain't yet. Sack me up somethin' to eat, will you, and I'll skin out of here again."

Sixto quickly filled Hewey's sack. He cautioned, "Those *rinches,* they have extra eyes. This one talks much and looks dumb, but I think he sees everything."

"He'll have to get up early in the mornin' to see me."

"Maybe he don't sleep at all."

Hewey said, "Tell my brother I'm doin' fine," and rode off in a long trot.

He found a suitable campsite near a windmill several miles farther on. The place had once been a homestead. He napped in the shade of a chinaberry tree some settler had planted, then shed his clothes and took a leisurely bath in the mill's earthen tank. His stomach began to talk to him, and he decided it was time to fix supper. He climbed out of the tank and walked to where he had left his clothes hanging on the bottom brace of the windmill.

They were not there.

A voice behind him asked, "Are these what you're lookin' for?"

He turned quickly, holding his breath. A tall, lanky man stood there, a round badge prominently displayed on his shirt. Hewey's clothes lay at his feet. "I reckon you'd be Bill Jones?"

Hewey recognized Len Tanner's broad grin.

Stammering at first, Hewey got over his surprise enough to say, "Where did you come from?"

"From all directions. Us rangers are everywhere. I figured you'd show up at the wagon sooner or later. I trailed you from there. Better get your clothes on while I decide whether you're Hewey Calloway or Bill Jones. I've got a warrant for Bill Jones."

"I'm back to bein' Hewey Calloway."

"I knew it had to be you as soon as I seen your brother Walter with that cattle herd. Everything fit. Naturally we didn't find anybody who'd admit to ever knowin' Bill Jones. Slocum doesn't know your real name, and I didn't see any reason to educate him."

"Thanks, Len." Hewey began putting on his clothes, starting with his hat. "I heard that you got yourself shot up by that cattle thief, what's-his-name."

"Olin Trumble. He just creased my ribs, maybe cracked one a little. It grabs me now and again when I move wrong. I made out like it was a lot worse because I wanted him to think he'd put me out of the way for a while."

"What brought you to this part of the country?"

"Trumble's a native of these parts. I had myself assigned down here where I could watch his white-trash kinfolks. I think I've got a lead on him."

"I hope so. It's on account of him that I'm on this drive. He threatened to get me for testifyin' against him. Some people thought they saw him back on the Pecos, so it was a good idea for me to go away."

"He *was* out there a while back, but he didn't stay long. Normally I wouldn't figure him to risk his neck for revenge against you, but them kind of yahoos don't think like us normal people. They can hate awful hard." He grimaced. "Sid Slocum for an instance. He's foamin' at the mouth like a hydrophoby coyote. He wants Bill Jones sent to the pen for life or a hundred and fifty years, whichever takes the longest."

Hewey tried to calculate how old he would be in a hundred and fifty years. "All that on account of me pullin' a little joke on him?"

"Some folks ain't got much sense of humor."

"What do you reckon I'd better do?"

"Keep doin' what you're doin' now till he gives up the hunt. If I was you I'd ride on ahead, take roundance on San Antone, and pick up the herd somewhere to the west, like over in the German settlements."

"You're not goin' to arrest me?"

"I'm carryin' a warrant for Bill Jones. I don't see anybody here by that name."

Hewey started breaking camp. "I'm much obliged."

Len shrugged. "For nothin'. Sid Slocum is a brass-plated son of a bitch. I just hope he don't find out that Bill Jones and Hewey Calloway wear the same size britches."

"Who's goin' to tell him? Padgett and the others,

they're honest men." He reconsidered. "All but maybe Fat Gervin."

He was tying his blankets behind the cantle of his saddle when he heard a gruff voice. "Well, ranger, I see you have apprehended the culprit."

Before he even turned, Hewey knew Sid Slocum had caught up with him.

{ FIFTEEN }

L en turned too quickly and grabbed at his side. He winced in pain, then said, "Sure did, Mr. Slocum. Caught him fair and square."

Slocum glowered. "He has a lot to pay for, leaving me to die. It will be my great pleasure to see him locked in the meanest cell of the Karnes County jail."

Len pressed his hand against his ribs, which had not yet fully healed. He said, "I'm afraid it ain't goin' to be quite that way. You see, I recognized him. His real name ain't Jones at all. It's Atwater, and his crimes take up half a page in the Rangers' fugitive book. He's wanted out in San Angelo for killin' a whiskey drummer just to get his sample case. They want him at Menardville for bustin' a teamster's skull in with a singletree."

Slocum's jaw sagged. "He did all that?"

"Sure 'nuff. He's a desperate man. Be thankful he didn't decide to kill you."

Slocum paled as he contemplated his narrow escape.

Len said, "I'll have to deliver him to Ranger headquarters in San Antone. They'll decide who gets to hang him first."

Slocum looked as if he were about to be sick.

Len said, "But I'll put your name on the list. You'll

get the use of him if there's anything left. Would you like to help me put the handcuffs on him?"

"I am not an officer. You'd better do that yourself."

Len locked the cuffs. He said, "You can tell the sheriff down there that Bill Jones has been took care of."

Slocum summoned up courage enough to say, "I should be entitled to strike him just once."

"It's contrary to regulations, but if he gives me any trouble I'll do it in your name."

Slocum mounted his horse. He said, "At least I shall have the pleasure of telling Jerome Padgett and his motley crowd that Bill Jones is getting what is coming to him."

"I wouldn't. They might do you some injury."

Slocum reconsidered. "You are probably right. I'll go around them." He took one more look at Hewey. "I hope they hang you so high that even the buzzards cannot find you."

Len promised, "He'll get his due."

When Slocum was well gone Len said, "I'd better leave the cuffs on you for a while. Slocum knows my ribs are still touchy, so he might circle back around to be sure you ain't taken advantage of my weakness. He threatened to get me fired if I didn't stop what I was doin' and hunt for you. His money gives him pull in high places."

"He's got a lot worse comin' to him than spendin' a night or two in the bottom of a cistern."

"Bad as they need it, sometimes you can't punish his kind. You have to leave them to heaven. He'll get his comeuppance someday, some way."

Hewey accepted it, though it was not good enough. "I'd better stay with you till Slocum has given up for sure."

"I'd be obliged for your company all the way to San Antone, but you'd better know that I'm goin' there after

Olin Trumble. His mother-in-law tipped me that he's hangin' around a low dive with a woman friend. The old lady wants me to shoot him so her daughter can marry a better man."

"Are you plannin' to shoot him?"

"Naw, I'd like to wake up every mornin' for the next twenty years and know he was fixin' to spend the whole day bustin' rocks in the state pen. The daughter can get herself a *dee*vorce."

Hewey rode alongside the skinny Ranger, imagining how it would be to wear the handcuffs for real. Though as a boy he had sometimes fantasized about romance and adventure in an outlaw life, the cuffs were a sobering reality. He said, "You're a natural born liar, tellin' Slocum that big windy about me bein' called Atwater."

"Wasn't much lie to it. There really was a Bill Atwater, and he does have half a page in my fugitive book. He got his light snuffed out a while back in Galveston."

"Shot?"

"Nope. Choked to death on a fish bone. Like I said, sometimes you have to leave them to heaven."

Arriving at the southern edge of San Antonio late in the afternoon, Len said, "I know you volunteered to go in with me, but are you still sure? I won't hold it against you if you decide to back out."

Hewey had begun to rethink the situation, but he had given Len a promise. He would swallow hard and keep it, the way Pa would have. "Just tell me what you want me to do."

"We'll stop here and wait till dark. Wouldn't want the quail to flush before the gun is loaded."

Hewey had no argument with that. A larger question nagged at him. Why in the hell had he given Len his word in the first place? He was no lawman. He wasn't even a top hand yet as a cowboy. He should be with Tarpley's herd, and he would be were it not for Sid Slocum.

He wished he were back on the Pecos. He would even settle for East Texas.

He said, "I'd better tell you, I'm real consistent with a pistol. I miss every time."

"I don't want you to carry one anyway. I'd sooner face a dozen Comanches than a well-meanin' cowboy with a gun in his hand."

Len untied his blanket roll and spread it in the shade of a tree. Though he moved carefully, he stirred up fresh pain and sucked in a sharp breath. He said, "I've got my ribs bound up tighter than the bark on a tree, but they can still hurt like hell."

"You oughtn't to be ridin'."

"You can't catch a fish if you don't keep your line in the water."

To Hewey's amazement, Len soon dropped off to sleep. He wondered how the ranger could do that with the hurting in his side and the knowledge that he might soon confront a wanted man who had already wounded him once. Hewey's stomach was in turmoil from just thinking about meeting up with Trumble. Sleep was out of the question. He would be lucky if he didn't toss up everything he had eaten the last two days. He thought of a dozen excuses for spurring away from San Antonio like a turpentined dog.

Pride made him stand hitched. He had walked away from fights, but he had never *run* away. Running was for cowards. Hewey was merely cautious.

When darkness came, Len awakened, yawned, then got up and rolled his blanket. "About suppertime. I know where there's a pretty good chili joint that don't try to get rich in one day."

"I don't think I could eat a thing."

"I've got a rule. Never get shot on an empty stomach if you can help it." He saw that Hewey took him seriously. "You ought to know I don't mean half of what I say. I just talk to keep the silence away."

Hewey tried to make sense of that, but he couldn't.

Len said, "Silence gives me the shivers. It's what it must be like when you're in your grave."

Len ate a hearty meal of tortillas, chili, and beans. Hewey sipped half a cup of coffee that kept churning after it went down. He said hopefully, "Maybe Trumble has gone someplace else."

"We'll find out directly. You ought to try some of this chili. It's hot enough to light a cigar without a match."

The thought of it brought the coffee halfway back up Hewey's throat.

Len stalled until his pocket watch told him it was nearly ten o'clock. "If he's goin' to be there at all, he ought to be there by now. You've still got time to back out."

Hewey felt that he had committed himself too deeply to back out. "I'll go." But his heart was not in it.

They tied their horses in front of a low stone building that had a sign reading EL GALLO ROJO.

Len said, "That means The Red Rooster. It's the kind of place where folks pick their teeth with a bowie knife."

"And we're goin' in?"

"Me through the back door, you through the front. I hope we don't set off a shootin' inside. Might hit some innocent party, if there's any innocent parties there."

"I'm an innocent party. What if he decides to shoot *me?*"

"I'm bettin' he'll want to sneak out without a ruckus. You go to the bar and order a whiskey. If you see Trumble, don't act like you recognize him. The main thing is for him to recognize *you*. I figure he'll head to the back door. I'll be waitin' there for him."

"What if he runs over me and goes out the front?"

"A fifty-fifty chance is about the best we get most of the time."

Len started around the building but turned for another word of advice. "Don't drink that whiskey. It's apt to burn a hole in your belly. In joints like this sometimes they sell it before the snake heads have dissolved."

"Thanks for worryin'."

"I ain't worried. This is what I do for a livin'. I don't like for life to get dull."

"Around you I doubt it ever does."

He watched Len turn the corner and disappear. He waited another minute or two, giving the ranger plenty of time to get in place. Putting down a strong urge to turn and run, he took a deep breath and stepped through the open door.

He wished his breath had been deeper, for the air inside was thick enough to slice. Whiskey, sweat, tobacco, and lamp smoke all mingled in a toxic mix that assaulted eyes, nose, and throat alike. He coughed and tried to blink away the sting.

Through the haze he saw that the cantina was crowded with men and women of many shades and hues. The aggregate noise of multiple conversations made it impossible to pick out any single voice. He worked his way to the bar and told the dark-complexioned bartender, "Whiskey."

The man waited, his brow furrowed expectantly. Hewey realized he wanted to see the money first. He dug a coin from his pocket. The man examined it distrustfully, then filled a clouded glass from a bottle beneath the bar. Hewey could not see the label, but it did not matter. The bottle had probably been refilled many times with something other than what the label claimed.

He pretended to taste the whiskey but remembered Len's admonition and barely let it touch his lips. He turned away from the bar and saw Trumble. His heart gave a jolt. He realized the cattle thief had seen him first, his eyes fixed on Hewey in sharp surprise. Hewey tried to pretend not to recognize him. He let his gaze sweep on past, but he continued to watch Trumble from the corner of his eye. The fugitive sat at a small table with a slender Mexican woman whose dark eyes had been accentuated with heavy black makeup, her cheeks crimson with an overdose of rouge.

Trumble pushed to his feet. He started to move toward the front door. Hewey forced himself to act casual, though his lungs felt about to explode with pent-up breath. He carried his drink toward a vacant small table and blocked Trumble's path. Trumble turned and started for the back door. He got there just in time to bump headlong into Len.

The ranger held a pistol, but the collision was violent enough to knock it out of his hand. He grappled with Trumble, then gasped and doubled over in pain. Trumble had somehow struck the sore ribs.

He was about to go out the door. Hewey had no time to think. He grabbed a chair out from under a patron. He threw it at Trumble, knocking him off his feet. The patron fell to the floor in front of Hewey, tripping him. Four were down in a tangle: Hewey, the protesting patron, Len, and the cattle thief.

Hewey was the first to his feet. Trumble struggled to his hands and knees, at the same time trying to draw a pistol from his waistband. Hewey managed to step on his fingers and then slide the weapon across the floor. He righted the chair and set it down so that its legs straddled Trumble. He seated himself in it and fought to regain his breath.

Trumble floundered and cursed, trying to free himself from the chair. He was pinned down by Hewey's weight.

When he gained enough voice to speak, Hewey said, "You all right, Len?"

Len sat up and saw that Trumble was helpless. He wheezed, "I think he rebusted my ribs. You sure you've got a tight hold on him?"

Trumble's woman companion recovered from her initial shock enough to fire off a tirade against Hewey and the ranger. Hewey recognized only a couple of words that he had heard the vaqueros use against the cattle. The tone told him she meant him no kindness.

He would not have been surprised if some of the bar patrons came to Trumble's aid, but none did except for the woman. Her opposition was entirely vocal. Word quickly went around the room that Len was a ranger. If Trumble had any friends here, their friendship was not strong enough to make them butt in. It was well known that trouble with one ranger meant trouble with all of them.

Nobody had touched Len's pistol. He got to his feet and retrieved it, holding a hand against his side. He said, "You've sat idle long enough, Hewey. Go out and get the handcuffs off of my saddle, would you?"

Len took Hewey's place on the chair that held Trumble down. He said, "Hold still. Faunchin' around like that is makin' my ribs hurt. Bartender, bring my prisoner a drink. Maybe it'll settle him down." He set the heel of his boot upon Trumble's hand and pretended not to hear the howl of protest.

Hewey leaned against Len's horse for a minute, trying to let his nerves settle. He found the handcuffs and took them back inside. Len arose and lifted the chair from his prisoner. He pulled Trumble's hands behind his back and locked the cuffs.

He said, "We'll take this gentleman down to the county jail till state headquarters decides what to do with him."

Hewey said, "We don't know if he's got a horse."

"He's got two good legs. A long walk will help him to think about the wages of sin."

Outside, Trumble stood with shoulders drooped as Len dropped a rope around his middle. Len swung up onto his horse. He said, "Well, Hewey, you won't have to worry about him anymore. You can go back to the Pecos River and not give him another thought."

Hewey shook his head. "I can't believe I let myself do what I just did. If I'd had time to think about it, I'd've lit out like a jackrabbit."

"You done fine, though. If you ever take a notion you want to be a peace officer, let me know. I'll put in a good word with the Rangers."

"Nobody can ever accuse me of bein' that foolish. I'll be happy if someday they can say I'm the best cowboy C.C. Tarpley has got, and maybe get raised to a dollar a day."

* * *

Len and Hewey spent the night in the county jail, though with the cell doors open. Hewey was tired enough that the hard cot felt like a feather bed.

After breakfast he bade Len good-bye. He did not stop to speak to Olin Trumble, for everything worth saying to him had been said. He saddled his horse and headed south on the road toward Laredo, hoping to strike the trail of the Tarpley herd. He encountered a woman and two towheaded youngsters traveling toward town in a farm wagon.

He asked, "Ma'am, you seen anything of a cowherd passin' this way?"

The question roused the woman to immediate anger. "You're damned . . . you're dern right I did. A bunch of them cows trampled my garden. What little they left behind, the cowboys ruined tryin' to drive them out. I'm on my way now to find the sheriff. I think I've got damages comin'."

"Yes, ma'am."

"Do you know who they belong to?"

Hewey thought quickly. "A man named Eli Jessup, out by Upton City."

"Mr. Jessup has got a surprise comin' to him when my lawyer sends him the bill."

"Yes, ma'am. I expect he'll be real surprised."

A herd of that size was not difficult to trail. Hewey cut across their sign and turned westward. He found them at noon, some of the men eating at Sixto's wagon, the rest continuing to push the cattle at a slow pace that did not tax the smaller calves.

Padgett noted Hewey's arrival with a casual nod and hardly looked up from his coffee. "Thought maybe you'd quit us."

"I couldn't do that. Ain't been paid yet."

Walter walked up carrying a plate of beans and some kind of meat. Hewey saw the freshly cut carcass of a kid goat hanging from the wagon. Probably a stray and fair game for whoever came along. Walter asked, "Are you sure you left Sid Slocum behind?"

"Did better than that. I left Olin Trumble in the San Antone jailhouse." He explained how he and Len had caught the cattle thief. Noting the eager reception his account received from Walter, Padgett, and a couple of the Mexican cowboys, he saw no harm in embellishing his own part a bit. Len probably wouldn't mind. Anyway, he wasn't here.

Walter said, "Now you won't have to keep lookin' back over your shoulder. You've got nothin' to worry about."

Hewey nodded, though he knew that was not entirely true. He still had to worry about Walter. His brother had not mentioned Eve in a while, but Hewey had sensed that he still thought about her often. A faraway look would come into Walter's eyes, and not even a clap of thunder would bring him back before he was ready. Hewey would try to distract him by talking about dreams of his own, dreams of being free as a pair of eagles, roaming the West wherever they pleased, visiting the Rocky Mountains, perhaps even wading barefoot in the California surf. The whole world was open to a man who carried no responsibilities except to himself, no baggage to tote that he could not wear or tie to his saddle.

He said, "I been thinkin', Walter. When we get these cattle delivered and draw our pay from C.C., let's quit and go see somethin'. I hear they're startin' up some big ranches out in Arizona. Been lots of Texas cattle gone up to Montana and Wyomin', too. I'll bet they're payin' a lot better wages than C.C. ever would."

"I thought you said money doesn't mean anything to you."

"It ain't the money, it's the excitement. A man can get bogged down in one place and never know what all's out there that he's been missin'. Like C.C. Tarpley. He doesn't know but what the whole world starts and ends along the Pecos River."

Walter frowned. "A man can also miss a lot by bein' always on the go. There's much to be said for takin' root in one place, buildin' somethin' of your own, raisin' a family and watchin' them grow with the country. It's the kind of life Pa and Ma had. They seemed to like it."

"Pa never got out of East Texas except for the war. He was always one crop short at the bank, and he died a poor man."

"Broke yes, but he never was poor. *Broke* just means out of money. *Poor* is when you're down in your spirit. Pa was always happy right where he was, him and Ma."

"Ain't many women like Ma, and there's few men lucky enough to find one."

"I believe I already did."

Hewey ran out of argument for a while.

Why wasn't Eve born fat and ugly? he wondered.

The terrain west of San Antonio quickly became hilly and rough, the rock-strewn road occasionally a challenge for the wagon. Padgett followed the old military route that would lead through Friedrichsburg and Fort McKavett, then on to San Angelo at the confluence of the Conchos.

Gabe had fallen moody and quiet. It was as if he isolated himself from the other riders, immersed in his own meditations much like Walter. Hewey pulled up beside him, hoping to strike up a conversation. Gabe offered none.

Hewey asked, "What you studyin' on so hard?"

Gabe was slow to answer, as if it took a minute to break through the invisible wall that surrounded him. "Walter's been tellin' me about a woman out in Upton City that he's took a shine to. Got me to thinkin' about the one we saw workin' for the old man who sold us that horse Belcher. What was his name?"

"It was Hickley, maybe, or Hickson. I believe it was Hickson."

"I keep studyin' about her. His cook's daughter, he said she was. Name of Belinda."

"You remember her name but you can't remember his?"

"She was a right smart the best lookin' of the two. Goin' by the landmarks, I think we'll be passin' that place again."

"Looks like it to me."

"Reckon it'd be all the same to Mr. Padgett if I was to stop off for a little visit?"

"I don't see how it could hurt, but he's bossin' this drive. You'll have to ask him. What's so special about that girl?"

"While you was out on the Pecos, did you see any women of my complexion?"

"I don't recall that I did."

Gabe nodded as if no more justification was needed.

Hewey said, "You and Walter have both got women on the brain. Women tie you down. They keep you from doin' all the things you want to do and goin' to the places you want to see."

Gabe shrugged. "It's different with you. You're white. You can go anywhere and be welcome. I can't. You've seen for yourself, there's places they won't even let me stay for a night. I've seen signs sayin' 'Nigger, don't let sundown catch you in this town.' "

"Matter of fact, I have, too."

"I'm out of work when this drive is over. That old man asked if any of us wanted a job. I'd like to see if he was just talkin' to you and Walter, or if he meant me, too."

"He'll have you wrestlin' with them goats."

"That's all right. Goats won't care what color I am."

Juanito rode close, bringing in a cow and a calf that had moved off to graze. Hewey asked, "How about you, Juanito? You thinkin' about leavin' us, too?"

Juanito seemed surprised by the question. "Mr. Dodge, he is dead. Mr. Slocum, he got his own vaqueros. I stay with Mr. Padgett."

Padgett was careful not to let the herd get close to Hickson's field. The goat man rode out and looked the cattle over, then pulled up beside Hewey and Gabe. "I'm glad they're yours and not mine. I can grab hold of a goat and throw it down. Can't do that with a cow."

Hewey said, "They're not exactly ours. They belong to Mr. C.C. Tarpley. We're deliverin' them to him."

"So you're all hired hands. I'm still lookin' for help. Anybody interested?"

Gabe tried to be casual, but his eagerness showed through. "I might be."

Hickson stared at him as if appraising a horse. "Are you a workin' hand or a smart hand? I've had some smart hands."

"I'm a workin' fool."

"I believe in payin' a man what he's worth. How about six bits a day?"

That was as much as Hewey was making, and Gabe didn't know anything about goats. Sometimes life was not fair.

Gabe asked Hickson, "Is your cook really good?"

Hickson rubbed his stomach. His belt was buckled at the last notch. "You can see for yourself. Her daughter is a pretty good hand in the kitchen, too."

"Then I ain't a cowboy no more."

{ SIXTEEN }

Padgett skirted south of San Angelo as he had skirted past San Antonio to avoid angry confrontations over trampled gardens and broken fences. He followed Dove and Spring Creeks past a village called Knickerbocker and a town known as Sherwood before bearing a little to the north and striking the Middle Concho.

He said, "I hope it's rained enough to fill up some water holes. Otherwise it's apt to be a dry drive from the head of the Middle Concho to the Pecos. Charlie Goodnight was one of the first to drive cattle this way, more than twenty years ago. He had all kinds of hell."

Hewey assured him, "There was water enough when we came this way, me and Walter. Even a few windmills that's been put up since the last time you were out here."

"Good. I was afraid I'd have to earn that extra commission I'm fixin' to charge C.C."

"What do you figure on doin' after we get these cattle delivered? You goin' to work for C.C.?"

"For that tight-twisted old hellion? No, I think I'll go on out to Pecos City and sign on with one of the big outfits. I'll take the Mexican hands with me. That way I can offer somebody a whole crew."

"Juanito, too?"

"I made Dodge a promise. I'll look after him till he's mature enough to look out for hisself."

That eased one of Hewey's concerns. He doubted that Tarpley would be hiring extra hands, and he had feared that Juanito might be left at loose ends. "You're good-hearted, Mr. Padgett."

Padgett seemed embarrassed. "Ain't nothin' good-hearted about it. It's just business. I'll be needin' Juanito and these other boys as bad as they may need me."

"How about Sixto?"

"There's times when cowboys are in surplus supply, but there ain't ever too many good cooks. Damn right I'm takin' him with me."

Hewey had been seeing travelers along the trail, so he paid little attention to a horseman coming from the west until he was close enough to recognize.

"Looky yonder, Walter," he said, "it's Snort Yarnell."

Snort stopped to talk to Padgett at the point of the herd. Hewey and Walter left the drags to Juanito and another hand and loped up to greet Snort. The gangly cowboy slouched in the saddle, his gold tooth gleaming in a foolish-looking grin that slanted across his homely face.

"Howdy, Hewey. How do, Walter."

Even before he was close enough to smell Snort's breath, Hewey knew he had been drinking. "Where you headed, Snort?"

Snort pointed in a vague easterly direction. "San Angelo. Thought it was about time I had me a good old-fashioned drinkin' spree and did somethin' I'll worry about from now till winter. I kind of dread it, though. I know how bad I'll feel when it's over."

Walter asked, "Why don't you quit it?"

"Can't. Got too much invested in it already." Snort reached inside his shirt and pulled out a half-empty bottle. "Drink, anybody?"

Padgett said, "Not till the drive is over."

Snort tipped the bottle, then stuck it back in his shirt. "It might be over sooner than you figured on. There's been hell to pay in Upton City."

Hewey pressed, "What're you talkin' about?"

"It's C.C. Tarpley and Eli Jessup. Them old jugheads got into a big cuss fight. Might've led to a shootin' if they'd been packin' iron, and there's liable to be a shootin' yet. I'd rather be someplace else for a while."

Hewey asked, "Aren't you workin' for Jessup?"

"Was. He fired me again. I figure by the time I've spent my wages he'll hire me back . . . if he's still alive."

Hewey remembered Tarpley's insistence upon secrecy about these cattle. "Were they fightin' about these cows?"

"The cows are part of it. Seems like there was a parcel of land the other side of the river that both of them wanted. Eli tried to buy it, but he was too chinchy to bid enough. So C.C. snuck in behind him and offered what the owner asked for. I gather he figured to stock the place with these cattle."

"That means we may be ridin' into a fight."

"You are if you keep goin' the direction you're pointed. You'll have to cross some of Eli's land to get to C.C.'s. Eli don't figure on lettin' you do it."

Padgett said, "The land's not fenced. I don't know where the boundaries are."

Snort considered. "Hewey and Walter can show you how to go around. It's an extra long way, but it'd be the safest thing to do." He touched fingers to the brim of his hat. "Adiós, fellers. I got friends workin' for both outfits. I ain't stayin' around to see them get hurt. Or me neither."

The cattle had not stopped moving. Padgett touched spurs to his horse to keep up with the leaders. He said, "This ain't a fightin' outfit. There ain't but one or two guns in the whole shebang. I reckon we'd better turn them. But whichaway?"

Hewey watched Snort leave and for a moment wished he were going, too. "South. We may've already crossed Jessup's line. I see a windmill off yonder that I think is one of his."

He was fairly sure it was the mill where he and Walter had shared coffee with Jessup their first night on the trip.

Padgett said, "I remember a time when the Comanches came close to takin' C.C.'s hair. I almost wish they had. It ain't right, them two drawin' their men into a private squabble . . . gettin' them hurt, maybe killed. At cowboy wages, it ain't worth it."

Especially on what we're making, Hewey thought.

Padgett added, "But as long as you ride for a brand, you ought to be willin' to fight for it."

Hewey and Walter helped Padgett turn the leaders southward. The cattle had been traveling west so long that they resisted. Hewey explained the reason for the change to the rest of the hands.

Fat took it like a death notice. He said, "I ain't bein' paid enough for this. I'll send for my wages." He put his horse into a trot back the way they had come.

Hewey shouted after him, "What about C.C.'s daughter?"

"There ain't no woman worth it," Fat shouted back.

Juanito asked, "What do we do now?"

"Just what we've been doin'. Keep drivin' these cattle. Except now we go south."

Hewey loped off to catch Sixto and turn the wagon.

Sixto pulled on the reins. "There is trouble?"

"There could be. We're changin' direction to try and go around it."

The cook reached into a canvas bag beneath the wagon seat and brought out the biggest pistol Hewey had ever seen. It was of an old cap and ball design and probably as old as Sixto.

Hewey whistled. "Was that cannon made in Mexico?"

"Sí, but it can kill anywhere. Many times it has done so."

"Better put it back in the bag. We're tryin' to go around a fight."

"Maybe the fight is already come." Sixto pointed westward.

Hewey saw eight or ten horsemen approaching. His mouth went dry. He said, "We can't afford to start anything. There ain't enough of us to finish it."

Sixto handed him the pistol. Hewey tried to give it back to him. He said, "I couldn't hit anything noway."

Sixto would not take the weapon. "Then better you give this to Padgett. I think he will need it."

Hewey loped back to join Padgett and Walter. They had already seen the riders. Padgett said, "Looks like your friend Yarnell didn't come soon enough."

Hewey gave him the pistol. "Sixto thought you ought to have this, just in case."

Padgett's eyes widened as he examined it. "This thing could kill an elephant." He checked to be certain it was loaded. "I hope I don't need to use this." He shoved it into his right boot.

Walter squinted, watching the oncoming horsemen. "That's C.C. and the boys, but I don't know whether to breathe easier or not."

Tarpley spurred out into the lead, slowing the last fifty yards to prevent frightening the cattle. He stood in his stirrups as if that would make up for his lack of size. He yelled, "Where the hell do you-all think you're goin'?" He pointed westward. "That's the way."

Padgett waited for Tarpley to come close enough that he did not have to shout. He said, "Howdy, C.C." His tone was civil but did not glow with friendship.

Tarpley grunted and turned angry eyes on Hewey. "You've worked for me long enough to know this ain't the shortest way to my ranch."

Hewey tried to keep his composure as Grady Welch and others of the Two Cs crew gathered around him. They were all armed. He said, "We figured it was the safest. We just found out that Eli Jessup intends to stop us from crossin' his country."

"I don't give a goddamn in hell what Eli Jessup intends. We ain't walkin' these cows two or three extra days just to suit him. Turn them."

Padgett flared. "You're the same blockheaded old fool I used to know, C.C. You're liable to get these cattle scattered and some good men hurt."

Tarpley flared back. "You've done your job, Jerome. I can do without your services from here on. I'll meet you in town and pay what I owe you after we get these cows settled where they belong."

Padgett did not retreat. "My job was to get these cattle bought for you and delivered onto your ranch. We ain't there yet. Till we get there and I get paid, I'm the boss of this drive."

Hewey had been in lightning and thunder storms when he could feel electricity crackling around him. He felt it now as the two men glared at one another. He looked at Walter but found no answers in his brother's worried countenance.

A distant movement caught his attention. He wiped a sleeve across his face and blinked away sweat that had rolled into his eyes.

He said, "You-all better come to a decision pretty quick. We got company comin'."

He saw at least a dozen horsemen, riding in a cluster. He knew they must belong to Jessup, for Tarpley had most of his crew here.

Tarpley looked at the men he had brought. "You boys check your guns. Make sure they're loaded."

Padgett exploded. "Now you *are* fixin' to get somebody killed. I thought when a man got older he was supposed to get smarter. You ain't learned a damned thing since the last time I saw you."

Tarpley gave no sign that he heard. "Get this herd movin'," he ordered. "Don't stop for nothin'."

The cattle had bunched up during the attempted turn southward and had not yet begun to string out again. Jessup and his men came on in a long trot, circling around them. Jessup drew rein with his horse and Tarpley's almost touching heads. His heavy mustache twitched like an angry black squirrel. He said, "You're on my land, C.C. Turn back, or we'll run them over you."

Tarpley's jaw jutted like a desert mountain rimrock. "This is a public road."

"The ruts are public, but the ground on either side of them ain't."

"These cows can't damage your land any. It's too sorry to hurt."

"If one of your cows travels a step farther west, I'll shoot her. And then I may decide to shoot *you*."

Tarpley leaned toward Jessup, eyes flashing defiance. "You won't get the chance. You'll be dead before you can pull the trigger a second time." Both men dropped their hands to the butts of their pistols.

Hewey felt a prickling up and down his spine. Looking anxiously at the J Bar cowboys, he suspected they felt the same way. Jessup's foreman Mitch was tense, his right hand frozen halfway between the reins and his pistol. Hewey sensed that the men on both sides wanted more than anything to turn around and ride away. They were held in check by the crackling animosity between the two older men.

Padgett drew Sixto's pistol from his boot and pushed his horse between the two men. He pointed the muzzle first at Jessup, then at Tarpley. "There ain't nobody shootin' anybody unless I do it myself. You two heathens get your hands up away from them guns."

Both ranchers cursed him roundly. Padgett waited until they had run down, then said, "Both of you drop them pistols to the ground." Neither man moved. Padgett quickly lifted Tarpley's pistol from its holster, then Jessup's. He tossed them away.

He said, "You've both been spoilin' for a fight, but you've always wanted somebody else to do it for you. Get down off of them horses." He poked the pistol toward Tarpley. The skinny rancher dismounted stiffly, his face flushed in indignation. Padgett turned to Jessup. "Now you, Eli."

Jessup defied him for a moment, but he could not hold out in the face of that formidable weapon. He said, "Padgett, you're as crazy as a bedbug."

Padgett said, "Crazy enough to shoot one of you. Maybe both. Now, damn you, fight." When they did not, he shouted, "Fight, I said." He fired the pistol, which made a report like a cannon. The slug flung up dust between their feet. It started the cattle to moving away.

Jessup struck the first blow. It glanced off Tarpley's chin and made his head jerk back. With a roar of fury Tarpley tore into Jessup. Though Jessup was a considerably heavier man, Tarpley's anger gave him strength. His fists sent Jessup staggering.

Mitch made a move as if to interfere. Hewey told him, "Best leave them be. War would be a lot less bloody if they made the generals fight it theirselves."

For two men past their youthful prime, the two ranchers managed to inflict considerable damage on each other. They cursed and grunted and groaned, alternately grappling, then stepping apart and swinging their fists. They gradually slowed, gasping for breath, wiping sweat and blood from their faces onto torn sleeves.

Jessup was the first to go to his knees and stay there. Tarpley swayed over him, clenching blood-smeared fists but barely able to raise his weary arms. His wiriness had won out over Jessup's bulk.

Padgett's anger eased a little. He shoved Sixto's pistol back into his boot. He said, "I hope you two get so sore you can't move for a week. Maybe next time you feel like a fight you'll remember this. Now we're takin' these cattle south. If we have to cross some of Eli's land to get there, so be it."

One of Jessup's eyes was beginning to swell. He pushed to his knees but had to lean on his horse for support. His other eye narrowed in resentment as he faced his men. "You-all just sat there and did nothin'. Every last one of you is fired."

"Everybody was more scared of Padgett than of you two," Hewey said. "Some people think he's crazy."

Tarpley retrieved his pistol. He tried twice to get back on his horse, but his legs were too wobbly. Hewey attempted to help. Tarpley blistered him with a curse. "Back away. I can do it myself." His third try put him up into the saddle.

"I still say we're takin' these cattle west." Tarpley looked toward his crew and shouted, "Stampede them, boys!" He ran his horse into the herd and fired his pistol into the air. The cattle shied away from him. A second shot put them into a run.

Tarpley kept firing until the pistol was empty. He commanded his men to do the same, but none did. The cattle were in full stampede.

Jessup shouted to his men, "Turn them. Get around them, dammit. Head them off." He spurred away in the wake of the fleeing herd.

Hewey lost track of other riders during the melee. Two Cs hands and J Bar punchers alike went after the cattle in a hard run, trying to move in front of them. They shouted and slapped coiled ropes against their leather chaps, trying to get them moving in a circle.

The run continued for the better part of a mile before the cowboys got the herd to milling. Jessup hollered, "Turn them south." Tarpley shouted, "Take them west."

Fuming, Padgett yelled, "Go to hell, the both of you."

Hewey was closest to him. Padgett said, "Better see if we got anybody hurt. It'll be the wonder of the world if we didn't."

Hewey immediately looked for Walter. He did not see him. He trotted up to Grady Welch and said anxiously, "Seen anything of Walter?"

Grady pointed. "He was over yonder way before I lost sight of him. I'm afraid his horse may have went down."

Hewey saw two horses limping with no riders on them. One was Walter's. The saddle was turned under its belly. Hewey's heart skipped. "Grady, help me find him."

The first man they found was Jessup's foreman, Mitch. He sat on the ground, one leg stretched crookedly in front of him. His face was pale in shock. Hewey said, "Grady, you better see what you can do for Mitch. I'll keep lookin' for Walter."

Grady dismounted, cursing. "Damned old rascals sure made a mess of it this time."

Hewey found Walter a little farther on. The first sight of him made Hewey's heart skip again. Walter lay on his side, one hand pressed against the other. Blood oozed out between his fingers. Hewey jumped to the ground, dropping the reins. He knelt beside his brother.

"Where are you hurt?"

Walter struggled to speak. "Horse fell. Then a cow ran a horn into me. Bleedin' like a stuck pig."

Hewey ripped Walter's shirt open. The wound still bled. Hewey could not tell how deep it was. He took a handkerchief from his pocket, wadded it, and pushed it partway into the hole.

Walter ground his teeth together. "If the puncture don't kill me, that handkerchief will."

"It's all I got." Walter's face was drained in shock, as Mitch's had been. Hewey looked up to see several riders coming to help him. He yelled, "Go get the wagon. We've got two men hurt."

Juanito wheeled around and loped off toward Sixto's chuckwagon. Two cowboys got down to see if they could help. Hewey recognized them as J Bar hands. In this emergency it did not matter which ranch they represented. They were cowboys together, the feuding owners be damned.

One of the men felt Walter's legs. "Don't seem to be broken," he said. "Looks like he got tromped on pretty good, though. He's probably bruised all to hell. Maybe got some hoof cuts."

Hewey told them about Mitch. One quickly rode off in Mitch's direction. The other declared, "They ought not to've stopped with a fistfight. I wish them two knotheads had shot one another."

Padgett rode up after a bit, his expression dark. He got down to examine Walter. He said, "As far as I can tell, there ain't but two men bad hurt."

Hewey said, "Two's more than enough." He saw Sixto's wagon coming. "We'll have to throw a lot of stuff off to make room for Walter and Mitch."

"Do it. If C.C. wants to bitch about it, let him. Right now I don't give a damn."

Tarpley rode up just before the wagon. Blood and sweat and dirt were smeared across his face. He launched an angry tirade against Padgett. "Them cattle are scattered all to hell, and you ain't doin' nothin' about it."

Padgett answered in kind. "And you can go to hell with them. Don't you see you've got a man hurt? And there's another one over yonder."

"That one's a J Bar man." Tarpley's tone indicated that Mitch was not his concern.

Hewey thought, *Some people learn awful slow.*

Sixto arrived with the wagon. He and Hewey and Juanito began throwing off bedrolls, dutch ovens, canned goods, and sacks to make room for the injured men. Tarpley shouted, "Wait a minute. Ain't that stuff mine?"

Padgett punched Tarpley's chest with the point of his finger. "If you ain't goin' to help, then get out of the way. Else I'm liable to forget that you're an older man than I am and finish what Eli started."

Sixto and Juanito spread a couple of blanket rolls while Hewey and Padgett gently lifted Walter into the wagon. Hewey told Sixto, "Mitch is layin' over yonder. We need to pick him up, too."

"We get him."

"What about them cattle?" Tarpley demanded.

Padgett said, "Let them graze Jessup's grass for a while. I'll take the boys and gather them when I get damned good and ready, only I ain't ready yet. Right now it's a good thing I've got no whiskey, or I'd get fallin'-down drunk."

{ SEVENTEEN }

Walter was running a strong fever before the wagon reached Upton City. He seemed to drift in and out of consciousness. Mitch was awake, his teeth gritted so he would not cry out in pain. Grady and a J Bar cowboy had improvised crude splints out of mesquite limbs and had set the broken bone the best they could.

Hewey and Grady rode alongside the wagon. The J Bar cowboys trailed behind it. Jessup had fired them but later had harangued them to stay and see the cattle driven off of his grass. They had all left him anyway. He sat on his horse, a man alone, hunched in misery from the beating he had taken. Tarpley had persuaded his own crew to remain and help the South Texans gather the herd.

The doctor decided that Walter was in the most immediate need of attention. He told Hewey, "Your brother may appear unconscious, but he's likely to thrash around when I start working on that wound. You'd better hold onto him."

Grady joined Hewey in holding Walter's shoulders and arms. Walter groaned and struggled as the doctor cleared dirt and shredded grass out of the hole in his side.

The doctor said, "I'm afraid he has a couple of broken ribs, too. It's lucky they didn't punch a hole in his lung."

Walter sank into deep unconsciousness. The doctor closed and stitched the wound. "I'll bandage him in a little while. Right now I'd best see to the other one. I'll have to reset that bone."

Hewey had made a strong effort to keep his nerves under control while Walter was being treated. He almost lost his hold when Mitch cried out. Mitch's face glistened with cold sweat after the doctor straightened the leg.

As the doctor applied splints and wrapped Mitch's leg, he said, "You waddies need to learn that those cow brutes aren't house pets. They outweigh you by four to one."

Hewey was in no mood for small talk. "What about Walter? Is he goin' to be all right?"

"I have sewed him up. That's about all I can do for him at the moment. The worry now is blood poisoning. I need to watch him for several days. But as you can see, this house is hardly a hospital. It has little room."

Grady suggested, "We can take him over to Mrs. Pearson's boardin' house."

"That would be a splendid idea," the doctor agreed.

Grady placed a heavy hand on Hewey's shoulder. "You stay here with him. I'll go talk to Mrs. Pearson."

"She'll need to make a place for Mitch, too," Hewey said.

"We may have to pay for this out of our own pockets. You know C.C."

"Who cares? Money's not good for nothin' except to spend."

Grady said, "While I'm at it, I'll take our horses over to Brandon's stable and wagonyard."

"Brandon? I thought the owner's name was Sandy."

"It was, but he got caught on Alvin Lawdermilk's place with a hot runnin' iron. He ought to've known that

a careful rancher like Alvin knows all his cows by name.
You remember the calves we found with hair brands on
them?"

"Yeah. We branded them over without lettin' C.C.
and Eli get wise."

"Turned out Sandy was the one who sleepered those
calves. Alvin caught him red-handed. On account of him
bein' a family man, the sheriff gave him a chance to quit
the country. He left last Saturday for California."

Hewey looked at his unconscious brother. "Just goes
to show what too much ambition can do to a man. And
all the time I suspicioned Alvin."

Grady had not been gone twenty minutes before Eve
rushed into the doctor's house. Mrs. Pearson huffed along
fifty feet behind her.

Eve demanded, "Where's Walter? How bad is he hurt?"

Hewey said, "The doctor can't say yet."

She accused him with her eyes. "Was this some of your
doin', Hewey Calloway?"

He raised his hands as if to defend himself. "No, it was
them two hardheaded old codgers, C.C. and Eli."

"I want to see him."

"He's in that room yonder asleep, or maybe unconscious. It's hard to tell the difference. But you'll be seein'
a right smart of him for a while. If it's all right with Mrs.
Pearson, we're fixin' to take him over to her place."

All the accusation had not left her eyes. "I think it was
your doin' that he went on that drive."

She had him there. He did not try to deny it. He said,
"I never figured on anything like this happenin'."

"I gather that you don't figure ahead about much of
anything."

"No, ma'am, I reckon not."

"Well, I'm goin' to take good care of him even if you don't. Is that your wagon outside?"

"I reckon it belongs to C.C., along with the cattle."

Her voice was crisp. "We'll haul him over there in it, him and Mitch. You go out and see that it's ready."

Hewey's face warmed. He was not used to being ordered around by a woman, especially one he barely knew.

God help Walter, he thought.

Walter's fever gradually subsided. Eve hovered over him, fetching for him, holding his hands when she was not needed in the kitchen or dining room. Hewey watched the two with deep misgivings.

Padgett showed up after a few days to inquire about Walter's progress. His red eyes and flushed face indicated he was suffering through a hangover.

Hewey said, "I suppose you got the cows delivered?"

"Yep, but I thought I was goin' to have to whip C.C. myself, all over again. It's a good thing he finally came to see things my way. I hated to hurt a skinny wart like him after Eli had already scarred him up so."

"Their fight has been buildin' for a long time, like a boil on the butt."

"Maybe they got it out of their system."

"I doubt it," Hewey said. "When the fight was over they were still the same two old hardheads they were before."

"At least maybe they'll call a truce till the sores heal up."

Hewey nodded. "I hope so. If it wasn't for you they would've got somebody killed, more than likely. What do you figure on doin' now that the drive is over?"

"Got a line on a job out in the Davis Mountains. They need a crew, so I'll take the South Texas boys with me. There's a good many Mexicans workin' out there. My bunch will fit right in."

"Takin' Juanito, too?"

"Sure. I promised Dodge. Anyway, the kid's got the makin's of a top hand."

Padgett walked to the door of Walter's room and looked in. Eve sat in a chair beside the bed, holding Walter's hand.

He asked, "Is that the girl Walter was talkin' about?"

"Yep. I don't know what I'm goin' to do about it."

"Why do anything? If Walter's found what he wants, you ought to holler hooray and get out of the road."

"It just ain't what I planned on. I thought me and Walter would see the country together, travel when the mood struck us, and light wherever we felt like."

"Maybe that ain't what *he* planned on."

"I fixed it for Walter to go with me to South Texas so he'd get away from her a while. I hoped he'd have time to get over this foolishness about bein' in love. Looks like things turned out just backwards from what I figured on."

"What *you* figured on? That's where you went wrong. Bein' brothers doesn't make you the same. You wanted to do the figurin' for both of you, but Walter has got a mind of his own. You were only thinkin' about what you wanted."

"It's just that we've always done everything together."

"But Walter is old enough to be weaned. You'd best cut him loose, or you'll eventually be just two grouchy old dried-up bachelors, like me and Dodge."

Hewey glanced toward the door to Walter's room. He

could hear Eve's soft voice, though he could not make out what she was saying.

He said, "Looks like it's been done for me."

Mitch frustrated the doctor by getting up on a set of crutches much too soon. Eli Jessup came to the boarding-house to visit him. His face was cut and bruised, one eye still swollen. He wasted no time on sympathy. He demanded, "How long are you goin' to lay there? Work's fallin' behind out at the ranch."

Mitch said, "You fired me, remember? You fired every-body."

"You'll be hired again when you can get back in the saddle. Till then you can understand why I can't afford to pay you for doin' nothin'."

Mitch's voice was bitter. "I understand real well."

Hewey bit his tongue and managed not to say any-thing, but he thought, *Even C. C. has got more human kindness in him than that.*

After Jessup left, Mitch said, "Padgett told me about findin' work out in the mountains. When I get up from here I think I'll go see for myself."

Tarpley came the same day, though fortunately not at the same time as Jessup. He, too, was bruised and bat-tered, but he offered Walter more understanding than Eli had shown to Mitch. He said, "Don't you worry, you're still on the payroll just the same as if you was out there workin'. By the way, how long before you *will* be back out there workin'?"

Walter said, "Doctor tells me I can go to the ranch in a few more days. May be a while before I can ride."

Hewey told Tarpley, "We heard you got those cows delivered to your new ranch all right."

"Yes, but I damn near had to whip Jerome Padgett.

He said he was in charge till we turned them loose and I wrote him a check. I didn't want a fight, so I finally let him have his way just to be shed of him."

Padgett would have made short work of Tarpley, but Hewey said, "It's a good thing you-all didn't tangle. You might've hurt him."

"That's what I was afraid of. I didn't want an old man like that on my conscience."

Tarpley turned back to Walter. "I'll need to put a camp man out at my new place to watch over them cows. It's got an adobe house. Would you be interested in the job?"

Walter perked up. "I might be. Is the house fit to bring a woman to?"

Tarpley blinked, confused. "The roof might need a little work. Women can be fussy about such as that. But where are you goin' to find a woman?"

"I've already found her. Just ain't asked her yet."

Hewey followed Tarpley out of the room and down the hall toward the front door. Tarpley shook his head. "A woman? The boy must still be runnin' a fever."

Hewey said glumly, "I'm afraid he is."

On the porch Hewey said, "After Walter goes to that camp job, you'll be shorthanded at headquarters."

"I figured I could pick up one or two of the J Bar hands that Eli fired and ain't unfired yet."

"If Walter gets married, he'll need a raise."

Tarpley considered. "I suppose a camp job does justify a little extra. Reckon he'd be satisfied with thirty a month?"

"*I* would. I'm only gettin' six bits a day."

Tarpley untied his horse from a post in front of the boarding house. He said, "I'll raise you someday when you're a cow*boy*. Right now you're still just a cow*hand*."

Hewey sat on the step and whittled a stick of wood into slivers while he watched Tarpley disappear on the road that led to the Two Cs.

Oh well, he thought, *money ain't everything. Look at the fun I'm having.*